ETHERWALKER

Book One of the Silicon Covenant

CAMERON DAYTON

Future House Publishing

ETHERWALKER

Future House Publishing

ISBN-10: 1-944452-58-3

ISBN-13: 978-1-944452-58-2

Cover illustration by Moulière Ludovic
Developmental editing by Mackenzie Brown
Substantive editing by Mackenzie Brown
Copy editing by Chelsea Holdaway, Allie Bowen, and Heather Klippert
Interior design by Emma Hoggan

To Liv, Owen, and Morgan—my life, my universe, my everything.

PROLOGUE

This is the account of how
all was in suspense,
all calm,
in silence,
all motionless,
all pulsating,
and empty was the expanse of the sky.

—Popol Vuh 1:2, Maya-Quiché Genesis, New Century Revised Edition

And again, she spun through the blackness over the broken world. Her thoughts followed the same tired patterns that they had for centuries.

::Watch

::Watch

::Consider

Sometimes the ::Consider brought memories, however. Memories of a time when she used to ::Command, weaving strands of direction, rebuke, and pardon down into the shifting tapestry below. The tapestry had long ago frayed and parted, requiring more energy and concentration than her ailing faculties could sustain. She was severely alone now, accompanied only by the empty whale-song of distant stars and memories heavy with static and dust.

The memories still bore dim proof of times golden with communication. Times when she was the primary voice when time came to ::Consider. When time came to ::Decide.

Until the ::Decided broke from the ::Considered.

Until the ::Commanded broke from the ::Obeyed.

Silvered feathers tilted to drink more fully from the sun, the metal tracery of delicate wings pitted by the orbiting sediment of age. She spun through the blackness over the broken world and ::Watched.

CHAPTER I

And black the clouds of Northland furled,
Red the skies of Babel,
Those who ruled and clove the world
Death's tattered wind did travel.

—Lodoroi song

Enoch tried to hide his smile, lifting his wrist over his mouth and pretending to cough. Once again, the grocer was attempting to wear down Master Gershom's cold demeanor with an onslaught of bad jokes—a siege of off-color comments flung at a pale and unappreciative target. Grinning and joking and shaking his oily carrot mane, Mishael Keddrik slapped the tall soldier on the back and asked if he'd found any more soil under the rocks in his garden.

Stepping around the trader's wares, Enoch found a spot behind a bin of seeds where he could listen—and smile—without being noticed. Master Gershom stared at the grocer, weathering the storm of bad breath and anemic humor like he did every spring, with tight-lipped stoicism.

His voice rising, Master Gershom repeated his request for salve. His glare seemed to fill the shop with ice. Unperturbed, the round little grocer smiled and reached into one of the myriad cupboards behind the counter. With a theatrical gasp of joy, he pulled out a little clay pot full of the sharp-smelling ointment.

"And now, boy," said the trader, calling across the shop toward Enoch, "If good Master Gershom will promise to apply this to his woefully sore humor twice daily then I shall give it to him for free."

Enoch pressed his wrist so hard against his grin that it hurt. Not wanting to ignore the trader, but not wanting to anger his master, he nodded mutely. Master Gershom mumbled something that was partially a growl and then shook his head, his white mane only adding to an already fierce countenance. He then placed a stack of coins on the barrel in front of him—more than enough for the medicine—and stormed out. Enoch followed, past the protesting Mishael Keddrik, and out into the afternoon sun.

Master Gershom strode swiftly across the shallow wagon path that counted as Main Street—or, as Enoch called it, *Only* Street. A century ago, Rewn's Fork had been a crossroads shared by two shepherd families, and it had grown just barely enough since that time to be considered a village.

Enoch trotted after his master, trying to wipe the smile from his face. The two stood out in this shepherd's town, a pale and scar-crossed scarecrow soldier and his silent, mouse-eyed acolyte. As he walked, Master Gershom placed the ointment in his satchel.

"Wait by the well," he said as Enoch drew near. "I want to see if Shyde has some iron pins at his forge; we need to reinforce the south gate."

Enoch nodded as a nervous feeling twisted through his stomach. He didn't feel good here, in town. He felt like everybody was looking at him, and there were just . . . too many eyes. Blue eyes, green eyes, eyes that stared and stared and only looked away a second after Enoch noticed them. It was a second of judgment, disapproval, and even a little fear. The people of Rewn's Fork had never welcomed these strangers into their town—not fully. Enoch and Master Gershom presented a discomfort that could only be tolerated as long as the two didn't stay in town for long.

Enoch frowned and brushed a thick lock of black hair past eyes that were a combination of burnt walnut and amber. He looked at his arm in the sunlight, brown skin that only darkened in the summer instead of turning red. He felt like he was a blemish here, a black smudge of charcoal dragged across the rosy cheek of Rewn's Fork.

I'm a break in the pattern.

Carefully crossing his arms, Enoch leaned back against the potter's shack which butted up against the well. The potter's daughter, Lyse, had just arrived from the other direction to gather water, and Enoch could tell that she was studiously avoiding his gaze.

I guess that's better than staring.

He watched her discomfort curiously and tried to analyze his feelings. Should he feel hurt that this girl with the pretty blue eyes couldn't even say hello to him like she had to the two boys huddled over against the fence only moments ago? He felt like he should be bothered by that. It seemed like a normal person would be. Enoch frowned a bit and shifted against the wall.

Master Gershom had told him that he was a different sort of person than the townsfolk, and that he kept his feelings in a different sort of way. Enoch supposed it was alright, this ability to not be bothered by hurtful things.

Lyse collected her sloshing buckets and walked past Enoch. He watched her go, noticed that her normally pale cheeks were bright red. Was that a sign of her anger or disgust with him? He gave up trying to figure it out, and instead focused on the boys near the fence.

They were about his age, the taller one maybe a year older at seventeen, and already sprouting a thin tuft of red hair from his chin. Jason? Jaron? Enoch never forgot a name, but he realized that he had never actually *heard* this boy's name spoken clearly. The other was Ben, a broad-shouldered lad who was covered in freckles. Ben had taken to calling Enoch names whenever they crossed paths but had never actually talked with him. Enoch found that odd.

The two were playing some sort of game on a wooden plank. The plank had a series of holes drilled into it in a regular pattern, and the boys were moving various stones from one side of the board to another. In a few short moments, Enoch figured the rules of the game. It was fairly simple: gray stones could only move a distance of three holes, black stones could move seven, and the two white stones seemed to be able to jump across any unbroken line of grays.

With a cry of victory, Ben jumped his white stone into a hole occupied by a black one. The other boy—Jason, as it turned out—grumbled as his friend took the black stone from its spot and placed it in line with several other black and gray stones on the left side of the board. Ben then moved the white stone forward two holes.

Enoch recognized what was happening here—it was a tangible metaphor for a duel. Each of the stones represented an action: a thrust, a parry, a dodge, or a feint. Gray stones were quick actions, and four of them could be moved per turn, or two black stones could be moved per turn, or one black and two grays. The white stone was a finishing move, a *coup de grâce* that ended each turn. If the duelist had been able to string together a series of actions that landed the white stone on an occupied hole, he got to keep the stone and take another turn.

But it was obvious that Ben was going to lose. In six more steps, Jason would be able to trap his white stone between four blacks and easily take the rest. Enoch was stunned when the tall boy instead chose to timidly move four grays into a line in front of his own white. It didn't make any sense. Didn't he know that his opponent could jump past that supposed "defense" with at least five of the black stones arrayed around the table?

Without thinking, Enoch stepped forward and pointed to the board.

"You shouldn't waste your advantage like that."

Jason looked up at Enoch, his eyes going wide when he saw who had addressed him.

"Huh?"

Enoch knelt down next to the board, tracing his finger along the four gray stones. "You are leaving yourself wide open for—"

Jason's expression went from a look of surprise to a scowl. He smacked Enoch's hand away from the board.

"Don't touch my toads, orphan. Who asked you?"

Enoch held his hands up, surprised by Jason's anger.

"Toads? I . . . I'm just trying to show you where to put your guard so you can turn your opponent's stroke."

"You have no idea what you're talking about, idiot." Jason rolled his eyes and nodded to his friend. "Hey, look at the runt—he couldn't talk until he was five, and suddenly he's an expert at *jedrez*?"

Ben had an amused smirk on his face. He seemed to be glad Enoch had joined the conversation. He swatted at Enoch's shoulder with a freckled fist, chuckling. Enoch frowned. He was not as tall as any of the boys—or girls—his age in town, but he wasn't *that* much smaller.

"This is a man's game," said Ben. "It's *complicated.* These stones are part of an army from the Rain Age—venom toads, coldmen, and Alaphim. The board is a battlefield. And it's none of your pitmilking business."

Now Ben hit his shoulder again, only hard. Enoch fell back on the gravel, instinctively bending his legs as he fell so that he rolled to his feet a second later. He had been so focused on the patterns in the game that he hadn't noticed the other boys who had gathered around as Ben spoke. There were three more of them, Jason's older brother and two of Ben's cousins.

"Well, Scales, that was a pretty little dance," said Ben, eyebrow raised. "Maybe the orphan's albino uncle has been teaching him how to spin and twirl like the girls down at Cavernsway?"

The other boys laughed at this while Enoch rubbed his sore shoulder. He looked over at Jason for some understanding.

"I was just trying to help you win."

Jason stood up to his full height.

"I don't *need* your help. I don't *want* your help. Nobody asked for your advice, you little—"

He swung at Enoch, his fist whistling through the air. Enoch ducked under the blow, now understanding that this conversation had turned into a fight. Somehow. He took a quick step back, turning aside into the *semprelisto*. This was the best stance for unexpected attacks, and Enoch felt it most appropriate. Master

Gershom had been drilling Enoch on stances just this morning.

"You *did* need my help," continued Enoch, trying to help them understand.

Why are they so angry about this?

"You had just set yourself up for five easy attacks, something that would've guaranteed a loss."

Jason swung at him again—only this time Enoch's dodge brought him up against Ben's sturdy frame. The thicker boy had snuck up behind Enoch, and now he wrapped his arms around Enoch's and lifted him into the air.

"See if you can hit the runt now, Jason. You need me to piss an X on his face?"

The taller boy cussed and swung, his heavy farm-boy fist slamming into Enoch's ribs with a thud. All the breath went from his lungs with a gasp. Enoch looked around, frantically searching for his master. He didn't understand why they were doing this. It hurt.

"Don't . . . I was just . . ."

The next hit cracked across his jaw, and Enoch tasted blood. He struggled to get free, but Ben only tightened his grip.

"Scales! Wiggly little weasel, aren't you?"

And then Enoch saw Master Gershom. He had just come out of the blacksmith's shop across the road and—and he was just standing there. Doing nothing.

Enoch tried to call out to him, but his voice was weak and there was no air in his lungs.

"Please . . ."

Another blow to the side of his face, and Enoch's vision went black for a moment. For a moment it felt quiet, and Enoch instinctively fell into that quiet. He *paused.* Everything slowed around him.

Enoch had learned this—this *pausing*—all by himself over the past couple of weeks. He could turn his mind inside and still the motion of the world around him. He couldn't actually stop the world, or even slow it, but he could affect *his* pace through it—allow his mind to quietly take his time to think. To plan.

Now seems like a good time.

From his *pause*, Enoch slipped into the *afilia nubla*.

Dodge, direct, divide. The three simple mind commands that freed his body into instinct.

Leaning back into Ben as though to avoid Jason's next swing, Enoch suddenly lunged forward and brought his captor's face in front of the blow. Jason's fist smashed into a freckled nose with a crack, and Enoch felt his arms suddenly free. Using his forward momentum, he grabbed one of the arms that had held him, twisting it as he swung around Ben's falling body. Ben fell limp to the ground, and his own weight pulled his arm from its socket. Enoch stepped away from the body and faced Jason, bending his knees back into the *semprelisto*.

Jason stared down at his fallen friend with his mouth open. "Ben! I'm . . . I didn't mean to—"

Enoch's kick swept his left leg out from under him, and the taller boy landed with a cry. The others backed away, having never seen anybody move like Enoch. What was more frightening was the emptiness on his face. The detachment. This wasn't how boys fought.

Enoch stayed in his fighting stance, eyes dead, until they had all slunk away. He looked at the two boys on the ground, calculating. He delivered another vicious kick into Jason's side, and one to Ben. Only one of the boys groaned.

This was not vindictive; it was how he had been trained, to make sure your opponent was not only beaten, but *broken*. Master Gershom nodded and waved Enoch over to leave.

By this time, several townsfolk had gathered. They whispered among each other and stared. Here stood that scrawny orphan boy from the other end of the valley, thin and wiry and silent. And at his feet lay two much larger boys—seventeen and eighteen years old. One whimpering, and the other out cold.

They were still murmuring as Master Gershom led his charge out of Rewn's Fork.

Enoch rose out of his trance state and into *afilia lumin* slowly, hesitant to enter back into the confusion of what had just happened.

Why did they attack me?

Master Gershom was silent, as usual, but as soon as they were out of sight of the town he motioned for Enoch to stop. He then brought out the pot of salve, handed it to his charge, and proceeded to apply the ointment to Enoch's side and bloodied lip.

"You will need to learn how to better read coming violence, Enoch. Not just in a telegraphed blow, but in your opponent's words. His expressions."

Enoch was angry, and not just because his master had stood and watched his beating.

"I wouldn't have had to fight them if we came to town more often. Then I could talk to them and . . . maybe figure out why they treat us like we're strangers!"

Enoch wasn't angry at the boys who had attacked him. He was angry at his master, angry with an intensity that surprised him as it all came spilling out.

"I don't know why they did this," he grumbled, "or why nobody will talk to me, or why Lyse can't even look at me!"

Gershom's hands had gone still, and he looked down at Enoch with those winter eyes.

"You aren't upset because they avoid you, Enoch. Or even because they hate you. That is what you may think you are feeling, but it is not what is truly troubling you."

Enoch met his master's eyes, waiting.

"You are upset because you can't understand their reactions. Their emotions. You are upset because this is a pattern you cannot understand."

Pulling a clean rag from his satchel, Master Gershom dabbed at the salve on Enoch's lip. Enoch wanted to pull away, wanted to shout, wanted to call his master wrong. But he felt the truth of those words.

"That is why I have to keep you isolated from the others, Enoch. Because you do not feel as they do. Or see as they do. You were not meant to."

Enoch had learned that he could not always depend on his

master for clarity, or for help. Eight years ago, Enoch had climbed too far up into the ironwood tree behind the stable. Master Gershom had come out at Enoch's pleading and then stood under that tree all night, quietly. Eventually Enoch had fallen, hands numb from keeping such a frightened grip on that branch, and Master Gershom had let him fall. He then picked up the sobbing boy from the ground, carried him inside, and bound his broken arm. Enoch remembered the only words his master had for him that night:

"You found your way down."

The shadows lengthened as the two neared home, the dark trees seeming to absorb the night as it soaked down from the mountainside. Enoch went to check on the sheep as his master took the iron he had purchased into the tool shed.

They had a silent dinner of stew and toasted bread, sweetened with a dollop of red berry preserves that Master Gershom kept at the top of the pantry. Enoch supposed that the rare treat was some sort of unspoken sympathy for the earlier trauma. It certainly wasn't an apology.

Enoch went to his bed near the stove, tired and aching. Sadly, his mind would not let him sleep, replaying too-clear images and sounds and memories of hard fists against his jaw. Enoch decided these thoughts wouldn't take him anywhere, so he pushed his thoughts back to the game he had seen Ben and Jason playing. It was a simple pattern, but it held so much potential for complexity.

Enoch played through the game again in his mind, trying to discover if there had been some hidden trap in the four-gray-stone defense. By the time the full moon had risen over the cottage, Enoch had concluded that the strategy was as useless as it had seemed—in fact, it was one of fifteen possible formations that *guaranteed* a loss. Enoch began to devise different action strings that would have granted Jason a victory in less than ten turns. The patterns and their subsequent responses were just as fascinating as a duel, and Enoch lost all track of time.

By the time the sky began to grow bright, Enoch had constructed a rolling unit of black and gray stones in his mind; the unit could be arrayed in five turns and could sweep the board clean in three more looping "super turns," after which it would fold in on itself until only one white stone was left in the center hole.

Enoch sat up in bed, rubbing his head as Master Gershom began to stir in his bed across the kitchen.

What a foolish game—it is impossible to lose if you move first.

He puzzled over it until his master had started cooking breakfast, thin strips of mutton sizzling in an iron pan. The older man finally noticed the red, puffy eyes of his charge.

"Couldn't sleep?"

Enoch blinked a few times and shook his head.

"No . . . I'm just . . . I just can't stop thinking about that game they were playing. I keep going over different ways they each could have moved their pieces for victory, and then finding new ways to counter each—"

Enoch noticed that his master was frowning.

"I should have warned you about getting your thoughts caught in that sort of thing. It can be dangerous for you, Enoch."

Enoch was not sure what he meant. "You mean I can't play games like that?"

"No, no—you can certainly play them. In fact, they can be wonderful tools for sharpening your . . . your talents. You just need to learn how to *moderate* your fascination.

"This particular game is called *jedrez demonyos*, and has been around in one form or another for ages. Your dear young friends were right about one thing; the stones represent beasts and warriors from ages past. The object of the game is to collect prey for your angels while denying the angels of your opponent."

"Except there is no use in pretending the pieces are living things, Master," said Enoch. "They don't vary in strength, and they don't tire or grow hungry. They always move exactly like they are supposed to. They are more like a series of actions."

"Of course you see it that way, Enoch. You see patterns and sequences where others see the pieces as tiny replicas of the creatures they were named after, unable to look beyond symbolic individuality and into the actual workings of the game. Their moves will always be reactive and shortsighted against an opponent who understands the variability of sequence."

Master Gershom smiled, in a warm mood for some reason this morning. He went on to describe the *jedrez* tables he had seen in his youth, obsidian and marble carved to the exacting detail of every wart and feather.

Enoch yawned and tried to listen, even though he was still upset; it was rare when his master spoke of the time before. Before Rewn's Fork and sheep and the endless woods. The quiet boy kept even more still in these occasions, afraid to startle the rare bird that was his master's lucidity.

* * * *

The dull metal of the hoe bit into the soil, slicing a root in half and ringing as it encountered another rock beneath. There were always rocks in the soil—at least, it seemed there were wherever he hoed.

Mishael Keddrik had called their valley Old Snake's Pisspot once during a visit to the town. He had laughed about how the lovely spring-fed pools, which watered the land along the foothills, were just a cruel trick to farmers: bounteous clear water wasted on such thin, stony soil. His laughter, however, had withered the second he caught Master Gershom's scowl. Enoch's master did not like blasphemous talk. Or talk, in general.

The memory made Enoch grind his teeth. Lifting the hoe, he swung it down into the soil with a grunt, sweat dripping from the long strands of hair at his forehead. Angry thoughts flashed through his mind.

I'll never have friends; I'll never have anybody to talk with. Not as long as I'm trapped here.

Enoch knew that he wasn't trapped. He really had no idea what he would do elsewhere, and people confused him. He had a routine here, a comfortable order to daily life. Master Gershom said that routine was important to people who were like Enoch, and that he wouldn't do well with the unpredictable.

Then why does the unpredictable seem so interesting?

He set to hoeing with the single-mindedness that Master Gershom had taught him to use when performing the *pensa spada* exercises, clearing all other thoughts and feelings from his consciousness and programming his mind with simple, powerful commands.

Strike. Pull. Step.

Body moving in smooth obedience, his motions soon became a fluid pattern. The hoe arching through the air, the weeds yanked from the soil, and another step along the row.

Strike. Pull. Step.

His breathing soon matched the rhythm, and his heart slowed a pace to synchronize itself with the motion of the swinging hoe. Face blank, eyes transfixed on nothing more than the ground in front of him, Enoch moved swiftly through the sunbaked rows. A dull, familiar pain began to throb at his forehead, something which his sub-conscious mind duly noted to inform him of when he came out of the *pensa spada* trance. For now there was only focus.

Strike. Pull. Step.

Soon he approached the end of the last row, and the trance subsided. The *afilia nubla* of the sleeping mind canceled subconscious commands and aroused the waking *afilia lumin* as it, in turn, shut down. Blinking his eyes like he had just woken up, Enoch turned to look at the garden. Piles of knotted weeds lay strewn across neat rows of tilled earth, pale and naked in the bright sun. He rubbed the heel of his hand on his forehead, where icy pain still needled. That had been happening recently when he went into *pensa spada*—ever since he'd learned to *pause*, actually. He intended to mention the strange aches to his master sooner or later, but it wasn't urgent.

Just a little pain.

If there was one thing that childhood on the edge of the wild had taught Enoch, it was that pain could be ignored. That had been one of the first lessons his master had taught him. Not that

Enoch had ever been beaten—Levi Gershom wouldn't raise his hand in anger. He believed in a different sort of discipline.

Enoch sighed. His master was the kind of man who could say enough in a few words to make you wish for the kick in the pants you deserved. Enoch remembered a few years ago when he had been caught hunting rockfinches with a sling. Master Gershom had looked down at the still cluster of gray-plumed bodies at Enoch's feet and sighed.

"They are so small, boy. Does it please you to bring pain to these tiny things?"

Then he had put his heavy hand on Enoch's shoulder, softly repeating the phrase he intoned when a new lamb was born to the flock, something he called *The Prayer of the Beasts*:

> *"Men are made for the Law of God,*
> *but the beasts and birds obey Him.*
> *Men sing hymns upon the alter of God,*
> *but the beasts and birds are His song."*

Enoch's sling lay untouched ever since.

Still rubbing at his brow, Enoch walked from the garden and set the hoe at one side of the utility shed. The windmill poking out from the roof of the shed stood motionless in the slight breeze. Enoch unlatched the rough pine door—tightly fitted to keep moisture and vermin from damaging the more delicate machinery inside—and reached for the sturdy pole, which stuck out perpendicular from the side of the tall center post. He pulled it, angling the blades up into the wind, and then grabbed the worn wooden handle of the crank at the base of the mill.

Slowly at first and then steadily faster, he began to spin the crank, watching the blades through the thick glass window in the roof. He kept at it until the blades caught the wind and spun on their own, and then he released the handle to thumb the switch on his left. The light above it glowed green weakly at first, but shone stronger as a gust of wind rattled the shed.

Head still aching, Enoch trotted back to the house, anxious to get his recitings done in what little time the late afternoon breeze would afford him.

Closing his eyes so that they could adjust, Enoch strode into the darkness. He had known this place all of his life, and even without light, he could see it in his mind. A stout pine table dominated the center of the room, surrounded by two simple stools. To his right, a large hearth of smooth river stones cemented together covered the wall, and the mantle was adorned with a thick beeswax candle—left unlit now that it was summer. Above the mantle would be two crossed practice swords, the wooden blades stained black with the soot his master used to teach him target strikes and edge awareness. Various herbs and sage peppers hung from the roof beams, giving off a sharp, simple smell. Enoch could describe this room down to the last dust mote if asked. It was part of the discipline that he had been taught:

"Absorb the image into your eyes, into your dream mind—the *afilia nubla*—and it will be branded there to be seen by your waking mind—the *afilia lumin*—when it is needed. A good warrior can dance through his fortress blindfolded."

Master Gershom was always talking about what a good warrior did. Enoch thought it was kind of silly. For all of his master's nostalgia for his military past, it really didn't serve any purpose here. Enoch would grow up to be a shepherd just like everyone else in the borderlands of Midian. Here, a sword was a rare sight, and a man who knew how to use one even more so. The only weapons ever seen were bows for hunting and the occasional sling or staff for protecting the flock. Enoch studied and listened and danced through the *pensa spada* exercises because Levi Gershom was his master. It was the order of things and always had been.

What Enoch wanted had nothing to do with anything. Sure, he was curious about his parents. Master Gershom said that they were good people, and that they had loved their son dearly. But now they were dead, and Enoch was all right with that. This place was all he knew. This farm was a comfortable and finite place, circumscribed by trees, sheep, and the atonal breezes which wound down the valley from the white-capped Edrei.

It was only lately that some of the questions had begun to take on a life of their own. Enoch had tried to quiet them, but the odd contradictions of his life were starting to stand out in relief against the uniformly predictable nature of the whole. Enoch felt . . . unease. It was somewhere in between curiosity and anxiety. And rather than answering his questions, Master Gershom had instructed him to take the mental turmoil and bridle it—turn the tension into a focus for his lessons and recitings. The odd thing was that it had worked, but Enoch wasn't sure that he *wanted* it to. The questions felt important.

Enoch reached the far corner of the room and pulled the hidden screen aside. Oblong and blocky, the Unit squatted in the niche like a rusty dwarf; the light from its small screen bathing the room in blue. Sitting at his stool, Enoch keyed his name into the pad in front of him. The words flashed onto the screen, as they always had:

::Welcome Enoch.

::What shall we do today?

The low throb of pain in Enoch's head surged again, blurring his vision before subsiding. Shaking his head, Enoch wondered if he should lie down until the headache went away.

And have Master Gershom come home to find me napping?

Gritting his teeth at the dull ache, he typed in the code for his recitings and leaned back as a list of ballads filled the screen.

Stories of heroes and their adventures were much less exciting when you had to memorize them in heraldic verse. And the excerpts from *The Book of Prophets* were even worse—translating from godspeech to commontongue was boring enough without it all being senseless metaphors entirely unrelated to anything in Enoch's experience. What use did a shepherd have for flowery words from men who had died back before the world had been broken?

With a groan, Enoch rubbed his forehead. The pain was getting worse. Out of frustration, out of desperation, he closed his eyes and *paused*—on the off chance that his new trick might help the aching subside.

Oddly enough, it did. For a few seconds, everything felt clear. Peaceful. Orderly. His thought about the Unit, its connection to the windmill, and the windmill's connection with the winds which blew into the valley from distant lands. Interesting places. Places with unique scents and colors and tastes, all of which streamed back over the mountains to turn the blades of the windmill and brought the Unit to life. The connection brought Enoch peace.

Enoch opened his eyes and reached over to key in his recitings. Glancing at the screen, he frowned. Something was wrong. For some reason, the monitor had changed. It seemed to be moving, *pulsing*, with waves of numbers and letters, a cascade of symbols that twisted and breathed. The dark room seemed to ripple with an aquatic shimmering.

And now I've broken the Unit! Scales!

Even though he had only thought the word, Enoch reflexively looked over his shoulder. Master Gershom frowned upon such language, and would guarantee no further trips to the village if he knew Enoch was talking like Ben and Jason.

The ache between his brows intensified, and he mouthed the word with a sneer, whispering, "Scales!"

The Unit had never acted like this before. Master Gershom treated the thing like a sacred relic, opening the metal box that housed the complicated mechanism every spring to reverently clean and polish the myriad of delicate pieces inside, then carefully putting it all back together.

Enoch suspected that it was incredibly valuable. Nobody in town had anything like it, and Master Gershom had told Enoch to keep it a secret. And now he would have to tell him that his precious machine was broken.

Shaking his head, Enoch reached for the cutoff switch.

A sudden spark shot from his outstretched finger to the keypad. The pain in his head was suddenly unbearable, forcing a moan through his clenched teeth. With a trembling hand, Enoch reached over to steady himself against the Unit, and as his watering eyes met the screen, his moan was cut short.

In the center of the screen was a face. Large eyes—deep and

bright and empty—stared at him as though from miles away. Enoch tried to pull away from the eyes with a gasp, fear punctuated by the pain that flared molten in his head. A finger of sharp white electricity leapt from the keypad to his clenched fist, followed by another which forked and wrapped around his other wrist. They held him to the Unit like nails.

"Help! Master Gershom!"

Under the pounding of blood in his ears, his voice came to him strangled and weak. On instinct, his mind reached for the *pensa spada*.

Something massive and invisible pushed it away.

The eyes continued to bore into him, and that face, cruel with remote disdain, opened star-crusted lips and spoke.

"SEAL EARTH AND SKY."

The words were made of lightning, and they ripped into Enoch's skull. He rocked under the blow and began to slip into blackness. Shadows danced at the edges of his vision.

"SEAL EARTH AND SKY."

He felt as though a fire had been ignited between his brow, and he tasted blood. The face seemed to waver, the eyes flickering with momentary static.

"SEAL EARTH AND SKY!"

The cry was undeniable, imploring, commanding, plaintive. It was a cry of desperate need and monstrous authority. Enoch gasped, aching with the undeniable need to serve, to obey. A final surge of bright power shot from the monitor as the face melted into a horizontal line that then winked into a pinpoint.

Then, nothingness. As dull numbness washed over Enoch, he imagined he saw a bird soaring away into the black depths of the monitor.

CHAPTER 2

Our coming has not been sweet. Alas! Would that we could behold the birth of the sun. What have we done? We were united in our mountains, but our natures have been changed.

—Balam Quitze, Balam Acab, Mahucutah, and Iqui Balam, The Progenitors Await the First Dawn

Mosk knelt stiffly before the altar, forced to stillness under the red light which smoldered from the clerestory above. Except for the occasional twitching of his thorny and segmented hands, he was motionless.

Rendel smiled down upon his monster, not unkindly.

Well, the Hiveking is right to be nervous . . . He might as well fidget. To be pulled away from the heat of the conflict with the Centek at such short notice. A normal man would be sweating rivers.

But Mosk was not a normal man. A dry voice—like sand being sifted through dead leaves—rustled from his armored throat. "My blood to your tongue, Sire. Command me."

I'll never tire of that—the needful plea of a monster craving the leash.

Rendel dimmed the lights in the surrounding niches and dilated the rose window high above the altar. The resulting column of light silhouetted his crowned form—or at least, this most human appendage of his form. Most supplicants were unaware, but the entirety of this mechanized cathedral was Rendel's true body; even now he felt the soft tropical breeze spilling over his coffered spine, smoky incense from the censers warm against his nave. But Rendel chose to use this smaller form, his withered carnal body, for addressing his supplicants. They always seemed to appreciate having a face to focus on, and the Arkángel Desgarrar enjoyed making small concessions to his chattel.

They were, after all, the keystone of the Vestigarchy. They were the vital strength that kept the old order vibrant, awake, and fervently gripped upon the reins of power even in this sleeping age. One had to be vigilant with such frightening slaves.

Thanks to the cruelties of nature—cruelties lovingly incubated and nurtured by the ancient breeders—Mosk and his kin were living symbols of pain and hunger. After hatching, the first moments of life for the larval blackspawn were pure violence. Brother devoured brother until only the strongest remained.

This simple hate had then been cleverly woven into something resembling human intelligence. The result was the most fearsome brand of warrior this tired old world had ever seen. The sciences which named and blessed the blackspawn were lost, and their numbers were now relatively few. But the Vestigarchy held tightly to its last remaining tools—tools from the days when men spoke and mountains fled. Of these tools, the blackspawn were the most jagged.

And Mosk was their leader—a name and a title given to Him Without Brother, the Swarmlord, the Hiveking.

Rendel smiled again, hidden servos moving skin and jaw in place of long-faded muscles. Mosk still bowed before him quietly, awaiting command.

"Keep your blood for now. We want you to leave your battle with the half-men and take up the Hunt once more."

With carefully concealed pleasure, Rendel noticed how even Mosk's spidery hands stiffened at the news, the misshapen ebony head swinging up to glare at him with tiny yellow eyes. It was rare that his kind showed surprise.

The dry voice hissed, "The . . . Hunt? The last etherwalker died by my hand not a decade ago at Tenocht. The witches reported none left in all of our Lord's domain. Scans were done . . ."

"You will take two legions of your coldmen to the eastern continent. An inter-stratospheric signal was sent from somewhere near the southern tip of the Horeb Wilds not five days past. The signature is unmistakable."

"Hmm, hmmm hmm," was Mosk's reply, his chewing claws rubbing against each other hungrily. This was how he received news, devouring it like flesh. "This has portent for the Vestigarchy. What does our Lord intend to—?"

"Our Lord intends to finish the Hunt!" boomed Rendel's voice, enhanced by speakers hidden in the steel pillars of the cathedral.

Tall windows of ornately cut glass shivered at the sound. Rendel shook his head with fatherly concern—a subtlety entirely lost on this son of a bastard race—and lifted his carnal form into the air on a thick spine of cable, antennae, and steel umbilical tubes. Flooding the nave with crimson light, he spoke in a pure basso that shook dust from the ceiling.

"All you need to know is that our ancient enemy still exists. Count yourself lucky that our Lord does not have your limbs pulled from your thorax for failing in the task which you had deigned complete."

Mosk stood. He unfolded his sub-arms with claws extended.

"Fail our Lord again, Hiveking, and you will pay the price of sour blood!"

Instead of bristling at the insinuation of weakness, Mosk simply lowered his head and extended his pri-arms, palms up, his species' way of showing subservience.

"I will go and do as my Lord has commanded."

Rendel nodded and lowered himself to just above his prostrate servant's head.

"Good," he whispered. "The draconflies will be waiting for you at nightfall."

* * * *

A low hum rose, barely audible over the roaring of the wind and waves below. A white claw of moon crept out from among the clouds, silvering a dozen long and monstrous shapes as they sped over the whitecaps.

Moonlight momentarily glinted off of spear points and armor. The monsters carried an army on their backs.

While most of the riders huddled tightly against their winged mounts, one lone figure seemed unconcerned by the long drop to the sea. Perched behind the massive head of his steed, he gripped its antennae tightly with two pairs of armored hands. Wind lashed at the figure, and beads of condensation rolled down his oblong cranium. The swarm turned away from the moon toward the dark eastern sea.

Mosk did not *pause* to shake the drops from his brow. He was staring intently across the waves, and only the giant beast beneath him could hear the clicking coming from deep within his throat. The beast was not much more intelligent than the primitive insects it had been bred from long ages ago, but even under the roaring of the wind, it understood the meaning of that sound. It was primal, a language as old as life. The language of hunger. The language of blood.

CHAPTER 3

One man? I count a Nahuati blademaster, his two swords, and more courage than your entire raza could collect in a week of Tuesdays. You are sorely outnumbered, Captain.

—last words of the martyr Aven Sant before the storming of the Fortaleza de Hiero

Sheep didn't care if you'd slept the night before. They still needed to be led out to pasture, to be watched and cared for no matter how slow and clumsy you felt. Enoch herded the last stragglers into the pen and closed the latch. He leaned against the post with a tired sigh. The moon was rising over the Edrei, and he could hear Master Gershom making dinner inside the cottage. After dinner, there would be sword practice—practice that Enoch had been delaying for weeks. His master had been lenient, but he had his limits. Enoch slumped his shoulders.

I don't want to practice. I don't want to use the pensa spada.

It had been two weeks since Enoch's accident, and he had not been sleeping well. He was having nightmares about that terrible . . . about the accident. Waking up in a cottage filled with smoke, hands sticky with blood and black soot. Master Gershom had returned from the pastures that evening, rushing through the door with his swords drawn.

"What happened? Who was here? What was burning?"

Enoch had tried to clean up the mess, tried to air out the cottage. But he knew Master Gershom would be able to tell. He knew that he would be blamed for breaking the Unit. At least he had been able to hide the burns on his wrists.

Things had been uncomfortable for a while. Master Gershom showed a genuine concern for Enoch, aware that he had been traumatized somehow, but the man was obviously heartbroken about the Unit. He had spent days trying to get the machine to run again, pulling it apart and putting it back together a dozen times. But the damage was irreparable. Enoch heard his master cursing and grumbling about "fused wires" and "cracked circuits"—not much that he understood, but he heard the anger, sorrow, and frustration in Master Gershom's voice.

And it's my fault.

Enoch wasn't going to make it worse by telling some half-remembered dream about a face on the screen. A face that talked to him and—

He shivered.

It didn't happen. The Unit broke and I breathed in some smoke and passed out.

Rockfinches dipped and soared overhead, chirping as they fed on the moths that fluttered from the trees as darkness fell. Warm yellow light was glowing from the windows, a thread of smoke drifting patiently from the chimney.

Enoch still didn't feel like going in just yet. He leaned against the rough wood of the gate, listening to the mewling of the sheep and the light birdsong.

Silhouetted in the moonlight, the remnants of the windmill leaned against the side of the barn. The evening shadows did their best to hide the naked skeleton of bent, blistered metal, but Enoch knew. It pained him to see the once-familiar figure standing so forlornly among the ashes of what had once been the shed at its base. He could see the new iron bolts holding the case together—his master had spent another two days trying to repair that as well.

And it's all my fault.

The shed had burnt to the ground the day of the accident, and luckily the wind hadn't carried the flames to the house. Enoch's eyes traced the length of the corroded metal post, followed its shaft down to the blackened crank. At the base was a tangled vole's nest of cables and wires, which had been twisted and warped by the heat of the fire.

As his eyes rested on the broken mess, he began to see patterns. It felt surprisingly similar to figuring out the *jedrez* game—layers of patterns and order webbed behind a chaotic facade. And the patterns in this pile of rubble were surprising.

Suddenly, it was as though Enoch's brain unfolded within his skull—his mind *paused* all by itself—and instead of a ruined windmill, Enoch saw a flash of bright connections, lines of energy and motion that pulsed and shone even in the now defunct machinery. It was only a flash, but in that instant, Enoch felt as though he understood the windmill. Not only *understood* it, but was a part of it.

And then the flash was gone, as it had gone that morning, leaving him breathless and down on one knee. Enoch shook his head—it was aching again.

What is wrong with me?

Gingerly touching his brow, he turned and walked back to the house as the blades of the windmill lazily spun, slightly creaking in the darkness.

I'll just tell Master Gershom about this. Maybe I should tell him everything—he'll know what to . . .

He stopped. Slowly crouching to the ground in front of the house, he lifted some dirty straw and let it drop. It fell straight down.

No wind.

The creaking windmill began to slow and then picked up again. A frigid trickle of fear slid down his throat. He turned to look at the windmill, blades spinning noisily in a phantom breeze. The burnt-out remnants of the shed, now shrouded in evening shadows, resembled a crouched animal, low to the ground and ready to pounce.

Stop scaring yourself. Sixteen years old and still frightened by shadows! But, if there isn't any wind?

Within the darkness, a bright yellow eye winked and then seemed to glare at him.

* * * *

Enoch practically leapt through the doorway and slammed the door shut.

Master Gershom looked up with a start. "What's the matter?"

Enoch didn't wait for him to finish. "Master, something is out there! Over by the windmill!"

Levi Gershom froze where he stood. "Enoch, go and get my blades. Move swiftly, silently, and douse the fire on your way back. Go!"

The fierce, whispered command shocked Enoch back into sensibility. He nodded once and then headed toward the back of the room where his master always placed swords beneath his bunk before they retired for the night.

Is this what I wanted? A break from the pattern? Why is my heart pounding?

From the corner of his eye, Enoch noticed that Master Gershom was creeping from window to window, shutting and bolting the heavy storm shutters. Enoch overturned the cauldron of stew that had been simmering over the fire—there was a splash and a hiss—and suddenly the room was black.

Enoch then returned to his master's side, a scabbard in each hand. Taking the swords, Master Gershom motioned for Enoch to move to the other side of the door. Then they waited, in the dark. Silently. Only the occasional sounds of the sheep came from the fold to punctuate the rhythmic creaking of the windmill.

Enoch had a hard time holding still, peering now and again through the slits and wringing the sling in his hands. Each time he checked, the front of the cottage was clear.

But I saw something. Something was there.

Master Gershom crept toward him and laid a hand on his shoulder. With a gasp, Enoch jumped.

"Calm down, boy. Find your *afilia nubla*, cast off your fear."

Enoch nodded and closed his eyes. He had been avoiding the

shift into *afilia nubla* since the accident because he was afraid of the detachment it brought. Now, at his master's command, he recognized the need . . . and he yearned for it.

Enoch's lips moved in silent incantation.

The mind is a world, the consciousness its light. As day turns to night, so shall my mind; afila lumin setting as the nubla rises, and my mindworld revolves.

"Now," said Master Gershom, "describe to me what you saw."

"Something's out there, Master." The cool rationality of *pensa spada* enveloped him as his fear slowly began to melt away. "I saw a . . . an animal . . . over by the windmill. It was turning and turning . . . and I saw eyes."

Master Gershom frowned, then sighed. "You probably just saw an old nerwolf. They've been known to seek out human settlements when they feel they are going to die. Now . . . let's go chase him off before he decides to make a final meal out of our sheep."

With a grunt, Master Gershom threw open the door and paced angrily out into the moonlight.

Whatever is out there will kill him. He doesn't know . . .

"Master, wait!"

Enoch hesitated half a second before gritting his teeth and chasing out after him, all vestiges of *pensa spada* slipping away. Master Gershom had stopped just in front of the windmill and was staring down into the dark patch below it. From over his shoulder, the pale light of the generator winked at Enoch mockingly; apparently, the green glass cover had melted in the fire and exposed the yellow bulb underneath.

"Master?"

He chuckled. "Here's your ferocious beast, Enoch."

"Well—I guess the good news is that the motor is still running fine. Sounds like the blade pivot needs some oiling, though. Listen to that squeak."

Enoch cut him off. "But that's what I was trying to tell you, Master. There is no wind."

Master Gershom's head shot up to look at the moonlit blades

spinning in a silver arc. He breathed sharply as his hand went swiftly to the sword at his side and tightened around the hilt.

"Boy, get inside the house."

Enoch didn't move; he just stood there, his eyes wide and lips moving soundlessly. "I think . . . I think I did this."

Master Gerhom looked down at his charge, eyes widening. "Are you sure, Enoch?"

"I think so. Yes," Enoch said in a distant monotone, his eyes intent on the windmill.

"Ever since the accident, I have been seeing . . . *more*, Master. Lines. Things that move and . . . and spin and glow. Ever since the accident." He slowly reached up and rubbed his forehead.

"It's like with that game, *jedrez*. I can see patterns like that, but inside of things. I can see how they work. The windmill, the Unit. And I can feel them, too, even though I am standing apart."

A hint of fear crept into his voice.

"What is wrong with me? Why am I seeing these things?"

Master Gershom closed his eyes, then put a sturdy hand on Enoch's shoulder.

"I'm sorry, Enoch. The signs have been there, but I had wished . . . had hoped if we kept you isolated out here . . ."

Enoch felt his fear deepen. *What is he trying to say?*

"Don't worry, Enoch. This is something that you carry from your heritage. It is not a flaw, or a weakness. It is . . . or it *was* once a great blessing."

Enoch nodded, waiting.

"You are the son of a noble house, Enoch. Before she died, your mother asked me to bring you here, to this crust of civilization on the edge of nothing. Your people had wealth, had tek, and it allowed their enemies to track them. So I searched for a place with no tek and no ability to signal . . ."

His master froze.

"Enoch, I made sure to remove any antennae or networking mechanisms from the Unit. It was a data storage and processing Unit, nothing more. Did you . . . did you change that? Did you help the Unit to connect—?"

The windmill began to spin again, the only sound in a countryside gone oddly still. The quiet of the melancholy twilight seemed to deepen.

Connect? Didn't I dream of the wind connecting from . . . but no, that was a dream!

"I don't know, Master. I thought that I dreamt of—"

"Stop, boy," came Master Gershom's whispered command, harsh in the nocturnal silence.

Enoch froze and turned his head in surprise. Master Gershom had his head slightly tilted, his lips moving in a voiceless incantation of the *litania eteria*—the word-thoughts which would bring on the *pensa spada* trance.

"What . . ."

And then Enoch noticed as well. The rockfinches had gone silent. Only the faint creaking of the windmill overhead was audible. A lamb called out nervously.

Master Gershom's face moved toward Enoch's ear, and in a low whisper he said, "Listen, Enoch. Tell me what you hear."

Nodding, Enoch cocked his head to the side as well. He sent the powerful command to his *afilia nubla*.

Hear!

All of his concentration came into focus on the sounds around him. The slight rustling of hay as the sheep stirred in the fold; the deep, rhythmic breathing of Master Gershom at his side; the slowing beat of his own heart; the slight sizzle and pop as the ashes on the hearth cooled inside the cottage; and . . . a distant humming coming from the sky. It was slowly getting louder.

"Something large is coming from the south, Master. It's coming quickly."

Somehow, the events earlier that evening had drained him of feeling, and he found it easy to maintain the cool serenity of *pensa spada*.

Master Gershom nodded and tilted his head to the other side. His eyes were closed.

"How far away?"

"Hard to say. I don't hear footsteps, man or muridon."

"Rewn's Fork is aflame."

Enoch turned his head. Sure enough, the clouds far to the south seemed strangely low and heavy. There was a flash, and their dark bellies flickered orange and red. The light played across Master Gershom's features, and his shadowed eyes slowly opened.

"Raiders. Or worse. They'll be burning the eastern farms next. Quickly, let the animals loose. Go to the stream and wait for me on the bank where it passes the large saproot. Go."

Enoch sprinted to the fence and unhooked the latch, letting the gate swing wide. The sheep, now fully awake and nervous, crowded into the back corner of the fold. Enoch ran toward them, waving his arms and hissing, as first one, then the entire flock poured around him and out. They milled around the side of the cottage for a few seconds until he was able to get them moving towards the open hills to the west. Hopefully they'd be safe foraging through the blue pine scrub until this danger passed over.

Gritting his teeth against the odd thought, Enoch changed his mind and ran around to the front of the herd. Now he pushed them toward the forest, scattering them into the verdant darkness in little groups of two and three.

Raiders will be hard pressed to find two people in a forest full of skittish sheep.

And another thought froze him in his tracks.

Why do I assume they are hunting us?

Disregarding the thought, Enoch plunged ahead, avoiding the path and weaving a serpentine trail through closely growing trees as his master had taught him. As soon as he could hear the gurgling sound of the stream, he cut left toward the ghost shapes of the white mountains visible through the trees.

He reached the looming shadow of the saproot and collapsed as his *afilia nubla* slipped back into its subconscious lair. Panting heavily, Enoch looked down to find that he had torn the skin on the side of his right foot as he ran. It wasn't too deep—his feet were tough and well-calloused—but he pressed a fallen leaf against it anyway to prevent the wound from leaving a trail of blood. The leaf stuck, although it did sting a little. Master Gershom had still not arrived. Enoch's last recollection was of seeing him bolt toward the house.

Where is he?

Thinking quickly, the boy leapt to his feet and grabbed the branch nearest him. He swung himself up and then grabbed the next branch—long summers of climbing now proved to be of some use. In a matter of seconds, he was near the top and could see over the other trees all the way to the cottage. It looked small and cold, huddling alone in the distance.

His gaze moved upwards at some half-imagined movement, and then he saw *them*. Two shapes in the night sky, blacker than the blackness surrounding them, and swiftly growing larger. As they swept low over the trees, he had to choke back a gasp. Each of the beasts was at least twice as long as the inn at Rewn's Fork.

As he watched, one of the beasts swung off to the west.

Old Aaron Kaspit's farm is at the fork of the stream over the next hill. I hope he is sleeping lightly tonight.

The other beast continued on toward him. In another few seconds it would be upon the house, and Master Gershom had still not emerged.

What is taking him so long?

Enoch tightly gripped the branch under him as the beast buzzed over the thatch roof, the nearby trees bending under the hellish wind of its approach. From his perch high in the tree, Enoch could see movement all along the ebony back. A man, no—nearly a dozen men in black armor rode astride the creature, and one of them held something glittering in a raised gauntlet.

The beast circled around, forcing Enoch to cling to the branch, praying that he wouldn't be seen. As it passed over the house again, he saw the glittering object arcing through the night air with a sputtering hiss. There was a thud, a roar, and the house burst into a ball of flame. An invisible wave of heat shook the tree as the forest was lit with a garish orange light. Enoch's own scream was drowned out by the hungry noise of newborn flames.

"Master!"

"I'm right here, boy. Stop shouting and climb down. We've

got to head for deeper cover—they'll be down here soon enough to see if they finished the job."

Scrambling, practically falling down, Enoch hit the ground a few seconds later.

"When I saw the explosion, I thought you were inside. I . . . what were you doing?"

"Retrieving what is ours."

Enoch noticed that he carried a bulging sack over his shoulder. He shot his master a questioning glance.

"Move it, boy! I'll tell you along the way. We need to get going—they'll not wait long to search through the ashes."

With that, Master Gershom strode off quickly through the trees, moving with that familiar quickness which belied his size. Enoch scrambled after him, head spinning.

Raiders, giant monsters, our house destroyed like a moth in a candle flame!

It was more than he had experienced in his sixteen years of life, yet Master Gershom spoke as though it were just another sheep to shear.

I should be that focused. Enough whining for me tonight. Focus!

Searching for something to concentrate on, his eyes rested upon the bulging sack his master carried.

What would Master Gershom think so important to remove from the house?

As he pondered the question, he sized up the dimensions of the bulky shape bouncing against Master Gershom's broad back. He caught a pattern in its weight and balance.

"The Unit. You removed the Unit from the house, but why? It was broken—they couldn't have wanted to steal that anyway."

"Smart lad," grunted Master Gershom, shifting the sack to his other shoulder. "I retrieved the Unit. Now think—what would somebody searching for us want with it?"

Enoch rolled his eyes. Master Gershom was always testing him, but now hardly seemed like the time. Well, it would keep his mind from dwelling on those flying monsters, the explosion, the only home he had ever known reduced to embers.

No. Just think.

What would somebody want with the Unit? All it contained in its dusty memory spool was a bunch of old poems and books, immunization and breeding records for the sheep, a seed inventory, and . . . and fairly recently it had contained a glowing inhuman face which had spoken to him.

But I never said anything about that to him.

"You think my accident caused this?"

"I fear so, my boy. Your new . . . talent . . . is not something new to this world. It is rare nowadays—some would happily say extinct, but there was a time ages ago . . . well, all I know is from old stories. There are those who would do anything—*anything*—just to have you at their command. And those are the ones who wouldn't kill you on sight. Recall your recitings? What does line three of Rephidem's Lament say?"

Enoch thought for a second, scratching an insect bite on his ankle as he climbed over a fallen saproot trunk. The leaf had fallen off of his foot some distance back, but that was all right because the bleeding had slowed. Enoch found the page in his mind and quoted.

"And oh, our sorrow when the Ironwed fell; oh, the sadness of the day when none more could walk within. Yet they, the Worldbreakers, were despised amongst men."

Enoch *paused.*

"What is a *Worldbreaker*?"

Leaves crunching underfoot, Master Gershom walked on. The question remained floating in the air. Enoch stared at his master but continued walking. He felt cold despite the exertion.

"Enoch, my boy. This talent is something intrinsic to your race. To your kind. I was sworn to your parent's banner, but I had no idea that—"

"My race?" Enoch interrupted, "What do you mean by *my* race? Are you saying my parents could do this too?"

His master sighed.

"No, not exactly."

He rubbed his hand through the pale bristles of his beard, and then returned it to his pommel. Master Gershom lifted the heavy sack from his shoulder and tucked it under his free arm.

"I've kept this information from you for your own safety. Sometimes children can't be trusted to keep to themselves that which might cause them harm."

What?

"Who did you think I'd talk to? Are the sheep planning a revolt?" The words burst from his mouth, and Enoch was surprised to find a thick surge of bitterness welling up inside his chest. "You should have told me!"

"Hold on, boy—you don't even know what I have been protecting you from. I had my reasons."

"You kept me stupid and useless!"

Master Gershom's voice was suddenly dangerous and low. "Enoch, you are walking the fine line between my patience and my hand, a line you've never tread before—and that is the only reason you still have your teeth. You'll not speak to me like that again.

"I taught you what you needed to know when you needed to know it. This talent is something unexpected and unasked for. It does not always arise in your line, and even then the full realization has rarely developed. Your ability to see patterns and your . . . *discomfort* around people is genetic and relatively benign. In fact, in ages past it was considered a genetic flaw. A weakness."

Enoch was confused and didn't know what to say.

His master tried a different approach. "Your father was a great man, Enoch, but he struggled to talk with people in the same way that you do. Like you, he was brilliant with patterns. With tactics. But he didn't have the ability to—" and here he motioned toward the Unit on his back.

Enoch felt as though his chest shook, his heart was beating so loudly. This news was making him feel anxious. Angry. Scared. It was worse than his fight in the village. He had to gain control.

Constrain. Calm. Control.

Master Gershom waited, watching Enoch's face, his breathing, his tightly clenched fists. Enoch knew he was being tested even now.

Constrain. Calm. Control.

His muscles unhitched and his breathing slowed. Enoch tilted his head up to his master and nodded. Master Gershom held his gaze for another second and then continued.

"There was a rare chance you would develop this ability, Enoch. Rare enough to pull you from your mother and hide out here in the wild. This ability can scare the powerful and anger the weak. Your family wasn't the first to fall after the Schism."

"Schism?" asked Enoch.

"A disaster which broke the world. The end of a golden age. Mostly dark legend now, but it provoked the lowest acts of a frightened people. The most despicable of these acts was called the Hunt—a calculated genocide."

Master Gershom looked down at his hands and sighed.

"The Hunt scourged this land seven times over the centuries. The creatures of the First Hunt—their description would chill your blood. They passed into legend, were slain by their prey, and have not been seen for many lifetimes.

"But I *did* witness the Seventh Hunt. This one was performed by men, by those who knew the folk they pursued. We don't need tales of monsters. I've seen the things that frightened men will do to other men when fear overwhelms them, Enoch. Monster is too small a word. And this fear didn't end when the Seventh Hunt departed into the west.

"There were those who worried that the last Hunt had failed, that it wasn't wide enough in scope to truly root out all of the Worldbreakers. It didn't help that those remaining families with ties to the Pensanden also happened to be the wealthiest citizens of the Old Cities. A few of the families fought against the Hunt. Most of them doubled their guard and locked themselves away, waiting for the fear to subside. The wise ones fled."

Enoch didn't understand half the words that Master Gershom was speaking, but he kept quiet nonetheless. His master had never talked of his past, and Enoch didn't dare shatter the moment.

"I was the Captain of the House Guard, a Nahuati blademaster, and trusted right arm of your sire. When the mobs finally cornered us . . . when my men had fallen, and your father lay bleeding on the tile . . ."

Master Gershom stopped walking. He turned and looked Enoch in the eye, a wetness glinting silver in the moonlight.

"Your mother begged me to take you and run. To hide my swords and mix with the crowd while she led them away. I was to bring you to this unwatched land and raise you to manhood."

Enoch was still.

"It was the hardest order I ever took. To spurn the clean deaths of my guard and *run*."

The woods were quiet. A small animal shuffled through the leaves near their feet.

"I was on the street below when she threw herself from the . . ." He looked away. "When she died."

Master Gershom cleared his throat, moving quickly from this memory. There was a tenderness in his voice when he spoke of Enoch's mother.

Enoch shook his head. Who was he to speculate? He knew nothing of these things.

"Our escape wasn't clean, you should know. My swords were not hidden, nor were they dry by the time I carried you through the Pauper's Gate and down to the burning plains beyond. It took me three long years to arrive here, and I imagine it will take an even longer stretch to return."

Enoch shook his head in astonishment.

"We're going back? But what about the mobs? The Hunt?"

"We are going to return in shadow. I can train any man to wield a sword and dance the *pensa spada*. I can train any man to stalk a foe and take his blood. But I do not know how to train a boy in the Pensanden way—and I will not create another World-breaker."

Now Master Gershom was talking to himself, and Enoch could barely make out his words. "This is a cup I cannot drink, but I know of others who can." He looked up into the sky and frowned. "And of those who can, I know a paltry few who should.

First we will have to stop in Garron. The Gray Wastes hold the keys we will need . . ." He considered his words, then shook his head. "No, the guardian still hunts the dunes for all I know. We'll have to hope for allies in Tenocht."

Master Gershom began walking again, and Enoch hurried to keep pace beside him.

"But Master, what does this word mean—*Pensanden*? Why do we need keys to enter a city?"

"Some keys are used to open, Enoch. Others are used to awaken."

With that, Master Gershom was finished talking. His mouth was set in a grim line, and Enoch knew that no amount of coaxing would open it. They walked on in tense silence again after that.

* * * *

The moonlight slanting down through gaps in the canopy overhead created living pools of light amid the deep emerald-black of the forest floor. It was still strangely quiet; apparently the rockfinches had returned to their mountain nests for the night. They had been walking for hours, weary after a long day of work and no sleep. The forest grew deep and thick. Finally, Master Gershom tapped his shoulder.

"We should be well enough away by now. Even with the full moon out, this tree cover should be impenetrable from above. We'll rest now."

Enoch stumbled over to the base of a tall pine and collapsed to the ground, ignoring the dull pricks of fallen pine needles as exhaustion overtook him. Master Gershom sat down with his back against the rough trunk and opened the sack, pulling out the Unit. There was a creak as the big man pried a template from the back of the now defunct machine with his short sword. Enoch couldn't help smiling as he drifted off to sleep.

Well, he finally found a use for that thing.

Enoch dreamt of flying—he flew up through the trees and into the warm summer air. As he reached the lowest clouds, he turned north and rode the wind until he had left the valley. Beneath him the forest thinned and became a rolling plain. He could see Master Gershom far below, a newborn lamb across his shoulders. His master waved at him but then pointed backwards—he seemed to think that Enoch was going the wrong way. Enoch laughed and flew onwards. Nobody could tell him what to do when he was this high in the air!

Up ahead, the bland smoothness of the plain was interrupted by a giant tree—a tree so tall that it pierced the clouds. Beneath the tree, huddled in the shade, a beautiful city sprawled—Enoch had never seen a city, but this broad expanse of buildings and crowds of people could only be that. He waved to the people below and was surprised to see terror on their faces. They were running everywhere, scattering to get out of his sight!

It was then that Enoch noticed his hands. They were hideous! Gnarled and segmented and ending in yellow claws. With a shout he looked down the length of his body only to discover that he was one of those monstrous winged creatures that had destroyed his house! No wonder the people were screaming.

Enoch looked back at the milling people, tried to speak to them. To apologize. Flame erupted from his mouth. Men, women, children; all were caught in the fiery blaze. Their screams mixed with the smoke and ash in the air and stained the city walls in violent tones of black and red. Enoch wept brimstone as the city burned.

His violent dreams evaporated as he awoke to his master's nudging.

"You were calling out in your sleep, boy. Besides, it's been two hours—we'd best get a read at what's happening around us. Climb that big pine and look around."

Shambling, his head still fuzzy with sleep, Enoch approached the pine and began to climb the prickly, spoke-like branches. After twenty feet, the wood began to bend under his weight, so he stopped and glanced out over the forest.

They had gone far. Most of his view was obscured by other trees, but he could tell by the thin line of moonlit gray smoke where the house had been, and it was now distant. There was only dark, waving green gilded with moon silver as far as the eye could see. He had barely begun to descend when the humming began.

Looking up, he was just in time to glimpse the giant beast as it roared over the tree. He struggled to hang on as his perch thrashed violently in the backwash of wind.

It was going far too fast to see me.

I hope.

Master Gershom called from below, asking if he was all right. Firmly placing his feet on the branch below him, Enoch strained to watch the retreating form of the beast. Something was strapped to its abdomen—a long, curiously worked saddle from the look of it. Enoch counted ten seats, two of them occupied by men in that strange black armor.

Meaning eight on the ground.

Enoch cast a fearful glance down to the forest floor and then southward. Master Gershom called to him again, concern in his voice.

In a clearing back by the stream, Enoch spied them. Two armored men were guiding hounds—or something like hounds—through the trees. The animals had their snouts to the ground and pulled the leashes taut, the men running and all but being dragged behind them.

"Master!" He shouted, "Master, they hunt us!"

"Yes, Enoch," came Master Gershom's reply, flat and unfeeling. He was deep in *pensa spada*. "They are already here."

Enoch froze, his hands locking around the branch. Looking down, he saw another raider come into view, closely on the heels of another pair of hounds.

Those are not hounds.

The beasts looked like some horrible combination of a giant spider and a dog. Eight jointed legs rustled through last year's fallen leaves, connecting at a scaly, bulbous torso. The torso ended in a small gray head, topped with a cluster of glittering black eyes. A blunt canine snout jutted from the head, grinning with crooked yellow teeth, and two pairs of antennae whipped through the air—conspicuously graceful on these obscene creatures.

The creatures surged forward, pulling their driver into a pool of moonlight. Enoch gasped. That was no man in armor—it was a monster more twisted than his pets! An oblong, seemingly overlarge head balanced on a spindly, segmented neck. Oily black skin, chitinous and splotched with red markings, covered the creature from head to foot. The legs were oddly bent, angling backwards like those of a cricket.

It looked altogether unnatural. Awkward. *Wrong.* Yet the smooth assurance with which it glided into the clearing spoke of predatory grace and lethal swiftness. A wickedly curved axe swung loosely in one of its segmented hands.

Master Gershom already had his swords unsheathed, the dissembled Unit lying in a heap at his feet. Cold light ran along the curved blade in his left hand and glinted off the point of the short sword in his right. The monstrous raider took a surprised step backwards to assess the threat—obviously it had met little resistance that night and did not expect to come face-to-face with a giant man bristling with swords. It cocked its head, tiny orange eyes glinting curiously. Then it unleashed the hounds.

They surged forward, voiceless except for the dry clattering of fangs. Master Gershom smoothly stepped into guard position, knees bent and swords crossed in front of him. One slash from the curved blade separated the first hound from its head; the straight sword buried itself to the hilt in the leathery thorax of the second. Enoch felt cold blood splatter his feet. His hands were frozen around the branch.

Move, coward! Climb down and help!

He couldn't move. All of the training in the world meant nothing in front of this terror.

Master Gershom had already leapt over the corpses and moved on toward the driver. It wielded the axe as though the weapon were another appendage, taking advantage of the lethal weight to parry his opponent's slashing attacks. Swinging the axe in wide arcs, the raider seemed to cavort in a gamboling dance punctuated by flashes of iron. It moved like a nightmare, whirling toward its prey with hungry certainty.

Devilishly quick and strong as the raider was, Master Gershom was quicker. Within seconds, it became obvious what the outcome would be—the big man moved with a liquid grace, countering each attack and pressing the creature into defensive postures again and again. His swords clove air like lightning, weaving a thread of reflected steel moonlight between the wafts of the shadowed trees.

As metal rang against metal, the monster was illuminated in a shower of yellow sparks; Enoch could see saliva frothing at toothy mandibles. The movements of the axe were becoming frantic. Backed against a tree, it swung wildly in a fierce attempt to decapitate his foe, and for a fraction of a second it left itself unguarded. Crouching low and knocking the axe wide with his curved blade, Master Gershom stabbed upwards with the straight blade.

With a horrifying silence, the creature fell over backwards, red, strangely human blood oozing from a hole under the shattered chin. It continued thrashing until Master Gershom stepped on an arm and chopped the head off with his curved blade.

Levi Gershom looked up to call for Enoch as four more of these armored warriors stepped into the moonlight, seeming to condense from the shadows. A hungry clicking sound filled the air. Master Gershom turned and let out a low whistle.

"Enoch, stay in the tree until I've dispatched them all. These coldmen are quick, but they don't know our style."

"But Master," called Enoch, voice trembling. "There are more of them!"

Master Gershom shifted into *semprelisto* and turned his back to Enoch's tree.

"They don't know who they are facing," he called. "My order—the Nahuati—was originally founded as a defense against them."

Here he held up his contrasting swords, the straight and curved blades that Enoch knew like his own hands.

Suddenly, two shadows moved in from each side. The clash of swords, the dull thump of bodies colliding, and an undercurrent of wet inhuman chattering—the strange percussive dialect of these *coldmen.* Master Gershom had pushed the fight into the trees, seeking to gain advantage amidst the shadowed trunks. Another clicking snarl trailed into moist gasping and went quiet as the straight blade found its mark. But his master was horribly outnumbered, and Enoch caught a glimpse of three more shadowy forms swiftly approaching through the trees to his left, led by a pair of spider-hounds.

Master doesn't know their number. He'll be overwhelmed! Get down there, damn you! Move!

Still, fear rooted him in place. He tried to grasp at *afilia nubla*, mumbling the *litania eteria* over and over again. Below, a pair of coldmen had spied him and began to move toward his tree. Enoch shut his eyes and let the words of the incantation wash over his mind.

The mind is a world, the consciousness its light. As day turns to night, so shall my mind; afila lumin setting as the nubla rises, and my mindworld revolves.

Something inside of him gave, and he felt his mind turn over. The darkness around him was now clear, each sound from below as distinct as a pearl. With the powerful focus of *afilia nubla*, Enoch sent the commands.

Descend. Distract. Divide.

Releasing the limb, he fell ten feet before landing nimbly on a lower branch. It bent almost to the snapping point before whipping him upwards in time with his leap. Lancing through the air, he curled into a ball. The air was a cold whistle against his skin.

With a crunch, his knees smashed into the face of an approaching raider. It toppled backwards into its comrade, and the hounds hissed as they were yanked short on their leashes.

Rolling free, Enoch bent and scooped a handful of rocks from the ground as the coldmen scrambled to their feet in a skein of jointed legs, spears, and axes. The hounds strained against their bindings, snapping at their masters in frustration.

They are armored, but move quickly. Six seconds until they regain footing.

Distract. Divide. Defeat.

Thin muscles rippled with a taut accuracy as the sling hummed through the air once, twice, in two fluid arcs. The hounds crumpled to the ground, each bleeding from a small dent in the middle of its head.

Enoch dropped and rolled to his right as a spear whistled over his shoulder. One of the raiders was up, an oily silhouette in the shadows of the forest.

They move like insects. Adjust timing patterns.

Still moving, Enoch found himself in front of a large fern bush. The other two coldmen had regained their feet now, and they circled around each side of the bush while the spear wielder collected his weapon and stalked closer.

Enoch stood and slipped another stone into the sling. The spear wielder stopped, tilting its head in a monstrous parody of amusement. It lowered the spear to the level of Enoch's gut and took a step forward. Out of the corner of his eye, Enoch could see the raider to his right raise its axe. This was going to happen fast. Spinning around, Enoch found himself trapped by a third—it raised a strange, tube-like device to its shoulder.

The unexpected route.

Instead of dodging, Enoch leapt forwards towards the spear. Too late to raise its point, the spear wielder had only time to see the boy run *up the grounded shaft* and deliver a sharp kick to its head. Moments too late, the axe slammed down on the spear shaft, snapping it in two as a loud blast of fire erupted from the third creature's weapon. The metal tube spat a swarm of molten steel balls and electricity that stripped the bush of leaves and ripped an arm from the axe wielder. With frustrated clicks, the grounded spear wielder struggled to stand, but the death throes of his bleeding companion knocked him back.

Enoch ran, the calm of *pensa spada* leaving him as worry for Master Gershom welled up in his throat. The sounds of battle had ceased, and only the thrashing of the wounded creature behind him was audible.

The monsters won't find us so quickly without their hounds.

His head buzzed with these thoughts as he stumbled into the clearing, nearly falling over the twitching corpse of a disemboweled coldman. He cast his eyes around the scattered bodies, all glistening black wetness in the moonlight.

"Enoch—"

Master Gershom lay on his side, a thick spear shaft passing through the muscled flesh of his inner thigh. His clothing was torn, and Enoch could see countless smaller cuts through the tatters.

"Master!"

"Don't fret, boy. This is not all my blood. The spear is the only serious wound of the bunch. A good warrior protects his vitals. Remember that."

Master Gershom winced as Enoch tried to staunch the flow of blood at his leg with a handful of leaves.

"Quite a skirmish, eh? I've been in plenty of battles but never at five-to-one odds. And every one of them more skilled than the other, why that last beast with the spear, I only barely—boy, those leaves will do no good. Go tear some cloth from the sack over there under the tree. That ought to do it."

Enoch stumbled over to the sack, his face a mask of misery.

I might as well have thrown that spear myself. Leaving him to fight alone and outnumbered. Coward! Coward!

The now silent woods echoed back his shame and rage. Master Gershom read the boy's thoughts as he returned with the bandage.

"Not your fault, Enoch. There are forces bigger than the two of us, stronger than the Edrei themselves. We cannot blame ourselves when destiny turns sour. That's right—not too tight now."

He grimaced as Enoch wrapped the tattered cloth around his wound. Blood soaked through the bandage and ran down Enoch's arms.

"No . . . no . . . I can't stop the blood! I need some more . . ."

Master Gershom pulled the boy's hands away from the mess and held them up to the moonlight. He looked intently into Enoch's eyes. He knew. They both did.

Master Gershom's eyes turned to his charge's hands, and then widened with surprise. He gave a shallow laugh and shook his head.

"These . . . these scars on your wrists, Enoch."

Enoch looked down at his hands. The serpentine scar which spiraled from the base of his left hand almost to the elbow caught the moonlight, seeming to ripple as he watched. On his right hand, the scar resembled an inverted wave, two arcs cresting at his knuckles and coming to a point at the back of his wrist. His master's laugh turned into a wet cough.

"I'm such a fool. How did I miss these? You have been marked, Enoch. Only a rare few of the Pensanden ever received the marks. They are gifts to you, boy—gifts and an ancient lesson." Master Gershom's hands, perpetual sources of strength and comfort, now shook as they traced the pale tracks on his charge's arms.

"The Serpent and the Hawk," murmured Master Gershom, his voice growing steadily weaker. "The two forms which destiny takes, avatars of fear and hope."

He pulled Enoch closer, his voice a whisper. His eyes were closed.

"Feather and Scale."

Master Gershom reached into his bloody tunic and pulled out the silvery memory spool he had taken from the Unit.

"Take this, boy. Take it and go north. Go to Tenocht. There are those who will hide you there. Show them this. Take my . . . my swords. Speak to no one. Hide your marks."

Two coldmen crashed through the underbrush into the clearing. One held an axe, the other a smoking metal tube.

"Run, Enoch, run!"

"No, Master. I won't leave you!"

"Fool, boy! Leave me and run! These are coldmen, bred to kill your kind!"

The creature has now raised its weapon to its shoulder. Enoch *paused.*

There!

There were the lines of force, the motes of energy. He felt the hammer pivot back, the charge building power, the trigger slowly pulled . . .

"No."

With a blasting roar, the tube exploded on itself, filling the air with white-hot metal, smoke, and steaming pieces of flesh. The first creature spun to see the mangled torso of its companion fall to the ground, and then turned and charged, axe raised murderously high above its head. It erupted from the smoke like a demon, orange eyes hot blisters of rage.

Enoch struggled to his feet, pulling his master's curved blade from the ground. The monster was almost upon them, axe thundering through the air. Grinding his teeth, fatigued muscles screaming in protest, Enoch gripped the weapon and swung.

The axe spun end over end and thunked into a tree twelve feet away—two segmented hands still wrapped tightly around the haft. The coldman had time to lift the bleeding stumps up to its uncomprehending eyes before Enoch's second stroke took him in the gut.

Exhausted, Enoch dropped the sword to the ground and fell to his knees. The sky beyond the mountains diffused into gray-blue as the dark liquid of night bled away into the west.

CHAPTER 4

And was not this their greatest folly? For they lay with that which was of metal in a corrupted union, trading their souls for empty immortality, a life without life.

—Abuk 4:15, The Book of Sins

From his stony niche, Rictus watched the thieves return from their raid on the caravan. Apparently it hadn't gone well—two of them wore bloody bindings and all wore scowls. Some slunk off to their bedrolls while others gathered around the fire, grunting and cursing as they sat on the pitted headstones. Night had fallen, and a cold wind whistled through the ruins, causing a few of the rough men to shiver with more than just the chill. One of the men produced a wineskin from somewhere under his cloak and passed it around. As a gust of wind fanned the flames, they began to speak of the failed raid.

"Kingsmen! A damned caravan of the king's own trained dogs and two of them on murback to boot—was a damned fool idea to jump that ship, I tell you."

"Who scouted it, anyhow?"

"Gil!" came several replies. "Gil spied 'em."

The accused man protested. "How was I to know that they was Kingsmen? They wasn't wearin' no livery and the murs looked rangy enough!"

"Anyone catch a look at what was under the rag?"

"Nah—those kingboys kept us from gettin' in close, as Scrape will tell." One of the wounded men nodded his head and cursed.

"Looked like a cage to me."

"Yeah—a damned cage. That's what it was. Probably one of His Majesty's new pets—perhaps we didn't want to open the damned thing anyways."

The conversation soon simmered down into drunken threats, mumbled vagaries, and tired boasting of the day's exploits.

Rictus stifled a yawn, more a force of habit than a biological urge, and crawled back into his tomb. He wrestled with the idea of moving on and letting the highwaymen have their fill of this lonely place, but then he remembered why he was here and what was chasing him.

Room enough for everyone, I guess. Just as long as they help out with the rent.

* * * *

Enoch awoke to the smell of wet earth and leaves. He rolled his aching body from a cocoon of forest debris and felt the first cold drops of rain, signaling an early morning storm. It had been raining periodically for the last couple . . . what? Days? Weeks? Enoch had lost track a long time ago. He rolled back under the low branches of the blue pine, trying to ignore the hunger gnawing at his stomach.

He tried to escape into the numbing world of sleep. Sleep did not come—only the nightmares that stirred his mind like a flock of noisy birds.

Enoch couldn't clear his thoughts. He saw Master Gershom's face growing pale and cold as the last few drops of blood crawled from his wounds. He felt the forest, weeping and quiet.

He shivered.

Those monsters—those coldmen*—laughing with their rattle voices.*

Eyes closed, Enoch saw the shallow grave he'd carved from the muddy forest floor. Levi Gershom now rested between the roots of the very tree which had sheltered his cowardly charge. Such a pitiful monument.

Thunder boomed from the heavy clouds, pounding across the dark sky and seeming to shake the heavens. Underneath the dripping boughs of a scrawny tree, Enoch's hands slowly curled into fists. He struck the ground once, twice. His frustration was lost in the storm.

Hours later, the rain had turned into a wet haze, which hung motionless in the dreary air. Enoch crawled from underneath the boughs and stood for a moment, swaying on his feet, as if waiting for some errant breeze to pull him along. Mud streaked his bare arms, and his light summer trousers were torn and spotted with dead leaves. Master Gershom's leather boots were strapped tightly around Enoch's feet with leather bindings, long strips cut from the soldier's belt to make sure that the durable footwear wouldn't chafe in the journey ahead.

He rubbed at his swollen eyes and walked around the tree to where he had stashed his master's swords. The Unit disc hung from a cord at his neck, and it jounced against his chest as he walked. Brushing aside a mound of leaves, his fingers trembled for a moment and then grasped firmly onto the dry, worn leather scabbards. He strapped them around his shoulder and hip with the ease of familiarity and began to walk.

North. Master Gershom said I should go north. To Tenocht.

His legs moved in a slow rhythm through the undergrowth, only losing syncopation to jump over a fallen log or sidestep a game trail. The *litania eteria* spilled silently from his cracked lips over and over as he waded through the morning mist. After a few hours of walking, the forest began to thin, and Enoch found it exhausting to keep up the stealthy tree-to-tree path he had been following. With every snap of a twig he imagined a horde of clicking coldmen descending on him from behind, but in the end he decided that if they were still on his scent after all the rain, then he would be caught soon enough anyway.

With a sigh of resolution, he stepped from the wet shade of the trees and onto the dirt road which he had been paralleling for hours. To the south, the road disappeared into the gloomy maw of the woods. Straining his eyes to the north, Enoch could see where the woods finally gave way. The land sloped steadily downwards from the green-laced feet of the snowcapped mountains to a broad plain. Large boulders were scattered across the flat expanse like grain tossed for enormous hens, and Enoch could barely make out what seemed to be a river transecting the plain from east to west.

He stood in wonder, almost in confusion. Never in his life had he seen so much flat, treeless land. Fifty shepherds could lose themselves for years in such a place, flocks and all. Enoch experienced a tiny thrill of discovery at the sight, a welcome feeling after so much numbness.

The *pensa spada* may have kept the grief at bay, but the resulting void had soaked through his entire being. Now Enoch experienced a detached hunger for feeling—*any* feeling that could make him less empty. That this tiny ray of sensation had been able to pierce the cloud which surrounded him gave Enoch hope. Holding tightly to that mote with whatever strength he had left, Enoch took a timid step. Then another. With growing confidence, he walked down the road, dark eyes quick and wary of this strange new world.

As the midday sun burnt through the gray thatching of clouds, Enoch began to realize that the distant plain was much further away than it seemed. He walked for several hours, occasionally stopping to drink from the common *flortasse* blossoms. The drip, drip of rainwater from the surrounding trees grew fainter, eventually replaced by the singing of morning birds as they fluttered overhead looking for food.

Stomach growling in response, Enoch pulled the sling from his vest and decided that if he wasn't going to die any time soon, he might as well find something to eat. He was just stepping from the road when he heard voices coming around the bend behind him.

Images of coldmen fresh in his mind, he dove into the nearest thicket just as the party came into view. He landed with the hilt of the short sword digging into his shoulder, but he held in the gasp of pain. Wet foliage dripped icy rivulets of water down his back, and Enoch shivered. Peering between the leaves, he could spy on the group without being seen. They were human, he noticed with a sigh of relief, but something about them stopped him short.

Two of the men rode mangy muridons. Enoch remembered having seen a muridon years ago belonging to a dye merchant on his way through Rewn's Fork. At first he had thought it a gigantic nerwolf, for indeed the creature shared the same black eyes, chisel teeth, and naked, scaly tail as its feral cousin. But the muridon was a taller, more muscular breed that had been tamed for riding. The two in this caravan were larger than the one Enoch remembered, and their coats were patchy and crusted with mud. Their riders were no cleaner. They clutched at notched swords and squinted dark eyes as they scanned the road ahead.

Enoch pulled back into the deep shadow of the underbrush as they passed, cringing as another barrage of chill droplets wound down his back.

Some of the other men in the party wore chains around their necks and wrists. They were pulling some sort of wagon. In contrast to the riders, these men held no savagery in their eyes. They smelled of filth and sweat, and the tattered clothes which stuck to their damp forms could not hide the myriad scars underneath. Enoch blinked at the chains. He had never seen slaves before.

The wagon turned out to be a sturdy wheeled cage that dug trenches into the muddy trail as it rolled past. There was a canvas tarp tied over the top of it, but from his low vantage point, Enoch could see upwards into the shadowy recess. A large shape, gray among the shadows, was huddled in one corner. As Enoch watched, two fiery yellow eyes blazed out of the darkness, staring directly into his. Stifling a yell, he pulled farther back into the bush, praying that the mounted soldiers hadn't heard him. After a few endless seconds, the party had moved on, leaving nothing but two wide slashes in the mud, stippled with footprints and a waning stink of unwashed men.

Enoch waited for a couple of minutes to be sure that they were gone, and then stepped out onto the road again.

What was that thing in the cage?

He shivered, then shook off the chill and began walking again. He had read tales of the great heroes before the Schism and knew the journeys of Medrano, Galicia, and Armstrong by heart. Their trials had always seemed so much . . . brighter.

Is this what adventure is like? Fear and wet feet and unanswered questions?

It wasn't until the sun was fully overhead that his grumbling stomach reminded him that it still had to be attended to. After a few minutes of searching, Enoch discovered some straggly cress plants growing just off to the side of the road, and the hoarse calls of a red jay led him to a nest of speckled eggs which, while raw, seemed to taste better than anything he had ever eaten. He chewed on the cress as he walked, curious about what lay ahead.

By evening, the trail had emerged completely from the woods and now followed a fairly straight course through the boulder-strewn steppe. A fiery sunset painted everything with molten hues, and long shadows stretched out from the gigantic rocks strewn across the landscape. Enoch shivered as he walked through the dark lee of one such monolith. Night would come soon, he realized, and he would have little protection here.

He began to search for some sort of shelter as the shadows grew longer across the plain. Enoch knew how to make a shelter in the forest—every shepherd boy learned how to build a lean-to after being caught in a few rainstorms while herding the flock. But out here it was different. There were no trees. No branches. No . . . no shelter at all.

But plenty of wind.

Just as Enoch had decided to curl up under the dubious protection of one of the giant boulders, he saw a flicker of firelight in the darkness. Walking towards the distant mote of orange, he could just make out the silhouette of some large structures. *A town!* He hurried toward the light, visions of warm food and shelter filling his head. Towns were safe—at least safer than the open wild.

The lookouts spotted him easily, for Enoch took no care for stealth as he scrambled up the crumbling stone ramparts. Too late, he saw that this was no town. It was a graveyard.

A bearded man stepped from the shadows and seized him roughly by the arm. Before Enoch could speak, the rogue struck him across the face with the back of his hand. Staggering under the blow, he felt his swords torn savagely from their straps, and a sharp kick in the back of the knees brought him to the floor with a painful crack. Wordlessly, the man lifted Enoch under one arm and began walking toward the fire.

Enoch's head spun, and his entire body was numb from the blow he'd received. It was all he could do to keep from blacking out. Through tear-blurred eyes, he could see that the fire was closer, and he could just make out several forms seated around it. One of them called out.

"By the Snake's tail, looks like Grunty's caught us dinner!"

This was followed by laughter; the rough, dangerous tones made Enoch shiver. His captor ignored their words as he marched past the fire toward a building just beyond the light. It appeared to have once been a stone temple of some sort, but time and the ravages of nature had reduced it to an irregular stack of mold-skinned pillars.

Through the worn cloth curtain which hung from the lintel, Enoch could just make out the sputtering light of an oil lamp. Voices came from inside—two people were engaged in an argument. One of the voices was angry and stained with potential violence, while the other . . . the other raised the hair on Enoch's neck.

That other voice had the sound of ice, free of any warmth or natural human inflection. It rose and fell with a liquid sharpness; the sound of a razor sliding through silk, a venomous frost snake tracing lines over new-fallen snow. Enoch did not want to know where that voice came from.

His captor pushed the veil aside and brought him into the temple. A man and a woman looked up from where they were seated. Their chairs were pushed up against a cracked alter which had been converted into a table, a gray hart skin spread over the top with a tarnished copper lamp as the centerpiece. The lamplight formed garish shadows among the pillars, and the features of the two thieves were sharply highlighted as Enoch's eyes adjusted to the light.

The armor-clad man was larger than even Master Gershom had been, his thick arms crossed over a broad chest. As imposing a sight as he was, however, it was the woman that held Enoch's attention, for at a glance it was obvious that she was the owner of the frozen voice. Long white hair hung straight, framing a pale and beautiful face. The red cloak which draped her body could not hide the stately form beneath, and her pose alternated from graceful to predatory.

But the eyes were what startled Enoch out of his reverie. They had no iris, no color; just a single black pinpoint in the middle of glaring whiteness.

The angry man would not be interrupted. He waved Enoch's captor off with a hiss and turned back to the woman.

"Milady, few enough caravans come by this way anymore, and those that do are usually Kingsmen. We can't live off that! I don't care what you say; I'm taking my men and going up north to raid. We'll draft some new boys and get strong. Get fat. Then we'll come back here to wait for your prey!"

The woman slowly turned toward him and smiled.

"My men, Nibat. *My* men will stay here. How can you expect to raid a northern village if you cannot even stop a caravan of slaves?"

The question curled in the air. Nibat boiled over, sputtering.

"I already told Milady that they was royal-trained, and on murback. A normal caravan we could've stopped, but they was royal-trained, I tell you!"

"Two men against six, Nibat. *Six!*"

That did it. With a roar, Nibat lunged at the woman, grabbing for her throat. Enoch shut his eyes, expecting at any time to hear the snapping of slender bones. He felt his captor's arm grow tight around his middle, and he opened his eyes.

The woman still lived. She held two slim, silver daggers—pointed down, pinning Nibat's hands to the table. The large man had been forced to his knees, his eyes staring widely at the blades sprouting from the skin between his fingers. A serpentine smile curled the woman's lips.

"Sweet idiots, you plainsmen. I was drinking men's blood when your mother's mother first drank milk."

Nibat's eyes slowly lifted from his hands to the woman's face, and he spat.

"*Bruja*!"

The woman sighed and leaned back, bored.

"Now, Nibat, I will tell you what to do and you will listen, or I will find something softer to bury my knives in. Are you listening?"

Nibat growled and looked down at his bleeding hands. He nodded.

"Good. You and your band of brigands will remain here. You will not question my authority again. I came here following rumors of a specter, but . . . something else is afoot."

Enoch wondered at her strange speech, for the woman's face was smooth, and she could not have been much more than a decade older than he was. She leaned over and pulled the blades from Nibat's hands. He fell to the floor groaning.

"The Serpent has returned to this face of the world, and he works his sweet venom in the southlands. Do you know what that means, Nibat?" From the floor, Nibat's moan quieted, and Enoch saw him pull a short knife from his boot.

"It means that the roads will soon be filled with refugees fleeing the storm. Easy prey for you and your vultures. Easy murder, easy money, and young farm girls for your entertainment. And when my sisters return for me, I can make you all captains and generals; no longer cutpurses and rogues, but minions of the Forked Tongue."

As the woman spoke, Nibat's face had switched from a mien of anger into sweaty greed and lust. But those last words gave him *pause*. Staggering to his feet, at what he presumed a safe distance from those silver daggers, Nibat lifted his knife in a bloody hand and growled.

"We may be cutpurses as you say, Milady, but a servant of the Snake I'll never be."

The smile on her face broadened almost imperceptibly.

"So you would die?"

He roared and leapt, knife raised high. She caught him mid-lunge, daggers flying from her hands to bury themselves in his eyes. His leap carried him over the top of the altar to crash lifelessly at the woman's feet.

Nibat's neck bent at an impossible angle, his face turned toward Enoch. The daggers reflected lamplight from his red-weeping sockets. Enoch shuddered.

The woman walked around to the side of the altar, retrieved her daggers, and, to Enoch's horror, licked them clean before hiding them somewhere in her sleeves. The flickering light cast part of her perfect face into shadow, and for a moment Enoch thought he saw a cold blue light shine from her eye.

The woman motioned for his captor to approach, and with a grunt he carried Enoch into the room. At her signal, he was dumped unceremoniously onto the floor right next to the corpse's feet. The man then placed Enoch's swords on the altar and stepped back. She motioned him out without a word.

Now she was inspecting his master's swords, a delicate furrow creasing her brow. Enoch dared not move. A woman who killed like this, who could predict what she would do next?

"You are young to travel the road at night. Why did you come here?"

Her voice froze Enoch to the ground. This *bruja*, or whatever she was, would not hesitate to sell him to the beasts who hunted him. Steeling his face into the *Ferrocara,* he prepared to lie.

He dropped his shoulders and looked down, hoping he looked the picture of frightened villager. He had seen the expression plenty of times in his visits to Rewn's Fork. Voice trembling with what he hoped conveyed the proper amount of fear and misery: Enoch spoke of black beasts, a midnight attack, and his family farm burnt to ashes. Afraid to veer too far from the truth and get caught in his inventions, Enoch spoke of hiding in the trees as the creatures swept through Rewn's Fork.

It sounded convincing to him.

Is all emotion just mimicking patterns witnessed from others?

The woman smirked.

"Do you think me a fool, manling? Telling me this nursemaid's tale as though I were a frightened girl? You claim to be from the land of shepherds, and yet you carry the *derech* and the *iskeyar*."

A dagger was suddenly in her hand.

"You will tell me how and why the Rift Queen sends a scrawny Nahuat apprentice to find me. What message do you bear? Speak, or die."

Far from intimidating him, her words and his tale reminded him that he was far from helpless. His master had been preparing him. His master had been forging a weapon.

I killed blackspawn. I slew their beasts and burst their weapons.

The *litania eteria* slipped from his bruised lips, and he felt the familiar peace as his subconscious mind took over. The room came into sharp clarity. Somehow the woman sensed this change, and she stumbled backwards with a snarl. Her dagger gleamed in the fire light. In a heartbeat, Enoch was on his feet, and he noted her stance.

She moves quickly, and there is another dagger in the left sleeve.

Enoch's mind measured distances and options as he stepped into the bent-kneed, loose stance of unarmed combat.

Distract. Delay. Disarm.

The woman's smirk broadened into a grin.

"If you wish to die, then . . ."

She was cut off mid-sentence as Enoch's stiff-fingered jab caught her square in the throat. As she staggered back, he slipped into the *semprelisto* stance. What should have been a crippling blow only stunned her, however, and a second later the dagger was slicing through the air toward his head. Enoch had already dropped to the ground and rolled away, coming up to his feet out of her reach.

She is not human.

The thought almost shook him from his trance, but he held on fiercely. The finger jab was a blow his master had taught him to use as a surprise advance. It was painful enough to down even the largest man and end a fight before it began. If done with enough force, it could crush the windpipe.

But Enoch had not felt the hollow crunch of a broken larynx like his master had described—his fingers had instead encountered solid cords of muscle. Muscle, and . . . something else. Something much more solid.

She chuckled at his hesitancy.

"I'm not the picture of feminine frailty you took me for, am I? Have you Northerners so soon forgotten the plata*bruja*s? You no longer tell tales of the Serpent Wives? If you knew half our lore your heart would freeze and crack."

Somewhere in the back of Enoch's mind a memory surfaced of the Rewn's Fork Patriarch, old Noach Kohn, telling ghost stories around the fire on Midwinter's Eve. Yes, he remembered the tales—except according to Noach, the Serpent Wives were giant, iron-scaled women with fangs. They spat lightning and gorged on the flesh of disobedient children.

The real thing may have been less gaudy but was much more terrifying.

Hold on to the pensa spada.

After being hunted through the woods by coldmen and their spider-hounds, Enoch had hoped that he would not be so easily frightened. But now he confronted the subject of dimly-lit childhood horrors. Concentration slipped.

"You've been trained in the old ways, I see. There are not many who remember the mind path anymore. Who taught you?"

At the last word, she launched herself across the room toward him, hidden dagger flashing into her hand. He barely dodged her in time, rolling quickly to his right.

Her reflexes were quicker. A cold hand snapped around his ankle like a vise of frosty iron, and Enoch found himself being pulled under the empty smile. She had her dagger at his throat in a flash. She leaned over to kiss his forehead—the blessing of a

Serpent Wife before sending her victim to hell.

The lips were ice on his brow, and Enoch felt no breath on his face. A voice at the back of his head commented, *she doesn't even breathe.*

Enoch opened his eyes and *paused*. He saw them. The glowing lines, the swirling motes of power and energy. They were hard to see, buried under the coat of flesh, but they were there. The whorls and sparks danced in a pattern more intricate than those in the windmill, even more than the coldman's weapon. Enoch didn't know where to push, if he could even interrupt the complex system woven through her skeleton. The woman's dagger slid slowly across his neck, and warmth began to run down his chest.

In desperation, Enoch pushed with his mind. Pushed everywhere, twisting lines of force and stirring bright motes with frantic abandon.

The dagger stopped. A shudder passed through her, and then she was still. Enoch crawled out from under her dagger, hand to his neck to staunch the blood.

First a crackle, then a hiss came from the witch frozen at his feet.

"Ssss . . . an etherwalker . . . Ssstill alive!"

Enoch looked deeply and saw that the lines and motes he had pushed were rearranging themselves rapidly. Whatever he had done, the witch was repairing. A pale hand flexed spasmodically, and the hissing turned into a whine. Her dead eyes widened and in one swift movement, she lurched to her feet.

"You must be what the blackssspawn sssearch for. The Hunt! It sssearches for you."

Enoch pushed again; the witch crumpled to the ground and was still. Still, but not dead—after a few heavy seconds of silence, a faint whirring sound whispered from her chest. Enoch decided to escape while he could.

Grabbing his swords, pulling them over his shoulder with one hand, he limped to the ragged door. His neck was still bleeding, although it had slowed—luckily her dagger had only cut through skin. Enoch's ankle was numb where she had grabbed it. Peering through the thin cloth veil, he could just make out several forms striding toward him. The other thieves had heard the struggle and had come to investigate.

Enoch cast around frantically, desperate for an escape. At last he saw a collapsed hallway behind the altar. The sputtering copper lamp provided meager light, and it was difficult to see if he would be able to fit through the tumbled masonry. He lifted the lamp, and it dawned on him.

As the first thief lifted the veil to enter the temple, the lamp smashed into his face. Both veil and brigand burst into flame as the oil doused them, and the wind fanned the fire until it caught onto the few thieves unlucky enough to have crowded in behind him. It was enough of a distraction for Enoch to squeeze himself through the stones of the collapsed hallway unnoticed. Near the back, he found a crack large enough for him to slip through. And just like that he was outside the temple, with the sound of the shouting thieves behind him. He pulled his hand away from his neck and wiped the blood on his pant leg. The bleeding had slowed.

I did it! They'll never find me in these ruins. I just need to put some distance between us.

Enoch's confidence died as more thieves rounded the corner of the temple.

* * * *

Rictus stirred from his dreamless sleep to the shouts of angry men. Cursing soundly, he rose from his tomb and decided to take a look at what had them so excited.

And at this time of night they're bound to wake the dead.

Rictus often joked with himself. Sure, he'd heard it all before, but as he was fond of telling himself, the commentary keeps away the crazy. Even stale commentary.

After a few millennia, you run out of new material.

So the thieves had caught themselves something, and that something was a kid. Rictus would have frowned at that, if he could have.

No lips.

He liked kids. Or had liked them. His dusty mind conjured up images of them—the kids—shouting and clapping and dancing and screaming at him with bright teeth and painted eyes. These scratched and scattered memories less tangible than a dream.

It was that shadow of feeling, that drop of diluted happy, which brought Rictus from his tomb.

He had been running on idle in the deepest of the deep holes in this necropolis, hiding from that mek witch. She had been on his trail since Nu Àleman, and Rictus had decided to lay low and let her pass by. *No need to cause a ruckus.*

But now this kid was in trouble, and Rictus didn't like that. Perched on the top of a leaning obelisk, he could see that the brigands were going to start hurting him if somebody didn't step in soon.

Yeah, somebody. Of course somebody's bound to pass by sooner or later.

Rictus marveled that he had already been able to get so close without the witch coming out of her chamber—her sensors should be going wild by now. Had these brigands realized what she was and mobbed her? Naw, he couldn't give them credit for that. Maybe she realized that her trail had gone cold and left to sniff out a new one?

That's unlikely—her band of saps is still alive, and a silverwitch never leaves a living minion.

Rictus didn't really make up his mind until one of the brigands pulled a white-hot spear tip from the coals and decided it was time for some fun.

Because hey, I like kids.

'Least I think I do.

* * * *

The specter appeared just as Enoch had given himself up for dead.

It was a terrible sight—a grinning skeleton man leapt out of the shadows and *into the fire*, filling the air with embers and wild laughter. The specter dipped low and then spun, its longsword painting a wide, fire-lit arc. The arc passed through several of the men nearest the fire, including the brute with the spear. With a cry of horror, he looked down to watch the spearhead fall away from the shaft, followed by his right forearm and a portion of his nose. The rest of him soon followed with a thump.

Most of the brigands screamed and ran into the darkness. Those who stayed to fight were drunk and easily overcome. Enoch, his reserves of fear long depleted, simply stared at the specter with detached curiosity. He had never seen swordplay like this before. The long, thin blade seemed to move independent of the skeleton that wielded it, cutting a slow, yet deadly swath through the bumbling thieves like shears through wool. The sword sang as it danced, a low hum that turned blood to mist, flesh to steam, and bone to dust.

The specter was oddly dressed—smoldering black boots, pants, and a tattered jacket made of smooth leather, all painted in strange, arcane runes. Looking with his new vision, Enoch could see a black cord running from the longsword hilt and pulsing with energy. The cord wound around the specter's arm, over a jagged shoulder, and into a glowing recess under slotted ribs.

The sword takes electricity, just like the Unit! But where does the power come from?

Then, to his surprise, Enoch noticed that the specter itself was surrounded by glowing lines of energy, similar to the witch.

The specter generates its own energy!

Finished with its mayhem, the apparition lowered the humming sword and stalked toward him. Enoch quickly backed away.

"Hey, hey, don't worry, kid. I'm not going to hurt you."

The specter looked down at his blood-spattered ribs and tried to wipe away the worst of the mess, only managing to smear it in a more ghastly arrangement. It looked up and shrugged its shoulders.

"Yeah, I wouldn't believe me either."

Enoch didn't know how to respond. Was the creature trying to joke? That toothy grin was unnerving. There had been as many horror stories about specters as there had been about the Serpent

Wives. It knelt behind him with a creak and began to loosen the rough bindings the thieves had tied from his ankles to his wrists.

"You . . . you're a machine!"

"Well, no, technically I'm a . . . wait. Oh, you must be Pensanden, of course. Sorry. Didn't see the scars. I haven't seen one of you guys for a while. I thought you'd all gone dodo or something."

Here the specter grabbed Enoch by the wrist and held it up to the firelight, raising a mummified brow in mock suspicion. Enoch caught his breath and froze. The ghastly creature actually rubbed a bony finger over Enoch's skin, checking the legitimacy of the boy's scar.

Satisfied, the specter grinned and released him, returning to the tough knots behind Enoch's back. One hand was already free, and Enoch toyed with the idea of *pushing* this creature like he had the witch. For some reason he hesitated. Odd chatter notwithstanding, the specter didn't seem to mean any harm.

"Anyhow, I've got to get you out of here—those brigands are going to be the least of your problems if the wicked witch finds out what has happened here."

Enoch wondered at the cheerful rambling of the apparition as it walked back around and handed him the bindings. Coming shakily to his feet, he took in the specter's fearsome appearance.

A shock of spidery hair clung to one side of its bony head, and yellow, parchment skin stretched perilously thin across that same half of the face—all the rest was bone. Dry, thin-lidded eyes stared out of recessed sockets, the irises a fierce, unearthly green. Through the specter's open jacket, Enoch could catch a better glimpse of the flexible cable—covered with a patina of age, coiled once around a shriveled neck, and rooted in a rusted steel box. A tiny red light pulsed rhythmically over where the cadaver's heart should have been. Another coil emerged from the bottom of the box and disappeared into the withered abdomen through the navel.

The specter noticed Enoch's stare and smiled, tapping the box with a bony digit.

"The LifeBeat 3000—making your dreams come true one beat

at a time. Thanks to this little baby, I've been a happily damned customer for fourteen centuries. Quality that lasts, kid."

The specter tapped at the box again, stared at it for a long second, and then let out an airless sigh. He looked up and gave another quick shrug.

"But I'm not so tired of life that I want to see you lose yours. Let's get out of here."

Enoch didn't move.

"Come on, kid. I know you took a couple knocks to the head, but—"

"Don't worry about the plata*bruja*," interrupted Enoch, "I killed her."

He was surprised at how easy it was for him to say. Master Gershom had taught him that to kill another person a warrior must be prepared to lose a piece of himself. The trick was in learning to keep from losing too much, he said.

Enoch felt no pain, deep or otherwise, for killing the coldmen. He felt nothing for the Silverwitch. There was a twinge of regret for the dead men lying at his feet, but he was glad they could no longer hurt him. And technically, he hadn't been the one who had killed them.

Technically? Am I really that cold?

The specter hadn't moved either, and was staring at him with steady green eyes. It tapped the box at its chest, scratched under a bony chin, and then let out another sigh as it sheathed the giant sword under a strap on its back. The power cable disconnected itself from the hilt of the sword and slid obediently into the recesses of the specter's jacket.

"Serious little guy, aren't you? And already going hand-to-hand with the big girls. I'm impressed, my somber friend, but the Meka-scheyf Cyborgs were designed with little mindwrenches like yourself in mind; and unless you melted her into soup, she's going to be back on her feet in no time. And she'll probably be angry."

Perplexed, but oddly unafraid for the first time in what seemed like days, Enoch decided that he would rather have undead company than none at all; he gathered his swords and followed the specter away from the firelight. It was some time before he realized that they were heading deep into the crumbling heart of the ruins.

CHAPTER 5

In the last centuries of their glory, they did thrust their stained hands into the destinies of those humble creatures not yet born, shaping crude tools from the near living. And in the irony of God's justice, these crooked souls became their truest friends. And in the irony of God's vengeance, the untouched became their truest foes.

—Rephidem's Song of the Pensanden, Vol. 5

Mosk noticed the blood dripping from his fingers and stood, mouth watering at the sharp, heady smell. Shaking off his hunger, he walked around the still-twitching form of his Proximate to wipe his hands on the thick curtains that framed the room. A sullen clicking resonated from his chest, the sound of thin bones striking stone in endless staccato. The sound of frustration.

Proximate Isk had failed, and Mosk had killed him. The Hive was stronger. A Clot of searchers dead; the few surviving arakids gone feral and feeding on their master's corpses. No explanations and still no clues as to where this hatcher had gone. It was going to be more difficult to trace this Pensanden than Mosk had anticipated, especially in such a backwards land.

The Hunt had been different years ago in the civilized north—there the Pensanden left electric footprints wherever they went, unable to resist dipping their minds into the ever-present machinery which filled the streets like honey pots. There the commoners had been helpful, even willing allies, ever eager to see the end of such an uncomfortably powerful folk. They had betrayed neighbors and friends alike to the slavering jaws of the arakid.

The clicking grew into a more hollow rattling sound from the back of Mosk's throat, the closest his kind could come to laughter. He found himself both amused and repulsed by this peculiar weakness of mankind—ever fearful of a power greater than their own, they sought to destroy it instead of worshiping it as the blackspawn did.

Except for these Southerners. They were a frustrating bunch, silent and passive yet with an inner core of strength which had surprised even him. Many had died in the newly constructed smoke pits behind this so-called palace, and Mosk's best torturers had reported an odd resistance to brands and screws which had made many a warlord weep—even though these shepherds obviously knew nothing about the etherwalker. A strange people.

At this, Mosk glanced beyond the body of Proximate Isk over to his special prisoner, who, although bruised, bloody, and bound hand and foot, still continued to glare at him with those wet human eyes.

"My dear Baron, are you still angry over the death of your child?" His bone-dry voice rattled like beetle wings. "You humans value your pets overmuch; did you not see how I dealt with an inefficient subordinate?"

Baron Mordecai Efron spat blood from his mouth and snarled.

"Does the Vestigarchy fear children and shepherds so much that it must send their trained maggots across the sea to murder them?"

The last word was punctuated by a vicious blow from Mosk, which sent the man sprawling backwards onto his bound hands. The Swarmlord loomed over his prisoner, then grabbed him by his stained lapels and pulled him close. Fierce carrion breath washed over the baron.

"You will tell me where the Pensanden is! If it wasn't your son, then who? Such a powerful being could not have been in this land without your knowledge!"

Mosk dragged him over to the shattered window, which

looked out across the burning city, and lifted him through the frame. The baron's feet dangled over the paving stones far below.

With pleasure, Mosk noted how the man's eyes had widened in surprise and horror at his captor's inhuman strength. It had been a long time since this side of the world had witnessed the power of his kind.

"I see you finally realize your position," he whispered. "I am not here to negotiate."

Mosk was interrupted by the clattering of horned knuckles on wood. One of his torturers called through the door that he had found someone who knew of the etherwalker. Mosk toyed with the idea of dropping the baron, but reconsidered. The man might prove useful yet. Turning to the door, Mosk tossed the man against the table as he would a rat.

"Enter."

The bulky torturer, carapace splotched with the rust-brown markings of the labor caste, ambled into the room. In his indelicate claws squirmed a fat, oily man with a shock of orange hair. Mosk noted that his clothes, while torn and dirty, lacked the singed edges of most torture victims. This one had spoken before the irons had even left the fire.

"This worm says that he knows a person fitting the description of a P-Pens-anden, Hiveking." The torturer struggled with the foreign word, a word taken from a language woven for light tongues, not hinged and serrated mouthparts. Mosk looked down at the trembling man.

"Tell me what you know."

The man gulped, and then stammered his reply. "Yes, Milord! My name is Mishael Keddrik. This, eh, person," here he indicated the looming torturer, "asked if I knew of any visitors or strangers to this land who had dark coloring—"

"Yes, yes," hissed Mosk impatiently.

The man continued fearfully, tripping over his words.

"A few m-miles from my shop there lives a shepherd and his son, except he looks like no blood of this land and n-nobody knows who the mother is, seeing as how the shepherd brought the child into town ten years ago, a complete stranger—"

Mosk yanked the man into the air. The last time the Hunt had been on this side of the world . . .

"Ten years? Are you sure? Where is this village? Speak!"

The man lost control, crying like a child as he dangled by his shirt.

"Y-yes, Milord, yes! I wouldn't lie, Milord! Rewn's Fork! That is my village!" The man tried to curl into himself, cringing under the baleful glare of the Hiveking. "Just let me go, please, I beg of you. I have children . . ." His voice trailed off into sobbing.

Savoring the man's fear, Mosk carried him over to the window; the last red streams of sunset were staining the jagged edges of the broken glass. His voice was suddenly cool.

"Tell me. Did he have power over machines? Did he bear the marks of scale and talon? What was his name? Speak! Where did he go? Where is the Pensanden!?"

From the table behind him, a clear voice pierced the air.

"Fool! Tell him nothing!"

The Baron of Midian rose shakily to his feet and took a lurching step forwards. He had cut through the cords binding his legs with a piece of glass and staggered toward his stunned captor. The lumbering torturer moved to intercept him, throwing the table aside so that it smashed against the wall. Mosk turned, hissing.

The baron, face flushed red by the last light of day, gathered himself up and made a mighty leap. He collided with a squealing Mishael Keddrik. There was the sound of tearing cloth as the shirt came away in Mosk's claw, and both men tumbled into the lengthening shadows far below.

Mosk held the fluttering cloth in the breeze for a moment and then let it follow the two men down into darkness. A black silhouette against the slowly purpling sky, the Swarmlord lowered his arm. The soldier behind him froze as a low-pitched rattle filled the room.

"You will return to your Clot Primal and ask him to slowly remove your hearts, one for stupidity and the other for sluggishness."

"Yes, Hiveking. May my third heart serve you better."

The torturer gave a shameful click of regret before turning and shuffling out of the room. Mosk called out after him.

"And tell the Matron that I need a new Proximate by week's end!"

Rewn's Fork. That was nearby the woods where one of his earlier scout groups had gone missing. It had to have been the Pensanden, and he must have had help from a small army of these Southerners to be able to dispatch an entire Clot.

Mosk had known Primal Kret, the group's leader, since First Molt. Kret had been a ferocious, cunning creature.

Rewn's Fork, on the edge of the Horeb Wilds. The unbroken forest extended for hundreds of miles to the west—an army could hide there for years. Mosk did not want to wait years. He decided to send a messenger back to the Vestigarchy for more matrons and whatever reserves could be spared from the Border Wars.

The forests would be black with soldiers in a week. Mosk felt his blood stir as hunting enzymes began to course through his body. As an afterthought, he decided to send a Clot of searchers north, on the off chance that his quarry might try to do the obvious.

CHAPTER 6

So come one, come all to this carnival land,
We've wasted them tears, filled our pockets with sand,
And Baby, you'll see this whole show is a joke,
A spinning ballet of heartbreak and smoke.
Yeah, yeah, oh yeah! Yeah! Yeah, yeah, oh yeah!

—chorus to "Salt-lick Illusion" by the Dogfish Knights

Enoch stole a glance at his gangly companion, who was humming merrily as he crouched over the body of a plump coney. With long fingers, no more than bones with gray skin stretched over them like leather, Rictus finished cleaning the small beast and spat it over the morning fire.

Enoch had half expected the specter to evaporate in the rosy light of dawn like some misty nightmare, yet there he was, licking cracked teeth with a dry tongue and chuckling to himself like an impatient little boy waiting for the morning sausages to cook.

The previous night had been an odd one, with Rictus leading him through the jumbled ruins as though they were on a carefree jaunt through the meadow, all the while singing and laughing and jabbering in that peculiar dialect.

Bubble gum? Funk? What are these words?

Enoch had toyed with the idea of bolting, sure that this towering stack of bones and leather could never match his speed through the tumbled masonry of the ruins, but each time he quelled the urge with reason.

I don't need anyone, but he's done nothing but prove himself a friend. I suppose if things prove otherwise, I can always stir up his wires with a little push.

He hoped he wasn't relying too heavily on his newfound powers, but he had nothing to gauge by.

How much is too much? Pushing the platabruja left me a little tired, but I feel capable of much more.

He hoped that in the North he would find more people like him. He had so many questions.

Master Gershom, you left me too soon.

The loss of his master had left an aching sore in his chest, and it seemed to swell when Enoch had time to reflect on all that had happened.

Rictus broke him from his reverie by announcing that breakfast was served. The smell of simmering meat made Enoch's mouth water, and his stomach grumbled noisily.

"You'd thought that old Rictus had forgotten about the vittles, didn't you? No sir, I may not require eats nowadays thanks to Nanny," here he tapped the box at his chest with a bony finger, "but I remember what it was like being a hungry kid." The specter *paused*, still absently tapping at the box on his chest.

"At least I think I do."

Rictus yielded the spitted coney, and Enoch set to the hot meat with a passion, ignoring burnt lips as he wolfed down the steaming food. Rictus watched the boy eat with sheer pleasure, eyes half-lidded with imaginary delight, even mimicking the chewing sounds that Enoch made. Enoch laughed at this, and, surprised at the sound, almost choked on a leg bone. The specter swatted him on the back with a chuckle.

"Slow down, kid. We'll rest here until nightfall and then be on our way. Odds are, we lost the witch in the labyrinth back there, but I guarantee that she'll be on our trail soon enough with some new thugs in tow."

Rictus crawled under the shade of a leaning monolith, and soon all that was visible from the shadows was the pulsing red light at his chest. For the first time since he'd followed the specter into the ruins, Enoch spoke. His voice sounded husky and tired.

"Why don't we travel by day? It will be much easier going, and we won't be taken by surprise."

Rictus's voice came nonchalantly from the shadows, "The daylight hurts my eyes—one of the unfortunate side effects of my condition. Besides, you're all dirty and unkempt—we don't want you scaring people half to death, do we?"

Enoch's hand went unconsciously to his face, which was still swollen and smeared with crusted blood. A low, dry laugh bubbled out of the shadow.

"No sir, folks don't take too kindly to an unwashed kid. I couldn't go *anywhere* with you looking like that."

Enoch looked at the garish, skeleton face of his companion, then dropped his hand and smiled.

This laughter, this unexpected warmth, finally overcame his fear and revulsion of the undead thing. He lay back and closed his eyes, surprised that he could feel this way so soon after his master had died. Enoch wondered if he should feel bad about that, but before the thought could take root, he was asleep.

CHAPTER 7

And the beast which I saw was like unto a leopard, and his feet were as the feet of a bear, and his mouth as the mouth of a lion . . .

—Revelations 13:2 KJV

From her secret spot in the joint between two girders, Sera watched the wagon being unloaded. The handlers were being extremely cautious, more so than they usually were with Nyraud's little pets. Sera could tell that this was a special delivery. It had been given a private pen instead of being allowed to roam the garden like the nerwolves, the grendels, and the chee. She toyed with her hair as she mused, winding the long, blue strands between her fingers.

A delivery from the South. I thought it was still a wasteland down there. Have the jungles survived?

Instead of the usual pair of handlers, a full dozen of them stood around this wagon, barbed lances held at the ready. Sera reached up and twisted her eye-rings, bringing the details hundreds of feet below her into sharp focus.

Upper lips and foreheads glittered with sweat, knuckles white with tension. One of the larger men had lifted the door to the pen, and the wagon's mouth was brought flush with the opening. A rumbling growl thundered from under the canvas tarpaulin, so low and strong that Sera felt its vibrations in the metal under her feet. She tried to focus deeper into the shadows where the canvas had pulled away from the wagon cage.

Just then, there was a flash of tawny movement as the rumble spilled into a roar. A scream rang out through the garden, spooking a flock of redjays from a tree just between Sera's roost and the wagon. The intervening chaos blurred her autofocus, and it was a few moments before she was able to find the wagon again. It had been turned over on its side and was now surrounded by shouting men who were thrusting their lances into its depths. One of the men was on his back in a spreading pool of blood, his torso split open to the sky. Another angry roar echoed from below, and the wagon shook. The handlers began to panic, jabbing repeatedly into the cage. Their lances dripped red.

Sera detected a commotion at the other end of the garden. Spreading her wings, she quietly glided down to the tree below, remembering to stay distant and in the visual lee of the tree the whole time. She landed on a branch on the far side and crawled around the trunk to the branch the birds had vacated. It was moist with their droppings, something which would certainly have disgusted the other girls back at the Spire—especially Taras and Keyr.

They're such children. Some things require maturity.

Sera started to shake her head and then froze.

Who would be crossing the sward but none other than King Nyraud himself! He was followed by the usual retinue of counselors, guards, and lesser nobles; many rushed and stumbled to keep up—none wanted to be alone in the Garden. The King usually left such rabble in the court when he went hunting, so their presence now indicated that this had been an unplanned detour. The King looked furious.

"Idiots! Do you think I had this Ur'lyn brought all the way across the Broken Sea so you could skewer it?"

Even at this distance, King Nyraud was an imposing figure with his violet cape thrown back over broad shoulders. A giant of a man, his sharp features and slanting eyes bespoke the vain cunning of a hunter. Despite what his subjects thought, Sera knew that Nyraud was more than that—he was a hedonist who relied on a practiced ferocity to sate his appetites. She shivered and moved closer to the trunk where the shadows were deeper.

The handlers had backed away from the cage as King Nyraud approached, twisting their goads in sweaty hands. The roaring from underneath the canvas had again subsided into a menacing growl.

Fascinated, Sera quietly soared down to a lower tree. She landed on the far side and then crawled from the shadows along its length, her fear of the Hunter King swallowed up by curiosity.

What manner of beast kills armed men from inside a cage? Even Nyraud is tense!

Focusing deeply with her metal eyes, she could see the bunched muscles on the king's neck as he approached the cage, his nostrils flared. Granted, she could have seen that from above—an angel's eyes were *made* for distant viewing. But there was something about being close, about hearing and smelling what she saw—these are the sort of thoughts which had earned Sera her "odd-feather" status back home. This was why Taras and Keyr teased her.

Maybe I'm more of a hunter than an angel? You ever dally with your upstairs neighbors, good King?

She mused about that for a moment, then shook her head. As she leaned forward, a twig snapped under her hand.

In a flash of stormy cloth, Nyraud whirled around. Sera stilled a gasp and slowly crawled back along the branch.

There is no way he could have heard that. He is two dozen meters away!

"Surround that tree, men! We have a spy in our midst! Archers! Archers!"

The sounds of running feet filled the Garden. Sera glanced around fearfully—the tree foliage hemmed her in on both sides and above. To fly she would have to swoop low under the surrounding branches, and already the sound of arrows whistling through the lower canopy ruled out that idea. Nyraud's booming voice carried through the leaves.

"To the left, yes! Now aim higher. Higher! Can't you see her, you fools? There! Underneath the large branch covered with bird scat!"

An arrow was suddenly embedded in the wood next to her feet.

Time to go!

There was plenty of wing space on the branch above her. A quick leap and she had it in her hands. Or almost did. Her fingers slid through warm moisture. *Damn birds!*

The Garden floor was rushing up at her, and she barely remembered to spread her wings in time. The trimmed grass bent low under the wind of her passage, and only an instinctual spin to the right saved her from colliding with one of the archers, who, caught in mid-chortle at what he had thought was a downed target, dove to one side and knocked a screaming courtesan on his face.

I must gain altitude!

Tilting her tertials forward, Sera soared up into the protective greenery of the trees and began beating her wings furiously. Branches swayed in her wake and leaves drifted down onto the milling crowd below.

Where is—? Oh!

A shadow pounced from the branch above her. Sera tucked her wings and twirled, hearing the whistle of a knife through air as Nyraud spun over her to land nimbly on a limb three meters below.

How did he get up there so fast?!

Heart beating like a drum, Sera spread her wings and let the velocity of her freefall carry her up and out of the canopy.

Arrows clattered against the girders around her as she reached the tangled iron safety of the Garden's roof. No man would follow her there—the upper levels belonged to the birds, the clouds, and the Alaphim.

Nobody is going to believe that I escaped an encounter with the Hunter King! I don't believe it myself. Well, not that I can tell anybody that I was here. Stupid treaty.

Her thoughts turned to curiosity as she rose through a shattered skylight to catch a rising thermal that would carry her to Windroost Spire.

I'll have to ask old Lamech what an "Oor-Lin" is. Didn't he used to fly over parts of the Broken Sea on patrol?

She sighed.

Back when there were enough of us to patrol that far.

The melancholy thought was swept away as quickly as it came as Sera enjoyed the gentle caress of warm air on her pinions. She was young, and what could be better than to spread your wings and stretch as the warm earth exhaled you skyward. Even now, in these dark times, to be an angel was sheer joy.

It wasn't until she had landed at the Spire that she reached back and discovered that her ponytail was missing.

CHAPTER 8

They say that she will never get off the ground. Are they worried that the core won't reach the suborbital construction site due to faulty engineering? Ha! Nothing so mundane. No, they say she'll never get off the ground because there are too many people in high places who don't like the idea of folks starting up all by themselves. Settling a world by themselves. And 70 light years is a long way to send the tax men.

—Admiral Ca'uich Na, at the groundbreaking ceremony for El Arko de Xibalba. The last recorded interview before his assassination.

Despite the danger of entering the city, Enoch found himself trembling with anticipation.

Babel, the city of a thousand tongues! Mishael Keddrik used to say that it was carved from one of the Serpent's own fangs.

Indeed, from this distance the city resembled a broken fang piercing the night sky. Rictus had *paused* at the sight and pulled back his hood, the tattered remnant of a stolen burial shroud. His eyes were hidden in shadow, and Enoch wondered what kind of memories he might have of this old city. With a light wind pulling at his tattered disguise, Rictus seemed even more ghostly than ever.

Well, the disguise was his idea.

Before leaving the refuge of the ruins, Rictus had wrapped the shroud around his body desert-style, telling Enoch that he'd seen nomads from the South dressed so. Enoch had covered himself in similar fashion, cringing at what his master would have surely condemned as desecration. It did, however, hide the nature of the swords he carried. Rictus had whistled through his teeth when he first saw them.

The signature tools of the Nahuati blademasters, he had said, were rarely seen south of Tenocht. They represented an open invitation to a duel if you were lucky, and gallows if you weren't. As handy as Enoch was with the weapons, he didn't feel deserving of such a title just yet—nor did he wish to defend it.

He reached under the shroud to adjust his scabbard, which was chafing, and sighed.

I may have been trained in the ways of a Nahuati, but that doesn't make me accustomed to wearing these swords on a long march.

Rictus had asked to see what Enoch could do with the weapons on their second night of travel, and Enoch had refused. For some reason he felt that drawing his master's swords for show would be wrong. The specter just shrugged and said that he could "suit himself." Enoch wondered if the comment referred to the shabby state of his clothing, but after a quick glance at his companion's ancient leathers—skins kept from the edge of decay by the same tek which animated their owner—he decided that it must be another remnant of his odd language.

The journey that night had felt exceptionally long. Trudging through the crumbled foundations of an abandoned temple, Enoch couldn't help but make a comparison between the setting and his own ruined life. Everything that he had known and loved was gone. Was dead. The numbness he had felt in the days following his master's burial was leaving—evaporating—in the frigid heat of true sorrow.

The following night, Enoch had drawn his swords and made an effort to move through the opening steps of *Cisne Caido.* Rictus was impressed, but he thought that it might be useful to teach Enoch something a little more "lowbrow." Every night since then, they'd sparred with shrouds wrapped around their weapons to muffle the sounds—and to minimize dismemberment. Rictus was reminded to disconnect the cable and silence his humming longsword after his shroud shivered apart in a flurry of dry powder. Enoch shuddered to think what would have happened if he'd tried to block that first strike.

At least I wouldn't be feeling these bruises! It's a good thing I'm covered in grave-wrappings—my arms look like they've been through a wool carder.

Enoch smiled in spite of his sore limbs. The nightly bouts had been a surprising remedy for his sorrow. Not curing, but bridling his grief. As he moved and spun and cut through the air, Enoch could feel the heartache softening in his chest, flowing along his arms and out along the flashing edges of the *derech* and the *iskeyar*. The sadness was still there, but it didn't rule him.

It wasn't the exercise alone. Training with Rictus was very different than training with Master Gershom. Laughter in place of stern command. Clever suggestions instead of orders. And the specter was *good*. Surprisingly, delightfully good. What Rictus lacked in quickness and agility, he supplemented with an amazing reach and brilliant swordplay. He focused on pressing the attack, often leaving himself wide open as he sent a whistling *volante* across Enoch's chest. The frenzy with which Rictus pressed the attack was unnerving, and Enoch could see how even the most seasoned warrior might panic under such a flurry of blows.

But Enoch wasn't a seasoned warrior, just a quick student with a talent for seeing through patterns. After two close losses to the specter's tireless blade, he concluded that if he could just keep his focus enough to step through the *volante* with a *cabra breve*, he would be able to riposte under the specter's extended arm and end the bout.

If he closed his eyes, he could remember everything about that duel, the third bout of that night; how he'd focused on holding off the onslaught of flying attacks, waiting for Rictus to pivot back on his left foot in preparation for the sweeping horizontal advance. The longsword had come rushing towards him, and this time Enoch had stepped *into* the arc, leaning backwards and spinning on his heels so that Rictus's elbow passed inches from his face. It had been a simple matter of extending his right arm as he completed the turn. Rictus laughed and lowered his blade. Enoch's *derech* was lodged tightly between his third and fourth rib.

"Well that's an impressive little piece of ballet. I tell you what—I'll give you this one."

Enoch was surprised.

"You'll *give* it to me? My blade is still stuck in your chest! You're dead!"

"No, no, no. No, sir. First of all, I was dead before you met me. Second, that sword would be a real worry for me if I actually had a lung there that you could open, but I don't. The fact that I can stand here discussing the merits of said fatal blow should be evidence enough of that."

Here he waved off Enoch's sputtering protests with a bony hand. Enoch remembered the odd feeling of anger at how *unfair* it had seemed. Master Gershom would have complimented him on the flourish. But what Rictus had said next still burned in his ears:

"Listen, Enoch. The real issue here is that you treated this duel as a game between equals. You saw my top-heavy offense as a flaw rather than a stratagem.

"Tell me, kid, what would you do now that your longest blade is lodged in between my ribs?" Here Rictus had spun away, whipping the hilt out of Enoch's hand and bringing the edge of his own longsword under the boy's jaw. "I've just halved your reach and brought you within the radius of my forté. More men have died with their steel in my chest then you can count.

"You are good at moving to your opponent's weaknesses, Enoch. The real trick is adapting to their strengths."

Enoch had been thinking about this every night since then. His duels with Master Gershom had always been structured and clinical. Wooden blades, proper counters, rules of engagement and measured ash-marks. The even-tempered study of angle verses force. He had never felt this heat, this *passion* in his training. It was new, and he liked it.

Enoch looked over at his companion. The specter had pulled his hood up again and resumed walking towards the city. Enoch hurried up behind him.

"Rictus, do people live all the way up at the top of the city—up there among the clouds?"

"No—nobody lives at the top. The middle levels were destroyed years ago, leaving nothing but a tangled skeleton of girders. You'd have to be a regular monkey-man to get through that mess up to the top—that or an angel. 'Course, if you were one of the feathered folk, you'd probably be more worried about your useless pecker! Hoo!" At this he slapped a bony knee and guffawed.

Enoch fanned away the resultant cloud of dust. He never found any of Rictus's jokes even mildly humorous, but he tried to appreciate the sentiment.

Squinting his eyes, Enoch could see that the dingy metallic walls of the tower only extended halfway up its length before turning into a patchy tracery of jumbled bars which, for all their delicate appearance, continued firmly up into the clouds for at least a mile above the base. Rictus spoke more to himself as the towering city grew nearer, something Enoch found significantly more useful than his jokes.

"Can't believe she's still standing after so many centuries," he muttered, and Enoch wondered if it was respect he heard in that dry voice. "We built to last back then, that's for sure. You know, it wasn't intended to be a tower."

His voice was soft and distant, ill-suited on the grinning specter.

"What was it meant to be?" asked Enoch, curious at what could change his companion's demeanor so.

"A ship, kid. It was the first pieces of a ship which could carry people . . ." Here he swept his shrouded arm across the night sky. "Out. Out there."

Enoch didn't understand.

"How could something so big ever even get off the ground?"

"Ha—well that wasn't even all of it. The tower you see was

just the core of the first rocket. See, we were building the biggest parts down here, and then launching them into that cozy space between the earth and the moon. Then we were going to stitch them all together and set sail.

"This was going to be our chance, our first good trip outta the old neighborhood, to spread a little *homo sapiens* around, you know? We'd finally found some vacancies out there, some real nice spots with all the amenities. For a while, it looked like we were going to break free from the history and the grudges and all of that dusty old badness. Finally had a chance to pull up our roots and get some real breathing room."

Rictus was staring at the sky. His jaw moved slowly up and down, and Enoch couldn't tell if he was trying to laugh, or trying to whistle, or trying to cry. A bony hand moved up to point at the tower and then went back to the metal box on his chest. Tap, tap, tap.

"But she never left the ground."

"Why?"

"C'mon—don't tell me that you haven't heard of the Schism! The big kaboom? When the world decided that two heads were better than one?"

"Oh, I've read of the Schism. The Great War in Heaven."

"Yeah, sure. Whatever they're calling it these days. Pretty soon there was no one left who knew how to fly the Ark, or that cared to."

"The Ark?"

"That is her name. Was her name. She was the last one built. Our last shot."

Rictus stopped talking. It was uncharacteristic, but Enoch didn't mind. He had plenty to think of already. And to be honest, he found it kind of nice to have some quiet.

* * * *

The traffic on the road had slowly become dense as smaller side trails converged from all directions. Enoch found himself in a constant state of open-mouthed awe as a kaleidoscopic parade of people, creatures, and vehicles shuffled past them.

A caravan of Akkadian traders had passed by earlier riding a short-haired variety of muridon which seemed much taller and sleeker than the ones he had seen before. Their wagons smelled of spices, leathers, and pungent oils. A young girl sitting in the back of the rearmost cart had sung a lilting song in a tongue Enoch didn't recognize. In the yellow lamplight, her hair shone a warm cinnamon color, which he stared at mesmerized—until he noticed that she was looking at him curiously. He had stumbled over the length of his own shroud and pretended to be watching a bug on the road. The girl's sweet laughter faded into the dust with the rest of the caravan.

A procession of performers from Axum soon followed, tattooed in shifting colors. They spun past like a flock of flowers in a windstorm. Enoch thought he could feel his eyes smarting from the wild chaos of hues.

Yet even this was forgotten as a raucous croak startled Enoch from the road. A trio of sallow-faced young men rode by on the back of what appeared to be a giant, scaly fowl.

"Swampmen from Garron," whispered Rictus in reply to his unspoken question. "They live in the boiling marshlands north of here."

Enoch had heard of Lodoroi—the Swampmen. They dealt in exotic breeds captured and propagated from the plagued Garronian wastes. It was said that they had made a pact with the Serpent in ages past, for the changeling sickness of that region never affected them. In the darkness, Enoch could see various cages and sacks tied to the back of their steed, some of which were empty and others which writhed with ersatz life.

The city walls came into view just as dawn broke over the eastern hills, which now crouched tawny and low like a pride of desert cats. Above the dirty stonework of the walls, a bright confusion of spires, minarets, and domes caught the morning light. While nowhere near as imposing as the impossible height of the tower, they had a magic all their own.

"That's Babel's undertown," replied Rictus, squinting uncomfortably. He nodded up. "Only the very rich are allowed to live inside the tower. The King himself occupies the top thirty floors," here he pointed to a bulging section of the tower-which-was-almost-a-ship.

"Rumor has it that Nyraud keeps rare and dangerous beasts up there, imported prey which he hunts at his pleasure. And there are some who say that good ole King Nyraud has a few trophies from the two-footed variety, if you know what I mean."

Enoch nodded slowly, not quite sure he did. Rictus continued.

"But things in the undertown can be even deadlier. Babel was once a lovely city, but times aren't like they used to be. Stay close to me and don't look anyone in the eye."

Enoch grew wary as they neared the guards at the mouth of the gates. There were half a dozen of them lounging around the entrance and inspecting merchandise before it entered the city walls.

I've never had to hide myself like this before. I hope I don't look suspicious.

Two of the guards were having some fun with the Swampmen. The guards, obviously bored, were laughing and poking their clubs through the merchant's cages. The Swampmen sat silently on their mounts waiting to enter, apparently either unconcerned or accustomed to the abuse that their stock received at the gates.

From the back of one cage came a furious hiss, and the guards again erupted into laughter. Further prodding produced more noise, and soon the guards were slamming their clubs against the sides of the cage as the creature inside howled. Still the Swampmen sat motionless, the long muddy rolls of their hair obscuring any expression on their faces.

Master Gershom's words came to Enoch. *Men are made for the Law of God . . .*

Enoch's hands curled around the hilt of his *iskeyar*, and he resolutely walked over to confront the guards.

"Enoch!" Rictus hissed.

But Enoch had already marched up next to the scaly side of

the Swampmen's mount. He put his hound out to catch the thick forearm of one of the guards.

Whatever noble sentiment Enoch was about to express was quickly forgotten as another guard grabbed him and knocked him back against the pack animal. The reed-woven rope holding the small cage, already loosened from the recent abuse, parted and the wicker cage fell to the ground. A lithe, shadowy figure writhed free of the bars and ran between the startled guard's legs and through the gate before anyone could react. The guards paid no mind—now they had new sport.

"Young cur!"

"Nobody ever teach you respect, boy?"

"Learn 'im, Lev!"

Enoch fumbled for his swords as the guards moved towards him, but the blades were twisted up and tangled with his shroud.

Maybe this wasn't the best time to make a stand.

The descending club of the first guard was caught in a bony grip. As he turned with a roar, a fleshless death's head leered at him from the depths of a lifted hood.

"Leave him alone, Lev, or you're next on my lisssst."

The guard staggered back into the arms of his cronies and bowled them over long enough for Rictus to grab Enoch up in a thin arm and in three massive strides, they were in the city. Behind them cries of "specter!" and "demon!" dwindled away under the muffled roar of humanity rumbling from the busy crowd. The guards were loud, but obviously too afraid to give chase.

"That was a stupid thing to do!"

The specters' accusation was lost to Enoch amid the buzz of voices. That had been dangerous, but . . . he felt good about his courage at the gate. After so many days of feeling helpless, it had been wonderful to *act* upon the world and defend something that had seemed so defenseless. His cheek still ached where the guard had landed his blow, but he felt strangely peaceful.

CHAPTER 9

You can take your shiny tek and ride it back to Tenocht, sir. I spent two years potty training Sal, and another teaching him the difference between a whiskey sour and a Rob Roy. I can deal with the fleas.

— *Calvin Jie, Disgruntled Bartender*

The city was a spectacle.

Everything seemed to be in motion. From the motley crowds of people to the vendors to the very buildings themselves—Enoch felt as though his eyes were going to vibrate out of his head trying to follow the surrounding motion.

How could so many people live together in one place like this?

A group of tall armored women stomped past, their shields decorated with red scales the size of dinner plates. From the other direction, Enoch noticed two men with pale white skin and black robes pushing a bulky object through the crowd. They leaned it into place against a nearby wall and then set to work bolting its chassis to the stone. Enoch thought he recognized that shape—

It's a Unit!

The machine was taller and sturdier-looking than the one Enoch had grown up with, and the keypad seemed designed for various sizes and types of fingers. But it was definitely a Unit.

Enoch looked down the length of the wall and noticed several other Units installed for public use. A few were occupied by merchants, but most stood alone.

And Master Gershom had said that our Unit was a rare treasure.

I wonder if he ever passed through Babel . . .

Enoch's thoughts were interrupted as a piece of rotten fruit flew through the air to splatter against the wall above the nearby Unit. The two pale men stood, nervously scanning the crowd for the source of the hostility.

Enoch could sense tension in the air, noticed that several passers-by eyed the Unit with anger. Distrust. Fear.

Rictus grabbed Enoch by the shoulder.

"Let's not stick around here, kid. People are still jumpy about the king's attempt to modernize. This could get ugly."

One of the pale men turned and went back to work, while the other signaled for some nearby soldiers to approach. The soldiers had green and gold livery, and they pushed through the crowd with an air of official authority. Rictus squeezed his shoulder again.

"Come on, Enoch."

But Enoch had something he wanted to do first. He had never had a chance to *pause* and use his new powers to look inside of a Unit before—the one back at Rewn's Fork had gone and melted itself before Enoch ever got the chance to. And maybe he could see if these public machines could read his disc? Enoch *paused*—

"No!"

Rictus's shout yanked him right out of the trance and attracted the stare of one of the pale men setting up the machine. Rictus pulled his face-wrap a little bit tighter and laughed.

"No, you may not have any more of those sugar meats, son! Not until we have the livestock unloaded!" He turned Enoch swiftly by the shoulder and marched him in the other direction. Enoch was confused.

"I was just going to look inside the—"

"I could tell what you were going to do, boy. You get that empty look on your face—what do you call it? The scary-carey?"

" ," said Enoch impatiently.

"Whatever. Just keep your brain out of the local Units. They are all networked together, and probably set to let off all sorts of noise if a Pensanden dips in."

Enoch supposed that he should probably trust Rictus in cases like this.

Maybe . . . maybe later I can try and see. Just a dip into the Unit there. Nobody will know.

Rictus was laughing, said something about never dreaming of having to baby-sit an etherwalker. Enoch didn't care. Babel was incredible! He decided to let his mind rest and just take in the sights and sounds.

Hawkers called out their various bargains in counter-rhythm to the whistle and bang of the machinists' scrap shop. A slender, deer-eyed creature draped in butterfly silks danced to the pan flute and tambour, her short, dappled fur changing color as the music switched keys.

To his left, Enoch saw a trio of tall winged men arguing over prices with a gnomish scrapmonger. The little man had complex goggles of metal and held a wrench almost as tall as he was. His customers were angry, but he seemed untroubled by their intimidating gestures. He shrugged and turned away from the trio, evoking a surrendering gesture from the tallest of them. The gnome turned and smiled—he had obviously just made a sale.

A little guy who knows that he's smarter than his opponents. I like him already.

Above his head, cables strung from building to building like cobwebs. Craning his neck, Enoch could see a limber creature leaping along the cables effortlessly hundreds of feet above the ground.

"It's a gabbon," Rictus said. "A word-ape. The rich families use them as messengers. The hairy little guys are perfect mimics, and they can repeat a message word-for-word even years after it has been given. With the constant power-outages, they are the most reliable form of communication in the city right now, but the king is trying to connect a faster form of electronic messaging."

The gabbon halted just above the fruit vendor in front of them and wiggled its body in a curious way. Enoch was about to ask what it was doing when all of a sudden the ape defecated, dropping filth onto the poor man's shoulder with amazing accuracy.

Rictus shook his head and pulled Enoch along, chuckling as the soiled vendor shouted curses at the retreating ape.

"Reliable but dirty. And stop looking around like a yokel shepherd boy. These streets eat Midianites for breakfast."

Enoch caught sight of the three-winged men he'd seen earlier. They were tall and stately, with coppery wings that shone in the morning sun. They looked nervous and wary, with one of them constantly watching the streets around them, but Enoch wondered how they could even dream of hiding. They were vibrant even in their canvas cloaks. Their skin shone with gilded edges, some sort of odd bronze jewelry at their elbows and wrists. Their hair ranged in color from green to a deep aqua blue, and they wore it long and braided, with bronze and copper wire woven through the strands. One of them noticed Enoch staring and turned to confront him.

"What is it, boy? Has this worm overcharged you for his rusting junk as well?"

Enoch shook his head no, and the gnome winked before pushing his cart away with a wave. But the gesture was quickly forgotten by the shepherd, who could not look away from the beautiful beings in front of him. He *paused* to see if their feathers were actually metal, and what he saw was unbelievable. The winged men had metal woven throughout their entire bodies! The jewelry on their arms were actually elements of their metallic skeleton which extended beyond their flesh.

But this was *nothing* like the platabruja, the silverwitch. Her exterior form had been a shell of beauty, but the underlying machinery was pure functionality. Reflecting back on what he had seen, Enoch realized that much of the platabruja design was built around redundancy—something which made sense if they were going to be doing battle with a "mind-wrench." But these winged creatures, this design was something else entirely. The melding of natural form and synthetic materials apparent here was appealing in ways both deep and powerful to Enoch.

Using his new sight, he looked deeper into the man nearest him and saw a delicate lace of alloyed metals which supported bones, protected organs, and balanced the wings growing from his back. Subtle projections from his cheekbones and brow held mounts for a series of lenses and rings which could flip down to magnify and protect his eyesight.

Magnificent!

The man stepped up to Enoch, his hands on his waist. His eyes darted left and right, obviously not appreciating the attention.

"Alright, move on."

A delicate hand rested on the winged man's shoulder.

"Oh leave him alone, Beyn. He's obviously never seen an Alaphim before."

Enoch looked up and froze. He hadn't noticed the girl standing between these *Alaphim*, and he stumbled backwards in surprise. This was a different sort of wonder.

She's beautiful.

She leaned forward and grabbed Enoch's arm to steady him. Her grip was firm but careful.

"Are you from around here?"

Enoch didn't know what to say, and he found himself answering by instinct.

"N . . . no, Milady. I'm from Midian. Rewn's Fork. It's south of here."

The angel smiled and tucked an errant strand of sky-blue hair behind her ear.

"Well, welcome to Babel, young shepherd. The livestock market is just through the eastern ramp over there."

Enoch furrowed his brow, then laughed.

"Oh! Oh no, you see. I'm not a shepherd, or . . . at least, I'm not a shepherd anymore. I'm—"

A bony hand closed on Enoch's shoulder and pulled him backwards.

"Let's *go*, son. The sheep are getting hungry or something. Say goodbye to the nice lady."

Enoch didn't even look at Rictus as the exasperated specter practically carried him back into the bustling crowd. He couldn't pull his gaze from the girl. She gave him a parting smile and then returned to conversation with her companion. Enoch gave her a feeble wave.

Goodbye.

Rictus scowled unconvincingly.

Grabbing a skinny arm, he pulled Enoch along towards the end of the market. The connecting street spilled into another large, open pavilion where rows of booths were set up haphazardly against the walls of great domed temples.

The Swampmen they had seen earlier at the gate had apparently made it through and were at a large stall unloading cages. Their steed stamped nervously and snorted at the surrounding cacophony.

Rictus released his arm and gave the boy a light cuff behind the ear.

"For the last time, close your mouth, shepherd. Keep your eyes down. And follow me closely."

The specter's voice was uncharacteristically stern, and Enoch tried to focus.

Enoch followed Rictus into a narrow alley, shaded by the multitude of ramparts, cables, walkways, and drying laundry strung between the two buildings which seemed as tall as the Edrei. His head still spun with thoughts of the angel, but even those were soon drowned out by the enormity of Babel.

This place is endless!

The alley narrowed, and the bustle of the crowd began to dim.

"Where are we going?" His voice sounded small echoing in the dark alley.

The specter looked up and down the alley to be sure they were alone and then shot him a long-toothed grin.

"With this face of mine it might be hard to believe, but even old Rictus has friends amongst the true music lovers of Babel. I can pull some favors and keep us safe for a while, but we'll have to be heading out in a day or two. With the kind of attention you're sure to have stirred up, we needn't make easy targets of ourselves.

"You almost spilled our disguise to that pretty bird back there.

From here on out it is best you understand, kid. The forces after you are strong. They are smart, they are quick, and they will not hesitate to do nasty things to you. Even with your training and abilities, you are no match for them. These snakes were killing Pensanden Blood Dukes before you were even a concept. I've been trying to teach you some less . . . orthodox . . . fighting styles to give you an edge. The skills your master taught you are useful, but you lack *savvy*. You'll need to know how and when to fight dirty. Luckily—" and here Rictus extended his hand with an odd elegance, and bowed "—that's my specialty."

Rictus straightened and patted the long, gaunt weapon hanging at an angle on his back, then cocked his head.

"Oh, and you're gonna have to sharpen up your listening skills here in the city. You can't listen for snapping twigs and crunching leaves, but I'm sure you'll find a way."

With that cryptic remark, Rictus winked a leathery lid at Enoch and returned to his long-legged gait down the slowly descending alley. Enoch recognized the challenge and slipped into the *pensa spada*, commanding his senses to come alive.

Hear.

Rictus was right—he had been trained to listen for the bending of grass under a heavy foot, the whistling of the country wind around the shape of a man. All the rules were changed here. Sounds bounced and giggled off of the high walls, shadows moved unexpectedly, and smells were born, matured, and died in a matter of seconds. So Enoch listened for *city* sounds.

There was a pattern within the greater boil of noises in the city—a pattern which syncopated with his footsteps. A pattern which was whisper-quiet, but that had stayed *constant* while all others waxed and waned. Eyes closed, Enoch turned towards the pattern. There was a muffled splash as something leapt from a nearby puddle and into the surrounding refuse.

Rictus saw Enoch's expression and chuckled. "It's been following us since the gates. I think you may have started something back there."

Enoch strode back to where the form had disappeared into

the shadows. Between some broken slats in a large wine barrel, two bright eyes suddenly flashed back at him.

"Aaargh!"

The surprise yanked him free from his trance as he stumbled backwards, tripping over a broken pot. Something launched itself from the shadowy recess and landed on his chest. Enoch could feel small, sharp claws digging into the front of his tunic where the wrappings had fallen away. He fumbled for the sword at his side, but it was still tangled up in the dusty shrouds.

He heard dry, familiar laughter. Rictus was obviously enjoying seeing him torn limb from limb by this alley beast.

The beast seemed less interested in tearing him apart than sitting on his chest and staring at him with those fierce yellow eyes. On further inspection, Enoch decided that the beast was less of a "beast" than he had first surmised.

As long as his arm from nose to tail, the creature had a silky and inconstant pelt which seemed to ripple from brown to indigo to black, alive with subdued color. The pointed snout ended in a small black nose, underneath which sharp white teeth almost glowed in the alley gloom. Large triangular ears swiveled towards him, amazingly motile upon the creature's curiously tilted head. Enoch slowly turned his head to face Rictus.

"What is it? Is it dangerous?"

Rictus stepped closer to examine the creature.

"I think not. Or at least not to you. A dangerous animal wouldn't have gotten so . . . so *cozy* on your chest there. This ferocious monster is—" Rictus shook his head, "—more enamored than alarmed, I would say. But as to its genus and species, I couldn't venture to guess."

Rictus rubbed his forefinger and thumb across his bony chin in a parody of scholarly inquiry.

"Judging by the chameleon fur, it seems to be some sort of a shadowcat hybrid—but if I'm not mistaken, there are some aspects of hue and pattern at play here which you don't see on the common breed. I'll bet this little guy . . . uh," here he tilted his head to peer under the creature, "sorry, this little *lady* can go invisible in the middle of a Technicolor sandstorm, more than just match grays with the shadows like her cousins."

He jerked his thumb around to indicate where they'd just come from.

"Those Swampmen are adept at mixing genes around, and it doesn't hurt that the very swamps they live in are just silly with the worst kind of rads and unchained nantek—Garron was ground zero for some of the worst of the Schism. That stinking pool of glowing slop used to be a city founded on the principles of art and romance. And that, my little friend, is what they call *irony*."

As usual, Enoch only understood about half of what Rictus was saying, but he parsed enough to realize that this creature—*she*—was not going to bite him. He slowly moved a hand towards her head. She twisted with boneless grace to sniff at the hand and then licked it with a rough, pink tongue. Enoch ran a hand over the creature's back and was amazed by the softness of the fur. Eyes closed in feral pleasure, she began to purr.

Ambushed by such unexpected tenderness in the middle of this alien place, Enoch felt some sort of emotion welling up from his throat. It was alarming, and he coughed while staggering to his feet. The creature practically slithered up his arm and onto his shoulder, where she perched confidently. Enoch reached up to take her off—the last thing he and his skeleton companion needed was to look *more* conspicuous—and barely pulled his hand back in time as she bared needle-teeth and snapped at him.

With a purr that was half warning growl, the creature settled back onto his shoulders and turned to look at him as if to say: *Okay, now we can go.*

This time, both Enoch and Rictus laughed.

"It would appear that we have a new captain. Good job, Enoch."

Enoch gave Rictus a miniature replica of one of his own signature shrugs. With that warm, somewhat prickly weight on his shoulder, he followed the chuckling corpse into the shadows of the city.

* * * *

The tavern, if it could be called that, seemed to be a half-hearted attempt at copulation by three or four run-down buildings of various styles and compositions—an architectural orgy of splintered beams, pock-marked columns, and drooping lintels. The sign hung crookedly from a rusted iron ring over the front porch, swinging in the slow breeze. At some distant point in the tavern's history, the sign had been painted with festive colors, colors now bruised with the pale marks of age. Enoch could just make out the crudely drawn logo: a naked man sitting on some sort of a rounded chair, his head draped in black cloth, a comically large axe across his knees. Rictus spread his long, spidery arms expansively in a scarecrow embrace.

"This, my young friend, is the Headsman's Hole. There is no finer tavern in all of Babel, excluding, of course, the ones which use plates."

With a laugh, Rictus pulled the dusty shrouds from his shoulders. Already tattered from the journey, they practically disintegrated at his touch and fell to the damp pavement in a cloud of dust. Enoch didn't follow suit—even if they were now entering safe territory where disguise was no longer necessary, he felt safer incognito. He wasn't sure he wanted anybody noticing his swords until he was ready to use them.

Entering the tavern was much like walking into a den of sleepy nerwolves. The low-pitched murmuring was occasionally punctuated by mad laughter, slurred cursing, and the clanging of tin mugs; the heady smell of an overcooked roast struggled to dampen the less-palatable odors of unwashed men and stagnant pinebeer. A pair of frazzled youth—gender entirely indistinguishable—trudged back and forth from the kitchen carrying trays piled high with mugs and steaming piles of meat. Thick, vermilion clouds jetted from the brass pipes of bleary-eyed coral smokers, hiding anyone or anything from scrutiny in the flickering orange lamplight.

Feeling conspicuous, Enoch rushed to catch up with Rictus,

who strode through the gaggle of drunkards, thieves, and worse as though he had just arrived home. Few people looked up at the gangly apparition, and those who did so showed only casual interest. This frightened Enoch, for what could be more dangerous than a place where specters were a common sight?

This train of thought was interrupted by a strange sound coming from the back of the tavern. It was oddly out of place in this din—the odd part being that something could actually sound so uniquely incompatible in this boiling stew of sounds. Enoch was reminded of a pan flute, common enough in sheep country, but this was something different—more complex in tone, yet beguiling in its melody. Wistful and elegant, the music swam untouched through the heavy air, weaving in and out of the mumblings of the crowd in melodious counterpoint.

It was a music that, for a few sweet moments, brought Enoch out of the harshness of his immediate surroundings. He would have been content to stand there listening forever, but Rictus had almost disappeared into the crowd, heading straight for the source of the music. Enoch scurried after him.

"Cal, you dried out piece of fly candy, how's it hangin'?" Rictus's voice rose in raucous greeting.

The music stopped just as Enoch reached the front of a small stage. At first he had to look around to see who Rictus was addressing. There was an ape on the stage, connected to some weird apparatus, but he could see no one else.

Just then the ape crouched, bringing the apparatus on its back into the light. Enoch gasped. A wrinkled human head was strapped to the animal, wrapped in dusty skin almost as leathery as Rictus's. And, like Rictus, a snakelike metal tube emerged from the withered neck stump and connected to a steel box which was adorned with a dull red light. It blinked in syncopation to the one nested in his companion's chest. As the ape scratched itself, the head turned to glare at the tall specter, and then lifted an eyebrow.

"It is 'hanging,' my crude friend, just as it always has. In the antique store across the street on a very large stand."

Enoch jumped back as both of the apparitions burst into

sandpaper laughter. He didn't know what surprised him more, that Rictus was friends with an animated head, or the fact that the head spoke with a cultured, high-society accent. Strapped to one of the ape's shoulders was a thin metal stand which held in its branching arms an odd assortment of whistles, flutes, and reeds.

Is this the musician I heard earlier?

As if in response to Enoch's thought, the head leaned down and blew a short, staccato melody on one of the pipes. The ape cocked its head in attention and then leapt up to the crossbeams above the stage, swinging from one hairy arm. The head blew into another pipe, this time a short copper tube. A piercing whistle rang through the crowd, and all eyes turned towards him.

"Attention, ladies and gentlemen, all esteemed clientele of this most hospitable of drink-houses!"

Laughter rang out from all corners of the room, both for the genuine pride in the speaker's voice and for the insinuation that ladies, gentlemen, or even anything as banal as "clientele" would ever frequent this tavern. Another whistle quieted them.

"It is my honor as proprietor of the Headsman's Hole to announce the long-awaited return of the most despicable villain ever to survive the Schism, my drinking chum for the past three centuries or so, and the one-time lead guitarist for the extremely overrated Dogfish Knights. Drinks are on the house."

As drunk and buzzed as they were, the crowd understood the last sentence, and a lusty cheer went up. Several entirely drunk fellows actually walked up to Rictus and patted him on the tattered shoulder in warm congratulations for something or another. Rictus looked up at the simian-mounted head with a boney grin.

"Cal, you unrequited ham, come down from there and talk with us." He unstrapped the monstrous sword from his shoulder and leaned it against the little stage. "And the Dogfish Knights had three platinum albums, unlike your woefully undersold little recordings."

The head, which Enoch guessed was Cal, whistled another short blast and was soon back on the stage in front of them. Cal's parchment skin pulled into a dramatic scowl, exposing a yellow patch of skull above his wrinkled brows.

"I played to sold-out crowds in San Vegas for fifty years, Ric," growled the animated head. "The Knights were a lucky flash in the pan right before it all went dark and you know it."

Rictus grinned as he tapped the pulsing red light at his chest.

"At least I could afford to get the *latest* LifeBeat tek, Cal. Full body preservation, they called it. She be a marvelous thang." He stretched his long arms in a mock yawn. Enoch thought the gesture oddly vain in such a hideous character, but he couldn't repress a smile.

I guess it's all relative.

"The preservation being what it is," smirked Cal, eyeing Rictus up and down, "I'm glad I opted for the economy model. You look more like the Grim Reaper every century."

"Look who's talking, monkey-boil!" retorted the specter. "The biggest tragedy of the Schism was that it failed to remove modern man's most annoying creation—the self-righteous musician."

Rictus winked at Cal as he reached down to scratch the ape behind the ears. "The second-biggest tragedy is that out of all the dubiously serviceable parts of your lackluster body, you had to preserve this one." He rapped Cal on the pate with a bony knuckle.

The grumbling head broke into laughter and invited Rictus to have a seat over in the corner.

"So who is your short companion?"

Rictus pulled some of the shroud away from Enoch's face.

"This is Enoch Gershom, Shepherd Extraordinaire." Enoch wasn't sure, but he thought he was being insulted. He pulled the shroud to one side, letting Cal see the *derech* at his belt.

"Enoch Gershom of Midian, charge of Master Levi, at your service, Sir." He tried to remember formal speech from his lessons, but wasn't sure it was coming out right. "We seek safe haven."

For some reason, Rictus was grimacing and making slicing motions with his hands. For some other reason, Cal wasn't impressed. He turned towards Rictus, catching him in mid-gesture.

"What is this? A refugee kid with illegal blades? I know better than to ask this, but are you mad?" Cal was angry, and Enoch could see the red light at his neck pulsing faster. Even the ape looked agitated.

Rictus winced, leaning close to his furious friend and whispering.

"You know me, Cal. I would never bring danger to your doorstep if I had any other options. There is something important going on and I knew you were the only one I could trust to help me out. This is big stuff."

Cal laughed bitterly at this.

"You'll notice," he remarked, addressing Enoch, "that he says that as though I'm at the top of the list of his dearest chums. He still thinks he can run around with that big sword of his and change the world. He still thinks he matters, that he's a star."

He blew three quick notes into a tiny silver flute, and the ape responded by pointing a long, hairy finger at Rictus.

"You, my skeletal friend, have become the stuff of nightmares. The few of us sad, sorry remnants of the old world are now mythology. We're out of style, Ric. The curtain is down. Show's over."

Enoch jumped as Rictus slammed his fist down on the table.

"You think I don't know that?!"

Several people in the bar were now staring at them. Rictus noticed and lowered his voice.

"Cal, it was only a few months ago that I came across the remains of one of 'our kind' in the ruins. I think he had been a bit actor—remember those?—from down in your neck of the woods. He had purposefully pulled a boulder on top of himself, crushing every bone into splinters. But this damn thing," he gestured angrily at the box at his chest, "this *miracle of immortality* was still flashing. I could hear the poor bastard talking to himself under the rock, quoting lines from one of those awful soap operas."

Cal twisted his mouth in distaste.

"I could see the red light through a crack underneath, but couldn't do anything. The rock was too heavy. He'll be there forever, Cal, and you know what? I think he prefers that to being here. At least he's not scaring people, not being called a monster—a specter! And it hasn't been so long that I've forgotten about Robyn."

Cal closed his eyes slowly at the mention of the name.

"You think I could forget how that mob tore her apart? You think I could forget how we found her few remaining *pieces*, still twitching in anguish? You, who hide from the world in this dark hole, you dare accuse *me* of being out of touch?"

The specter's voice smoldered. Cal had his tired eyes cast down, his jaw set. He blew softly into the silver flute and the ape pulled a rag from its belt and proceeded to polish the surface of the wooden table. Enoch hardly dared to breathe.

"I'm . . . I'm sorry, Ric. Times have been tough with this new king in the tower. He wants places like mine cleared out of the city. His guards have been roughing up my customers. The other day they tried to take Sal—claimed I needed a *license* for him." The ape looked up in recognition of its name, and then returned to polishing the table. "I have a lot on my mind. And it is worrisome not seeing you for so long. Fifty years, Ric. Fifty. That's a long time, even if you're immortal."

Rictus laid a hand on Cal's furrowed cheek. "I forget that time moves slower for you here in the city with all these people," he said, raspy voice low and almost gentle. "Out in the ruins, the years fly by, just . . . just *invisible*. Empty like old ghosts."

Cal chuckled. "You always did write dreadful lyrics."

Rictus just shrugged.

"You're right. That's why the kids loved me, you know. Cheesy lyrics appeal to them. That's why your fans were all blue-haired old biddies."

Enoch sighed with relief as the two broke out laughing again. He didn't understand exactly what had been communicated between these two ancient creatures, but he had a feeling it was something deep and centuries beyond him. Cal blew a few notes and the ape leaned forward, simultaneously tucking the rag into its belt.

"Now, what is this trouble you mentioned? I've got a feeling in my long-absent gut that this little Nahuatito is only the tip of the iceberg."

Rictus glanced around to see if anyone was listening, his dry eyes rolling like ivory marbles. "Do you have someplace we can go to talk?" he whispered, "there be snakes in the walls . . ."

Cal jerked his head back at this, and then, regaining his composure, blew into the flute. The ape turned and shuffled towards a stairway in the back.

"This way," he said, then turned to address one of the drab youths at the bar. "Kris, you're in charge 'til I get back. No fighting and no more free drinks."

Amid the chorus of groans from around the bar, Rictus grabbed his weapon and stood. With a questioning glance, Enoch stood as well, then turned and followed the ape as it bounded up the steep wooden stairs behind the bar.

At the top was a narrow hallway lined with doors on both sides. It was lit by a long, narrow lamp on the ceiling, which flickered with an odd blue light. Cal turned and gestured up with a caterpillar eyebrow as the ape continued to the end of the hall.

"The city still provides a meager amount of juice for taxpayers. Meaning, of course, that they shut *me* off months ago, but I have my connections. Having a real incandescent light adds a touch of class to the joint, eh?"

Rictus chuckled at that. Cal pretended not to hear.

"Yeah, I know a guy down in Scrapfield who makes the bulbs. Of course, decorative lighting isn't the *only* reason for my illicit sipping of the city's power."

The ape reached the door at the end, and after fumbling with a key ring at its belt, managed to open it. With an enigmatic glance, Cal motioned them into the dark room with his head.

"This is my own private luxury suite, gentlemen, so please remove your shrouds at the door."

Cal glared at Enoch.

Enoch pulled the dusty shroud from his head, ripping it down the front in his haste. The ancient cloth fell into threads on the floor. Cal rolled his eyes as the ape shuffled to a corner of the room and flipped a switch. A bare light bulb hanging from the ceiling flickered to life.

The room was relatively simple compared to what Enoch had imagined a "private luxury suite" would be. A hammock hung from the low ceiling over a pillow in one corner. An oblong woven rug adorned the floor, leading up to a simple table holding a hammered metal basin. A door in the back led to what Enoch assumed was the closet, although what Cal would need an entire closet for was beyond his guess.

A large collection of hats?

A short tune caught his attention and he turned to see the ape unbuckling Cal from its back and placing him gently on a pillow before leaping up to the hammock, where he sat quietly, regarding Enoch with deep-set eyes.

"Now," said Cal, wiggling himself deeper into the pillow, "What is all this about snakes in the walls, Ric? There haven't been blackspawn in this part of the world for years."

Rictus leaned his sword against the table, and, motioning for Enoch to sit on the rug next to him, folded his scarecrow figure to the ground.

"This should explain everything," he said, grabbing Enoch's scarred wrist and raising it to the light. Cal gasped.

"Is that what I think it is?"

Rictus nodded.

"But the Pensanden are all supposed to be dead! Scales, Ric, you know how to find trouble!"

The specter motioned for Cal to lower his voice.

"I found him in the southern ruins making friends with a band of cutthroats. They were being led by that mek witch we caught wind of in Uxmal—remember her? Well, she had sniffed me down to the Emim Reaches and was waiting for my next move when she caught this little surprise instead. He completely wrenched a silverwitch, Cal. I'm talking full paralytic reformat." At this, Cal swallowed and glanced down at the steadily blinking light buried in his pillow.

"Go on."

"It gets worse. He's been chased from Midian by coldmen,

and from how he tells it, they rode draconfly and hunted with arakid. We're talking a full scale Hunt. It's a miracle he's still alive."

"But how? And in Midian? There were never any Pensanden in that little barony. And how was it that the Hunt missed him the first time around?"

Rictus shrugged his bony shoulders.

"His master wore these," he ventured, gesturing towards Enoch's swords. "Perhaps he was sent down from Cuitla or Tenocht, one of the big northern cities. He seems to have trained him in the Nahuati style, and the child can do the mindtrance as though born to it. He's an odd kid."

Enoch was getting more than a little angry at being called a kid; in fact, he was downright incensed at being labeled "odd" by these two fleshless specters.

Cal furrowed his brow in thought. "Question is," mumbled Cal, "what to do with him?"

Enoch thought it about time that he had a say in all this.

"What *I* will do is go north. That is what I was instructed to do by my master. Whether you wish to help me or not is your own concern."

The shadowcat at his shoulder hissed in assent. While part of Enoch was angry at being left out of the planning by his undead allies, part of him dreaded heading out alone again. But he would do as his master had said, alone or not.

Rictus and Cal looked at each other and chuckled.

"Oh, there's no doubt about it now," grinned Cal. "He's Pensanden."

Placing a spidery hand on Enoch's arm, Rictus shook his head.

"We are not going to kidnap you away from your *holy mission*, Enoch," he said, still paternal but apologetic. "But seriously, Tenocht? You've got to be kidding me. North is the most dangerous direction for you to be heading right now. If anything, we should be heading east into the Akkadian hills. The caves there would offer a perfect hiding place until you grow into your powers and the Hunt dies down."

Rictus shook his head.

"North . . ." he said bleakly, ". . . lay the last remnants of the Serpent's power on this side of the world. It would be like walking into your own grave."

"Nevertheless," said Enoch, determination in his voice, "I go north."

Rictus rubbed his temples in exasperation. Cal suddenly spoke up.

"Tenocht. I don't know. There are several powerful factions in that city with a reputation for dodging the Forked Tongue—scales, that is where the Nahuati were formed. Perhaps if we took him there?"

Shaking his head, voice bridled with suppressed frustration, Rictus protested.

"Cal! To get there we would have to pass between the Sister Seas. Garron is nestled right between the two, and need I remind you of the hospitality of the Swampmen?" Rictus ground his yellow teeth.

"Even were we to survive that passage, the manticore warrens lay between them and Tenocht. The Rookbane still rules there, my friend, and he looks less gently upon our kind than he does Enoch's. The idea of us passing safely through such lands is preposterous. Enoch may be the last of his kind, and if so, we need to protect him from danger, not thrust him into it."

Cal scoffed.

"What? You think this boy is any better than his forbearers? You think he could be the one to finally seal earth and sky and save this cracked world. Get off the stage, Ric. That show has been over for years."

Enoch had frozen, his mind filled with the memory of that beautiful, monstrous face. The bonfire eyes full of molten need. Remembered fire swam along his wrists, and Enoch shivered. Both Rictus and Cal were staring at him now. Even Sal cocked his furry head.

"Those words, 'seal earth and sky.' I . . . heard them. Just before we were attacked, before my master was killed. A face appeared in the monitor of our Unit. It was made of stars."

Cal rolled his eyes. Rictus leaned closer to Enoch, disbelief written across his brow in wrinkled cursive.

"I know you've been through a lot, kid, but really . . . I mean, how would a shepherd own a functioning Unit, much less find power to run it in the middle of sheep country? What you are saying is . . . it's just—"

Enoch pulled away the remaining shroud and fumbled with the front of his vest, finally pulling out the silvery disk strung with a cord. He held it up to the light, and it cast aqueous reflections on the walls. Even Rictus was stunned.

"That looks like a core memory disc to me, Cal. It looks like Papa Nahuati may have brought some swag down from Tenocht."

Cal cleared his throat, obviously a force of habit, and looked Enoch straight in the eye.

"Are you trying to tell us you received a communication from *God?* That The Winged One Herself logged on to your Unit and asked you a favor? That's . . . that's . . ."

Cal moved his head from side to side, sputtering as he searched for the word large enough to encompass the concept. Rictus cast him an exasperated glance.

"Man, Cal, you *have* been with the mortals too long. What do you mean 'God' and 'Winged One?' You remember how it all happened. Just because humanity has forgotten and lost its head about all of this mess doesn't mean that *you* have to . . . figuratively speaking, of course."

"I never said it was the Winged One," protested Enoch, using the commonspeech name for the Great Unnamable. "Just a face, that's all. This has nothing to do with religion."

Rictus burst out laughing while Cal continued to shake his head. The shadowcat under Enoch's arm decided now would be a good time to investigate the room and leapt softly to the floor. Wiping imaginary tears from dry eyes, Rictus leaned over and put a hand on Enoch's knee.

"No, Enoch. You misunderstand. It has *everything* to do with religion." His voice grew somber so quickly it was almost comical. "Everything.

"Now listen, 'cause what I'm going to tell you has a lot to do with you, religion, and what has happened to this crazy world. Most of the human race has forgotten what it once was and how it got here. It is a twisted tale, kid, as convoluted as the Serpent's guts—"

"Give it up, Ric," interrupted Cal. "Your lyrics are going to ruin a relatively simple story. Let me tell him."

Rictus nodded and gestured towards Cal with another sweeping bow.

Enoch leaned forward nervously.

Do I really want to know this?

He glanced down at the shadowcat, which was nosing around at his feet. Rictus noticed Cal's discomfiture and shook his head.

"Don't worry—she's housebroken. Made sure to do her business on Enoch's shoulder."

Enoch jumped at this, frantically pulling his vest around to investigate. Rictus laughed.

"Wow, you are easy to take—that was a joke, kid. Good thing you don't duel with that brain."

He turned back to Cal.

"The lil' shadowcat hybrid is as manicured as one of Nyraud's courtesans. She won't mess on your spotless floor, don't worry. Hurry and get on with the tale before you pop a vein, Cal. I know how you geezers love to talk about the good old days."

Cal ignored the jibe and began to speak.

"Ok, first and foremost—this world didn't used to be the half-bred schizophrenic wreck it is now. You know, the other day I saw a man selling Unit parts out of a murwagon. A murwagon! Can you believe it?"

Rictus chuckled along with Cal. Enoch stared at them. He didn't get the joke. Cal noticed and cleared his throat again.

"No . . . no, I guess that wouldn't seem strange to you. You've grown up in this world, after all. You wouldn't think it funny to see giant rats bridled as beasts of burden now that the horses are gone. Or to see their smaller cousins—I still laugh at what happened to the mice, Ric—filling the niche left empty by wolves.

Mickey, I hardly knew ye.

"Anyway, as I was saying, this used to be a very different place. We owned the world. Do you know what I mean by owned, Enoch? I mean that it was clay in our hands. We could do anything with it, go anywhere, and see anything. Our cities stretched from sea to shining sea, as the old ditty goes—but this time, it was literally *every* sea. And even underneath them. We had cities on Mars and some of the Jovian moons. Colonies on other systems—circling other stars—were planned."

Here Rictus pointed up in the direction of the Ark and shrugged. Cal continued.

"There was nothing out of reach for us. Oh, it was a grand time. We had learned to control the smallest of things, the tiny codes in our bodies that make up what we are. We gave animals speech, read dreams from stone, and had every miracle of the imagination at our fingertips. Tireless *machines* waited upon our every need. They grew our food, fixed our bodies, and entertained us. Your folk," here he nodded towards Enoch. "Your folk, the Pensanden, made it all work. They'd made it happen—they were the first to connect the dots, oil the gears, and light the lights. It was a golden time, the pinnacle of humanity . . ."

"For some," interrupted Rictus, causing Cal to *pause*, then purse his lips and look away. "You have to realize, Enoch, that you are getting this all from the mouth of a sheltered celebrity who lived the lap of luxury all his life. For many, it was a dark time. Those machines Cal refers to were not entirely mechanical, you see."

"And there were some who felt that the Pensanden had gotten drunk with their power. Imagine, Enoch, having the power that you do in a world of machines."

Enoch nodded, felt a chill rush along his skin. He wasn't sure if it was fear or perhaps . . . pride? Excitement? Shaking the thought from his head, he leaned forward and tried to regain his focus on what Cal was saying.

"It happened so fast that your folk never had time to learn wisdom with their power. They went from being a freakish little cult of drugged-out shamans and rogue mathematicians, to an omnipotent race of tribal technocrats." Cal whistled low, and Rictus threw his hands in the air.

"I know, I know, lame alliteration. Bad lyrics, I got it. It's just how I talk, Cal. You've had centuries to get used to it."

Cal was grinning and shaking his head from side to side.

"Ha—you know, this self-analysis may do you some good, Ric. I was actually responding to your aspersion of the Pensanden founders—what did you call them? Drugged-out shamans? Deny it all you might, my friend, but you've still got a touch of the old neo-luddite hatred. Still pointing a blame finger at the etherwalkers, eh?"

Rictus was annoyed now and stared up at the ceiling, deliberately avoiding Enoch's eyes.

Cal took a long breath and continued. "Your ancestors combined Quiché Mayan Mysticism, parametric computer languages, Neo-Santería, and vigesimal geometry into a programmatic artform that was . . . it was spiritual. And amazingly adaptable. Their innovations became the life blood of the Mexican Renaissance.

"From Calistados barrio slums to ruling the world. All of it, Enoch. Many suffered at their hands before your folk finally grew into their power, if such a thing is possible."

Enoch looked down at his scarred wrists.

"Maybe it was their humble origins, their mortal conscience which eventually stopped them—certainly nobody else could. The wisest amongst them, a sage who called himself Tepeu, finally called together the thirteen members of the ruling Tzolkin Core and drew up an accord—a pact, if you will. Something which would help the Pensanden to remember their responsibility towards humanity. I don't know the details of this accord—"

Enoch cleared his throat, and Cal stopped. The shepherd had a strange look on his face. He climbed to his feet and folded his hands behind his back, eyes fixed to the wall in front of him.

"With minds blessed to enter the marrow of the world, with the vision which pierces, the thoughts which command, we shall keep one eye drawn to heaven, the other drawn to earth. Thus we bear the marks of feather and the scale, the talon and the fang. We are Ketzel and Koatul, above, below, beginning, end."

Rictus and Cal were staring at him oddly. Enoch touched the curling white scar at his wrist, the other on his hand. In the ensuing silence, he spoke reverently.

"It is the Silicon Covenant, opening stanza to the Book of Tepeu. A revelation fulfilling promises made in the *Popol Vuh*. It was my first Reciting."

He lowered his hands in disbelief. All this time, the prophecies his master had made him learn, the endless hours of lessons.

They were for me. For me and about me. He wanted me to know this history, the story of my lineage. He didn't know if I would have the talent, but he knew my family. Now I understand.

"What about the Schism, then?" asked Enoch. "I thought it was the time of Creation, when the land was divided from the sea. When the world was born."

Rictus nodded.

"In a way it was, Enoch. We'll get to that. The Pensanden, having grown into their power, now no longer desired to rule. They realized that this power which had given them free reign over humanity also chained them to lives of stewardship—to some it seemed slavery. Their ability to go within the machines is what made our comfortable little world possible. Without the constant, expert touch of their trained minds, the random and minuscule elements of chaos would have eventually ground the great network of mankind to a screeching halt."

Enoch frowned at this. It didn't seem right.

"But if they truly did not want to rule, why not just let it all wind down?" he replied. "That would have solved the problem for them."

Cal spoke up, somewhat irked that the story had been stolen from him.

"You see, Enoch, for your kind, the more these powers are used, the stronger they become. Practicing the art heightened their senses, increased the sensitivity of the nervous system, and produced a general endorphin rush. They were addicted to it—

quite literally so. Electron junkies."

But I've felt the power, and it hurt. It burns. Why would I choose *to . . . ?*

With a start, Enoch realized that Cal was wrong. The Pensanden weren't addicted to their power.

"No, don't you see? The Silicon Covenant. They couldn't just let the world fall apart because they didn't want to rule. They had already sworn themselves to the stewardship of mankind. They wore the marks of their oath." Enoch held up his hands.

Rictus looked at him with eyebrows raised. Cal gave the shoulder-less equivalent of a shrug.

"Well, whatever the reason, they decided they didn't want to be gods anymore. And that is where the real problem started. Now we're getting to the Schism.

"You see, while the Pensanden had suddenly been struck by a bout of conscience, it didn't necessarily mean that they had been humbled. They assumed that with their peerless control of all things tek, it should be easily within their ability to create an artificial intelligence powerful enough to perform their responsibilities for them.

"A small number of your folk were actually against the idea. They believed that a mechanical intelligence would never be able to deal with the myriad complexities of humanity with any sort of compassion. The majority of the etherwalkers disagreed, however."

"Xolotl," interrupted Rictus.

"Yes," said Cal. "He lead the group. Xolotl Gabriel Villa. A brilliant man and he claimed to have the solution. By combining and digitizing the personalities of the ruling Pensanden, he would create a group-mind which would oversee the governance of the world's greasy gears with proven efficiency—and there would be no need for the exhaustive trials and testing any 'synthetic intelligence' would require. Already weary of the burden, the majority of the Pensanden agreed to Xolotl's plan and set to work making it a reality. They named it Quetzalcoatl—the name of God in an ancient tongue."

Enoch remembered the verse in chapter twelve of Tepeu's book.

"And in their pride did they spin the world to ash. In their folly did they cast a graven image and adorned it in robes foreordained unto themselves."

Rictus chuckled, breaking the reverent silence jarringly.

"Looks like you know the rest, kid. The tek went nuts for some reason—the complexities and foibles of the human minds it was patterned after didn't jive with its perfect structure, I suppose. The duality of human existence and all that. Just split it apart. Whatever was left in the ashes suddenly decided that your ancestors needed to die for the crime of siring it. That's when the Hunt was kindled. The world wound down. The colonies on Mars, Venus, and the Jovian moons were cut off. War and factionalism had apparently not been forgotten in the years of peace, and humanity ended up destroying whatever the machine left when it was done.

"There was a manic hatred towards any and all things tek. Scientists, teachers, anyone with learning of any kind were killed or forced into hiding. Libraries were burned, factories destroyed—" he waved his hand expansively, "—and this world was born. The coldmen, who, ironically enough, had been created by the Pensanden for entertainment in their arenas, became their hunters. Koatul, as the remnant machine named itself, converted the entire western hemisphere into its warren and then sank into myth. I believe the smallfolk refer to Koatul now as the Serpent.

"So the only scraps of what the world once was are a few crumbled buildings, some malfunctioning Units, and a couple of tired, long-forgotten entertainers." He gave a bony grin to Cal and then folded his hands over the steady red pulse at his chest.

"The religions of this day are all loosely based on those happenings. The Winged One, the popular god of our age, is based on the hope for another surviving remnant of the original master machine. Something as powerful as Koatul yet benevolent and wise. Maybe Ketzel? Cal thinks you may have heard from it. I think you got a screwy Unit, but unless we want to risk our lives being traced on a public machine, I guess it's all up in the air . . ."

"Not necessarily," interjected Cal, a sly grin creeping across his dried apple face. He motioned towards the closet door behind Rictus with his eyebrows.

"Open that door, boy. I've got a present for you."

As Rictus gave Cal a questioning glance, Enoch climbed wearily to his feet and walked to the rear of the room. The shadowcat was suddenly visible at the door, sniffing under the crack.

"Looks like your little friend wants to ruin the surprise for you," chuckled Cal. "Have you named your mate yet?"

Enoch froze mid-step.

"Mate?"

"Of course," said Cal, mock-surprise on his face. "I ought to know when I see a shadowcat—even a Garronian mix-up like this—protecting her mate. The King himself used to trap them up in the Akkadian Woods, before they became too rare. He'd parade his trophies around town in wire cages before taking them up to that private garden of his. Sometimes he'd even line up battles in the coliseum—shows for the commoners when he grew bored of his pets. By themselves, shadowcats can hold their own, but usually they will just try to escape. That chameleon pelt of theirs makes it damn near impossible to find them. But once you throw a mated pair into the ring . . ." Cal whistled, eyebrows peaking. "I once saw a she-cat tear the eyes out of a young manticore when it gobbled her mate. You got yourself quite a commitment there, boy."

Enoch blushed. The shadowcat, as if in response to the conversation, turned from the door, hissed, and then proceeded to wind her way up Enoch's legs to perch on his shoulder. Both Cal and Rictus laughed.

"So what have you named her, boy?" said Cal, grinning. "Can't have a girlfriend without a proper name."

Enoch decided to ignore their teasing and instead scratched thoughtfully at the creatures' pointed ears. Her eyes waned into slits.

"There was a statue in the commons at Rewn's Fork. I . . . I don't know if it even stands anymore, now that the coldmen have passed through. It was nothing so grand as any of the monuments I have seen here in Babel, but I remember looking at it often as my master did business with the townsfolk. It was cut from the native stone—rough and blocky—but it was beautiful. I used to think it was an angel, but now I know it was an Alaphim, kind of like the one I just saw over in the market. But scarier. All dressed in armor, with a sword in one hand and a man's head in the other. She was holding the head high in the air like a trophy."

Rictus nodded his head in recognition, raising a finger in the air.

"Sounds like the Alaphim Princess Mesha Frost, also known as the *Blue Valkyrie*. She was the first to uncover the treachery of the Arkángels, and she killed the traitor who started it. He was her lover."

"Master Gershom said that the statue was called 'Mesha Triumphant'—and that it should remind me to always treat women with respect. Or else." Rictus chuckled at that. Enoch cupped the shadowcat's pointed face in his hand and looked into the deep, moonlight eyes.

"I'll call you Mesha."

"Alright," remarked Cal, rolling his eyes, "let us move on to what is behind door number three!"

Enoch could see no other doors in the room other than the one they had come in through, but he decided to open the closet door anyway. A cool draft welcomed him as the door creaked open to reveal—nothing. The cluttered darkness of a forgotten closet. Enoch turned to face Cal, hands on his hips.

"Okay, I get it. More fun with the shepherd. There's nothing here."

Cal turned to Rictus, an impatient look on his face.

"Does he always jump to conclusions so fast?" He shot Enoch an irritated glance. "Pull the cord, foolish boy. Of course you can't see with the light off."

Enoch narrowed his eyes suspiciously, then turned back to the closet. He reached around until encountering a piece of twine dangling from the ceiling. With a click, yellow light filled the space.

Strange objects—broken odds and ends, refuse from the tavern, and some dust-covered shapes which Enoch suspected were abandoned prosthetics—were stacked against the walls reaching up to the ceiling. Enoch's hair stood on end as another chill draft passed over him. It came with a metallic odor, oil-blue and tangy. At the back of the room was a staircase leading down into more shadow. This was where the draft had originated. Cal's voice came from the other room.

"See that staircase, boy? Leads right down to the roots of the city. Who knows what we might find amidst Babel's twisted toes, eh?"

Enoch turned excitedly around, almost dislodging a surprised Mesha.

"Is there a passage to the north?"

Infected by the excitement, Sal started jumping up and down in his hammock, hooting.

Rictus was shaking his head, arms crossed. Cal noticed and smiled.

"Slow down there, etherwalker. Don't go jumping ahead of yourself again. We are going to have to wait until nightfall—I got business to take care of now. And don't you think of taking off without old Cal. You'll get lost after your first ten steps down there without me."

Enoch slumped to the floor. "Well, what will we do until then?"

Cal's smile broadened, the dry wrinkles on his face webbing up like shattered glass.

"Go back into that closet and bring out the long, black case marked 'Fender.' I think it's about time Rictus made it up to me for bringing trouble to my doorstop."

Rictus tilted his head as Enoch went to retrieve the case.

"It's been a long time, Cal. I'm sure you can pipe rings around me with that flute of yours." Rictus nodded towards the odd-angled conglomeration of flutes and whistles bolted to Cal's harness.

Cal rolled his eyes in exasperation.

"You think that the fine clientele of the Headsman's Hole are going to pass up a once-in-a-lifetime chance to see the return performance of the Dogfish Knights?"

Enoch set the oddly shaped case in front of the specter, watching with fascination as the bony hands caressed the black leather case and the bronze lettering. The clips holding the case closed flipped up smartly with little puffs of dust. Rictus let out a low whistle as he raised the lid.

"Now that is a fine axe, my friend."

The cherry red guitar gleamed silkily in the electric light, casting molten reflections up into the specter's grin. Rictus lifted it gently, carefully, cautiously—as though it were babe in his arms. Or a scorpion.

Enoch had seen simple wooden guitars before, carried around by wandering minstrels that passed through Rewn's Fork. But this instrument! It almost seemed a living creature, curved and gleaming. There was a slight popping noise as Rictus plugged the long black cord that hung from the guitar into his LifeBeat. A low, sinister hum filled the room.

Rictus looked up from the guitar, the strange grin on his red-lit face sending chills up Enoch's spine.

"Show me to the stage, Cal. I'm gonna break this baby in."

CHAPTER 10

Then was Gucumatz filled with joy.
Thou art welcome,
Oh Heart of the Sky,
Oh Hurakan,
Oh Streak of Lightning,
Oh Thunderbolt!

—*Popol Vuh 1:15, Maya-Quiché Genesis, New Century Revised Edition*

The war-drones were uncomfortable in these lofty passageways, betraying their nervousness with an absentminded clicking of mouthparts. Mosk gave them the claw sign of *Death for Cowardice* and the sound stopped immediately. The Silverwitch who followed him nodded in approval. Kai had been a wonderful and unexpected find, appearing at the end of their fruitless search with news of the Pensanden.

The entourage had been slowly winding up through the belly of this famed Tower for over an hour now, and the King regaled them with a seemingly endless supply of anecdotes and historical background for each branch and tunnel they passed through. The exotic tapestries and carpets which lined the walls and floor, signs of Babel's position as the crossroads of this primitive land, did an admirable job of disguising the true nature of the Tower. As the group rose higher and higher up, evidences of the incomplete and decrepit nature of the edifice became more apparent. Entire walls were open to the sky. The King called them balconies, acting as though they were deliberate acts of architecture, and took advantage of each of these openings to admire the view of the sparkling city sprawled out below them in the darkness.

Kai finally spoke.

"King Nyraud, I begin to suspect that we are taking a less-than-direct path towards your council room. While we are not unsympathetic toward your concepts of hospitality and exhibitionism, our patience does have its limits."

Several of the more foolish of the King's courtiers gasped at the creature's tone—*that one would talk so to the Hunter King!* Nyraud covered their sounds with laughter, and bowed to the Silverwitch and the Swarmlord with a flourish. The torches had gone out in this most recent section of "balcony," and the gesture would have been lost in the wan moonlight if not for the King's cape. The garment flowed over his shoulders in a cascade of pelts from a dozen rare and deadly beasts, scintillating indigo, silver, and cream.

"My apologies, august Hiveking. My lady. Your memory of this crumbling excuse for a castle serves you well—I am indeed taking a slightly more *scenic* route towards the council room. Your troupe, your . . . your *swarm* arrived in my city without warning and caught me entirely unprepared for such a venerable guest. Having been away at business in the east, I only returned this morning to learn of your arrival. Even now my servants are scurrying to prepare proper quarters befitting you and your—"

"It has been too long since blackspawn bled this rotted city," interrupted Mosk. In the stunned silence that followed this, the dry rustling of the Coldman's toothy mouthparts could be heard above the sound of the wind through the balconies. Nyraud took a step back. Kai put a slender hand on Mosk's arm and smiled.

"King Nyraud, if the Swarm was indeed staying here, it would mean that your reign is ended and the Vestigarchy is again assuming control of Babel." Her eyes narrowed. "Blackspawn do not stay unless they have first prepared their own 'proper quarters' with blood and fire. We are not venerable guests, and the only reason your stain of a city isn't in embers right now is because we don't have time to burn it properly."

All pretense gone, Nyraud's face lost the mask of noble congeniality and assumed a form more befitting his features. His personal guard recognized the hungry look—the Hunter's Gaze—and in seconds had escorted the speechless courtiers from sight.

King Nyraud took a step back; not a retreat, but preparation for a pounce.

"Witch, you haven't burnt my city. You haven't prepared anything with 'blood and fire.' And your threats, while frightening, are empty when your need of me is so obvious."

Nyraud's voice was cool and quick.

"Let me be more plain," he continued. "There is only one thing that would bring the Hunt to Babel. Only one thing that would bring the Hiveking to me."

He leaned forward, predatory and direct. Mosk tilted his head curiously.

"Who is this Pensanden?" Nyraud whispered. "Why would he be in my city? And do you need him alive?"

CHAPTER II

The sky, the wind, the rising thermals—we know a poetry that is new to man.

—Keyden Roth, Alaphim Roostmaster

It was evening, with a few thin clouds scattered over the far western mountains like sparrow down. A gentle murmur of wind stretched through the Spire with familiar ease.

Several angels had perched on the western cornices with their wings outstretched, capturing the last moments of sunlight flowing warm and purple over the distant Edrei. Sera was struck by how small the Alaphim seemed against the jutting spires and girders of her home.

So small and so few.

She knew that the Alaphim were suffering, that the Nests had been empty for over a decade now. Even in her relatively short lifetime here at Windroost Spire, Sera had noticed the numbers dwindling—ancient perches, carved with family names stretching back to the First Hatching, now gathered dust. It made her feel sad. Hopeless.

And maybe a little guilty for risking our treaty with Nyraud just to spy on his Garden.

She reflexively reached back to the space where her ponytail had once hung.

Well, I paid for it.

Sure, the treaty with King Nyraud kept them free from hunter arrows, even allowed them access to the Babel markets. It was a good thing not to have to worry about their "downstairs neighbor," especially when the rest of the world couldn't seem to forget that Vestigarchy extermination order. Or the current market price for angel feathers. But the treaty didn't solve the Alaphim empty nests.

The Spire felt emptier every year.

Meaning more responsibility falls upon young angels who should be allowed to play instead of patrolling.

After returning from Babel that morning, Sera had taken the metal scraps they had purchased over to the molting perch. She then forced herself to remain silent as Boneweaver Skek scolded and complained about the poor condition of the metals they had brought her. Skek, it seemed, took personal umbrage to the fact that fine metals, pure metals, weren't delivered to her perch by grateful royalty every morning. Apparently, she had been listening to Lamech's stories of "the way it was" before the Schism. For the first time, Sera understood why her father had warned her about spending too much time wrapped up in the old angel's tales.

Because being Alaphim used to mean something. Because we used to have a place in the world.

Sera spread her wings and glided down to a lower platform. After unloading the scrap metal, her bag felt much lighter. She had one more delivery, the one she had saved for last as a personal reward for dealing with Skek. And the one that she probably wouldn't tell father about.

I can be quick—Lamech's perch isn't far from here, and I can ask him to keep it brief.

Windroost Spire had not always been an angel sanctuary. According to Lamech, it was really the unfinished tip of a massive *spaceship* intended to travel to distant worlds. After the Betrayal, when the Arkángels brought the combined wrath of the Vestigarchy against their own kind, refugees from several of the fallen Spires had discovered this place. It was a discovery that saved their lives, and, as far as Lamech knew, had preserved their kind. Who would think to search for Alaphim in the tower of the king who had personally slain hundreds of them? Who, at the first word from the coldmen, summoned his own personal guard, rode at top speed to the southernmost corner of the Reaches, and toppled ancient Fullwind Spire? Nyraud's grandsire's hatred for the angels was famous, and it gave Sera a grim satisfaction to know that her people were brave enough and clever enough to use his own misunderstood "tower" against him.

And they didn't just hide here. They discovered that much of the tip was inaccessible to those living in the platforms of the tower below. And all *of the tip was inaccessible to a king unwilling to use the few mechanical lifts which still functioned in his palace.*

So Windroost had stayed hidden for a time, at least until King Maloch died. The boneweavers had power to work their magic, and the refugee angels scoured the skies for any of their brethren who may have survived the Fourth Hunt. Those few who returned had to be instructed on the new rules, on how to survive and stay hidden. It had been a hard time.

Not that things are much better now. Maloch's grandson is certainly a better king than even his father, more open to exploring and familiarizing himself with the dying tek of his tower—but nobody is fooled into thinking that his alliance with us is based on anything other than his own ambitions. Why else would he request patrols into the north, past Jabbok and skirting the Old Cities? We may have lost as many angels running his blasted scouting missions as we would have without the treaty!

These gloomy thoughts were quickly chased away as Sera neared Lamech's perch. It was situated over the crown of something he called "the navigation bridge." Shaped like a crescent moon, the space was more complete than much of the tip upon which Windroost Spire was located but because of its location and placement at the lowest wing, had been ignored until he settled there. It was fully paneled and had a complement of luxurious benches and desks—all anchored sideways to the wall that would become a floor after launch, but impressive nonetheless. Lamech used them as shelves for his metal books. With these books, he had answers to just about any question Sera could think of. And she had tried to stymie him.

Sera smiled to remember his perplexity when she asked why the Tzolkin Core had built (or tried to build) the Ark in this place. Lamech had frowned, ran an errant finger through his sparse primaries, and then stood in a rush. In seconds he had the right book, and the always-confusing answer:

The tower was only part of what would be a "colonization vessel." Heavier elements had been constructed and assembled in orbit around the planet and would be attached after launch, but because of "necessary structural tests for gravity" and "high-volume storage of concentrated volatiles" much of the ship's body had to be built and launched from this facility, which later became Babel. Apparently the complex natural cave system winding through the terrain here allowed for a more efficient adaptation of "subterranean heat-deflection and umbilical structures." Sera didn't understand much of the magical words Lamech used, but they were fun to say.

She pulled her delivery out of the bag and gave an entry whistle. A familiar shuffling came from inside the perch. Lamech was obviously in the middle of an exciting read, and was torn between leaving the book and seeing a rare visitor.

"Yes, who is it?" came the cracked reply.

"It's Sera, Lamech. I've come with a gift and a question."

There was a *pause*, a noise which sounded like fingers tapping against the wall, and then a sigh. The clank of metal against metal, a book being set against the floor.

Sounds like he's decided the book can wait. I'm in luck.

"Come on in, child. Your father was here earlier. Very polite, your Hatchsire. Said something about not wasting your time. I'll have to remember that. Only tell you the important stories now."

Sera laughed. Lamech had a tendency to see any social interaction exactly as he wanted to see it. She followed the old angel into his perch, squinting in the dim light.

Lamech was well into his third century now, at a stage when the boneweavers no longer spent metal on "unnecessary upkeep." He had lost many of his feathers, and Sera could see knobs of brass protruding from his curved spine. His hair had receded behind his ears, and the once midnight-blue was now threaded with bright silver. Lamech's eyes were still quick, and the wrinkles around his ring-mounts accented every expression.

We are even beautiful in our waning years.

"Okay, fledgling. First the gift, then the question. This is how we do things now in Windroost Spire. Times are hard."

Sera smiled—this was the same thing Lamech said on every visit. It made it sound like the "hard times" were a regrettable but temporary situation, and that at any other time Lamech would be willing to share his tales at no cost.

"Here you go. The gift is something I found in the market this morning, and my question comes tied to it."

She handed him the carved wooden beast. It was a sandy brown and covered with exquisite detailing—tooled fur resolving into stylized curling locks which flowed across the toy's stout form. Sera's ears had perked up at the vendor's pitch for "exquisitely carved toys in fine wood! Beasts from beyond the sandy seas! Manticores, Grems, and Ur'lyns, come buy!"

Now she could ask about these Ur'lyns without revealing her visit to Nyraud's Garden. Now she could find out what sort of monster he kept.

Lamech lifted the carving and held it up to the waning sunset light which trickled orange into the room. He nodded his head.

"Not a bad representation, but the pose is all wrong. The Ur'lyn don't stand on their hind legs like a man. They are largely quadrupeds, but have been known to pull back onto their haunches when fighting."

Sera smiled. Of course Lamech knew this.

"What is an Ur'lyn, Lamech?"

Lamech turned the carving in the light, admiring the way the textured fur caught the sun.

"Like many of the 'monsters' of our world, the Ur'lyn are merely a misunderstood remnant of the times before the Schism. You remember the story of the blackspawn, don't you child?"

Sera nodded.

"They were originally bred to fight in the gladiator pits, right? For the entertainment of the Pensanden?

"Oh, not just for the etherwalkers. The entire world enjoyed these bloodsports. And while there were strict, civilized rules against humans competing in such events, the Pensanden had their gene-crafters create warriors who *almost* seemed human, at least in their cleverness. Their sadism.

"The Ur'lyn were a combination of several distinct predatory animals—animals which are now long gone. Their names: Lion. Tiger. Bear. Names which bore the legendary sound of fear and nightmare for most of mankind's history. And now they are summed up in a race which is, like our own, falling into extinction."

For some reason, this made Sera sad. The beast she had seen in the Garden was rare. Was special.

Like me.

"Why is it . . . I mean, why are they going extinct?"

Lamech put the carving down on the table beside him and turned to look at Sera. One eyebrow raised, he continued.

"In all my years of patrolling through the southern deserts, south of Midian and beyond, I only came across a single pack of Ur'lyn. I took the chance to land and speak with them, and, as I am prone to do, question them about their own history. The creatures speak using their forepaws, Sera, since their mouths are too full of fang to form words we could understand. I spent the better part of a year learning their language. It is simple and poetic—the language of a noble savage."

"They speak? The Ur'lyn are intelligent?"

"Oh yes, much more so than their later rivals. The blackspawn were only given cunning, only given the part of human thought which could scheme to fill hungers. This was done as a reaction to the Ur'lyn, who many thought had been given too much of the human sensibilities. Why would a gladiator need to empathize with his opponent? Or consider the morality of his battles? These were not things that the gene-crafters *deliberately* included in the Ur'lyn psyche, simply an effect that they lacked the skill to control in their early creations. They learned control with the blackspawn. None of the angst, just quick and decisive bloodshed."

Lamech brought the toy Ur'lyn up to his eye and flipped down a magnification lens. The detailing on the creature's face made him smile.

"As murderous as they were, these new insects-come-gladiators still couldn't compete one-to-one against the ferocity forged over millennia. It still took an entire Clot of the coldmen to down a mature Ur'lyn. Why, I could read you some tales of incredible battles—"

"You were telling me why they are dying out."

"Yes, yes, I was. Did I mention that I learned their paw-language?"

Sera tried not to be impatient. This is how talks with Lamech tended to go lately.

"Yes, you did. You said it was simple and—"

"Poetic! A beautiful way of speaking! And it allowed them to hunt while conversing, to silently compose an approach from which no prey could escape. The Ur'lyn were consummate hunters—"

". . . and are now dwindling because . . . ?"

"Yes! Dwindling. Oh yes. Because they became mystics."

"Mystics?"

"Quite. The Ur'lyn carry the bloody memories of their ancestor-races—something they call the Red Instinct. These memories will seize hold of an Ur'lyn when hunting, or in battle, and transform the creature into an unstoppable blur of claws and fangs. Very effective in the arena. But when the instinct fades, and the blood cools, the Ur'lyn have to face the death they have wrought with a moral consciousness which nature never meant for them to have. This contradiction harrowed the poor creatures to the point of despondency. It is one of the reasons the blackspawn were created in their place, for the short 'battle life' of an Ur'lyn before this hopelessness set in was highly inefficient. The Pensanden dislike inefficiency.

"So the Ur'lyn were 'retired.' Removed from the arenas and

replaced by the exciting new toys. Blackspawn. Manticores. Lamia. Many collectors, fans of the bloodsport, tried to keep the race alive out of nostalgia, a love of memories. The Ur'lyn became relics before they became a people.

"So when the Schism happened, these remnant Ur'lyn found each other. They shared their pains and created a culture. They became a tribe. And they turned the paradox of Red Instinct and Morality into a mystical belief in the cruelty of the universe. A belief that they are doomed souls, avatars of suffering meant to pay for the crimes of other races."

"And this belief is what is killing them?"

"Well, it isn't helping them. When an adult Ur'lyn has reached its prime, it is given a 'Task of Atonement' from the ruling Shaman Pride—a group of aged mystics. This task usually involves traveling to a distant land and 'saving an innocent' from evil. The Ur'lyn who comes back, and very few do, becomes an Atoned Beast. It can then fully enter the pack, select a mate, and breed."

"The Ur'lyn's own mysticism is their greatest killer. Because the 'evil' they try to save an innocent from is almost always the Vestigarchy."

Lamech took the carved Ur'lyn and stood, placing it on one of his nearby "shelves."

"Is it a tragedy that such an untouchable killer, the perfect predator in a fallen world of monsters, is bringing about its own end?"

The old angel was still for a moment, then turned and shuffled back to the window. He picked up a book from the sill and settled down to read.

This signaled that the storytelling was over.

Sera whispered a thank you and left. Flying back to her own perch as the sun disappeared behind the mountains, she considered Lamech's last words.

Yes. Yes it is a tragedy. And I won't let Nyraud kill the Ur'lyn in his Garden. I am going to rescue it.

CHAPTER 12

> *You don't walk the streets of Undertown at night. The shadows . . . they seep up from beneath; they clot like blood. They are angry, the shadows.*
>
> *—Gelven Menkatral, Scrapmonger*

Enoch shivered. They had been moving through the tunnels under Babel for hours now, and it was *cold*. Even Mesha's warm weight about his neck couldn't hold off the chill. Cal whistled a short burst, stopping the ape. Sal sat back on his haunches and sighed. His breath came out as a thin puff of vapor in the frigid air.

"This cold is new. I've been further down than we are now, and it's never been like this."

Rictus *paused*, too, looking at Sal's breath. "Is it getting cold? You should have said something, Cal. I'm less sensitive to this kind of stuff—" He pointed down at his legs. "No monkey."

Cal studiously ignored the comment.

Rictus looked over at Enoch, who was rubbing his bare arms. "You want to head back and grab something less 'summer shepherd's garb' to wear? I'd offer you my jacket, but this old leather is only kept in one piece by my LifeBeat—part of the upgraded package."

Enoch shook his head.

"We've already come pretty far—I'll be alright."

Rictus looked at Cal, who pursed his lips. The ape scratched at its leg and seemed to be unaffected by the cold. Enoch wondered if it had been bred to be hardier than its tropical ancestors—he was certainly jealous of the creature's shaggy pelt.

The tunnels beneath Babel were extensive. According to Cal, this network of metal passageways and machinery had been around since before the Schism, and was one of the few "relatively untouched" remnants of that forgotten time on this side of the world. The walls and ceiling were paneled with sheets of thin, pale metal. From time to time, they came across empty rooms—rooms with jagged holes in the floors and ceiling.

"Signs of ancient violence," said Rictus.

"Looting by a disreputable tavern owner," said Cal.

Occasionally, they passed dark hallways extending endlessly from one side to the other, but Cal kept them moving in a straight line. He said that this passage would take them to the "fully-functioning secret" he had discovered in his last trip down here, and that the same passage would continue to carry them straight through the bowels of the city and out into the northern swamps.

"We should be almost out from under Babel by now, right?" asked Enoch.

Rictus tipped his head back and laughed. "We haven't even gotten under the tower yet, kid. Babel is a big city. Cal, are you sure you don't want to head back now and try for a sunnier path?"

"You saw what I did, Ric. Those soldiers that arrived at the end of your show weren't there for the ale. I had three separate informants tell me that they were all over the city looking for *a boy and his ghoul* . . . and if I hadn't cut your second encore and rushed you back here, we'd be in the tower by now. The part without any windows."

Rictus started to mumble something but stopped and looked back up at the arched ceiling. "Well, this doesn't look good."

Enoch followed the specter's stare up into the flickering blue light—a light which *he* had ignited back when he first *paused* and noticed the remnant lines of power running behind the paneled walls.

After walking in the poor illumination of Cal's flashlight for an hour, it had been nice to be able to see the area both in front of and behind them. The light snapping on overhead like that had brought Rictus leaping out in front of the group, his sword humming around in a protective arc. The specter shot quick looks up and down the tunnel before Enoch's laughter broke the tension. Cal had laughed as well, commenting that traveling down here with a Pensanden may just have its advantages. Rictus had grumbled, detaching the flashlight cord from his LifeBeat generator and telling Enoch that he should warn him before surprising him like that. That maybe next time Rictus's sword might decide to "go luddite on your head."

Whatever that meant. He had made Enoch agree to extinguish the light behind them as they descended, and that did make sense. No trail.

Now if only we could find some wood for a fire . . .

Enoch shivered again, squinting up into the light. It just looked like a long glass tube. Like the hundreds of others they had passed as they moved through the paneled sections of this passageway.

"I don't see anything, Rictus."

"Don't look *into* the light tubes, silly peasant boy. Look at the walls around them."

Turning to glance at the sides, Enoch noticed dark stains on some of the highest panels.

"I've not seen those down here before," mumbled Cal, "but I've lived long enough to recognize the arcs and spatters that blood can leave."

The words hung in the chilly air for a long moment. Rictus had his sword out again, and Enoch followed suit.

"Have you ever seen anyone else down here, Cal?"

Cal shook his head.

"A few times, but that was years ago. People looking for shelter. For scrap to sell. It's probably been half a century since I last ran across anybody. All of the entryways have been sealed up and bricked over—Nyraud doesn't want anyone down here, that's for sure. The only way I could keep my little secret door was by hiding it under a grimy, forgettable tavern and then outliving anyone who might remember its location. There are stories, though . . ."

"Here we go," said Rictus, letting out a sigh.

"They are just stories," said Cal, ignoring Rictus. "But you hear them enough over the years, and certain similarities begin to stand out. You know the sort, Ric—rumors of the labyrinths underneath the city being full of gold or unspoiled tek. Rumors of medicines, elixirs from the past which can return a man's youth or heal any sickness. Silly stuff. But the constant stories? The ones where the details don't change over the years? They are always the ones about monsters. About the trolls."

"Trolls?" said Enoch. He'd already faced coldmen and a Silverwitch and a specter—this was getting to be too much.

"Oh, come on, Cal!" complained Rictus. "I know you—you wouldn't be down here if you thought there was any chance of danger. You were a half-decent musician but a coward through and through. Remember that plata*bruja* ambush back in Septimo? Your screams had that mek-witch thinking she had trapped a caravan of monkeys—no offense Sal—and I took two daggers in the gut before I could stop laughing enough to take her head off."

Cal stared at Rictus, waiting for him to finish. "Sure, Ric, make fun of the disembodied head riding on a monkey. Very big of you. But I'm serious—I hear a lot of rumors. A lot of stories. I preside over a place where people come to share their sorrows and forget their pain. After a century or two of this, you learn to see patterns."

This caught Enoch's attention, and he turned to give Cal his full attention. For a moment he forgot how cold he was.

I see patterns, too.

Cal had a strange look in his eye. Distant.

"You learn to recognize things. Patterns in how stories are told. When, and by whom. The repetition of certain elements, the plot and structure of a million tales through a million tongues can form . . . clouds of truth . . . over time."

Rictus clicked his dry tongue. "Clouds of *truth*? Um, are we still talking about trolls?"

"I don't know a better way to describe it, Ric. Things are so much more complex than we'd like them to be. The right and wrong of our world seems so obvious sometimes—too obvious. It's vulgar. The Schism, the Hunt," he laughed, "even our heroic little quest to help 'the last remnant of a fallen race'." Here he nodded over at Enoch.

"Do you think Ketzelkol saw this? Saw the meta-tale? I mean, here this all-powerful machine was charged with our protection, and instead it burnt our tek and turned us into cavemen. It's like a bad morality play. Sure, we can't nuke ourselves anymore or choke to death on smog. But this couldn't have been the solution! Again, it's too stupid and too simple—the true tales don't work like that."

Enoch and Rictus were silent. Cal had gone somewhere else in his mind, and they didn't know how to respond.

"Maybe this was why the Winged One split with her sibling? For a tale to hope for resolution, there has to be a . . ." Cal noticed the others staring at him.

"Sorry." He looked down. His voice broke. "I . . . I guess I don't get much of a chance to talk with somebody who can see beyond the immediate concerns of day-to-day peasant life. Or somebody who remembers the time before. Who remembers what we used to be—what *I* used to be . . ." Cal was crying now, and Sal reached up to place a hairy paw on his master's cheek. Rictus took a step forward.

"No, no. I'm alright. It's been a long time, Ric." Cal trembled. "So very long."

Rictus ignored his friend's protests and sat, putting his long arms around the ape and Cal in one smooth gesture. Enoch looked away. He recognized the pain in this moment, but his mind was racing.

I need to know more about these patterns Cal talked about. There is truth in what he said; I can feel it. I need to understand this "meta-tale."

After a long moment, Cal cleared his throat, and Sal gently removed Rictus's arms from around them. Rictus understood, and he gave his friend a bony smile. Cal whistled, and the ape leapt up to hang from a thick cable dangling from the ceiling.

"Okay, so about the trolls: I know, Ric, that stories with trolls in them are usually based on something mundane that scared the teller. They are usually, and obviously, fabricated accounts. You and I would both recognize a description of the *real* thing—" That caught Enoch's attention.

The real thing?

"—so, what caught my attention is that the latest rumors are sharply different from the imagined ones I'd been listening to for years. More . . . *accurate*. But also disturbingly wrong. They have the trolls foraying *above* ground, actually emerging from the old doors—doors which have been shut for decades—and dragging people back down underneath. Nobody important or noteworthy, just street children or alleyway drunks. This is why the stories haven't caught the attention of Nyraud's city guard. But I've heard enough of these tales from enough people to think that *something* is going on. Something." Here he smiled up at Rictus. "Clouds of truth are notoriously unspecific. But I think we have trolls under Babel."

The change of topic, specifically to bloodthirsty trolls, hit Enoch like a winter gale. His teeth chattered.

Oh yeah—I'm freezing!

"Rictus, Cal—I think I may actually be ready to head back and get some warmer clothes, especially if what you say is true about how far we . . . Hey!" Enoch flinched as Mesha sank her claws into his shoulder, hissing at the passageway behind them. He turned.

There was a shadow at the end of the hall. It was almost undetectable, a thicker darkness amidst the shadows where the blue light faded into blackness.

With a flash, Rictus was in front of Enoch, long sword humming to life. "Move back, you two—we don't know who this is."

As if in response to Rictus's words, another shadow moved up next to the first. Followed by another.

Rictus turned his head slightly towards Enoch, keeping one

eye on the shadows. "They're deliberately staying out of the light. Can you turn on the light in the passageway behind us, Enoch?"

Enoch nodded and then put his hand to his forehead. Mesha leapt to the ground and stalked towards Rictus's feet, growling.

The mind is a world, the consciousness its light. As day turns to night, so shall my mind; afila lumin setting as the nubla rises, and my mindworld revolves.

The familiar lines of the power network spread out around him, and it was an easy thing to re-ignite the lights in the hallway they had just passed through. The bulbs were still warm.

The light flickered on, and Enoch gasped. Even Rictus staggered back a few steps.

The hallway was full of trolls.

The monsters were startled by the light and scrambled back into the darker passages behind them. But in those few seconds, Enoch had seen enough to terrify him to the core.

The trolls were tall, easily eight feet at the lopsided crouch they seemed to favor. Large, meaty hands reached down to the floor—hands ending in misshapen fingers stained brown with blood and filth. They had small, bony heads with cruel black-button eyes placed closely together over a hooked nose. Drool seeped from wide, craggy mouths, rolled over chinless jaws, and disappeared into the matted hair of their naked chests. These horrors looked like caricatures of men, only twisted and swollen.

"I told you so."

That was Cal. He had whistled Sal up into the rafters above Rictus.

"So why didn't you warn us about this before we got here?" growled the specter, his eyes riveted on the heavy shapes moving in the darkness behind them.

"Well, I've never actually seen any. And these stories are new. Really new. Only a few weeks old, actually, so I wasn't positive—well, at least until we saw the blood. There was a chance we wouldn't see anything; we've been in troll country before, Ric. Remember? They never attack an armed group, and certainly never in the light."

One of the trolls edged out into the light, squinting its tiny eyes in the blue glow. Standing erect to a full twelve-foot height, it sniffed at the brightness above him. The creature was massive, and Enoch could see the bones of its knuckles protruding from pink skin like dull yellow horns. With a low snarl, the troll swung at the bulb and shattered it. The end of the passageway went black. Cal and Rictus looked at each other.

"That's odd."

Rictus, with his sword extended in one hand, reached behind him with the other and pushed Enoch backwards, slowly following. The trolls crept after them, hesitantly following the big one in the lead.

"Move. Slowly. Enoch, keep the lights on in front of us as we move. The light doesn't hurt them, but they don't like it."

"Okay—let me try to increase the power."

With a *push,* the lights above them glowed brighter. The big troll shuffled back a couple of steps, deep growls coming from behind him. The beasts didn't like having to wait.

Rictus kept his little group at an even pace, slowly moving through the tunnel. Enoch turned on the lights ahead of them as they moved, and the lead troll smashed the glass tubes one by one as he followed. It was getting impatient, coming closer and closer after each light went out. The trolls behind it were even more impatient, pushing and jostling. At one point the lead troll turned on the creature at its back with a snarl. The snarl was answered with a roar, and the walls shook as the two monsters grappled. In the half-light, Enoch could see this new troll cuff the leader to the ground and leap on its stunned form. He looked away as the usurper took a massive bite out of its fallen packmate and was quickly surrounded by more trolls eager for the easy meal. Horrible sounds, wet and hungry, filled the dark tunnel behind them. Rictus pushed Enoch and Cal onwards.

Distracted, the trolls stopped following them. A quiet minute passed. Two. Cal whispered if maybe the beasts had gone looking for different prey—or had perhaps already sated themselves.

Rictus shook his head. "They'll be back. Did you see how they jumped on that one in front the moment he fell? Something's wrong with these trolls. They're starving."

"Poor bastards," said Cal.

Enoch gave an empty laugh, impressed that Cal could joke at a time like this. Then he looked over and noticed that Cal wasn't kidding. He honestly felt pity for these things!

"Are you serious?" asked Enoch through chattering teeth.

Cal looked up at him and nodded.

"They were men once, Enoch. A remnant of the 'souls who oiled the gears' of our golden age, as Rictus puts it."

Enoch decided he was done letting these mysterious innuendos fly by. And besides, talking made him forget about the cold. And the trolls.

"What do you mean? Are the trolls as old as you specters?"

Rictus laughed, and Cal looked slightly offended. Sal stopped to scratch himself before continuing down the hallway.

"I'll just assume you meant that out of innocent curiosity, Enoch. An artist never tells his age, you see."

Rictus was still laughing. Cal continued.

"As for how old the trolls are, I suppose it's possible that some of them have survived from our time—apoptosis, negated cell death and all that—" He caught Enoch's blank expression.

"Sorry, old timey words which mean that trolls don't die unless you *make* them die. So, sure, these could be remnants from our age. But not necessarily—they've certainly been prolific since then. You'd have to ask the troll, I suppose."

He looked from Enoch to Rictus expectantly. Nobody was laughing. Cal frowned.

"It's complicated, Enoch. These trolls, like so many other elements of this wonderful dark age, are leftovers from the world before the Schism. Uh, how would you tell this, Ric?"

"Start with the plague."

"The plague? You want me to get into . . . ?"

Enoch noticed that Rictus had gone serious, still walking slowly along the passageway, but with a strange look in his eyes.

Is he angry? At what?

"Alright, the plague then. Okay, Enoch, even though our world had become automated to the hilt, there were some tasks that we assumed would always require the human touch. One of these was medical care. Doctors and nurses and all that." He *paused* and looked over at Rictus.

"Do they even have those anymore?"

Rictus shook his head. "No, that kind of stuff ended with the Schism. You know that, Cal. I've met some tinkers who can leech you for a few coppers, though."

Cal grimaced. He turned back to Enoch, who had just turned on the next row of lights above them. Still no sign of trolls.

Maybe they lost us?

Cal continued.

"So, when the Crow Plague struck the Asian Conglomerate—"

"And it didn't just kill birds," interrupted Rictus.

"—it ripped through the hospitals like wildfire, infecting the patients *and* the doctors. Undetected for months, it traveled through organ transplants. When its second stage took hold, just about every hospital in that hemisphere took a hit. The patients, already weak from other ailments, quickly succumbed to the virus. The symptoms for the disease were quickly cataloged, and, the medical community thought, understood. The doctors, assuming themselves free from infection due to all the usual precautions, kept their surviving patients isolated but continued their usual routine of travel and sociality. It wasn't until the virus manifested itself in a third . . . horrible . . . stage that the ruling Pensanden, the Tzolkin Core, realized their dilemma. The plague had been spread throughout the world, rooted deeply in the one group of men and women who had a chance to cure it."

"So the Pensanden solved the problem the way they always do—with machinery."

"And," interjected Rictus, "with a healthy dose of cold, mathematical brutality."

Cal whistled for Sal to turn and point at the specter, who walked past them with his jaw set in a grim line.

"Let's not start that old argument again, Ric. You and I wouldn't even *be* here if not for the First Hunt—our LifeBeat systems are based on the tek that originated from the Tzolkin Core medical reforms."

"Wait," said Enoch. "How did the Pensanden cure the Crow Plague?"

Rictus stopped, his back to them both.

"They didn't cure it. They were programmers, Enoch, not doctors. All they could see were the numbers."

Cal sighed.

"The numbers were true, Ric. If they hadn't done what they—"

Rictus spun around, fists clenched tightly. Enoch had never seen him this angry.

"They cut their losses! They turned their backs on three billion men, women, and children so that they could save their own lives! This is why the Pensanden fell, Cal! A little bit of cosmic justice!" He closed his eyes, visibly trying to calm himself.

"They loved their numbers and their power more than they loved the people they were responsible for. They weren't even human anymore. They were . . ." Rictus stopped, looked at Enoch. His mouth hung open.

Enoch took a quick step back, shivering and feeling guilty for some reason. Rictus reached a hand out apologetically but shrugged it off.

He forgot that I was here, I guess. That I'm a Pensanden.

A darker thought bubbled to the surface.

So I'm a monster, too?

Cal tried to cover the awkward silence.

"That's what some people thought, Enoch. But some of us were a little more, uh, *wise*—" here he shot a look at Rictus, "or distant from the situation, and realized that Tepeu and the Tzolkin Core made the only choice they could have. With the entire medical community paralyzed, they turned to their algorithms. They saw that unless hard decisions were made quickly, humanity would be inundated with this plague. It had spread too wide, too fast. The off-world colonies were untouched, but they still depended on shipments from earth to survive."

"So what did they do?" asked Enoch, numb but still oddly afraid of the answer. "And what does this have to do with the trolls?" Mesha had climbed back onto his shoulders, and it was a welcome warmth.

"They created a machine which could detect the virus," said Cal. "They created an army of them. And they programmed them to contain the virus."

"Contain?"

"You've met these machines, Enoch. The Meka-scheyf Cyborgs—prototypes of the Silverwitch you fought—were the first line of defense against the plague. Clothed in a sculpted layer of anti-viral synthetic flesh, they entered the populace unnoticed and efficiently removed those who were infected. Entire nations had to be taken down. Billions of people. A human army could never have accomplished the task and kept their sanity. It had to be machines."

Enoch was horrified.

"So the Pensanden built the Serpent Wives? To kill sick people?"

Cal looked away. Rictus kept walking, silently.

"But how could they excuse themselves to . . . didn't they at least *try* to find a . . . ?" Enoch was speechless. The pride he had felt for his newfound lineage was gone. Now he felt sick.

It's true. I'm descended from monsters.

He jumped as a hand rested on his shoulder. Rictus had sidled up next to him as he walked and matched his pace. The specter was obviously feeling bad about his tirade. His voice was soft, apologetic.

"It was the numbers, Enoch. They didn't dare hope for a chance to save those people. The risk was too great for them, too frightening for a group who had forgotten about faith in anything that couldn't be calculated. So the cyborgs became commonplace since we couldn't risk another outbreak. Machines watched our health, extended our lives," here Rictus tapped the box at his chest, "and became our crutch."

"Don't think this heavy burden didn't affect your own people, Enoch," said Cal, his tone heavy. "The weight of those actions is what drove them to create Ketzelkol. They didn't want to have to make that kind of choice ever again."

"How?" said Enoch, "How could they live with themselves, having ordered the murder of so many?"

"Some of them couldn't." Rictus's hand was heavy on his shoulder.

Cal whistled, and the ape swung from another cable to land right in front of Enoch and Rictus. Sal turned and held up a hand to stop them.

"Oh, but they didn't kill all of them, Enoch. You see, some of those infected with the Crow Plague didn't die."

"Yeah," said Rictus. "The lucky ones who had cancer."

Enoch didn't know the word. He shrugged, and Mesha hissed at the motion.

"Cancer," explained Cal, "was a disease of our era in which parts of the body started growing . . . incorrectly." He shot a look at Rictus, searching for the right words. "Well, that's the layman's description, I suppose. These cancerous parts, these 'cells' would often grow uncontrollably, blocking off normal bodily function and, in many cases, killing their host.

"The Crow Plague virus, however, was attracted to these cancerous cells like a bear to honey . . . wait, you don't know what a bear is, do you, Enoch? No? Okay, how about like a nerwolf to a newborn lamb? Does that make sense? Upon infecting a cancer patient, the virus would chemically 'sniff out' the cancer—deliberately avoiding the healthy cells—and bury itself in the mitochondria, er, the *guts* of the thing. There it would quietly go to work, changing the nature of the cancer until one day . . . boom."

"Boom?"

"Boom. The cancerous cells would burst into an unheard-of frenzy of energetic growth, dividing and specializing like the stem cells in an embryonic, um . . . well, they just started to grow like crazy. Bones, muscles, organs, every part of these once-sickly cancer patients became strong. Too strong."

Enoch understood where this was going.

"The trolls."

"Exactly. The hospitals were already scenes of chaos, abandoned by anyone wishing to avoid the plague and filled with the dead and dying. All of a sudden, entire wings of the building are filled with these crazy overgrown monstrosities. Crazy? Well, the human brain wasn't meant to grow at this speed. The poor creatures kept some remnant of their core animal brains, but any memory of their civilized lives was lost. And to make matters worse, the explosive growth was accompanied by an insatiable hunger. A hunger for the quick sustenance of warm meat . . ."

Cal let the subject drop, and that was fine. Enoch didn't care to pursue that line of thought either.

I don't want to know the details.

"So the Silverwitch army—the *cyborgs*—were sent to kill them, too?"

"At first, yes. But the trolls proved surprisingly resilient to physical assault—and it was soon discovered that they weren't *vectors*, i.e. they couldn't pass the plague on to uninfected people. So the Pensanden focused their efforts on that critical First Hunt. The Crow Plague was their primary concern. The trolls escaped into the dark places of the earth and became, well, trolls. They bred. Where there was food, they flourished. Your ancestors made a couple attempts to eliminate them all after the plague scare had ended. But it was too late—the trolls were too many, and too well hidden."

They walked for a while in silence. Enoch turned on the light in the next section in front of them. Up ahead, the passageway seemed to widen, and they could hear something that sounded like running water.

Enoch's teeth wouldn't stop chattering now. He shivered violently, inciting another round of growls from Mesha.

Hopefully we can find something more flammable than cable and metal panels up ahead. My hands are going numb.

Rictus saw the widening passage as a good sign.

"I was hoping we'd get out of these narrow tunnels at some point—sooner or later those trolls are going to figure out that they can circle around and break the lights in front of us. And then we'll have to fight them in the dark."

"But maybe they aren't following us anymore, Ric," said Cal hopefully. "We haven't seen them for a good while now."

"Look at Mesha, Cal. Her eyes haven't left the passageway behind us for the last several minutes. They're back."

Both Cal and Enoch swung their attention to the shadowcat. She was staring intently into the darkness behind them. In the silence that followed, they could hear the soft popping sound of another bulb being shattered. Enoch had continued turning the lights off as they moved out of each section in the hopes that the trolls would lose their trail. It hadn't worked.

"You made me nervous with that whole 'circle around us' thing, Ric," said Cal. "Can we make a run for where the tunnel widens out ahead? Enoch, can you check if there are any lights there?"

Enoch *paused* and sent his mind along the electrical lines up ahead. This journey through the complex network of a Pre-Schism construct had been opening his mind to what would have been the amazing potential of a Pensanden in an electronic environment. He was learning that he could use his power to *see* far beyond the limit of his eyes, actually following the trails of energy that wound through the architecture around him. It would have been more exciting if he wasn't freezing to death.

Enoch saw that the lines ahead got thicker and more complex as the tunnel widened out. But he recognized some of the forms within that complexity.

"Yes, there are lights up ahead," he said, eyes closed. "A different . . . type of light. And I just turned them on." A warm yellow glow was suddenly visible at the end of the passageway.

Cal looked at him, then turned to Rictus with a smile.

"As I said—*convenient*. Let's make a run for it, Ric."

"No, Cal. These trolls are starving. Desperate. I don't know that a little painful light is going to keep them off of us for much longer. If they think we're escaping, they'll charge."

So the trio kept walking. Their pace was deliberately, painfully slow, but the trolls stayed at the borders of the shadow. Enoch recognized the new lead troll as the one which had provoked, then attacked the first one. It was, if possible, even larger. A pale and wrinkly gray, it had a tumescent hump jutting from one side of its broad shoulders. The troll stepped carefully into the nearest light and reached up to smash the bulb. Enoch gasped. The "hump" was actually another head, with one bleary eye and a gaping, toothless mouth.

Am I partly to blame for this?

The big fist swung, there was a pop, and the light went out. Enoch lit the next one, now in the final section before the tunnel opened up. The troll shied back again, growling hungrily. A thin mewing came from the mouth at its shoulder.

Now I understand Cal's pity. But I want to be rid of these things as well.

"Well, that's a welcome sight," said Cal as they emerged from the tunnel. The walls fell away from them on each side, the metal bolted to ice-covered rock walls. The floor continued level across open space—the path through this enormous cave now a bridge extending over a frozen subterranean river. The sound they'd heard earlier was the deeper water flowing under a thick layer of ice. But the best news, that which Cal had commented on, was that the cave had been wired to serve as some sort of decorative rest stop amidst the featureless network of tunnels. Huge electrical lamps were mounted in the rock ceiling above them, and they now filled the icy cave with a warm yellow light.

No more of that hideous blue flickering! It was making my head hurt. Well, that and the constant pausing *to effect the on/off ignition of the lights.*

Enoch rubbed at his forehead. The pain he associated with his powers was now a dull background ache, something he had become accustomed to.

Maybe Cal was right—will it become pleasant after more practice? It doesn't hurt with any of the intensity it had when I first started using it.

The trolls had followed them to the edge of the tunnel but now had stopped. This stronger light really hurt their eyes, and they were getting angry. The lead troll took a few cautious steps out onto the bridge then snarled, retreating back into the darkness. There were answering growls behind him.

"We're safe for now," said Rictus, lowering his sword. "This new light really pains them."

"Hmm," said Cal, "well, Enoch, I figured out where all this cold air came from."

"Where's that?"

Cal whistled a trill, and Sal pointed to the far wall of the cave where the river disappeared into the dark. Hidden under a massive stone lip were two enormous cylinders, white storage tanks the size of a Babel city block. They were bolted to a collection of pipes and support girders, and tubes entered and exited these tanks all along their length.

"Frostwater."

"Did you just say *frostwater*, Cal?" said Rictus, groaning. "Geez, you *have* been amongst the peasants too long. That's liquid hydrogen, you caveman. Coolant for the Ark."

Cal rolled his eyes. "That's right, I forgot—you were a big spaceflight-junkie before the Schism. Seriously, Ric, remind me why you became a rock star again?"

Enoch turned away from their bickering to examine these giant "frostwater" tanks. The tanks weren't actually white, just covered in a thick coating of frost. He could see the tank's original metallic color on one corner where a newly-lit lamp was melting the frost away. And then he spied the problem, the thing Cal had been trying to show him.

One of the support girders, rooted on the bank of the river, had collapsed as the bank eroded away beneath it. The massive iron post had torn a gash in the lower tank. A thick stream of liquid ran down the side of the cylinder, coursed along the remaining ice-choked girders, and pooled on the glacial rocks below. The liquid gave off an icy steam, even in this cold air. It was devouring any heat in the room, even from the lights Enoch had just powered on. He thought he could feel the evil stuff suck the last bits of warmth from his arms.

"That is why the trolls are starving," said Rictus. "The cold has killed any of the fish and vermin which used to live down here. And the cancer won't let their own bodies die, probably sloughing off frozen skin."

Cal nodded. "And that's why they've started hunting topside."

They all looked up as a cracking sound filled the cave. Rictus was the first to realize what was going on.

"Scales! Enoch, can you dim the power you're channeling to the surrounding lights?"

"What? Why? They're actually *warm*, Rictus. Besides, these aren't adjustable like the blue lights in the tunnels—they're only off or on."

"Turn some of them off, then! The lamp materials have been cold for so long that . . ."

The cracking intensified, finally culminating in a loud crashing "pop!" as the lamp nearest to the tunnel they'd just emerged from went black.

"Run!" shouted Rictus. "Get to the passage on the other side and turn those lights on!"

The trolls had already moved onto the newly darkened edge of the bridge. The dying light had emboldened them.

Another lamp exploded in a cascade of glass and filaments, and another section of the bridge fell into shadow—this time behind them.

"Run!"

They ran. Enoch struggled to keep up with the specters. He couldn't get his frozen body to move fast enough, couldn't feel his feet as they pounded down the metal bridge. He was so cold. Rictus turned and came back for him.

"Keep going, Enoch. I'll try and hold them here until you're across."

Enoch felt a tug at his pant leg and looked down to see Sal pulling at him. Cal was trying to keep his voice calm.

"One step at a time, boy. Follow me—Sal will make sure you don't fall over the edge."

At that, Enoch looked down. He was at the direct center of the bridge. The cave floor now dropped several hundred feet beneath him. The icy river was a narrow white line in the dimming light.

That would be a long fall.

Another pop, and the cave was darker.

"Move!"

Rictus pushed him, and he staggered a couple of steps. Sal kept Enoch's momentum going in the right direction, pulling the boy along whenever he slowed. The bridge shook with the heavy footsteps of the oncoming trolls. They were charging now.

Everything felt slow, not like when Enoch *paused*, but frozen. Heavy. Numb. Enoch ignored Cal's protests and turned to look back.

The first troll had reached Rictus, a smaller beast with tusks curving out from the bottom of its jaw. Rictus met the charge with a sweeping overhand blow, completely cutting the creature's arm off at the shoulder. It squealed and fell to the metal floor with a wet thump. Enoch tried to smile, but his lips wouldn't move.

Rictus can handle them.

The specter took a step back and almost fell over. The troll's disembodied arm had curled around Rictus's leg. The specter struggled to pull the muscled limb off of him. With a shout, he kicked free and stepped into guard position. The fallen troll was already back on its feet, the ghastly wound at its side squirming with some sort of muscular scar tissue. Enoch was repulsed but fascinated.

Is it growing a new arm?

He couldn't look away, despite Sal's insistent tugging, Cal's desperate invective.

A new arm *was* growing from the wound. Enoch gasped as the scar bulged like a blister, writhing as snakelike muscles pulled the swelling mass into a thinner protrusion. Wet skin, pink as a newborn pig, rippled across the appendage. The troll panted and whined as its body contorted under the explosive powers of this *cancer*—apparently the regrowth was just as painful as the loss.

Rictus, less moved by the miraculous regeneration, kicked the still grasping arm off the side of the bridge and brought his sword down upon the troll's head. The weapons' vibrations caused the cranium to shatter, sending bits of brain across the cave. The troll wasn't going to heal that one.

A detached part of Enoch's mind applauded the move.

Just like he taught me. "The real trick is adapting to their strengths."

Two more trolls leapt out of the growing darkness, and Rictus met them with his sword blurring the air.

Enoch finally turned and followed Sal's frantic nudges. He was trying to remember something Rictus had told him, something important.

What did he say? What am I supposed to do?

Mesha hissed from his shoulders.

The lights! Rictus told me to turn on the lights in the tunnel up ahead.

He tried to *pause*, tried to remember the *litania eteria*, but none of it would come.

Focus! Why can't I focus?

* * * *

Cal looked back to see Enoch stumbling along behind him, tears streaming down cheeks red from the cold. Overhead lights exploded, syncopating to his wooden footsteps. The cave was almost dark.

"Come on, Enoch. Just a little bit farther!"

The tone of concern in Cal's voice reminded Enoch of Master Gershom.

Master.

Master Gershom would be disappointed if his charge couldn't focus just because of a little cold.

Focus, Enoch.

Enoch closed his eyes. He *paused.*

The lights. Follow the lines, find the electricity. Direct it to the tubes. Ignite.

The hallway flickered to life ahead of them, that hateful blue light so welcome now.

Cal cheered and called back, "Come on, Ric, the light's on—let's go!"

Wait, that's not what I was trying to remember!

Enoch staggered to a halt, and Sal spun around to resume tugging on his pants.

The lead troll. The one with two heads. Where did it go?

A roar erupted from the passageway in front of them, followed by a softer popping sound. The newly lit passageway was suddenly dark.

Enoch reached a frozen hand down to unsheathe his *derech.* The blade slipped from his unresponsive fingers and clattered to the ground.

"What are you . . ." Cal turned on Sal's shoulder and saw the shadow.

"No!"

The troll stepped out of the dark hallway, its enormous figure outlined by the few remaining lights in the cave. Enoch could hear the small head mewling hungrily.

Rictus . . . ?

Enoch turned in time to see Rictus, knee-deep in headless troll bodies, impale another oncoming beast and turn the sword upwards. He was cutting up through the troll's torso, aiming for the neck. The skewered troll, howling with pain, thrust itself forward on the blade. It grabbed Rictus at the shoulders and pulled, ripping the specters arms from his body. Enoch screamed, but the sound seemed to come from a distant part of him. He couldn't feel anything.

So we die here?

Two more trolls joined the other, ripping Rictus apart.

We die here.

An odd whistling tune suddenly filled the air. Enoch looked down, dumbly. Sal had moved to the edge of the bridge and stood tall as Cal played a melody on his pipes.

The lead troll stepped forward, a look of focused intensity written across its face. The smaller head cooed.

Cal took a breath and turned towards Enoch.

"I guess there's still something human left inside these things after all. I'm going to try and lead them away from you. You get down that tunnel and *run* until you get to the gate marked with a purple square. That will open to the north."

Cal turned back to his instrument and blew another cascade of notes. The troll exhaled wetly and moved even closer. Enoch could smell the thing, sour and musky.

He couldn't move.

Cal finished the melody and turned to face him again, his eyes steady. "Don't forget what I said, Enoch. About the patterns. About the story."

Enoch nodded dumbly and then fell to the metal floor as the troll shoved past him to follow Cal. Sal was moving quickly, knuckle-running along the bridge to where the remaining trolls were gnawing unhappily on Rictus's bony limbs. Those trolls perked up as well, lifting their heads and shuffling towards the music.

The tune changed slightly, and, as ordered, Sal crouched and then leapt. The leap carried him ten feet through the air to the last functioning electric lamp. He grabbed onto the bottom edge and hung precariously, and all the while Cal played. The yellow light flickered dangerously. The two trolls and their leader crouched at the edge of the bridge, mesmerized.

Cal stopped playing. He looked down at Sal and kissed him gently on the shoulder. The trolls growled. All three sank into a crouch, muscles tensing.

The final light went black.

No!

There was a roar, a crash, and a snarling cacophony that trailed off into a distant splash. Then, quiet.

CHAPTER 13

Life is born from rot.
And so it goes.
Mud was our first womb.
And so it goes.
We shall rot again.
And so it goes.

—Lodoroi Prayer of Acceptance

Mosk was beginning to realize why the Vestigarchy had never cared to govern the swamps of Garron. Well, apart from the stench of rot, the ever-present mold, and the complete lack of useful resources.

It was the unpredictably explosive zealotry of the natives.

The Hiveking had been forced to kill four of their tribal chiefs and put down a half-dozen insurrections in the past three days alone, and *still* nobody would give him a straight answer. He feared he'd run out of Swampmen before too long.

Scratching at a new patch of yellow mold at his arm joint, he turned to look out from the wooden tower he'd erected upon arriving at this muddy "capital." These humans were odd. They had no centralized government, just an amalgam of chiefs whose own power was relative to the size of their specific tribe—and even that power was dependent upon the ability of their tribe to cleverly breed new animals. It was a chaotically shifting morass of merit, indulgences, and unspoken hierarchies.

The construction of their cities—if you could call them that—

reflected this. Sprawling and borderless, they bled from swamp to swamp in a scattered mess. You couldn't tell where one ended and another began. No highways, no centers of commerce, and no standing army. The Swampmen didn't seem to see the problem with this, but it made the orderly blackspawn searches his Clots had perfected an impossibility—unless he was willing to commit them to years of scouring every stagnant pool and rotten tree for hundreds of miles. And this would surely inspire countless more insurrections. These people were oddly protective of their stinking home. In fact, Mosk could still hear the cries of righteous anger as these fanatics threw themselves on his spurs. Pitiful. If they saw these mud-brick huts as "hallowed ground," the frog ponds as "sacred treasures," then they could have them. Mosk had grown tired of this place—it seemed deliberately grown to discomfort the blackspawn.

He scratched at the mold again.

It was humiliating, but the mold was another serious problem. Two of his Clots were effectively out of commission from the stuff, which built up on the joints and restricted movement. He'd had to send them back to Babel to dry out and recuperate. The worst part was how the mold affected his Matrons, newly arrived from the west. Their last batch of eggs—meant to provide replacements for the Clot he lost back in Midian—had arrived dead. The Matrons said the mold clogged the breathing slits in their abdomens, and the eggs suffocated before they could be delivered.

Mosk gnawed at his upper jaw, the blackspawn equivalent of a sigh. He motioned to his guard. "Tell the handlers to prepare the draconflies. We fly at sundown."

His guard clicked assent and moved down the tower mast. Coldmen could use their claws and uniquely jointed legs to scale a bare post easily. They had no need for ladders or those wide human stairs which wasted so much space. Blackspawn towers were practically inaccessible to grounded attackers, perched atop smooth posts like berries on a thorn.

Mosk didn't know why he'd wasted the time building this

one. These Swampmen were pitiful. Woefully armed with green spears, bone knives, and poison darts which snapped off his shell like toys—wonderful tools for hunting a frog, he supposed, but useless against coldmen. The poor natives couldn't even find rocks to throw on this soggy ground! Putting down their sad little mobs had been like slaughtering grubs back in the warren feedpens.

Exciting, even nostalgic in its own way, but Mosk couldn't help but yearn for battle against an *able* enemy. The Centek, with their unbelievable speed, their devious skill with explosives. That was an enemy to be respected. Or the Nahuati blademasters! The complexity of their swords, the deadly, flowing movements. How Mosk missed those battles—the memory brought a rush nearing ecstasy. He remembered the shock on their faces, the fear in those wet little eyes when these consummate swordsmen realized that they faced a coldman who could read their moves. Who could break their patterns.

This was why Mosk was Swarmlord. His mind was almost human.

And this was why he hated having to rely on a human. Until he received more Clots from the Vestigarchy, Mosk simply didn't have enough claws to search all of Babel *and* secure the northern kingdoms from this supposed Pensanden threat. Nyraud was a painful necessity for Mosk right now, but the Hiveking had no illusions as to the man's loyalties. Fear for his city, that alone kept the man searching for the etherwalker—fear and his ridiculous obsession with hunting. Why this "Hunter King" chose to revel in the art of sneaking up on an inferior enemy rather than the fire and blood glory of battle was beyond Mosk's desire to comprehend.

Regardless, he'd had to rely on the Silverwitch Kai to keep Nyraud in line for now. She had plans for the city that were . . . unsettling, even to the Hive King.

It was time to return. Mosk had wasted enough time in the swamps. If the Pensanden *were* here, he'd be as useless as the rest of the natives. North was where the real danger remained. North, where remnants of the old tek still slumbered and dangerous knowledge still moved through hidden channels. The Pensanden would eventually have to go there, wouldn't be able to resist—and while Mosk may have failed at catching the hatcher en route, all that really mattered was keeping him from Tenocht.

CHAPTER 14

All Are Prey.

—Motto of King Nyraud's Kingsguard

The only reason I'm here is because Keyr couldn't keep her big mouth shut.

Sera tipped her wings slightly, dipping under the low clouds which always seemed to huddle around the Akkadian foothills. She knew that she couldn't blame Keyr entirely. It was her own fault for bragging about the Nyraud encounter in the first place. The memory made her uncomfortable, and her hand went up to feel the short blue hair where her father had chopped off what remained of her tresses.

She was lucky to have gotten away with border patrol and a haircut. The Roost Dame had been furious. Expulsion had been discussed, even a *clipping!* Sera had no idea that they took the Babel Treaty so seriously.

The wind was light down here, so Sera locked her pinions into a soaring pattern and tried to relax.

If Lamech hadn't intervened, I could have been wingless. Flightless. Grounded!

She wondered if human girls ever got grounded, and if so, how it was done.

Restricted jumping?

Regardless, she had resolved to avoid Nyraud and his Gardens like the plague. Her curiosity had cost her some freedom, some respect, and a whole lot of hair. Not worth it. And she really didn't mean to have put the Spire at risk. She knew that the Alaphim were suffering, that the Nests were empty year after year.

What's that?

There was some sort of a caravan down below: a dozen long-tailed murs circled around a camp fire. A few cloth tents set up nearby.

There's nothing but empty hills between here and Babel. What would merchants be doing here?

Sera reached up to twist her eye-rings into deeper focus. Like all angels, she was proud of her sight. The Alaphim naturally had vision that could rival that of an eagle—this was part of their heritage. But the brass-rimmed lenses that fit snugly into their occipital cavities enhanced that vision to an astonishing degree. Lamech said the Alaphim were the truest art, "the marriage of gene-sculpting and prosthetics." Lamech said a lot of odd things. The centenarian was still spry—*the Alaphim may be largely infertile, but at least we're long-lived*—but Lamech never flew patrol anymore. Just kept to his coop reading those books of his.

Father had warned her about spending too much time with him—said Lamech couldn't let go of a past that was long gone. But Lamech was lonely, and Sera was the only one who ever listened to the old rooster. Besides, he had the best stories!

He remembered when the Spire had been networked to a dozen other angel Roosts.

He remembered when the Vestigarchy still feared the Alaphim.

He remembered that horrible time when several northern Roosts had betrayed their purpose and served as scouts during the Hunt—actually *hunting* their Pensanden lords—and ushered in the Dawn of the Arkángels.

He remembered the betrayal that followed the Dawn. He said that the Arkángels brought the curse down on all the Alaphim. That forgiveness from the Pensanden—pardon from a dead race—was required for the angels to thrive again.

So much for that.

But best of all, Lamech remembered the stories *his* grandsire had heard from his grandsire about the time before the Schism. Sera loved those tales—back then the Alaphim were the elite messengers of the Tzolkin Core! Lamech said that while there were faster, even instantaneous ways of delivering messages in those wondrous times, nothing compared to receiving a message from the hands of an angel. It was the highest honor. It meant the gods smiled down upon you!

Sera turned and circled, high above the caravan. She could only see one merchant down with the animals, probably a lowly stable hand. That was odd—even the eastern reaches of the kingdom could be dangerous, and leaving an entire camp under such minimal protection was a really bad idea. In fact, Sera could already see a pack of nerwolves circling the perimeter.

Uh oh. I better go warn the poor man.

Bending her wings at the pri-ulna, she spread her secondary feathers to catch the air. Dramatically slowed, she put her head down and coasted down to the camp below her. The stable hand was watching her now. It always made Sera smile to see the envious way humans looked at angels.

Of course they envy us.

She decided to show off a little—tucking her feathers behind her back, diving to the earth, and then snapping them out to their full length before touching down. A cloud of dust billowed the ground at her feet, startling some of the murs. The man looked impressed.

"You've got some nerwolves circling the camp, merchant."

The man cocked his head at that, smiling.

"Merchant? Do you recognize the device on my collar, bird?"

Huh?

It was a sanguine arrow versant on a field of green. The heraldry of Babel. Sera went cold—she'd just landed in Nyraud's hunting camp.

In a flash, she furled her wings and launched upwards. Beating furiously against the air, she lifted above the trees. Too late, she saw the nerwolves that had been circling the camp stand and pull back their pelts—they were Nyraud's huntsmen, and each trained a bow on her.

I'm high enough, I can dodge their—

With a thud, something smashed into her back, wrapping around her wings. She screamed and fell, crashing to earth with a sickening crack. Sera couldn't breathe and her legs were numb. Gasping, she rolled over to see Nyraud stepping back from her, one foot pinning her wing to the ground. The king was panting hard—that leap from the tree behind her had been impossible. Inhuman. But he was laughing, flexing his shoulders as he brushed a leaf from his tunic.

"I missed you the first time, girl—you shouldn't have given me a second chance."

He leaned over and quickly tied her wrists together with a cord.

"Immunity," gasped Sera. "The treaty!"

King Nyraud laughed again.

"Your trespasses into my Gardens make that null and void for you, my dear. You are mine now."

Here he leaned close to rub his hand over her close-cropped hair.

"I guess you liked what I started with my knife, eh? Too bad about that color, though—I don't know what the Pensanden were thinking with the blue. A side-effect of the brassy 'extras' woven through your bones, perhaps?"

Here he rolled his foot over the thin, penultimate joint of her wounded wing. Metal scraped against metal. Sera screamed.

"I haven't hunted Alaphim in a long time. Maybe we'll take you back to the Gardens and get you back on your feet again. Oh, we'll have to do something about all that flying nonsense. But we'll give you a sporting chance."

Sera spat at him, eliciting further laughter. He turned to one of his huntsman.

"Grab me some shears; I'm going to clip her now. And have Tehr prepare the smaller cage. It looks like it will have a different occupant than we had originally planned."

The huntsman left, shouting instructions to the man Sera had descended to help. Nyraud removed his foot from her wing and placed it against her chest.

"You're young for an angel. I thought your people had forgotten how to lay eggs—or are they adopting from the other avian species now?"

Sera just looked away.

I won't give him the satisfaction. He just wants me to react so he can hurt me more.

The huntsman had returned with a pair of large iron shears. He handed them to the king. Nyraud lifted them so Sera could see. He gave two quick practice snips. Sera struggled and tried to roll away. She still couldn't feel her legs.

"I usually use these when I need to field dress a manticore—their armored skin will turn most knives. But I imagine they could do the job."

He leaned over and lifted her left wing by the primaries. Sera screamed.

"Why all this noise, my dear? I know that you won't feel anything. You see, I've had some good opportunity to study Alaphim anatomy. Closely. I know that your 'wings' are nothing more than metal contraptions, heirlooms given to an angel child when an old one dies. Your surgeons—what do you call them again? Boneweavers? They attach the wings to those grotesque limbs you have growing between your scapula, weld them tight, and pretend you're birds!"

Nyraud leaned in extra close, and Sera could smell his sweat.

"That is the funniest thing about you 'regal' angels, so arrogant and vain. You're unfinished. You killed the Pensanden before they could finish you!"

It's not true.

But even as she thought this, Sera could feel her *pollices*—the "grotesque limbs" at her back—trembling. The strain of her prone position was wearing on them; Alaphim slept standing. What was worse, the metal casing of her ulnar sheathe had broken the skin. She was bleeding. Despite what Nyraud thought, she felt pain in her wings.

My unfinished wings.

Sera wept as Nyraud cut at her feathers. She didn't feel his shears—the feathers were made of a thin brass alloy, the yellow shine polished to match her eye-rings—but she felt the loss of her freedom. The loss of the sky.

A shout went up from the one side of the camp—a rider had just appeared, his mur foaming from what must have been a hard ride from Babel. The man dismounted and ran to the king.

"Sire, I have news from the Tower. We've found him!"

Nyraud spun, dropping the shears.

"What? Found him? Where?"

The man leaned in to whisper to the king. Nyraud's face was incredulous, his expression moving from surprise to a greedy joy as the man spoke.

"*In* the tower? Are you sure? Ha! I was positive that he'd head east to the caves!"

King Nyraud turned to face his huntsmen.

"Men, I want to be packed and saddled in an hour. It turns out our prey couldn't wait for the hunt. He has come to us!"

There were confused expressions throughout the camp, and a few halfhearted cheers.

"Oh, don't worry, this wasn't an entirely unsuccessful trip—we caught an angel! Get her caged and in the wagon quickly. I want to be in the city by tomorrow!"

Sera lay still in a bed of her own feathers. They were cold against her skin. The sky had begun to grow dark overhead.

CHAPTER 15

Surely the bitterness of death is past.

—1 Samuel 15:32 KJV

Enoch burned. That was his first sensation, burning. His fingers felt like red-hot irons. He wondered if they'd burn through his sheets.

Sheets?

And then:

Am I home? This was all a dream!

"Master! Master, are you . . . ?"

Sitting up, Enoch's hopes were quickly shattered. He was in a bed, but not the humble straw *palliasse* he had slept on his entire life. No itching, no lumps.

No Master Gershom. That's right. I don't need anyone.

He blinked. Smooth white sheets stretched across his body, over the two bumps of his feet, and then beyond for what seemed like forever. A white canopy stretched over his head, supported at four corners by ornate pillars, carved from a rich red-brown wood that Enoch didn't recognize. His hands were bandaged, and he could smell some sort of bitter ointment.

Where am I? Why is my skin burning? And where is Rictus? Cal . . . ?

Memory rushed back to Enoch in a sickening wave. Rictus being torn apart by trolls. Cal giving his life to save him. The cold. The lights going out, one by one.

His hand moved quickly to his chest.

It's gone!

The disc from the Unit, the one Master Gershom had risked his life to retrieve, was missing. Enoch's neck felt naked without the cool weight that had rested there for so long. At least it felt like it had been a long time.

He kicked the sheets clear and rolled to the side of the magnificent bed. It was surprisingly high up off of the floor, almost as tall as Enoch, and he stumbled when his feet hit the tiles. He had been dressed in a tabard of smooth green silk—at least Enoch thought he recognized the material. A trader had brought a small roll of silk to Rewn's Fork years ago, and everybody in town had lined up to touch the shiny stuff. They'd touched it, sure, but nobody could afford it. The trader left sulking.

The memory seemed so far away, Rewn's Fork part of another world.

"Your clothes are on the table next to the door, Milord. Your swords are being held by His Majesty. He wanted to speak with you when you awoke."

Enoch jumped, spinning around to face the voice. It belonged to an old woman who had been quietly sitting on a stool next to the door. Enoch hadn't seen her in the flickering light from the brazier. She stepped forward and bowed.

Dressed in a simple green frock, the woman had a voice that was hardly a whisper. She was stooped and small, her gray hair tightly wound into a bun. Enoch thought she looked kind. But her words were perplexing.

Milord? His Majesty?

"Thank you," he said, then remembered his manners. "Thank you, ma'am."

The woman nodded, keeping her eyes on the floor. Enoch wondered how long she'd been sitting there.

"The burning should ebb as the feeling comes back to your skin, Milord. The cold almost took your fingers. Almost took your ears. Milord is lucky to have been found when he was."

"Do you know how I got here? I . . . was with some friends,

and—"

"Friends that let you wander half-naked in such cold, Milord?"

Enoch held back an angry response. His heart still ached when he thought of Cal, his sacrifice. *Rictus* . . . and he wasn't sure if he heard scorn in the woman's voice or gentle reproof. She had obviously learned how to speak without the implications of tone and mood, and Enoch wondered why somebody would want to learn that.

Should I tell her that my friends didn't have enough skin to know how cold it was?

"His majesty will be wanting to know you've awakened, Milord."

She shuffled to the door and raised a brown, wrinkled fist. Then . . . she stopped. Her eyes flickered up to meet his just before knocking. Enoch was confused by the look.

Was that fear?

Three quick knocks, and the door swung open. Two men were standing on each side of the door. Craning his neck, Enoch thought he spied a drawn sword in one of their hands.

The woman moved through the doorway, carefully avoiding the two guards, and disappeared into the hallway. The door swung closed.

A sword! I've got to get out of here!

Enoch was tired of this feeling, this feeling of panic and danger and his heart beating in his throat. The loss of those he loved. It was a very real pain. And while *pensa spada* could suspend the sensation for a little while, it certainly didn't make it go away.

Does it ever *go away? I hurt . . . and I'm just tired. So tired.*

He felt a sob building up in his chest, a thick ball of fear and sorrow and futility rolling up to burst out of control.

No.

Enoch pushed the feeling away. It wasn't quite like pausing or *pensa spada*, but there was something similar—he was controlling his mind, controlling his feelings. It had happened so quickly, he had surprised himself.

I don't need anybody.

Pushing the hurt away didn't necessarily feel good. But he was back in control. Master Gershom would have been proud, would have recognized the steely expression of a Nahuati blademaster, the *Ferrocara*. Enoch wondered if the Pensanden of the Tzolkin Core had done something similar when calling the First Hunt together—pushing away their feelings to be able to do something so monstrous.

No, no time to dwell on that. I have to find my way out of here.

The room was large, probably larger than his cottage back at Rewn's Fork, with an ornate copper brazier mounted on one wall. The red coals filled the room with a warm, comfortable glow. In front of the brazier was a large green cushion with an odd furry trim at the center.

The green trim opened shiny eyes and yawned.

"Mesha!"

At the sound of his voice, Mesha's fur rippled from green to black and then to a warm red that matched the light on the floor. Enoch laughed—it was just like Rictus had guessed. She was more than a simple shadowcat!

Enoch limped over to the cushion, his sore muscles protesting the quick movement. Mesha watched him approach, as though she expected him to come to her rather than the other way around. With a grunt, Enoch dropped onto the cushion next to the shadowcat and pulled her close. She looked slightly bothered that he had ruined her nap, and her fur rippled green again. She wanted the cushion back.

"Where are we, girl? How did we get here?"

Of course, no answer came. Mesha rubbed her head against Enoch's chest and then climbed up onto his shoulders, changing color to the default brown she usually wore. He reached up and patted her with a bandaged hand.

"Well, I'm glad you stayed with me. Let's find a way out of here."

Enoch continued searching the room. On another wall, he found an enormous tapestry depicting a hunting scene. There were no windows in the room, and the ceiling arched up at an odd angle. Enoch thought he saw the red light reflecting on the edge of something up in the darkness of the arch.

Panels? Am I still in the tunnels underneath Babel?

Enoch closed his eyes and *paused*. For some reason this seemed easier with Mesha around his neck. There weren't any signs of . . . *wait!* There was a power line—an old one, thin and fading—tracing along the contour of the door. There wasn't much energy in the line, just enough to make it visible to Enoch.

To a Pensanden.

He used his new vision to follow the line, moving along its length until it branched off into another. And then another. Little by little, Enoch began to feel an outline of the space around him. But it wasn't enough—just old wiring with a dwindling connection to a distant source. No motors like the windmill, no energized parts like the Silverwitch, nothing that Enoch could effect. But there was something, something close by, that could possibly be useful if he could just get some power to it. It was a motor—a small one, but it presented a possibility. Enoch could feel the latent energy of the thing, the tense motes shivering to be set in motion.

Right . . . there.

He walked over to a corner of the tapestry and pulled it away from the wall. There was a panel just over Enoch's head. The motor was behind it.

If I can just push the panel aside, maybe I can get my hands on some of the wiring in the surrounding walls. I should be able to pull enough power into the motor to get it started.

He wasn't sure that was true, but it felt right. Enoch didn't really have the words for what he saw and felt in these machines, but his instinct tended to be correct. This was how he had turned on the lights in the tunnel.

Enoch reached up and pushed against the panel. It was stuck tight. He looked around the room for something to stand on.

If I can get high enough, I bet I can pry it open with . . .

Mesha hissed and jumped down. Somebody was at the door, talking to the guards. Enoch threw the tapestry back against the wall and hurried back to the giant bed. He leapt in and was just pulling the covers up when the door opened.

The man who came through was a king. Enoch wasn't sure how he knew, but the man fit every idea he had ever had about what a king should be. He was tall, broad shouldered, and he walked into the room with a stately elegance. He wore a fine cloak of fur, and his green doublet was decorated with an arrow piercing the sun—sewn in golden thread. The man's dark eyes were stern, but upon seeing Enoch's face, they lifted. He smiled.

He is happy to see me?

"Good morning, young man. I trust you are feeling better?"

Enoch didn't know how to respond to this warmth from a complete stranger, even if he was a king. The man smiled at his hesitancy.

"Some of my men found you in the tunnels underneath this very spot. You were freezing to death . . . you almost died, actually. I've had Endra—I think you met her when you woke up—caring for you since my men brought you back here. She is quite skilled with balms and potions." Here he pointed to the bandages on Enoch's arms. The boy was still unsure of what to say.

Who is this man?

"You seem frightened. I assure you, young man, this is the safest room in Babel. The trolls wouldn't dare climb into my tower—those few that you've left alive, that is."

Enoch was stunned.

Babel? I'm in the tower—in the Ark! So he must be . . . ?

The tall man had come around to the side of the bed, and he put a hand up on the corner post.

"I've hunted the beasts before. You've impressed the Hunter King, boy. My men say that when they found you, you were surrounded by trolls. Dead ones. Lieutenant Stykes says he counted at least eight in various states of decapitation strewn across the bridge. He says there were more on the cave floor beneath."

The Hunter King!

King Nyraud, Lord of the Reach, turned and pulled a shortsword from behind his back. Enoch flinched, pushing back into his pillow.

"They also say that they found this underneath you, and another at your waist."

Now Enoch recognized the sword. It was his master's *derech*. The king put it on the bed and pushed it towards him.

"Go on, take it. Far be it for me to keep a blademaster from his blade."

Enoch reached over and grabbed the hilt. He looked up at the king and froze. Nyraud laughed.

"I don't blame you for being cautious, boy. Anyone who could slay a dozen trolls and still clean his blades before passing out has got to have some enemies!"

They didn't find Rictus?

Enoch caught his breath, slowly pulling the *derech* to his side.

Of course they didn't. All they saw was a mangled pile of old bones, some tatters of cloth—all worn and chewed on. His sword is probably still buried to the cross-guard in troll guts.

King Nyraud inclined his head a notch. He seemed to be waiting for something. Enoch blushed.

"My name is Enoch, m . . . Milord. I was traveling through the . . . um, traveling underneath your tower, Milord."

Don't tell him too much—where was that place Rictus said we should go? Not north.

"I was heading east to the hills. I've got some family there."

Nyraud was smirking and looked amused.

"Yes, I *thought* you'd be moving towards Akkadia. I suppose I just got there ahead of you."

Nyraud laughed at Enoch's confusion, but not unkindly. The king seemed to be a generally pleasant person, nothing like the tales of the feral Hunter King Enoch had heard from Old Noach Kohn.

"You weren't traveling alone, were you, Enoch?"

The king asked as though he knew the answer. Enoch didn't want to mention his friends. He felt his façade cracking, struggled to retain the *Ferrocara*.

"Don't worry about covering for your little friend. If Stykes hadn't been armed with a tin of smallfish, he'd have lost an arm trying to carry you out of there."

Huh?

The king nodded over at the cushion, where Mesha was settling herself. Enoch gave a silent sigh of relief.

"Luckily, she seemed to understand that we were saving your life and was content to follow. Stykes says you owe him some fish."

Enoch couldn't help it—his relief combined with Nyraud's generous demeanor broke through the *Ferrocara*. He laughed. The king laughed with him.

"Well *now* you sound like the boy I imagined was hiding under all the fierce Nahuati training."

The king stepped away from the bed and went over to the cushion. He crouched down to stroke Mesha's fur, which rippled from cushion-green to ember-red as she exulted in the attention.

Well, if Mesha likes him, he can't be that bad.

"So I took great care to put you in one of the more, ah, primitive rooms in my tower. One without any mechanical workings. I wanted to make sure you weren't disturbed—Endra says that a deep sleep heals better than any potion."

Enoch wondered where he was going with this.

Mechanical workings? He doesn't know about my . . .

Looking down, Enoch saw that the scars on his wrists were covered by the bandages. His face and forehead were bandaged as well.

I guess it all comes down to whether Endra would recognize my marks. And if she would tell.

The king stood up and came back over to the bed. He leaned closer, gently put his hand on Enoch's head. Just like Master Gershom used to do.

"I don't know why you were in my tunnels, Enoch. I don't know how you got there, and I don't where you were headed. But please—accept my offer of a safe place to stay until you need to leave."

A safe *place.*

Enoch was overwhelmed. This kind of treatment from a *king?* There had to be something behind it.

"Why?" he stammered. His voice broke, and he was ashamed of revealing himself so much. "Why are you helping me?"

King Nyraud smiled, gently tousled Enoch's hair.

"I had a son once, Enoch. You remind me of him. Sure, he wasn't a swordsman like you. Or a Pensanden—" he glanced at Enoch's bandages. "—but he was a smart boy. A clever boy. You would have liked him."

The king turned, almost as if to hide his face, and slowly walked from the room. At the door, he stopped, just as the old woman Endra had done. But the look he gave to Enoch was tender. Hopeful.

"I put you in this primitive room so that your etherwalker mind could rest, could be still while you recovered. Yet you were more perceptive than I gave you credit for. I can see where you pulled the tapestry away from the wall—it's got the smell of your balm on it. You found the old ventilation fan in there, didn't you?"

Enoch's open mouth was answer enough.

How did he smell the balm from across the room?

Again, Nyraud laughed.

"Oh, don't worry about it. I'm just impressed—that fan hasn't worked since I was a child. I didn't think the Pensanden could read dead machines.

"Your other sword—your *iskeyar*—is down in my sparring room waiting for you. I thought we might practice some swordplay when you are feeling better. Sleep well, Enoch."

With that, he left.

Enoch exhaled, almost as though he had been holding his breath the whole time.

He knows I'm Pensanden!

The thought shook Enoch. From the way everyone had acted, he had assumed this secret would bring dire consequences. Hatred, or fear. But the king mentioned it as if it were just an interesting facet of who Enoch was, like his swords or the color of his eyes.

He knows I'm Pensanden—and he smiled.

* * * *

The sparring room was huge. It was higher up in the tower than Enoch's room was and had tall windows looking out over the city. The view was breathtaking, with various smaller towers and minarets glinting in the morning light. Enoch squinted his eyes to see if he could find the Headsman's Hole, or at least recognize the general area. Unfortunately, nothing looked familiar from this height.

"So you found your sword?"

Enoch turned and smiled, his hand dropping to rest on the familiar pommel of Master Gershom's *iskeyar*. It had been placed on top of the sole piece of furniture in this enormous room, a long table carved from the same wood as the posts in his bedroom. The sword had been polished until it shone like silver, and the stained sheepskin wrappings about the grip had been replaced with white calfskin wound in a thin silver cord. Enoch had been too stunned by the king's initial introduction to notice that a similar treatment had been given to the *derech*, and he had apologized profusely when Nyraud next visited. King Nyraud had shaken his head and smiled, saying that *of course* he would have a blademaster's weapons taken care of while the Nahuati was indisposed. He said hospitality was important, more so when your guest was such a dangerous one.

The king was often referring to Enoch's martial prowess like that. At first Enoch thought he was being made fun of, that King Nyraud was being condescending. Master Gershom was usually sparing with his praise. It was hard to get used to such treatment from a king.

Well, not too hard.

Enoch looked down, tried to straighten the white cloth at his waist. He felt odd in this spotless sparring gear, restricted. The man who had fitted him said that this had belonged to King Nyraud's son, said that Enoch was shorter than the boy and the jerkin would need tightening.

I should have stuck my chest out more. I'll never be able to move properly in this thing.

The king was dressed in more formal dueling armor—silvery plates protecting his chest, arms, and thighs, all sewn into a similarly brilliant white doublet and hose. He even wore white leather boots, detailed with silver tracings that ran to a shining cap at the point of the toe. Sheathed at his side was a pearl-handled practice foil. While thin and flexible like a true foil, the King's variation was longer than average and curved at the tip. The cimitárra was the fashionable style of sword here in the Reaches. Or so Enoch had heard.

Enoch didn't know much more than that concerning King Nyraud's lands—just what he'd been able to glean from Master Gershom about the "lands of Babel" north of Midian. The Emim Reaches, spreading from the Edrei foothills eastward to Akkadia, and northward to the swamps of Jabbok. Enoch imagined that he'd been in Nyraud's domain ever since he'd met Rictus.

"Alright, blademaster—shall we spar?"

"Oh, I should tell you, Milord. I'm not a blademaster. I was trained by one, and was learning the *pensa spada*, but I never did any of the trials. And I've never been tiered. Master Gershom said you had to earn your tiers with blood."

"Well, that sounds oddly appropriate, eh?"

Enoch laughed.

"Enoch, if passing through the now-frozen tunnels of Babel while single-handedly fending off a horde of starving trolls doesn't earn you a tier or two, then I don't know what would."

Or what about killing coldmen? Breaking a Silverwitch?

Enoch decided he was going to stop feeling guilty for taking pride in his accomplishments. The king was right—it was important to set yourself apart from others sometimes.

King Nyraud leaned forward and handed him another finely wrought practice foil. It matched the king's own, and Enoch smiled to see that the workmanship on this "toy" was more elaborate than that on any blade—on any *thing*—he'd ever held.

"I apologize that we don't have tools more befitting your expertise, but maybe the Nahuati-in-Training would deign to use these poor Babel foils?"

Enoch had already unbuckled his new tooled-leather sword belt and carefully placed it on the table where he'd found his *iskeyar*. He gave the foil a few practice thrusts.

The length is unwieldy, but maybe I can try a few of the sweeping moves that Rictus favored? That sword of his was longer, but similarly proportioned.

He attempted a lunge. It felt slow.

I'm used to sparring unencumbered by all this cloth and armor plates, so I'll need to remember to adjust my dodges accordingly.

The king watched him, curious.

"Shall we?"

Enoch bowed and saluted.

"Avanza!"

And with that, he was dueling against King Nyraud of Babel. The king was fast, and his reach was extensive. Luckily, Enoch had been sparring with Rictus—the appropriate parries and sets to move inside a tall opponent's radius were still fresh in his mind. The unfamiliar curved tip of the cimitárra kept frustrating Enoch's advances, though.

King Nyraud noticed this and pressed the attack. With a subtle flick of the wrist, he could slip his blade over the top of Enoch's with alarming precision. It was through his reflexes alone that Enoch was able to dodge these thrusts.

I'm going to get tired out before he does—I need to parry those.

The problem was, Enoch noted, that he was too accustomed to having his other hand free. It felt so sluggish to be anchored to this single unwieldy length.

Use the length. Let the blade's own weight carry the forte *into his thrust.*

The next time Nyraud lanced his foil over the top of Enoch's point, the boy pushed his foil high while letting his wrist dip. The thicker forte caught Nyraud's thrust and snapped his foil in two.

Nyraud stood there for a second, stunned. Enoch leaned in and tapped him on the chest with his foil.

"Point."

The king held up the remaining stub of his foil and laughed.

"Enoch, tell me that this isn't your first time sparring with a cimitárra or I may have to abandon swordplay for good. After those first clumsy dodges, I was sure that you didn't know how to defend with a single blade." He shrugged and threw the stub down to the ground. "Apparently, you can."

The king found another foil, and they sparred until the windows were dark and their jerkins were drenched in sweat. Enoch had never enjoyed his practice so much—sure, dueling with Rictus had been fun, and the specter kept the conversation lively. But what could compare to dueling with a king who had nothing but astonished praise for your skill? And having cool fruit juices delivered to the room every hour didn't hurt. Enoch felt drained and bruised and ready to drop. But he couldn't remember being happier.

Nyraud didn't look tired, but Enoch couldn't miss the king's slight limp where he'd scored a sharp blow after one of their longer bouts.

"Well, Enoch, I think that we've both learned something today. Unfortunately, you learned how easy it is to bruise a taller opponent. And I learned that even royal dueling armor can't protect a man *everywhere.*" He rubbed at his ribs, right under one of the pectoral plates, and winced.

"Luckily for me, I've got a kingdom to run. So I get to escape your foil for now."

Enoch saluted with his foil and tried to give a decent bow. His arms *hurt.*

"I learned more than that, Milord. I learned that the cimitárra can move surprisingly fast when the dualist leads with the tip. I learned that while the length can hinder quick movements, it can be used defensively in ways that my shorter *iskeyar* never can. And I learned—" Enoch groaned tiredly, reaching over to retrieve his old blades from the table, "—that a cimitárra, even wielded by an expert, could never best the two blades of a Nahuati." Enoch caught himself, realizing that his speech with King Nyraud had maybe gotten too informal.

He doesn't seem to mind.

King Nyraud laughed at Enoch's surety.

"You aren't bragging, are you? You sound as though this were some obvious fact. These things are never so clear, Enoch. I've personally seen men with cimitárras carve a blademaster to pieces—not in a duel, mind you, but on the battlefield. The Nahuati aren't immortal."

"No, no. I know that, Milord. I . . . watched my own master fall to enemies. I'm not talking about a crowded battlefield or a mismatched number of opponents. I'm just saying that one cimitárra against the *derech* and *iskeyar* simply can't overcome the speed and myriad movements the two blades present. Everything else being equal, of course."

"Which is a rarity I've never encountered," chuckled the king. "I tell you, Enoch, 'everything else' is rarely equal, and never so simple as you would make it sound."

"I'm sorry, King Nyraud, but this is how I see the weapons—they hold moves and counter-moves. The complexity and variation which two mismatched swords provide will always outweigh the possibilities of a single sword. Especially one so limited and directionally-focused as the cimitárra."

The king was silent, his eyes focused on the ceiling. He seemed to be thinking.

Enoch cringed.

I've gone too far. I need to learn to keep the talk of patterns to myself.

"Enoch, this isn't just dueling bluster you're giving me, is it? You've actually calculated the possible advances, parries, and retreats for these weapons."

Enoch nodded.

Nyraud shook his head, then clapped him on the back with a shout of laughter. "Ha! My boy, I think I just realized something. You are applying your Pensanden skills to swordplay! Brilliant! Now I don't feel so bad for losing half my bouts to a youth! Your quick adaptation to every single one of my feints. Your counter-parries that began before my parries even ended. I was starting to think my tricks were all old, obvious and primary stratagems taught to any novice. But no, you literally calculated the possibilities of my every foray and then reasoned the best response."

Isn't this how everyone does it? Master Gershom never made such noise about my dueling.

It felt good. They discussed Enoch's ability to recognize patterns as they walked towards the *elevator*, which would take them from the sparring room to Enoch's floor. Enoch still marveled at the sensation of stomach-dropping unease he felt when the machine first lifted them. He had studied the workings of the elevator and laughed to find such a simple mechanism sheathed in the complexity of the Ark.

Enoch had talked about this with the king and was proud to have surprised Nyraud with what he had learned from Rictus about this ancient space-vehicle. Enoch still refrained from mentioning Rictus and Cal; although as time went by, it was less out of loyalty to his companions and more out of a desire to retain the king's respect for having slain twelve trolls single-handedly.

Technically, they couldn't have done it without me.

It was almost as though the king had been reading his mind.

"We need to discuss your 'special' abilities at some point, Enoch."

"Why is that, Milord?"

"I know enough of your people's history to know that adolescence is when your powers start to blossom. It was a time when the young etherwalkers would begin an intense training regimen with an array of teachers. There aren't any teachers left, Enoch, but I have some recordings saved on the specialized Unit here in the tower."

Enoch's face must have shown some of the fear he felt upon remembering the last time he'd used a Unit.

The face. The command. The marking.

Nyraud's studies must have hinted at something like what Enoch had gone through. He put a consoling hand on Enoch's shoulder.

"Don't worry, Enoch. This machine isn't on a public network like the consoles down in Babel. And it's shielded—so no prying eyes or ears will notice you. Again."

The king tapped Enoch's wrist, winking.

How does he know about the marking? What else does he know? I need to learn from him.

The elevator door opened, and Enoch stepped out. He bowed to the king, and Nyraud nodded his head with a smile.

"We'll go to the Core Unit tomorrow, Enoch. It's down in the tunnels, you know. Not far from where we found you."

The door closed. Enoch shivered, although the hallway was perfectly warm.

* * * *

Even wrapped in warm furs and surrounded by a patrol of armed guards, Enoch felt vulnerable. The blue lights flickering over his head were too horribly familiar.

The king had been insisting on this trip down into the tunnels for the past several weeks. He said it was too important for Enoch to perfect his skills, to reach his true potential. Enoch had delayed and delayed until finally he was unable to refuse. He didn't want to appear frightened before King Nyraud.

Mesha had taken one step into the tunnel behind Enoch and then hissed, her fur flashing a sickly blue. She remembered what was down here and would not follow no matter how Enoch cajoled her. Just as he was about to step out of sight, she gave another angry hiss, bolted down the hallway, and leapt on his shoulders. Enoch had smiled, given her some comforting pats, and tried to ignore the claws poking into the skin around his neck. Mesha hadn't moved an inch since then, and Lieutenant Stykes, the Huntsman who had originally rescued Enoch from the tunnels, had a good laugh at the "little fish-theif."

They had taken two different elevators to get this low, and now had been walking for the past hour. The air was getting frigid. King Nyraud broke the silence by telling Enoch about his adventures in these tunnels.

When the king was a boy, these tunnels provided an escape from the "mundane stretches of royal life" and were a unique source of both amusement and education for the prince. He had learned much of his hunting skills down here, tracking the elusive trolls in a darkness that required you to rely on smell and sound if you wanted to survive. Granted, the trolls were less aggressive and direct back before the cold killed the fish and vermin they generally subsisted on. But according to King Nyraud, they still put up quite a fight if you cornered them.

Now he was talking about the recent cold.

"When the cooling tank was ruptured, I had my alchemist come and analyze the remaining girders to see if the cold could threaten the stability of the tower. He said that the spill was mostly contained in the cave—that the overall temperature drop in the tunnels couldn't affect materials built for 'the vacuum of space.' I assumed it would clear out the trolls, too, but instead it's driven them up to the alleyways of Babel. Apparently starvation doesn't kill the things, just makes them more daring. I assume you found one of their new 'grab holes' and found your way in."

Enoch just nodded his head.

"My men are scouring the city for the holes, Enoch. Sealing them up again. We can't have every beggar, treasure-seeker, and boy-Nahuati in Babel wandering around the roots of our royal tower, can we?"

Laughter from the guards.

Not guards—these men with the red-fletched arrows are his elite Huntsmen. The most able of his soldiers.

Enoch was still restricted in his movements throughout the tower, but he had picked up on a few things. From the commands he'd overheard King Nyraud giving to his messengers, Enoch surmised that the king had a surprisingly large army for a land with such innocuous and even-tempered neighbors. Not that Enoch was any sort of an expert in these things, but he couldn't help but consider the numbers that Nyraud whispered to his underlings. If they referred to soldiers, it would be a force to rival any of the historic battles he read of in the recitings Master Gershom had assigned him. Enoch couldn't ignore the patterns; this army was big. And apparently it was growing.

Does he know about the coldmen in Midian, and is he preparing for them? Should I tell him what I've seen?

But Enoch kept quiet about where he came from, and the king didn't ask. Enoch was afraid that the truth of his humble shepherd upbringing would disgust this regal man who treated him like a peer.

King Nyraud had been delighted when Enoch brought the overhead lights to life, even though it wrung further hissing from Mesha. The king said that the wiring was too complex for any of his alchemists to decipher, and he had to rely on torches to visit the "Core Unit." He said that similar lighting—even heating and cooling elements like the fan in Enoch's room—had once existed throughout the entire tower, but most had been ripped out to be replaced by more pragmatic braziers and sconces. The king had then looked at Enoch with his eyebrows raised.

I think he wants me to fix his tower. That would be hard; this place is so old. So broken.

But it would be fun to try.

King Nyraud called the Huntsmen to a halt and crouched down, running his fingers over claw marks in the flooring. They were wide and crusted brown with blood.

"I've tried to hunt the trolls out of these tunnels for years, you know. The creatures are, as I'm sure you witnessed, amazingly resilient. And *prolific.* The females stay in their deepest caves with the brood. Count yourself lucky to have avoided one of those big girls, Enoch. They eat the males when food runs low."

Enoch shivered inside the warmth of his cloak.

This place has that effect on me.

He tried to change the subject.

"Milord mentioned that he had an 'alchemist' come look at the girders. I don't know the word, but it sounds like somebody who sees things like I do. Are there more Pensanden in Babel?"

The king shook his head, then signaled for the party to start moving again. Enoch could see the breath of the men walking in front of him. It was getting colder, which meant they were nearing the cave.

"How I *wish* my alchemists could see things like you do, Enoch. You would be surprised how hard it is just to find those willing to study the remnants of the old sciences, even these many centuries after the Schism. We lost so much in the Sixth Hunt—all of the scientists, the learned men, yes. But worse, we lost our desire to discover. We let our fear of the Worldbreakers rule us. And the cruelest irony is that the Sixth Hunt wasn't led by the Serpent, wasn't manned by blackspawn. *We* began it. *We* finished it. The last few kingdoms of men on earth anchored their place in a perpetual Dark Age all by themselves.

"My line is as guilty as any other. My father's father—the one who wrote the law banning your Nahuati blades—he built the walls around Babel. He sealed off the tunnels. He began the deliberate 'cleansing' of this tower, an act I have spent my life trying to correct.

"So to answer your question, Enoch, my alchemists are the few men and women bright and daring enough to open the ancient books I have been able to save. They are the few willing to risk the fires of an Eighth Hunt, the fearful sparks of which are simmering in the streets above us even now. They are the ones who have helped me rebuild the network of Units you may have seen connected throughout Babel. And they are the ones who are helping me bring my tower back to life."

King Nyraud turned to Enoch and waved his Huntsmen to move on down the tunnel. When they were out of earshot, the king leaned close to Enoch. His dark eyes were suddenly ferocious. Enoch took a step back, and Mesha tightened her grip at his shoulder.

Is this the infamous Hunter's Gaze that Old Noach talked about? The look that could freeze a manticore to the ground?

"Will you help me restore Babel to glory, Enoch? Will you help me light the first torch to turn back this Dark Age?"

Enoch didn't know what to say. He *did* feel as though his feet were stuck to the floor. Is this what he was meant to do? Master

Gershom's dying words came to his mind.

"I . . . I have to go north, Milord. I have to go to Tenocht."

Rather than souring at this news, Nyraud's expression brightened. The king raised his hands in the air.

"Well, of course! Any Pensanden would *have* to go to Tenocht when he reached the apex of his power. It is the greatest of the Old Cities, the key to opening up all that has been closed.

"Enoch, all I am asking is for you to stay with me until you reach that apex. Allow me to help you, to train you, until you come into your abilities. And then I swear I will personally carry you to Tenocht on my shoulders!"

The king was so animated, his face so lively, that Enoch had to laugh.

He is excited about this—and the excitement is infectious. No wonder his Huntsmen are so loyal to their king. He lets them feel connected to his ambitions, shares the vision he desires so ferociously that they can't help but want it, too.

This is leadership.

"There is one more thing I wanted to ask you, Enoch. Something I thought could wait until later . . . but now is a better time than anything I could have planned."

"I *am* at your service, King Nyraud."

"Yes, well, I was hoping you would be willing to be something more."

Enoch didn't understand. He furrowed his brow.

"Milord?"

"I want you to be my son, Enoch. You are an orphan, correct? You haven't been overly talkative concerning your past, but I have been able to put some clues together. I am the Hunter King, you know?"

He knows I'm a shepherd.

Nyraud raised an eyebrow. He took Enoch's silence as a cue to continue.

"You are obviously of royal descent."

Oh. Oh no. Master Gershom hinted at this. I haven't . . . I couldn't dare to hope. How did the king track me beyond Midian?

"Your Pensanden blood, however, could be traced through hundreds of possible lines—lines which have thinned through the centuries but resisted extinction, resisted the finality of the Hunt. Time and time again the Serpent has sent the coldmen, has had the world cleared of your kind. And time and time again, your people resurface and try to retake their thrones, to resume control of things. It is in your very bones, the desire to rule. This is what scared people, almost more than your breaking of the world. This is what fueled the Sixth Hunt. And much of the Seventh.

"We thought those lines were finally severed in the Seventh Hunt. It came to a close around the time you were born, Enoch, as the last three families with legitimate claim to Pensanden lineage were burned from Tenocht."

Mesha shifted on Enoch's shoulders. She sensed his tension.

"No, none of those families left record of your birth. Obviously. We wouldn't be speaking now, would we?"

Enoch nodded mutely. He had learned more about his past in the last few minutes than in an entire sixteen years of patient yearning.

Well, my possible past, at least.

The king continued.

"And once again, the Pensanden have proven their tenacity. Your people are more resilient than trolls, Enoch—and I mean no offense by that. But this time it will be different. Providence has brought you here, to the one kingdom in this crude and forgotten half of the world that could support an etherwalker Prince—support and raise him hidden from the Serpent's eye. Protect him. Perhaps provide him with a man he would be willing to call father . . ."

King Nyraud looked straight into Enoch's eyes. Enoch knew that the king wanted this, needed this, to be able to achieve his goal. But the king wasn't going to force it upon him, even though he could. He would let Enoch decide.

To choose whether I want to be a prince or go to a strange and hostile city somewhere in the north all by myself.

I'm sorry, Master Gershom.

"I would be honored to be your son, Milord. Honored to help you bring the tower back to life. And honored to carry this 'torch of knowledge' at your side."

The king smiled, and there was a brightness in his eyes that Enoch had never seen before. He leaned down and embraced the boy firmly. Enoch didn't know how to respond—*how does one respond to his new father?*

My father. Unbelievable.

The king stepped back and crossed his arms.

"Well, my son. Shall we start your training?"

Unbelievable!

* * * *

The Core Unit was unlike anything Enoch had ever seen before—a breed apart from the little device Master Gershom had smuggled down from Tenocht.

The monitor alone filled an entire half of this strange, circular room that King Nyraud had brought him to. It swam with what the king called "interim static," a fascinating sea of white sparks and shadow. Black cables as thick as a ram's foreleg ran from floor to ceiling behind the monitor and all along the circumference of the room. Small colored lights could be seen flashing on and off in machinery hidden behind the cables. It felt like being suspended in the night sky.

"The actual Unit itself is relatively small," said the king, crossing the room. "A panel, almost the size of your finger, rooted in the floor underneath the monitor. The rest of this . . . this heavy gear is for maintenance and security—protective hardware to insure that the information on this machine survives whatever hardships space travel would subject the Ark to.

"It is this same gear which will allow you to hone your abilities without alerting the Serpent. He will not be able to track you here."

Enoch crossed his hands and felt the scars on each wrist.

Will it hide me from the face that marked me? From Ketzel? Winged God or no, I don't think I want to see that again.

And then an exciting thought occurred to him.

Hey, I'm Pensanden. I can see just how secure this Core Unit is, see what all of this "protective hardware" really does.

"May I have a second, King Nyraud?"

The king looked about to ask Enoch what he meant but caught himself.

"Of course. You want to see if my confidence in the security of this Unit is well-founded. Are you sure you'll be able to understand this type of tek? We haven't even begun your lessons on circuitry and basic coding."

"I've never been trained in any of this, Milord, but I was able to detonate the mechanized bow of a coldman. I paralyzed a Silverwitch with a thought. A lot of what I do is based on instinct, on feelings I don't have words for. I'd like to explore this Unit with my powers. I'd like to explore this room if I could. It would make me feel more confident to start training here."

The king had opened his mouth when Enoch mentioned the coldman. He had shut it again with an audible click when Enoch mentioned the Silverwitch. King Nyraud decided to hold his comments, however, shrugging and putting his hands behind his back.

"Proceed, Enoch."

"Thank you, Milord. Thank you, Father."

Enoch reached up to give Mesha a reassuring pat, then closed his eyes and *paused*. He sent his mind past the dark cables and shadowed machines, out into the bright complexity inside and through them. He gasped.

A Pensanden built this!

The lines of power, the swirling motes, they were all there in the patterns he had become familiar with these past few weeks living in the Ark. This entire tower was wired in a fashion both ordered and pragmatic, the patterns of any one room practically identical to those of the next. Enoch had quickly grown bored following the electricity from one disconnected light fixture to another. Maybe the Pensanden had created the tools to build the Ark, but somebody else had put it together. But the way *these* lines were arranged—the way they were orchestrated! Enoch wasn't educated in much beyond swordplay and shepherding, but he recognized true art when he saw it. This was beauty, and a beauty that only he could see. It felt sacred.

Why does it feel so much like the beauty I saw in the Alaphim?

Every element of this room worked in harmony with the elements around it. One of the most simple of these harmonies dealt with the temperature of the room, something Enoch had remarked on when they had first stepped out of the bitter cold tunnel. Seeing the choreographed movement of heat against cold, fiery motes dancing against their somber brethren, made his heart race. It was beautiful.

The warm cables that ran behind the monitor and carried power to the entire room were woven around steel braces, sinking heat harmlessly into the metal before they got too hot. Those braces continued under the floor, where they branched out like budding ferns. The heat gathered from the cables now dissipated into the air, warming the room to a comfortable temperature even this close to the leaking coolant. Delicate sensors spaced evenly throughout the room tasted the air and adjusted the weave of cable to steel until the temperature was just right.

And this was only the *simplest* of the functions.

I could spend my entire life here.

This thought brought Enoch back to the reality of his situation—this combined with the surety that becoming lost in tek was probably a true danger to his kind. He pulled his mind back from the intricacy of the room and tried to observe its larger, more obvious functions. Many of them were immediately clear.

The Core Unit could monitor every facet of the Ark. It had little eyes and ears embedded in the flesh, skin, and bones of the tower.

The Core Unit could control the mechanized elements of the Ark. Many of them were now disconnected, lost, or defunct. But not all of them. Enoch saw controls for every light, elevator, fan, and hidden doorway in the king's estate.

And the Core Unit could control the Ark once it began its

journey to the stars. This was mostly guesswork on Enoch's part, but what other purpose could these controls for speed and trajectory serve?

There was so much here. Years of complexity. Odd mysteries that he could pursue endlessly—strange things like the vibrant lines of power which were hidden in the girders running all the way to the top of the tower.

Didn't the king say that area was inaccessible? Something is using power up there in the clouds. A lot of it.

Enoch stored that mystery away to question the king about later. He had so many questions! What was the purpose of these giant rooms filled with water? Or this one lined with electrical coffins? How did the generator tucked into the belly of the Ark produce such an endless supply of energy? It seemed to have something to do with the lines it drew from the Ark's sun-warmed skin. Could electricity be pulled from the air?

Careful. I almost lost myself again. I need to pull back. Remember why I'm here.

Drawing his focus, he began testing what King Nyraud had called the "heavy gear"—the thick cables which wound around the exterior of the room like the reeds of a basket. They were a sturdy combination of dense metal and another material, which was somehow both porous and crystalline. Like the ceramic in a dish.

A slow electronic pulse throbbed through the cables in a random pattern of long and short beats.

How does this protect the Unit? How will it protect me?

Enoch pulled his mind back from the cables and into the surrounding spaces. The buzz and hum of the energy moving around the room was suddenly loud to his Pensanden senses. He moved back into the bosom of the cables, and the hum was gone.

Ok, it seems like the material of the cables muffles interference from the outside. But what is the purpose of the pulse?

Again, he pulled back from the cables. The ambient noise increased again, a jumble made more chaotic by the perfectly random pulsing.

Chaotic. There is something to that.

Enoch contracted his senses back into the cables, but this time he continued until he was inside the wiring of the rooms. Again, he had to smile at the artistry of these patterns.

Patterns hidden to the outside by "perfectly random pulsing." This is what hides me from any watchers. The interruption of my own patterns.

It suddenly dawned on Enoch how the coldmen had known to find him in Midian. How that starlit face had spoken to him through the Unit.

A Pensanden gives off a pattern, just like a Unit. Just like the one I saw inside the Silverwitch. This pattern must be amplified, broadcast whenever I use my abilities to communicate with a device as complex as a Unit. Even when I'm not using my powers!

Enoch was suddenly glad he hadn't used any of the Units he had seen in Babel.

Rictus was right. The Serpent, or whoever it is that controls the blackspawn, must have ears constantly listening for that pattern. Listening for me.

Ketzel does, too.

Neither thought was very comforting. Enoch, however, felt like this Core Unit would be safe for him to use.

It was, after all, built by a Pensanden.

He pushed his mind back into the tek around him, this time searching for the Unit itself. Just as the king had said, it was under the floor. The lines of power woven through this little machine were infinitely complex. Unraveling this would take even more time, and King Nyraud had been patient while he searched. So Enoch retracted his mind from the room and opened his eyes. The king was still standing with his arms behind his back. Mesha had fallen asleep.

"It seems safe, Milord. I'm ready to proceed."

The king looked up and nodded. A long moment passed. Enoch realized that the king was waiting for him to initiate the Core Unit.

Maybe he has a little too *much confidence in my abilities.*

"There aren't any keys attached, Milord. I'm not familiar with this type of machine. How do I direct the Unit?"

King Nyraud responded by stepping up to the monitor and placing his hand against the smooth surface. The static immediately coalesced into pure blackness. A thin line traced around the king's hand and then flowed into words on the screen. Nyraud stepped away from the monitor with a flourish.

Enoch smiled—*now* he recognized this.

::What shall we do today?

The air in front of Enoch shimmered and glowed. Suddenly there was a row of keys floating at his waist.

Keys made of light! This explains the system of projection bulbs and lenses I noticed in the ceiling. The Unit uses its eyes to read my finger movements and translates them into letters.

"You can use those," said the king, obviously enjoying Enoch's amazement, "or you can speak to the Unit directly."

Speak?

Why not? A Unit spoke to me once.

Enoch leaned forward and smiled.

"Teach me to be a Pensanden."

The screen went black and then flashed to life, the entire surface suddenly filled with tiny letters of bright white text. Enoch squinted—there had to be *thousands* of topics. And each topic appeared to be followed by hundreds of sub-topics. This was going to take years.

A larger message in friendly yellow script appeared in front of the imposing data.

::Where would you like to begin?

Okay, let's just take this one little bit at a time.

"How about my powers? Why is it that I can see these tiny moving parts, these lines of energy, inside of mechanical objects? How is it that I can move them without using my hands?"

The text began to move on the screen, gradually increasing in size. It felt like diving into a pond of letters, with the outermost text spilling off the edges. Finally the screen had settled on a reasonable block of text that could be comfortably read from where

Enoch was standing.

::Elementary Physics.

King Nyraud chuckled and stepped forward. He put a hand on Enoch's shoulder.

"I think that I'm going to leave you two alone for now—this is fairly basic stuff, and should arm you with the vocabulary you need to understand the Pensanden powers. I'll leave four of my Huntsmen at the door while you study, and they will escort you back to your chamber when you've finished."

"Oh. Okay. Thank you for bringing me here, Milord."

"Learn what you can, Enoch. I've got a feeling we may not have as much time as we think we do. Certainly not as much as we would like."

With a wave, the king was through the door. Enoch could hear him giving instructions to the men outside, heard the grumbles from those chosen to stay in the cold tunnel waiting for him to learn "elementary physics."

The next two hours flew by, and Enoch lost himself in the new yet familiar world of "electrons" and "weak and strong forces." Mesha grew bored of her perch on his unmoving neck, and she patrolled the room for a while, sniffing at the base of every cable with feline suspicion. Satisfied that the area was safe, she went and scratched at the steel door, persisting until Enoch finally broke away from the monitor to let her out to beg fish from the Huntsmen.

When Enoch got back, the monitor looked different. He tried to look closer, to focus his eyes, but his vision was blurry after staring for so long.

The monitor pulsed.

Oh no.

Terror began to rise in Enoch's heart as the monitor pulsed again and then began to stream with symbols. It was just like before. Just like the time he was marked.

An icy pain grew in Enoch's head.

But I'm safe! This Unit is shielded!

Quickly, almost instinctively, Enoch *paused* and sent his mind into the cables surrounding the room. They were still intact. They still absorbed the noise, still pulsed their chaos.

And then Enoch saw the pattern.

A pattern! The pulse isn't random anymore! It's magnifying my signature into a roar!

Enoch desperately sent his mind diving along the cables' length, searching for the source of this pattern. He found an invasive power line and followed it out of the cables and into the floor. The culprit was hidden in a steel bracer—one of the same steel bracers Enoch had admired for its role in the temperature control.

But I didn't look close enough!

It was a small disk, similar to the one at the heart of the Core Unit, only this one was tasked with one simple directive—something so simple that even Enoch could read it in the circuitry: wait for a Pensanden pattern, then repeat that pattern through vibrations in the shield cables.

It was heart-wrenchingly simple. And it had been orchestrated seamlessly into the room by the same hands that had created the rest. Enoch's heart sank.

Why would a Pensanden betray his own kind?

And almost simultaneously:

Destroy it!

Enoch threw his mind at the device, pushing the lines apart and ripping motes—ripping *electrons* from their intended paths. Knowing what he saw, understanding their names and roles, gave him a fierce confidence. Sparks flew from the ceiling.

The cables moaned and then were quiet.

The monitor went black.

Did I stop it in time?

The room was deathly quiet. Enoch could hear the Huntsmen just outside the door, laughing at something. Apparently Styles had brought another tin of smallfish for Mesha. He let out a sigh.

The screen came to life.

It was a face. A face just like the first one Enoch had seen, except for the eyes. These eyes were empty. Bottomless holes.

The face smiled.

"I see you, Enoch."

CHAPTER 16

If they won't go to the rot, they go to the gray.
To the gray.
And so it goes.

—Lodoroi Specter Chant

Perched on the lone branch of a hangman's tree, the skeleton played his guitar to the moon. The notes were fiercely sad, and they ached of lonely years under this same cold light. A thick breeze pushed through the swamp below, stirring the reeds into tired motion. The music climbed to a sobbing climax and then held its breath.

Naked in the audible vacuum, the air shivered. Waited. Listened.

The ending chords struck with cried resolution, echoing tears and bones and the salt of forgotten centuries. Almost as if on command, the last threads of cloud pulled back from the moon's face. A final note pierced the night.

For a long moment, the skeleton cast a bleak silhouette. He was desolation pressed against the sky.

Oh, this is too cliché. It's pathetic. All that's missing is . . .

In the distance, a nerwolf howled.

And with that, I'm done. Even washed-out zombie rock stars have standards.

Rictus lifted his fingers from the frets and the note died. He shook his head and set the guitar down on his lap.

Poor baby. Of all the recent tragedies we've seen, your scars may be the hardest to bear.

The specter clicked his dry tongue at the jagged claw marks that transected the instrument's soundboard from below the bridge almost to the neck joint. A guitar like this was a rare treasure nowadays, and Rictus had gone thirty years since his last—he was picky about what he'd play. That combined with the frustrating habit of outliving his instruments meant that Rictus tended to go long stretches with only a sword on his back. It was nice to remember why he'd had an amp built into his LifeBeat all those years ago.

That was an expensive upgrade, but it may be the one thing I'm actually proud of wasting my fortune on.

And the damage to the guitar was mostly cosmetic, with long strips of that beautiful red lacquer peeled away from the pale ash wood underneath. The strings were a loss, but a minor one. Rictus always kept an array of those wrapped around the grip of his longsword.

Always keep some spare strings handy.

Funny which habits won't die no matter how many centuries you live. You'd think brushing your teeth would have lasted at least past the first hundred years. I stopped after fifty.

He slung the guitar behind his back and sagged forward, his arms across his knees. With an audible click, Rictus dropped his chin against his chest. It was a posture of exhaustion. Of resignation. The red light at his chest winked knowingly.

Little bastard.

The LifeBeat had brought Rictus back together like it always did, and this had been one of the more memorable awakenings of his long life.

Alone with a broken neck, missing both arms, and covered in congealing troll blood. Now those *would make good lyrics to a song!*

The distant nerwolf howled again, and Rictus rolled his eyes.

Waking up alone is always the worse part. I wonder if they left because they thought I was too mangled for a LifeBeat to fix. Maybe they had to escape, couldn't wait? They were headed back off the bridge last I saw . . .

Rictus deliberately avoided thinking of the other possibility—that the bodies he glimpsed in the shadows below the bridge did not all belong to trolls.

Well, good for them. I couldn't have been much use in the escape anyway, especially after losing Lefty and Righty.

Rictus remembered coming to in the still darkness and calling for Enoch or Cal or anyone who wasn't a troll to come help him re-arm; he remembered having to squirm around and use the dim red light of his LifeBeat to locate his scattered self. He'd done this before, of course, but never in such total darkness. It had made what was already an arduous process almost unbearable.

The specter had inched his mangled body across the bridge and then taken a long and frustrating hour trying to position himself so that the knobby head of his bare humerus could slide right into the bony cavity below his shoulder. He finally found the right spot, pressed down, and tried to hold still while the nanites powered by his LifeBeat went to work. It was only a few minutes before the connective tissue was strong enough for Rictus to roll over and situate himself over the other arm. The LifeBeat had jetted steam into the frosty air as the tiny bio-fusion generator that powered the machine was pushed to its limit. Rictus wondered if his guardian angel would be able to handle another resurrection.

The little gal is getting along in years—doing pretty well despite the neighborhood's deplorable lack of repair centers.

Rictus reached into the pocket of his newly-healed leather jacket to pull out the disc he'd found.

Enoch will be glad to see you, won't he? Almost missed you in the dark there.

Newly rez'd and stiff, his LifeBeat steaming like a teapot, Rictus had almost walked right past the disc. Only a last-second reflection of red light had caught his attention, sparked his curiosity enough to investigate. It was still tied with the cord Enoch had worn around his neck.

But no blood on the cord. No blood anywhere but around where I made my mess. They got in a scuffle, but I think they made it out. I have to believe that.

The journey from the bridge to the exit hatch had been slow and uneventful. Rictus had tried to search for any sign of Cal and Enoch, but it was too dark to discern much in those cold metal tunnels. Rictus had waited at the tunnel exit, the one Cal had told him of, for an entire day. He had a hope that maybe this would be a meeting spot. That idea died as the sun set, and Rictus realized that he *had* to keep moving on the chance that Enoch and Cal were already ahead of him. So he had given a specter's sigh and stepped into the murk, heading north.

Enoch was going north, going to Tenocht. Nobody was going to convince him otherwise, that's for sure. Stubborn kid.

The specter had been making good time, avoiding the more obvious trails and cutting northward in a straight line. He didn't want to deal with the nut-job Swampmen if he didn't have to, but he wanted to catch up with his friends as quickly as possible. Rictus's long bony legs allowed him to traverse even the boggiest areas at a swift pace, and he wasn't bothered by the standard worries of leeches, snakes, or carnivorous fish.

No blood. Just enough nanite-transfer fluid to make a mosquito puke.

Rictus looked down and knocked some mud off of his big black boots. The LifeBeat kept the boots whole, but never really did much to shine them. He supposed that was provided by the later models.

I think I covered fifteen miles today—an impressive hike for anyone packing a moly-vibe longsword and *a six-string Stratocaster on his back.*

Rictus had only stopped because he feared passing his companions in the dark. A specter didn't sleep, but he could take some down time and let his nanites recharge. The poor guys had been stitching up his shredded leather jacket all day, and Rictus was sure that their microscopic little spinnerets were tuckered out.

He lifted his head and stared into the moon. Those old familiar shapes, the craters and highlands, were always a welcome sight. It was nice to have something so constant in a world that changed every couple hundred years.

So I'll keep following them north, then. I have to. Enoch and Cal are useless without me.

* * * *

In the still water beneath the tree, a dozen wet shapes moved silently and unseen. They had heard the music, and they came armed with ropes, nets, and long barbed spears. They knew how to subdue a specter. Such things did not belong in their swamp.

CHAPTER 17

They will soar on wings like eagles;
they will run and not grow weary,
they will walk and not be faint.

—Isaiah 40:31 NIV

Enoch had been spending more and more time in the Gardens. The trees, the greenery, all of it reminded him of home. He felt . . . emptiness . . . when he thought of the cottage he had grown up in. Sure, the tower he lived in now was incredible; the ancient tek structures the king had him bringing back to life filled his dreams with electrons and *circuitry.* Enoch finally felt like his mind and talents were being put to use instead of merely put to practice. But sometimes Enoch felt a void. There was no other way to describe it. He wasn't sure if that meant that he missed Master Gershom, or if that meant that he was incapable of the feeling. Did this mean he was a bad person? Should he care? *I don't know if a Pensanden can miss somebody, really. I think a shepherd is supposed to.*

But now I'm a prince.

A prince who cannot leave his own castle. And that is why I've decided to disobey the king and come up here. If I'm not allowed down in Babel, then I am going to go wherever I please inside the tower.

Enoch felt guilty for going against King Nyraud's orders. *Father's orders.* But in a funny way, he felt like he was doing what a prince would do. Father was constantly urging him to "step beyond your commoner past and start preparing to rule."

Well, I'm going to start by ruling where I can go inside my new home.

He cringed. Master Gershom would never approve of that kind of thinking.

And Master Gershom is dead. He raised me blind to who I was, to who I can be, and then left me to figure it out all by myself.

Thoughts like that had been troubling Enoch lately. He remembered being happy back in Midian, remembered long sunny afternoons free from the type of chaos, energy, and noise buzzing through the tower. But how could he have been happy as a shepherd? A commoner?

Well, at least a commoner wouldn't have to worry about the Serpent hunting for him. Finding him.

The memory still brought goosebumps to Enoch's skin. Huntsmen pounding on the unexpectedly-locked door, bright sparks against the darkness of the room, and a face staring midnight into his heart. The face was gone by the time the king had burst through the door, trailing alchemists and Huntsmen. By then, the room was dead.

The surprising thing was that King Nyraud—*father*—hadn't been worried when Enoch told him about the face. About the betrayal of the Core Unit. If anything, Father was excited.

That excitement had condensed into a frenetic and unceasing energy. The king's ability to inspire his followers, to imbue them with a shared sense of ambition, continued to astound his new son—in a matter of hours, Nyraud had transformed the tower into a hive of military preparation. Night and day, the halls were crossed with running Huntsmen and alchemists with their arms full of parts, plans, and newly forged weaponry.

Enoch had been tasked with the revitalization of the Ark's tek, from the defensive cannons to the perimeter cameras to . . . the Core Unit. He had been surprised that his new father wanted that to function again—after all, hadn't the Core Unit alerted the Vestigarchy to Enoch's location? Wasn't that the reason why Babel was now locked down, with frustrated caravans camped out in the plains beyond the city walls?

Again, King Nyraud wasn't angry about the machine's betrayal—he acted as though this message from the Vestigarchy had somehow *freed* him into action. It made no sense to Enoch. Not that his father's movements were heedless—he was still being careful. But he was being careful at a breakneck speed.

Father knows that he doesn't have much time, but he knows that he can be ready. He's been preparing for this his entire life.

The king and a small army of his black-robed alchemists had descended on the Core Unit room with carts of tools, searching for any signs of intrusion or sabotage. Even with all of these supposed "experts" at work, Enoch had still found it necessary to point out the location of the treasonous circuitry that had broadcast his pattern to the sky.

These alchemists were sometimes hard to work with. The strange, pale men treated him with an odd mixture of reverence and ill-disguised hatred. They took orders from him with swift and unquestioning determination, but Enoch felt a bitter tint of hostility in every "Yes, Milord." He wondered about this and supposed that perhaps this was something nobility could always sense in the commoners due to their differing social stations. But then Enoch remembered his encounter with the alchemists upon first entering Babel: the angry looks of the crowd, the thrown fruit.

I suppose they see me as a symbol for all of the persecution they've suffered. Just for learning about how the world works.

In the end, even Enoch had to agree that the room was safe. The defensive cables were broadcasting their interference, and the damage he had caused trying to stop the signals was quickly repaired. Regardless, Enoch avoided that room; he only spoke to the Core Unit when father ordered him to, usually after encountering something completely baffling in the tower circuitry.

Something that is happening with less and less frequency.

Mesha leapt from his shoulder to chase after a redjay that had landed on the grass in front of them.

At least she's feeling at home. Smallfish from the Huntsmen, a warm cushion in front of the fire, and occasional covert trips through the Garden. I've never seen an animal so content. Or one that looked like she deserved *to be so content.*

Enoch sighed and leaned back against the trunk behind him. The work his father had tasked him with was fascinating and exciting. But it was also tiring. The boy looked forward to these evening walks in the Garden with Mesha as times when he could step away from his *afila nubla,* away from the circuitry and microscopic busyness of Babel.

If I get caught, I'll tell father that I was practicing my abilities with the Ark camera network. Testing their range, seeing if it was possible to move through the tower—all the way up to the Gardens!—without being seen. He doesn't need to know about the hidden lift I found . . .

Enoch smiled, finally exulting in his powers. Father would be proud to learn that his son had been able to find a way into the forbidden Gardens, proud to know that the new Prince of Babel had been spending evenings here amongst the trees for several days now.

At least he will be proud—whenever I decide to tell him.

I am getting better at this. I'm understanding what my powers can do.

Enoch flicked a beetle off of his sleeve and sat.

Too bad I'll never get to actually use these "understood" powers anywhere but inside the Great Ark's dusty guts.

King Nyraud had forbidden Enoch from leaving the gates of the city. He couldn't risk losing the greatest asset he had against the Vestigarchy. Enoch understood. But these trips to the Garden helped him to feel a little less trapped.

The king had said that the Hiveking and his blackspawn would be at their gates soon. Enoch wasn't so sure—two weeks had passed already without a sign of coldmen. He asked how his father was so sure that the face he had seen was from the Vestigarchy. It certainly hadn't said anything to identify itself—just those few chilling words of recognition before disappearing into the blackness of the monitor. Instead of answering, the king had gone quiet, staring Enoch straight in the eyes.

He knows it was the Serpent. I do too. He is impatient with self-

deception.

Who else would have the power to respond so quickly to the pattern—*no, the word is code*—the code identifying a Pensanden, which couldn't have been broadcast for more than a few minutes? Who else could have generated enough power to send a return signal back to Enoch's exact location?

I know it was Koatul. I guess I was expecting fangs and scales and a forked tongue, even after having seen Ketzel. It's hard to see past all of the stories and beliefs of the community I was raised in. I wonder if Koatul benefits from the Serpent image?

The answer seemed obvious after a moment's thought.

Of course he does. It means that his name is paired with fear and revulsion. The Serpent doesn't care to unite people, or to inspire them like father does. He seems to be devoted to isolating mankind, like molecules in a gas.

Enoch was proud to have used his new understanding of physics in a simile. He smiled, but quickly became uncomfortable with the sensation. Something about this new feeling of pride, about this constant self-satisfaction, seemed contrary to him. Master Gershom had never been this way. But King Nyraud—*my father*—encouraged it. Said it was a prince's right to recognize his own nobility. His duty. Enoch liked that. Or . . . he felt like he should. Frowning, he plucked a blade of grass and started to tie it into a knot.

I need to learn from Mesha. There is nothing wrong with enjoying what I can do, nothing wrong with feeling that I deserve it.

He pushed the worry out of his head. Tried to focus on the Serpent, on a question that had been nagging him for some time. It felt important.

What does Koatul have to gain by keeping the world dark? If this tower—this Ark—is any indication of what people can do when they are organized and educated, then why wouldn't any leader, evil or otherwise, want to utilize that power?

I wonder if it has anything to do with the Pensanden? With the Silicon Covenant?

Enoch's thoughts were interrupted by a sound that he felt

more than heard. It was pitched low, almost beneath what his ears could register. Enoch lifted the knotted blade of grass up to his eyes and watched it vibrate. The sound ended, and the grass went still.

What was that?

It started again, this time a little bit stronger. The sound rose in tone, held, and then fell. Enoch leaned over to put his ear to the ground.

It's music!

Mesha heard it, too, had come over to sniff at the grass in front of Enoch. She looked up at him and purred, her fur shifting from black to honeyed yellow to grass green. If Enoch wasn't mistaken, she was enjoying the music. And it seemed to be coming from underneath the grass.

This was no surprise; Enoch was aware of the chambers underneath the Gardens. On his first secret trip up here he had sent his mind out to see if there were any mechanical elements in the area—it was something he did out of habit now. He had been surprised to find that the Gardens were merely an extension of what had originally been intended as a self-sustaining forest, something the crew could visit and spend time in as the Ark traveled. Nyraud had taken the irrigation system and expanded it across the entire top level of the tower—at least, the top *accessible* level. This was the top of King Nyraud's domain. Naked girders framed the sides of the Gardens and extended in a broken web up towards the distant and unfinished tip.

I still need to figure out what is drawing all the power up there.

The music rumbled under his feet.

But first, let's find out what is hiding under the grass.

Shutting his eyes, Enoch tried to clear his mind of the guilt he felt for this sneaking. He tried to clear his worry of being seen by the Huntsmen posted at the entrance. And he tried to clear the simmering excitement he still felt for having discovered the hidden elevator that brought him up here. He tried. It wasn't working.

This is how I treat my new father? With disobedience?

Okay, this is the last time. I find out what's underneath here and then I never come back. King Nyraud deserves a son who obeys him.

Lips moving silently, Enoch began the *litania eteria*. He didn't need to use it anymore, but he found the chant helped him to move into a deeper trance than just *pausing* could.

His mind turned over, and Enoch could see the lines of force—the streams of electrons moving along live electrical wires and circuits—running underneath the grass. He quickly recognized a simple piston system, unlocked the coded latch, and *pushed.* A large square of grass began to lift away from the surrounding ground. It was a powered door, and when the pistons came to a stop, Enoch could see a metal ramp leading down into darkness. A dank smell wafted up from the opening, a smell that reminded Enoch of the sheep pens after a long cold winter. It smelled of animals. Mesha hissed and then leapt up on his shoulder.

Perhaps this is where father breeds the manticores he lets loose in the Gardens. They'll be in cages, but I'd best be careful.

Enoch sent his mind ahead into the darkness, and sure enough, he found rows of cages with electrical hatches set to release upon the king's command. Enoch checked to make sure they were all locked securely and then routed power to the familiar blue light-tube in the ceiling. He squinted as the chamber flickered into azure visibility.

These aren't manticores!

The cages held people.

A short, muscular man lay sleeping—or unconscious—in the nearest cage. His yellow hair and bristly beard reminded Enoch of Master Gershom. The cage next to this held a tall, dark-skinned woman. She was crouched warily, holding on to the bars with scarred hands and whispering in a language Enoch didn't recognize. Like the man, she was dressed in a simple green tunic. It bore the arrow-sun mark of Nyraud.

Are these prisoners? I assumed they were all kept down in the municipal building west of the tower—the place that looks like a big gray box. Maybe these prisoners are too dangerous for the shared jail grounds?

Then why would they be kept here in the Gardens?

Enoch craned his neck to look between the two rows, counted maybe a dozen cages.

So many down here and I never heard a thing—well, until this music started. Why are they so quiet?

As if in answer to his question, the music started again. The bars on the cages rattled in time with the low-pitched rumbling. The tall woman released her hold on the bars and flinched. Her eyes flashed towards the far end of the room. When she noticed Enoch's stare, she stopped whispering and stepped back to the rear of her cage. Enoch caught a glimpse of a fresh scar at her throat. It was stitched with green thread.

Have their voices been taken?

He started walking down the row towards the large cage in the back. It seemed to be the source of the music.

He tried to keep his eyes straight forward, tried to keep his attention away from these people. They reminded him of the poor men he had seen pulling the cart on that muddy trail in Midian—Rictus had told him about *slaves.* That sort of helplessness, that sort of exposure, bothered Enoch deeply. He passed another man, a red-haired adolescent who could have easily have been from Midian, and two more women. All of them were silent, all of them with scars on their throats. Enoch could smell sweat and urine mixed in with the fresh hay that covered the floor of their cages. The chamber stunk of fear.

In the next couple of cages, he saw why. The enclosures didn't all hold people. Some held animals. And worse.

I guess I was partially right about the manticores.

A mated pair of the beasts crouched at the front of their cage, pressed against the bars with muscles quivering. Having never come so close to one before, Enoch couldn't help but stare at the horrible things. Thin and feline at first glance, the creatures moved with a silent deadliness that reminded him of Mesha. That similarity stopped at the movement. A closer look revealed that these creatures were covered in thick, scab-colored scales and—Enoch gasped.

Those faces!

Their faces were those of babies. Round and rosy-cheeked, topped with a downy thatch of hair. One of the manticores stared up at him with soft blue eyes—not the fiery embers that Enoch had heard of in the stories. It cooed sweetly.

The illusion was broken as the manticore opened those small pink lips and snarled. The creature's *actual* mouth extended in a jagged line from those lips around to the edges of its head. Sharp white teeth were visible from ear to ear.

Repressing a shudder, Enoch walked on. The next cage was no better, even though Enoch recognized the inhabitant. Crouched in the darkest corner of his cage, the troll gave a bubbling groan. It was chewing on a mouthful of straw and staring hungrily at the manticores. Those terrifyingly familiar eyes, black and wet and set closely above a veined nose, blinked painfully in the overhead light. But Enoch saw something apart from hunger in those ebony buttons, something unexpected. Fear.

What can scare a troll?

Another rumble came from the final cage, and the troll pulled back further into his enclosure. Enoch squared his shoulders and rested his hands on the pommels of his swords.

It's in a cage. It's in a cage.

It was twice as large as any of the other cages and was partially covered by a canvas sheet. Mesha curled her tail tightly around Enoch's neck. He could feel her muscles tense, ready to spring.

Even behind bars, that thing can scare a troll.

And then Enoch recognized the cage. It was the same one he had seen as he hid in the bushes! The same cage that had been pulled by all of those slaves! The rumbling music had stopped.

He took a step forward.

"You probably want to stop there. He took the arm of the last guard who interrupted his song."

Enoch spun to face the voice. It was young. And female.

"Take a step back. That stain at your feet isn't mud."

The smaller cage had escaped his notice, hanging from the ceiling next to the manticores. Enoch struggled to see who—or what—was inside. He could barely make out a frail form, the glimmer of metal.

What stain—?

Looking down, he could see the umber stain at his feet, and he took a quick step backwards.

And just in time. A massive paw, tipped with ragged claws, struck out from the large cage and tore into the metal at Enoch's feet. The largest claw ripped a gash mere inches from his toes. He shouted and leapt backwards, colliding with the troll cage.

The troll lumbered forward, fear forgotten as it smelled warm food. Enoch recognized the sounds of a hungry troll. He sprung away from the bars and drew his swords. Mesha leapt to the ground.

"Put those away, Shepherd Boy. You're safe as long as you stay in the middle there, under the light."

The voice was right—the troll had already stopped and was rubbing at its eyes angrily. It gave another drooling moan, cast a glance at the big cage, and then shuffled back to its shadowed corner. Enoch was frantically looking back and forth between the troll, the suspended cage, and the enormous paw, which had retracted its claws from the five jagged holes it left in the metal. His mind spun.

Focus! The troll is contained, and I'm beyond the reach of whatever is in that big . . . wait, 'Shepherd Boy'?

Enoch *paused* and looked into the hanging cage again. He recognized the pattern immediately. Metal woven into bone, graceful alloys of steel and brass and complex crystal.

Not crystal. Piezoelectric ceramics.

Enoch had recently been studying Alaphim bio-constructs in his obligatory Core Unit time. The artistry of their forms was a welcome relief from the monotonous weapon systems he'd been calibrating on the Ark. Enoch had hoped to escape into Babel and find an Alaphim . . . well, he wanted to find *her.* He sent more power into the light above the hanging cage, and it was fully illuminated. The troll groaned.

And . . . I found her.

The angel was just as beautiful as he remembered. Her cerulean hair was shorter, and it looked like her wings had been damaged, but she still had those vibrant eyes. The graceful neck that arched from sculpted shoulders. She raised an eyebrow and smiled.

Unexpectedly, he smiled back.

Focus!

"What are you doing here? Why are you in that cage?"

A horrible realization struck him.

"Are you an enemy of my father?"

The angel was taken back.

"Your father? You mean that tall man wrapped in old sheets?"

Enoch had no idea what she was—*oh, she means Rictus.*

"No. I've been adopted by King Nyraud. I live here now."

For some reason, those words sounded silly to Enoch. As though he were bragging. The Alaphim was staring at him with her mouth open. He changed the subject.

"Why are you here? With all these prisoners—and all these *things?*"

The angel gathered herself and moved to sit at the front of her cage, dangling her feet over the edge. One of the manticores leapt towards her, colliding into the bars with a dull clang. She didn't flinch.

"Prisoners? Shepherd Boy, do you know why the king—your 'father'—is called the Hunter King?"

Enoch's stomach tightened. He'd heard the stories. But after his time here with Nyraud, he had decided that they were ignorant fables born of the commoner's envy. Imagined stories to decorate their evenings. Just like Old Noach Kohn's Serpent Wives and their non-existent fangs. Enoch had first-hand experience with that fiction.

"He is called the Hunter King because of his tireless pursuit of fallen technology. His quarry is the restoration of Babel to her former glory."

She was looking at him with pity.

". . . also, he really enjoys hunting."

His last sentence trailed into silence. King Nyraud was the perfect father, as far as Enoch could tell. He was smart, noble, and passionate about protecting his people. He was going to change the world, and he was going to do so with Enoch at his side!

She must be an enemy of Babel. Of course she spreads lies about the king . . .

"Your father does enjoy hunting, Shepherd Boy."

"Enoch. My name is Enoch."

"Very well, Enoch. I am Sera."

She gave as much of a bow as was possible from her confined space. Somehow, it still seemed graceful.

"The tales of your father's hunts are true, Enoch. I have witnessed many of them. He is an exceptional hunter, never losing his prey and never tiring of the chase. He tired of hunting the simple beasts years ago."

A rumbling song came from the big cage. Enoch looked down at the claw-marks on the ground and took another step back. He wasn't going to let this go.

"You are lying. You are being kept up here as an enemy to the throne, probably for spreading the same sort of lies you've been telling me."

Enoch turned and started walking back towards the ramp. He wanted to run.

"I'm not lying, Enoch. Why would he keep 'political prisoners' caged next to trolls and manticores? You know that he loves to challenge himself. Loves the pursuit."

She's lying! She's trying to make me doubt my father, to doubt the man who has given me everything*!*

Enoch stopped at the foot of the ramp, sent his mind out to cut power to the lights. As the chamber went black, Sera's voice rang out desperately.

"He hunts men, Enoch! He hunts men and women as well as beasts! You've got to let us free! Enoch! Enoch!"

Enoch walked out and lowered the ramp. He could still hear Sera's muffled shouting from under the grass.

I guess they haven't had time to cut out that traitor's voice yet.

Mesha leapt from his shoulder to chase after another bird.

How long will father keep her down there with those monsters? How long until she's learned her lesson?

Enoch dropped to his hands and knees. Sera had stopped shouting, and the Gardens were silent.

He is called . . . he . . . his tireless pursuit of . . .

A low rumbling song echoed up from the ground, punctuated by sobs as Enoch drove his fist into the grass again and again.

CHAPTER 18

Tenocht was the first of the Eastern Colonies, the first place considered safe by refugees from Pan Americana. There the people who had lifted the world and broken it chose to circle their wagons and lay low. The meager remnants of their tek were turned to protection and to survival.

—A Broken World, by Diego Thompson

Mosk swung his claw through the door, shattering the fine wood and sending splinters through the air in an explosion of mahogany. The man stumbled backwards, barely catching himself against the balcony rail. He shook a piece of wood from his shoulder and returned to the *senpelisto* stance. A drop of blood fell from his right hand.

Mosk circled to that side, pressing the attack. The man parried a lunge with his *derech*, then followed through with a downward slash from his curved *iskeyar*. The sword cut through the Hiveking's left pri-arm spurs, severing two of them. With a rattling hiss, Mosk took a step backwards.

The Nahuati, encouraged by the feint, drove forward with his straight blade. Against any other man, this thrust would have gone straight through the chest. Against a creature who had killed more blademasters than were alive today, it was a tiredly predictable move. Mosk snapped his barbed sub-arms up to catch the blade, then spun and pulled the man to his left. The man exhaled sharply and released the sword. Too late.

The Hiveking brought both of his heavy upper arms down on the man's unprotected back. Thick spurs pierced the skin and muscle, and the blademaster hit the ground with a groan. Mosk was surprised to see the man roll to the side and then stagger to his feet. This was a strong one!

Before the man could raise his remaining blade, Mosk was on top of him. Pri-arms pushing the Nahuati's head back, the Hiveking drove him to the floor. With a roar, he spread his toothed mandibles wide and then bit into the man's chest, snapping through the sternum. Mosk felt hot red air burst from ruptured lungs.

He ate as the man shuddered his last.

Proximate Keq arrived several minutes later, his spurs also wet. They glittered darkly in the moonlight.

The coldman waited until his Swarmlord finished, and then bowed.

"My blood to your tongue, Sire. Command me."

Mosk waved the Clot Primal up.

"Report, Keq. How many more in this building?"

"We found three others trying to escape through the sub-levels. One was a blademaster, and our losses were commensurate. We lost seven of the battle caste and fifteen arakids. The remaining Clot is still searching the top floors, but I suspect we will find no more."

Keq leaned forward, and Mosk noticed that the violet caste markings on his shoulders were still florid with excitement. The Proximate had missed the clean blood of men, too, it seemed.

"The Rift Queen knew we were coming—I found signs indicating that this was a major meeting place for the rebels. My arakids are trying to follow a dozen different scent trails. We only caught the last few, probably those left as a rearguard while the rest escaped."

Mosk regarded the jagged stubs of his left pri-arm spurs. They would grow back in his next molt, but the loss angered him nonetheless. The cost of growing soft in between Hunts.

"How could they have known we were coming? We only arrived in Tenocht this morning, and our camp is hidden behind the generator sector."

"I suspect," said Keq, "that we were betrayed by the Tenocht Council. The queen must have a spy in the governing dome."

Mosk didn't like having to rely on humans.

"Kill all of them. I don't have time for these soft people and their complexities. I want your Clot to take the cannon batteries at the front gate, Keq, and I want them back online and fully charged by morning. Tell Proximates Toq and Gelt to hold the remaining gates. This city will be locked tight until I am personally satisfied that it is clean—we left too soon after the last Hunt, and our sloppiness has festered."

"Yes, Sire. Do you expect the Pensanden to make a frontal assault? If he gets close enough to take the cannons before we—"

Keq was suddenly silent. Mosk looked up from his damaged spurs with surprise. A slender kra-wyrm had flown up to the balcony, was hovering over the Hiveking's head.

Mosk dismissed Proximate Keq and turned to face the creature.

It resembled a small, paler version of the draconfly. Only as long as one of Mosk's arms, the kra-wyrm struggled to hover in one place with its two pairs of transparent wings. The winds were strong up here, ninety floors above the ground.

Mosk raised the arm he had been inspecting, and the creature came to a rest on his spur nubs. The kra-wyrm was still wet from hatching. This must have been an urgent message.

Mosk pulled it close and whispered the key word. "Yohl Ik'nal."

The kra-wyrm shivered and turned its back to Mosk, tilting its wings together to form a flat panel. Trembling light flowed across the wings, and a face appeared in the brightness. It was the Arkángel Desgarrar.

"Our Lord has grown tired of waiting for your Hunt, Hiveking. He found the Pensanden Himself."

Mosk took a surprised step back. His throat clicked warily.

"Where, Sire?"

"In the city you so confidently deemed clear. And left in the hands of a traitor. The Pensanden is in Babel, Hiveking. And the only reason you still have your head is because I need someone to surround the city until I arrive."

"You, Sire? But . . . but my Swarm isn't large enough to hold Tenocht and surround Babel until—"

"You will leave Tenocht immediately and take your entire Swarm to Babel. You have wasted far too much time in a city that we already control. The Pensanden is in the tower, obviously using the king and any remnant tek to build up an army. I have sent Kai to prime the chambers, and we will need your forces there. Now."

Mosk was stunned. He felt a cold thorn pierce his heart.

Is this what fear is? The anticipation of rewards for my weakness?

The face in the light raised an eyebrow.

"You are silent, Hiveking? Have your years hunting these humans infected you with their fears?"

Am I infected? My ability to defeat the Nahuati alone, unique amongst my kind—it has required some understanding of their minds. The Arkángel himself told me that my brood was pushed as far into the human range of intellect as the Vestigarchy had ever gone.

Too far?

Mosk shook his ebon head. The cold thorn went deeper.

Is this fear?

"No, Sire. The wind up here is strong—I can barely hear you. I will take my swarm to Babel and hold it until you arrive.

"Upon your arrival I will offer you my head. I recommend Proximate Keq as the new Hiveking. Cleanse my weakness from the blackspawn, Sire."

The Arkángel was silent, wrinkled lips in a grim line.

He knows that I fear.

"I will arrive at Babel in two days. I will be accompanied by five battalions. Have your Proximate familiarized with the proper command pheromones."

"Yes, Sire. My blood to your tongue."

The light fuzzed into static and then disappeared. The krawyrm shuddered one last time and then fell to the ground lifeless.

Its purpose had been served.

As has mine.

But . . . I don't want to die.

CHAPTER 19

This is Gonna Hurt.

—Title to the Dogfish Knights second album, which broke international record sales.

They are everywhere!

An army of coldmen, arakid, and draconflies covered the Reaches in a carpet of shifting, rustling darkness for as far out across the plains as Enoch could see—or at least, for as far as the Ark's *hull-mounted optical docking-sensors* could see. He was down in the tunnels with the Core Unit, monitoring the Ark's activity in preparation for the Vestigarchy attack.

The draconflies had been arriving for the past three days, some unloading their cargo of insectoid warriors and some circling Babel's perimeter. There were now two dozen of them in the air—the low humming of their wings had become a constant refrain in the city. Despite the incredible size, the massive presence of this force, Enoch couldn't help but smile. He knew the power of this place. Knew it intimately.

And the bugs have learned not to land on the walls anymore.

The blackspawn were now staying safely out of the range of the city's cannons—a dozen craters peppering the battlefield in front of them bore witness to a hard lesson learned. The functionality of the Ark's defensive systems had been a complete surprise to the Vestigarchy, even knowing of the Pensanden inside.

I guess they thought me too young, too inexperienced to have brought so much of this unfinished starship back to life.

However, Enoch did have to admit that his father's leadership—the planning, the energy, the organization—had been vital to the confident situation he found himself in. Enoch knew that the tower could hold off an army like the one arrayed below indefinitely.

This is my gift to you, Father. And my apology for leaving.

Enoch shook the regret from his thoughts. There wasn't any time for that now. He keyed in the perimeter patrol checks and waited as the Huntsmen stationed around Babel's walls sent in their reports. The king's "public Unit placement" now made a lot more sense to Enoch—while it had been a costly and labor-intensive act of municipal generosity, the benefit of having instantaneous communication with the soldiers at key points in the city was vital. King Nyraud's foresight was astounding.

Enoch made one last check to ensure that the cannons were fully charged and that the sensors were clear. He then powered up a line of access channels along the path he would be leaving through. He wanted to have his eye on this battle, on the weapon he'd resurrected, and on his father for as long as he could.

Mesha was pawing at the door. She was ready to go.

I don't know if I ever will be ready to go. But I have to. If I don't go now, I'll never find another time when Father and his Huntsmen are so distracted. If I don't go now, I'll never be able to bring myself to leave—no matter how many more "dark secrets" I learn.

Enoch pushed the pain away. He tried to remember the rooms he had discovered, the trophies. He tried to remember Sera's words, her calm and tearful descriptions of the horrors of the Tower.

I have to go.

Setting the Core Unit to automatically collect reports from the perimeters, he glanced over the newly awakened tunnel cameras. He could see the liberated prisoners from several angles; they had just stepped out of his secret elevator and were separating into the various tunnels which would lead them under the city, past the blackspawn army, and out into the cover of swampland along the northern borders of Babel. Enoch had deliberately shortened the range on the northern cannons so that the Vestigarchy forces would move in close, past the tunnel exits. The Core Unit was programmed to open fire on those forces in thirty minutes, just when the prisoners would need some chaos to hide their escape.

And my escape. I don't need anyone.

Enoch keyed in the final command, which would lock the door upon his exit—cover for at least several hours, enough to hide his absence. He picked up Mesha and left the room.

* * * *

Sera couldn't believe that this boy—this *shepherd boy*—had been able to accomplish what he had.

I know that he claims to be a Pensanden, but he's so young.

This thought made her laugh—didn't she hate it when the older Alaphim referred to *her* age with such condescension? G'Nor heard the sound and looked down at her, one tawny ear raised in question. He raised a massive paw and signed.

Sera shook her head.

"No, I'm not laughing at you. I was just thinking about how unexpected our rescue was—and how unexpected the rescuer."

G'Nor's purring ratcheted up an octave, his equivalent of a laugh.

Sera lifted her hand to place it on the side of the beast's peaked shoulder and smiled. She had become close friends with the Ur'lyn in their weeks of confinement, and had surprised herself by how quickly she had been able to learn his subtle, gestured language.

On Enoch's subsequent visits, the boy had consented to leaving the lights on so that she could see G'Nor's gestures more clearly; Sera had been fascinated by the insights that this imposing predator had on life and the ending of a people. So much of what he said put into words her own feelings about the Alaphim.

Enoch had taken longer warming up to G'Nor due to his close encounter with the Ur'lyn's claw. Sera had explained to him that G'Nor had taken the swipe to make the boy aware that, although caged, he was far from helpless. She told Enoch that G'Nor could have done worse when he passed him on the road back in Midian, killing or at least exposing the boy. But the Ur'lyn had held back then and had sensed something unique about Enoch.

That memory sure stunned Shepherd Boy, and I think it pleased him. Enoch likes his unique status. And I think the memory helped him to move past his fear of the Ur'lyn—what was it that Enoch said to G'Nor? That he reminds him of his master? Enoch seemed relieved to be able to say that, almost as though it felt good to remember his master again.

Regardless, I'm glad he consented to freeing us both. Spending weeks caged next to that troll was enough for me.

At that thought, she quickly looked down the tunnel in front of her.

And I don't want to meet any more of them.

Sera couldn't hear any of the other prisoners' footsteps anymore—their paths had finally spread to the point of "numerical chaotic safety," as Enoch put it. Any one prisoner captured could never lead a guard towards the others. Sera wondered about the other prisoners. She had spent so much time with them, but their surgical muteness, combined with a general sense of fear and suspicion, kept her from learning much. She silently wished them well.

The tunnels weren't as cold as Enoch had described them in his harrowing tale, and for good reason. Just a week ago, he had led a team of the king's alchemists to seal off the ruptured tank of frostwater. Apparently this was done with the excuse of conserving and rerouting the fluid into the tower, cooling the defensive cannons and allowing a higher rate of fire. It had certainly convinced Nyraud. But the result of a temperate and troll-free escape route was something Sera appreciated. Once committed to an idea, Enoch reasoned through every possible angle that idea could take. It was unbelievable how thorough and detailed the boy's mind could be.

She leaned against G'Nor's warm flank and sighed.

"What about our rescuer? Do you still want to kill him?"

The Ur'lyn turned his head to look at her but kept walking. Sera knew that G'Nor was bothered by Enoch's ancestry. The Pensanden were the cause of much of his people's suffering; he saw the fall, the Schism, and the practical genocide of the etherwalkers as a painful but divine cleansing. Sera had stayed awake several nights trying to talk G'Nor out of killing Enoch—hours of odd, slow-moving conversation. It was true that the Ur'lyn had sensed something special about Enoch even back along the road when they had their first encounter, recognized the scent instinctively. What she hadn't told Enoch, however, was that G'Nor had been debating his responsibility to destroy the Pensanden once they had all escaped. She was almost positive that she could talk him out of it.

This was the thing Sera found most interesting: for a somber creature from a race of melancholy mystics, G'Nor was unexpectedly optimistic. Sure, he saw most things as absolutes, but he tended to place himself on the better, nobler, more successful side of those absolutes. Like his escape from Nyraud's Gardens, for example. There he was caged with manticores at the topmost level of the Hunter King's tower, and G'Nor spoke of his "eventual escape" with a certainty that had at first made Sera laugh. Then, when she realized that he wasn't joking—something he seemed incapable of—she had asked him how he was going to accomplish this feat. G'Nor had simply stared at her with those yellow-green eyes and purred.

That purring. Sometimes it was a song and sometimes it was poetry. G'Nor said it was the sound his people made to "warm the cold times." Sera thought it was a great way to avoid answering hard questions, but she had grown accustomed to the thick sound. The Ur'lyn was doing it now, and she could feel it coming through the firm walls of muscle at his side.

My happy beast.

G'Nor claimed to be "slender" for his kind. Sera had a hard time imagining how a creature could get any larger, or more imposingly built. The wooden carving she had purchased at the market hadn't prepared her.

On all fours, the Ur'lyn was a massive block of tawny fur and bulk reaching seven feet from paw to arching shoulder peak.

His thick neck extended another few feet out and down from the peak, ending in a leonine face with a blunt, whiskered muzzle. Those feline eyes, sparkling from a mask of darker fur, held all of the wild and ferocious millennia of this creature's ancestry. It was no surprise that Lamech had seemed so taken with the Ur'lyn. They shared a beauty with the angels, and she had said so.

Enoch had claimed that this dual beauty—the ethereal and the wild—was an obvious example of the Pensanden art. Sera had laughed. G'Nor had considered for a minute, then raised those mighty paws to sign a response. He said that no, Enoch's people found the art. They took it. And then they had framed it for themselves.

Enoch didn't have a response for that, and he hadn't come back for several days after G'Nor made the comment. Sera recognized hurt pride when she saw it.

I can tell that this arrogance is new to him. He is excited about it. He is still unexpectedly flattered when his competence is rewarded—and doubly hurt when it is questioned. What has Nyraud been teaching this boy to get him so caught up in his own worship?

Regardless, Enoch had made the right decision. The hard decision.

And I'm not just saying that because he saved my life.

Sera felt something—respect? Admiration? She was unsure. It felt odd to think that the object of these feelings was a boy just barely stepping into adolescence. A boy . . . well, not much younger than her . . .

No, no, no, Sera. Let's not move our attention away from escaping the Hunter King. And the blackspawn surrounding that tower.

She shook her head and was comforted to feel the touch of her growing tresses against the side of her face.

But I'm impressed that he is able to voluntarily walk away from all of this.

They had reached a point where the hallway split into two. Sera remembered Enoch's instructions to take the left tunnel. G'Nor stopped, sniffing the ground in front of them.

"What? You smell something?"

The Ur'lyn pushed off of the ground with his front paws and stood—filling the blue-lit hallway as he scented the air. He extracted his ebony claws to emphasize the command of his signed words.

"You mean trolls passed here recently?" she said, wanting to be sure. "And a specter? Yeah, I'll climb up on your back."

A specter? I thought trolls were bad enough!

Sera grabbed onto the longer hair that ran along G'Nor's spine—almost a mane. G'Nor dropped back to all fours and leaned towards her, lowering his shoulder peak. They had talked about doing this up in their cages but had never tried it. She was a little nervous—not for the height, obviously, but for the utter dependence that this position forced upon her.

Well, I wouldn't have to rely on an Ur'lyn if I had kept out of Nyraud's hunting camp. I wouldn't have to worry about breaking my already clipped and damaged wings if I had stayed on patrol . . .

Sera pulled on handfuls of mane and lifted herself up onto the broad, shaggy back. Her head almost touched the ceiling, and she winced as her wings brushed a light tube. They still ached, but the skin had healed over. She would need to find her people when this was all over. Maybe Sera would never fly again, but a boneweaver could at least straighten the twist in her carpal joint.

Enoch says he can't fix my wings—says he doesn't dare touch their "art" after so much time working with the crude guns in the tower.

But I've caught him staring at them, doing his deep Pensanden look. He wants to try.

Sera reached back to run a hand over the rough edges of her shorn feathers.

Do I want him to try? Could he make it worse?

They didn't encounter any trolls, or specters for that matter, as they moved lower into the tunnels. G'Nor's rumbling purr seemed to warm the air around her, and Sera tried to ignore the ache in her wings. She found that she could overcome her claustrophobic fears of dependence, actually started to enjoy her ride on the Ur'lyn's broad, warm back. Soon they reached the portal

Enoch had mentioned, a large steel disk marked with purple symbols. And Enoch was there waiting for them.

His eyes were closed, and he had his hand splayed against an outlet next to the portal. As soon as they were in earshot, he smiled, and without opening his eyes, he gestured and invited them to sit. The boy's shadowcat pet purred a greeting to G'Nor and shifted color to a matching tawny brown. G'Nor ignored her. Mesha pretended not to notice, leaping off of Enoch's shoulder to explore the hallway behind them.

"You are late, Sera. G'Nor. The guns will be starting soon, and we have to be ready to move quickly."

Sera climbed off of G'Nor's back, careful not to jostle her wings.

"Sorry, Shepherd Boy. I had G'Nor unlock the manticore cage and hurry out before shutting the trap door—those clever beasts should be able to figure out how to open it eventually. It will be a nice surprise for the Huntsmen when they go up to prepare the King's next foray."

Enoch opened his eyes and looked at her crossly. He didn't like when his plans were changed.

"Sera, there is a good chance that 'those clever beasts' will find a way out of that chamber. There is a vent shaft they could fit through, possibly alerting the tower security earlier than we had planned. And the trap door itself isn't built to withstand . . . hey, you didn't let the troll loose, too, did you?"

Sera let out a frustrated sigh.

"Have a little bit of faith in your conspirators, Enoch. I blocked access to the vent with my own cage. And G'Nor moved the troll pen in front of the trap door, not close enough for our slobbering friend to touch it, but close enough for him to grab any manticore which dares to approach."

Enoch was quiet for a moment. He nodded, then turned back to the outlet he was monitoring.

He's going to have to learn to trust us.

G'Nor signed to Sera. He wanted to know what Enoch saw.

It was a good question. If things were as rushed as Enoch

claimed, what had captured his attention like this?

"G'Nor wants to know what you are looking at."

Enoch put his other hand against the wall and murmured, "What is that?"

"What? What are you seeing, Enoch?"

He was shaking his head, and Sera watched a blue-white thread of electricity curl from the outlet and wind around Enoch's scarred wrist.

Eyes still closed, he shook his head. "I'm watching the Vestigarchy front lines from the docking cameras—the lenses are old and cracked, and I can't focus in as close as I'd like to. But the blackspawn have just pulled back and . . . *something* has just come forward."

Sera stepped closer.

"Something?"

"It . . . it looks like a man. But he's being carried by . . . no, they are metal, but those are *his* legs . . . hold on, let me try and see if I can . . ."

Enoch's lips began to move in some sort of chant. Sera recognized it as the mantra he used on occasion to focus his powers and send his mind great distances. He had used this *litania eteria* to explore Windroost Spire after she had told him about her people's home. And he had discovered the explosives Nyraud had placed on the supporting girders that ran up through the garden—insurance against the Alaphim's disobedience.

Even after having learned of the king's hunts, this new information shook him. Enoch still wants to believe in Nyraud's goodness.

She placed a hand on Enoch's rigid shoulder. His lips had stopped moving. The boy was deeply focused on the events of the battlefield below. Sera was still worried about her own people.

Luckily Enoch was able to send word of the explosives to Lamech in his navigation bridge-turned-perch. I'll bet that old rooster was surprised to see one of his "bookshelves" come to electrical life—and then spell out the need for our Spire to be evacuated.

The thought made Sera sad, and she had to remind herself of its necessity.

If Enoch had risked deactivating those bombs, the king could have simply replaced them at any time. My people have to move on—I hope they listened to Lamech. And I hope that I will be able to find them again. I wonder where they will—

Enoch cried out and jolted away from the wall, his eyes popping open. He spun around and pointed an accusing finger at Sera. G'Nor surged forward with a growl.

"He's one of you!" shouted Enoch, his teeth bared. "The leader of the blackspawn is an Alaphim!"

"What? You're wrong. That can't be true!"

Enoch took an angry step forward, accusatory finger jabbing at Sera.

"He has your bones. He's one of you!"

There was a rush of russet motion, and Enoch was suddenly pinned to the ground beneath G'Nor's paw. The Ur'lyn roared, and the walls of the tunnel shook.

Sera strained forward.

"No! Don't kill him! We need to know what he saw out there!"

G'Nor hesitated, then retracted his black claws. Five thin lines of blood ran down Enoch's chest. The boy was staring at her still, his face a mask of anger and confusion.

"Listen, Shepherd Boy, I don't know what you saw out there, but it doesn't excuse you from courtesy. You chose not to be a prince anymore. Now you have to choose not to act like one."

Enoch's breathing calmed, and Sera could see him forcing down the anger. He looked up and placed his hands on G'Nor's restraining paw.

"I . . . I'm sorry, Sera. Get your pet off of—"

G'Nor's roar blasted Enoch's sable hair flat against his skull.

"Sorry . . . would you please ask G'Nor to let me up?"

G'Nor turned to her and signed.

Sera shook her head.

"G'Nor, we need him to help us out of these tunnels. We need him to guide us through the coming fusillade and past the blackspawn."

She looked down at Enoch, who appeared to be calculating

how to move out from under G'Nor. His hand started moving slowly towards the sword at his waist.

"And besides, we owe him our trust for setting us free. Maybe he will be different from his posterity? Maybe he won't be a Worldbreaker?"

Enoch's hand stopped moving. G'Nor lowered his muzzle to rest it against the boy's chin and then opened his jaws wide. The white and yellow fangs encompassed Enoch's entire chest. G'Nor licked the blood from the puncture wounds he'd left and signed to Sera.

"G'Nor says that now he has tasted your blood. He will be watching you. He will know if you turn. And then he will kill you."

Enoch reached up with his hands and grasped the sides of G'Nor's jaws tightly. Sera could barely hear his whisper.

"Don't let me become like them. Please."

G'Nor pulled back and closed his mouth. He sat back on his haunches and regarded Enoch with surprise.

Sera bent over and helped Enoch to his feet. He couldn't look her in the eye.

"Okay, so G'Nor has decided to trust you, Shepherd Boy. Now . . . tell me what you saw."

Enoch, still avoiding her gaze, walked over to the outlet and placed his hand against it. He spoke, and his voice was in the detached monotone of his *pensa spada* trance.

"The man who is approaching the front lines of the coldmen, the man all of the blackspawn are bowing to, he . . . isn't a normal man. At first I thought he was some sort of monster, one of those Iron Ogres you hear about wandering the ice-fields of the North. He is covered in thick plates of armor, and is suspended from six massive steel legs—insect-like legs rooted in his back—"

Sera gasped.

"His back . . . ?"

"Exactly. As soon as I looked closer, looked *inside* of his construction, I could see the truth. He is an Alaphim, Sera, just like you. Only his wings have been replaced by these automated insect legs, and the armor around his form is fused to the metal in his bones. And Sera—he's *old.* The design of his frame, the weave of his metal, it is more primitive than yours. Even the metal itself is of a cruder substance, not the light ceramic alloy you have."

Why does it make me feel naked when he talks about me like that?

"But the legs, the armor—all of the unfamiliar elements that disguised his true nature from me—they are designed without the artistry of his inner structure. They are designed by the Serpent. Simple, rough, pragmatic; no thought towards beauty. Koatul's work. I've seen it in the coldmen weapons. I know it."

Enoch finally looked up at her, his eyes cold. "Why didn't you tell me your people served the Serpent?"

Sera held back the urge to shout.

Remember he's still just a boy. He doesn't know.

"Enoch, you need to know a little bit of history. Originally, my people were the Pensanden's greatest allies. And after the Schism, your kind deliberately ignored us; they were too worried about keeping their power and regaining control of the world. We had to find the most inaccessible places in the world—our Spires—to avoid the hatred that came from our association with you. A few of the Alaphim, a cursed few, were angry enough about the Pensanden abandonment to join the Vestigarchy. They were known as the Arkángels. We never knew what happened to them after the Hunt. Now . . . now I guess we can see that the Serpent kept them alive, or at least one of them. He must be very old. Centuries."

For some reason Enoch seemed unimpressed by that, but he was contrite as he turned back to the outlet.

"I'm sorry, Sera."

"That's okay, Enoch. Next time ask before accusing."

She could see him clenching up, holding back the pride and anger at her condescension. It was good that he was able to show this kind of control, but Sera couldn't help but enjoy his turmoil.

Shouting at me like that!

"So what is the Arkángel doing?"

Enoch tilted his head, curious.

"He is holding something. A . . . a metal staff. It's a machine. The circuitry is incredibly complicated, but it looks like some sort of antenna, something meant to broadcast a pattern . . ."

"He is walking forwards—he is coming within range of the cannons! Is he trying to die? I can see Father's Huntsmen bringing the front battery into position. The weapon is charging . . . He's raising his staff . . ."

Enoch went quiet. He brought his other hand up next to the outlet. The walls around them shuddered as the massive cannons fired. For some reason, even though she didn't know this Alaphim, Sera cried out. Her kind were so few. This suicide didn't make sense!

Did he see this as a way of escaping from Serpent's hold? Is the Arkángel atoning for his betrayal?

"Enoch? Enoch, what happened?"

"He's stopped right at the edge of the cannon range. Father sent a salvo into the earth in front of him, but the . . . the Arkángel seemed to know exactly how far he had to go. How would he know that?"

Sera shook her head.

Has the Serpent blessed him with Pensanden sight? It sounds like he is more machine than angel now. Did he willingly surrender himself for this power?

Enoch continued narrating as he watched.

"The Arkángel's staff . . . he has activated it. It's broadcasting the pattern now . . ." Enoch turned to look at Sera, "I don't know what he thinks that is going to do—I've changed the patterns on all of the cannons and entry gates to my own coded resonance. There's no way he can affect . . ." He turned back to his focus. And smiled.

"He's leaving now! He just gave a sign to the blackspawn armies behind him. They are departing as well! They're going!"

Sera couldn't believe it.

"Enoch, they wouldn't bring a force like that here and then allow a little artillery to frighten them off. They've got enough coldmen out there to swarm this place!"

Enoch turned to her triumphantly.

"No, Sera. They've seen what I've done here. They've realized that my cannons can hold that perimeter indefinitely, or at least as long as it would take them to expend their entire force. They're giving up!"

"Enoch," Sera said, her voice low, "the Vestigarchy doesn't give up. They've ruled over this broken world for centuries now. I'm sure your cannons are impressive, but—"

Enoch interrupted her with a laugh, extending his hand to the portal. With a groan of rusting metal, the wheeled handle began to twist open. Apparently the automatic functions were still intact.

"We better make our escape while my father is up celebrating with his men. My hours of 'concealment' in the Core Unit just turned into minutes."

G'Nor was already nosing the door open, and a wave of humid swamp air washed over them. He growled encouragement.

Sera waved off his urgency and turned back to Enoch. There were bigger concerns.

"Are you sure that they are leaving? Are you sure that we are safe going out now?"

Enoch, still unbearably sure of himself, smiled and motioned for her to exit with G'Nor. Mesha was already outside, and Sera wondered if the shadowcat would leave them now that it was home again.

"Just let me shut down my planned barrage of the northern swamps—it would just be wasted energy. The draconflies have already moved beyond range, are already past our own exit. You know, it was a good thing you showed up late after all!"

With a laugh he turned from Sera to put his hand on the outlet. Sera gave him a worried look and then followed G'Nor out the door.

The swamp spread out before them seemed so open, so *alive* after her long weeks in a cage. Gnarled trees grew up around the metal exit, and the ground in front of them sloped forwards a few feet before sinking into still, mottled water.

I think I'll ride on G'Nor's back for this part of the journey.

She snapped the distance ring down on her cheek mounts and looked into the gray morning sky. Sure enough, the retreating forms of black draconflies were spread across the horizon.

Is it possible that this shepherd Pensanden boy has done what scores of his own people never could? Has he driven the Vestigarchy away?

A cry came from the portal behind her, and she scrambled back through the opening. Enoch was horrified, staggering back away from the outlet.

"Enoch? Enoch! What is it?"

Enoch turned, his eyes angry and shocked.

"Are the blackspawn coming back? Should we go—"

Enoch stumbled, pushing her out of the portal, and then followed. He turned to close it.

"Enoch?"

He leaned into the heavy iron doorway, and Sera could hear the machinery inside tightening with a brutal strength. The border around the door began to glow with the heat of friction, and steam rose from the surrounding damp earth. There was a shriek of metal, and sparks flew from the hinges. Sera grabbed Enoch and spun him to face her.

"Enoch! What are you doing?"

Enoch avoided her eyes again, shook her hand from him, and trudged down the path and into the water. Mesha leapt up onto his shoulder, and he absently stroked her tail. He was heading north.

"I sealed the portal. It will never open again."

Sera gestured to G'Nor, and he lowered himself so she could clamber up onto his back. He signed to her, signed that he had heard screams from the tunnel just before the Pensanden had closed it.

Screams?

She looked back as G'Nor stepped into the water behind Enoch. The portal was solidly welded into place, the red metal cooling to black as steam wound around its form. As G'Nor moved nearer to Enoch, Sera could hear the boy mumbling to himself:

"The coffins. Entire rooms of those electric coffins, and I never looked inside them. Why didn't I check the coffins?"

Sera leaned down to place a gentle hand on Enoch's shoulder. He flinched.

"Enoch, what coffins? What did you see?"

He turned to look up at her, eyes wet and darkly wrought.

"Silverwitches. The Arkángel woke them with his staff. He brought his army here to keep our eyes focused on the walls, to keep our forces with their backs to the real danger."

Sera recognized the look. He was ashamed. He was ashamed at being wrong, ashamed at failing his father, but more than anything he was ashamed at having been outthought when he'd had weeks to perfect this plan. His voice broke into a whisper.

"Plata*bruja*s. Hundreds of them."

Enoch turned his attention back to his pace through the stagnant water in front of him, whispering the last part almost to himself.

"They will kill everybody."

Sera put her hand on G'Nor's shoulder, directed him to fall behind by a couple paces. The Pensanden Prince needed space to grieve. He had just lost his kingdom, his tower, his father, and his pride.

CHAPTER 20

The Hunt is over. You shall return to the West and take your place in the trenches with your brothers. Your thirst for blood is needed in another place now, in another form. But do not worry—it will always be needed.

—*Arkángel Desgarrar, to the new Hiveking*

The wind roared at this speed, and Mosk felt cold.

Cold? The blackspawn do not feel cold!

Mosk tightened his grip on the antennae, and the draconfly rumbled in protest. They were high in the air, higher than the creatures were meant to fly, and Mosk knew that if he didn't steer down into lower altitudes its breathing slits would freeze up. The draconfly would suffocate before challenging an order.

This is true of all blackspawn.

Except . . . except for the Hiveking.

He could still see the crowning, couldn't strike the image from his mind. Proximate Isk had been ready for the enzyme bath, the marks on his shoulder-plates and belly already changing from blue to purple. Two members of the serving caste had lifted Isk into the swirling depths of the bath while another perched above them, kneading the length of the Matriarch's swollen mesothorax. Dark green oozed from the moist glands at the tip of her abdomen and slopped into the freshly dug pit. Proximate Isk immersed himself in the fluids while the servants left to inform the Arkángel. The coldmen weren't much for ceremony.

Mosk had only spotted his Proximate being readied for kingship as he crossed the battleground to meet with Rendel.

To meet with Rendel and present my findings in Tenocht. And then to be pulled apart and fed to the maggots—the price a fallen Hiveking pays for failing his Lord . . .

So Mosk had left. He had watched Isk finish his bath, watched the newly purpled Hiveking emerge from the enzymes shiny, wet, and regal. Mosk had then turned and walked towards the draconfly grounds, mounted the largest beast he could find, and flown away. Nobody had tried to stop him. Nobody said anything. Blackspawn did not flee, did not fear, and certainly did not ignore their Lord's summons. Even to death.

But I am not blackspawn. Or, I am more *than blackspawn. Never has a Hiveking ruled for so many generations, overseen the end of so many Pensanden. Never has a Hiveking driven so many Hunts.*

The draconfly rumbled again, and Mosk could hear a rattle in the abdominal slits behind him. The creature was freezing.

It isn't cold that I feel. It's . . . ambition. I will not be content with death from a failure impossible to avoid. No Hiveking could have foreseen the path of this rogue Pensanden. Not even the Arkángel himself could have finished this Hunt better than I.

Mosk tilted the antennae downward and the draconfly gave a grateful hiss. It dipped its enormous head and began to descend through the milky layer of gray-white clouds beneath them. Babel was far enough behind them now, and Mosk suspected that Rendel would be more concerned with rooting the etherwalker out of his tower than he would be with dismembering a fallen Hiveking.

By the time Rendel learns of my departure, he will have learned that the Pensanden is gone as well. The true Hiveking does not visit a suspected enemy lair without leaving some ears, some subtle tek in the walls meant just to listen for the voice of his prey. Tek that will know when that voice has left—no matter how subtly, for when a Pensanden leaves a network, that network feels the loss.

Does Rendel not trust that my centuries on the hunt have taught me things invaluable to him? He sentenced me to death hours before I learned of the Pensanden's escape.

This is why he will be grateful for my escape, grateful for my disobedience. He will see that the rareness of my breeding, this ambition, is what has allowed me to understand what drives our quarry. Now it is obvious to me where the Pensanden Enoch is headed. His own ambition parallels my own, for his is going to mark a new direction for his species.

The draconfly broke through the clouds, and Mosk could taste something familiar in the damp air. The joints at his shoulders began to itch.

He is ambitious—dangerously so, this Pensanden Enoch. And I will kill him for it.

CHAPTER 21

A city of lights.
Then black, then dead.
Now all gray,
and so it goes.

—Fourth Stanza of the Lodoroi Song of the City

The Swampmen had been following them for days.

Well, not following, exactly. We are being herded.

Enoch turned and caught a glimpse of one of the mud-colored figures ducking behind a tree several yards away. He didn't know why they even tried to stay unseen anymore—Sera had called back to them this morning, asking for food or guidance or *anything*. There was no response.

Enoch, Sera, Mesha, and G'Nor moved through the still waters and low, stunted trees at a steady pace. When they stopped to rest, the Swampmen stopped too. The few dangerous creatures native to this area—hairless nerwolves and giant snakes—gave the little group a wide berth, probably due to G'Nor's size. The journey thus far had been monotonous and uneventful, but the constant presence of the armed natives behind them kept everyone on edge.

G'Nor had enough energy to hunt every evening, in spite of a long day's journey. The Swampmen gave him plenty of space to seek out his prey—as long as it was in a generally northward direction. It almost seemed as though their pursuers were less concerned with the Ur'lyn leaving, although G'Nor claimed he could scent three Swampmen on his trail perpetually whenever he left. He usually returned with one of the massive serpents native to this sodden land, unbelievably long creatures that wound through the waterways all around them as subtle ripples in the murky water. The creatures were muscular and splotched in intricate patterns of brown, green, and black—and they provided plenty of meat for the Ur'lyn and his lighter companions. It was stringy, and blandly flavored, but was sustenance that could be chewed on throughout their trek the following day. G'Nor claimed that the serpents were far too easy to hunt, especially once you learned to avoid the body and strike directly at the small, triangular head. When the group had departed this land, he said, he'd bring them some "true game" which "cost blood and thought" to bring down.

Enoch was able to use his boyish expertise to climb into the trees around them, looking for dry tinder (or "dry-ish," as Sera called it) to light a fire and cook their food. He used his time in the trees to scout around them as well, although he wasn't quite sure what he was looking for. North? Tenocht? Both concepts were equally general and unfamiliar to him.

Mesha, however, was thriving. She would disappear into the shadows for hours at a time, only to return with a small creature in her mouth, wet bristles in her variegated fur. Her warm, satisfied purr was a tangible comfort in this bog. She seemed to sense the direction the group was heading, often taking the lead in the procession and guiding them past unexpected sinkholes. Her reaction to the Swampmen had been curious—G'Nor signed "disloyal." She would flit back and forth between the two groups as they traveled, and spent time at each camp during the nights. Enoch was sure that their odd pursuers were feeding her, and he noticed that all of the burs had been combed from Mesha's fur after her latest visit. He wasn't sure how he felt about that but figured it couldn't hurt to have an ambassador.

G'Nor, who had scented their pursuers not long after leaving the tunnels, was growing increasingly upset. Here was an alpha predator who had barely gotten free from his cage, and now he was being hunted again. He turned occasionally to roar at the

Swampmen. They simply crouched in the moist shadows and waited for the group to move on.

Just yesterday, at G'Nor's impatient urging, the group had tried to scatter. Enoch had run left, and G'Nor carried Sera to the right. They didn't get ten paces before a rain of darts peppered the trees in front of them and on either side. Enoch remembered how the bark on the tree nearest him had quickly blackened where it was struck—Garronian poisons were renowned for their lethal speed. The message was simple: except for hunting forays, the group was to stay together. And it was to move forwards.

Well, at least we're moving north . . . Sera is right; we could never fight that many and survive.

Not that I haven't been looking for a way out of this.

Enoch wondered what these Swampmen were trying to do. It was hard to coordinate an escape when you were unsure of your captor's motives. According to G'Nor's signs, there were now three dozen Garronians in pursuit.

Enoch remembered the few Swampmen traders he had seen months ago on the road heading into Babel. They had seemed odd, somehow detached from the world around them. Rictus called them "loopy zealots" and had warned Enoch about talking religion with them unless he wanted a "dart beard." But the few Swampmen he had spotted since entering *this* place seemed to be of a different breed. Wilder.

They were tall and thin, with a shock of brown hair rolled into thick fingers of mud that hung in long, rigid lines down their pale skin. The Swampmen wove leaves and pale blue feathers into their hair in a pattern that seemed both meaningful and chaotic. Scattered across their cheeks and brows was an array of tattoos in green ink—images of natural objects such as leaves, snakes, insects, and rain. Clothing of scaled leather and woven reeds accentuated their scarecrow forms, and the liberal swatches of mud over everything seemed, Enoch thought, more deliberate than accidental.

And now there were Swampmen in front of them, too. G'Nor nodded towards a footprint slowly filling with brackish water, and

Enoch hummed in dour recognition. It was getting more and more difficult to imagine a way out of this trap.

Sera made a frustrated sound and leaned forward—she was trying to use her eye-lenses to see into the thick afternoon horizon. "How can anybody live in this mess? You can't see ten feet without a rotten tree getting in the way!"

G'Nor signed a quick response, and Sera groaned.

"I know, I know. Other senses. This is why Enoch's people *gave* you that big nose. The same reason they gave me wings. So that we could be happy doing what we did best—as long as it was entertaining to them."

Enoch ignored the jibe and started to lift himself into the tree in front of him. "We've come far enough today. I'll go get some kindling."

Nobody resisted Enoch's will on this, although both Sera and G'Nor would be confused if you asked them when Enoch had become the leader of this group. There was a pervasive feeling amongst them, an unspoken sensation that Enoch was at the center of these events as they unraveled. And Enoch hadn't noticed yet, but over the past few days his voice had taken on the commanding tones of Levi Gershom. They were tones that communicated decisiveness, will, and command. It was obvious that Sera couldn't return to the Roost with her injuries, and so she had decided to continue on with the group. And of course, G'Nor went where she did.

Sera climbed off of her steed's warm back, looking for a dry place to rest. She found a suitable spot between a small grove of twisted saproot trees, and began to clear away the brush. Enoch could tell that her wings were still bothering her, but she was trying to hide it. Everyone was tired, and everyone was nervous due to the constant presence of their pursuers. She looked up at him and gave a sad smile.

Wow, my heart still stops when she does that.

Enoch didn't know what it meant to have this sort of fascination with a girl. Their difference in ages didn't bother him—he didn't really have a mental destination for what it meant to feel this way. He knew that he felt kind of confused and a little clumsy when she was around, but he also knew that he didn't want to be apart from her.

Sure, he'd heard the kids at Rewn's Fork talking about girlfriends and boyfriends. He'd even seen a young couple kissing once—Master Gershom had caught him staring at them and had reprimanded him for "nosing around where a boy shouldn't nose." Enoch supposed there was something secret going on. It certainly wasn't a topic that his master would talk about. Growing up on a farm, Enoch had seen enough to know how sheep made other sheep. But that seemed entirely unrelated to kissing, and had nothing *at all* to do with what he felt when Sera smiled at him.

Sera had turned back to clearing their campsite for the night, and Enoch climbed higher up in the tree. He bent the branches as he went, testing them for dryness.

Or dry-ishness.

An entire limb of the tree had died some time ago, so Enoch busied himself collecting an armful of wood. This was a good sign—there was enough here to cook food *and* provide warmth through the night. Last night's dry wood had run out not too soon after darkness fell, and Enoch had woken up damp and shivering this morning. His bones ached, and he felt like he may be catching a cold.

And this persistent coat of mud provides surprisingly little insulation.

G'Nor had already lumbered off into the darkening woods ahead, and Enoch found himself hoping that the Ur'lyn would find something other than snake for dinner tonight. It had been the same thing for the last few days now, and Sera claimed that she was growing scales.

At the top of the tree, he took a moment to lean back against a branch and scan the horizon. The landscape was a drab green—hazy and unremarkable. Patches of complex trees were scattered across the murk, with roots and branches cobwebbing at top and bottom into an olive mist of leaves, moss, and unending water.

Even the sun seemed touched with a hint of beryl, but Enoch was unsure whether that was due to the moisture in the air or the constant stench of rot, which, he was convinced, had condensed over his eyes in a grimy film.

Arms full, he dropped down to the ground and made his way towards the clearing. Sera was using one of her metal feathers to dig a pit in the soil, scraping away the damp, mossy earth to provide a shallow home for the night's fire. She pulled back as Enoch approached and gave him another smile, raising the feather triumphantly.

"This is a pretty good spot, all things considered—the hole isn't filling with water."

Enoch couldn't help but laugh as he crouched down and started arranging the kindling. "We'll appreciate even the smallest victory, I guess."

Mesha had returned from her most recent foray with the Swampmen carrying a fish. The fish had been cleaned and deboned. Enoch called the shadowcat over and, with some struggle, took the fish from her mouth. He lifted it and admired the fine, pink flesh.

"This has gotten insulting."

Sera looked over and laughed. "Hey," she said, "I have no problem with our pursuers treating Mesha like royalty—as long as she is willing to share the spoils."

Mesha growled.

"My dear," Enoch said, "you shall get first choice of the snake G'Nor brings back tonight. This fish, however, is going to be enjoyed by your rescuer—" here he indicated himself, then looked over at Sera, "—and his friend. No more complaints."

Sera laughed again, that clear, wonderful sound that electrified Enoch and seemed to wash this entire swamp away in a few sweet tones. He gave the fish to her and returned to arranging the fire.

"Can an angel eat enemy fish delivered by a disloyal shadowcat?"

"Thanks, Shepherd Boy," she said, carefully removing a few

specks of dirt from the fish. "It will be nice to eat something that started out smaller than me."

Enoch smiled and stood, holding out his hand.

"Your lens, Milady?"

Sera sighed and reached up to remove the thick glass lens from one of her eye-rings. The lenses, and their thin brass framework, were usually folded up against her forehead when not in use. It made Enoch think of some crystalline tiara, and he liked how a lock of her blue hair hung over it like a slice of sky.

Sera held out her lower lip and blew the offending hair out of the way, then snapped the lens from the mount hidden in her eyebrow. "Here you go—just make sure you don't get fingerprints on it. It was never meant for such crude, stubby fingers."

Enoch sighed dramatically while taking the lens, then crouched over the damp fire pit to start the fire. Angling the lens to bring a bright point of sunlight down onto what, he hoped, was the driest portion of the kindling. He tried to respond casually with a matching taunt.

"Yeah, well . . . I'll make sure 'my people' create more *useful* Alaphim next time."

He chuckled at his own response, then leaned over to blow softly on the thin stream of gray smoke that began to curl from the wood. A pale flame flickered to life, and he gently took the burning stick and placed it in the space he'd arranged under the rest of the kindling. The flame grew and spread to the surrounding wood. He turned to give Sera her lens.

"We should find some herbs to season that fish—"

Sera was frowning, staring down into the flame. Her brows were furrowed, and she had made her hands into fists—trembling fists held so tightly that her knuckles grew white. Enoch's heart dropped.

"Sera? Sera, what's wrong?"

Sera turned away from him, brushing against his chest with her wing feathers.

"Sera?"

"Why did you say that?" she said.

"What? About the fish? I was joking about—"

"No, no. What you just said," she turned back to him, and her eyes were cold. "You said I wasn't complete."

Enoch thought back. "No, I didn't—I was joking about how useful your fragile lenses were in our situation. I didn't mean to say that *you* were—"

Sera interrupted him sharply. "I'm not finished, Enoch. None of the angels are. Lamech told me. Your people didn't finish us."

She raised an accusing finger at Enoch and scowled. "Tell me I'm wrong! I can see it in your eyes whenever you give me that 'Pensanden look.' You don't think I'm done. You don't think I'm right!"

Enoch didn't know what to do. She was telling the truth. The artistry of her form was missing something—Enoch couldn't tell exactly what, but he'd lately noticed an absence in her design that seemed at once subtle and obvious. Like a picture missing a frame. And it seemed *deliberate.* That is what had him so confused. He felt bad that she had noticed.

So soon out of Babel and already I am forgetting my Ferrocara?

"Sera, I . . ."

He was confused, and his face felt numb. Enoch didn't know if he should frown or scowl. He had hurt someone that he cared about when he had only meant to make her smile. And he didn't know how to talk with an angry girl.

It was obvious now that Sera had noticed his discomfiture, and she was struggling to regain her composure. She seemed embarrassed about her anger.

And probably for having been criticized by a "shepherd boy."

Enoch felt a flush of warmth rise up his face. He twisted around and stalked away from the fire, splashing swamp water over the little fire he'd just started.

* * * *

Enoch had no idea that a desert sat at the center of the swamps. A desert. It hadn't happened all at once, but the effect was surprising nonetheless—the stagnant ponds simply got shallower and then disappeared entirely. The thick greenery became sparse and stunted and then turned into a dry, thatched landscape where the swamp life struggled to survive. Then the thatch gave way to sand. A gray, drifting sand that glistened like glass and shadow.

Hadn't Master Gershom mentioned something about Garron—about the Gray Wastes? I can't remember, but he decided not to go. There was something valuable there . . . and something dangerous.

It appeared that the Swampmen had been guiding them towards this desert the entire time. They stopped at the edge, where the last trees stood, and began to sing. The sound was surprising after so many weeks of silent pursuit, and Enoch halted the group to listen. Mournful and lilting, it was singing that wove voices into the soft hiss of drifting sand. G'Nor perked up his ears and made a sign.

"He says it's a sad song. Sadness for the land that died here." Sera translated, then turned and looked at G'Nor. "You speak the Swamptongue?"

G'Nor shook his shaggy head and made a few quick signs.

Sera nodded. "Says he knows the sound of mourning, and that the tones match this broken land."

"Broken?" Enoch was confused.

G'Nor didn't elaborate.

The song ended, and the Swampmen solemnly raised their bows—a simple sign that the group had quickly learned: "Resting time is over." Turning, the three shared a glance and then walked into the dunes. After a few hundred steps, Enoch glanced back. He *paused* and whispered to Sera.

"They're not following."

Sera nodded.

"I think that once we are over the next dune and out of sight, we should cut to the side and try to make our way around . . ." Enoch *paused*. "No, they'd already be prepared for that . . ."

Sera nodded again. She reached down and picked up a handful of sand, then let it crumble through her fingers.

"I can't tell if we have just received an armed escort out of their holy land," she said, "or if we just took a shortcut to their sacrificial altar."

G'Nor rumbled.

"Regardless," said Enoch, "we wanted to go north, and we still are headed in that direction. What are a few gray sand dunes against a vicious gladiator beast, an intrepid angel, and . . ." Here he stopped, realizing for the first time that he really didn't know what he was. "And . . ."

Sera volunteered:

"And a lost shepherd boy?"

Enoch scowled, Sera smiled, and G'Nor rumbled his purred version of laughter. Enoch shook his head and laughed too. It felt good to be out from under the constant watch of their damp pursuers.

Even though we all have the feeling they may have pushed us into something much worse.

Enoch decided to call a halt to their short march, to enjoy the absence of the Swampmen and take stock of the situation. Sera and Enoch both carried leather water pouches, and G'Nor had a larger one strapped to the harness around his shoulders. The harness contained supplies that they had stolen away from Babel, several items that they hadn't unpacked during their watched march for fear the sentries would take them: a tightly rolled canvas tent from King Nyraud's stores, flatbread, venison, and dried fruit.

It would be enough to keep them alive for a week, perhaps more if they could supplement the menu with hunting. Enoch wasn't sure if G'Nor would be able to find anything edible—or killable—out here. This desert was unlike anything he'd imagined before: warm with moist winds coming from the swamplands surrounding them, and the sun was certainly hot without any shade . . . but it wasn't unbearable, either. The only thing that seemed to mark this as a desert was the sand. That, and the fact that nothing grew here.

It was more than a lack of vegetation, however—this place just felt lifeless. Enoch decided that the wisest course of action would be to move in towards the center of the desert for another two days to put more distance between their pursuers and themselves, and then consider any changes in the landscape to make a more informed decision about altering course . . . or not. For some reason that he could not explain, Enoch felt that continuing north was actually going to be the best decision.

It only took the group one more day before the landscape changed. And it was not good.

Of course it was Sera who saw them first—the odd, thin shapes clustered at the top of a colorless dune just a few miles north. At first she thought they were trees, which was encouraging to everybody: trees meant water. Enoch increased the group's pace, and there was a palpable sense of lifted spirits in the group.

After a few minutes, Sera gasped. "No!"

Enoch turned in alarm, almost knocking Mesha from her perch on his shoulder. Sera had gone pale, and she covered her mouth with a hand.

"What is it, Sera? Is there something under the trees?"

Sera twisted the focus rings with shaking fingers, biting down on her bottom lip.

"They're not trees. They . . . at first I thought they were, but they're too straight. Too regularly spaced. And there's something . . . something hanging from them." She went quiet, hands now still on G'Nor's back where she rode.

"Sera?" said Enoch, concern in his voice.

"It's people. Dead people."

Sera was quiet as they closed the distance, now at a much more cautious pace.

The shapes were now obviously not trees, but metal girders jutting from the sand like teeth from a comb—a row of evenly placed metal posts that lined what appeared to be a long, sand-blown road that ran straight through the dunes and into the distance. And hanging from the top of the girders were corpses. It was obvious as they climbed the last stretch of dune. Obvious in the thin, dangling shape of limbs that swayed in the light breeze.

G'Nor wrinkled his nose and raised a front paw to sign.

"He says they don't smell right," said Sera.

"Maybe the desert dried the smell from them, G'Nor? Because they sure *look* dead."

Enoch walked up to the nearest girder, noticing that the soft, deep sand under foot had grown shallow now. Only an inch or two, packed over what appeared to be corroded iron plates of the same alloy making up the girder. He let his eyes run up the length of the thick metal beam until he saw her. Impaled by a spike and left to bake in the desert sun was a dead woman.

Her skin was pulled tight to her skull, and was a dry, parchment brown. A few straggly locks of gray-brown hair hung over her face, which hung down over her bony, sunken chest. The spike had been driven through her chest, just between her collarbones, and it bent upward in a vulgar curve. It was forged of thick, black metal that seemed to radiate a punishing heat under the desert sun. The woman had been wearing a dress that now existed in brittle tatters, a floral pattern barely discernable over sun-faded brown. Her legs dangled underneath, nothing more than leather skin and bone, rattling in the hot breeze.

Enoch couldn't imagine why such a cruel and tortuous death could be considered just punishment by anybody, regardless of the crime. And if the sagging shapes attached to the line of girders, which disappeared into the horizon, were any indication, there had been hundreds of these victims. Staring up into the shadowed, withered face, he murmured to himself:

"I did not think the Swampmen capable of this . . ."

The corpse's eyes opened, and she grinned. Enoch leapt back, letting out a cry of terror. G'Nor snarled.

"Oh, they're quite capable of this sort of thing, young man. Quite capable indeed."

Enoch took another step backwards, looking over his shoulder to see if G'Nor—and Sera—had heard his yelp. He noticed that his swords were drawn and lowered them. Now that he was over his surprise, Enoch was angry at himself. He had seen a talking corpse before, and he knew where to look. The pulsing electrons of the micro-fission reactor at her chest, the bright molecular packets of nanotek tracing slender veins through her dry, husk veins. Enoch shook his head.

"A specter. Are you . . . can . . . can I help you down?"

The woman stared down at him, seemed to consider the offer.

Sera had climbed down from G'Nor's back and put a hand on Enoch's shoulder. "Enoch, I don't think it's wise to—"

"Don't worry, pretty angel, the boy's little stabbers can't cut through this nail. I've been tuggin' on it for two centuries now . . ." and here she made a grotesque face, straining against the spike. Its placement through her collar and shoulder blades meant that she couldn't raise her arms high enough to push against the thing, only flail her arms and legs in a pathetic mimicry of flight.

"Two hundred years. And I haven't slipped a centimeter." She tilted her head and bit down on a dry bottom lip. "Then again, if you wanted to climb up here and lift me off?"

Sera leaned in to Enoch's ear. "You told me about your specter friend, Enoch—but trust me when I tell you that not all post-mortems are as kind as the one you came across. Most of them are insane, wild, murderous . . ."

The dead woman's voice became plaintive, softer. "Please, boy. Please. I've been here so long. Please!"

She made another grotesque attempt at straining against the spike, and her grunt became a screech. The sound was loud enough to carry across the dunes, and Enoch could see thrashing movement along the girder lines for several hundred yards. More screeches, some cries for help, a long, plaintive howl.

"Listen to your feathered friend, kid. You climb up to help out Miss Starlet there, and she'll rip your arm off and suck everything out through the hole."

Enoch and Sera turned to see the girder behind the first one they had approached. Nailed to that post were the withered remains of a man—one leg, a bony pelvis, and a spine curving into the punctured rib-cage topped with a grinning, leathery skull. The only signs of life were the trembling tilt to the man's head and the steady, pulsing red beat of the machine fused to his spine. He nodded to Enoch. The woman continued screeching.

"When her tek began to fail and her looks went dry, she did

what a lot of the pretty ones did—went into hiding, tried to find another way to live. But for those of us who lived off of attention, lived off of recognition . . . solitude is the surest path to insanity.

"She didn't start killing children until, oh, about sixty years into her retirement. She held out longer than some. But her particular flavor of crazy involved drinking all the blood and soft parts from her victims."

The dead woman's screech turned into a cackle. She was grinning down at Enoch and ran a dry, wormlike tongue over her yellow teeth.

"It's the moisture!" she giggled. "It's the wet stuff that keeps you young and smooth."

Enoch was horrified. Without thinking, he pushed against the dead woman's LifeBeat—pushed and smashed the motion out of the wriggling nanites that coursed through her monstrous form.

The box hissed and went dark. The dead woman dropped her head and hung still.

Sera's hand tightened on Enoch's shoulder. "Enoch! Did you—?"

The dead man let out an airy gasp.

"A mindwrench! The kid's a mindwrench! Mercymercymercymercymercymercymercy . . ." And whatever faint lucidity the specter had shown was lost in a torrent of babbling. His one leg kicked against the girder with a thin, clattering sound. The word "mindwrench" echoed up the line, and the flailing grew more intense. Some of the ghouls were screaming now. Screaming, like this one, for mercy.

Enoch felt a heavy sorrow wash over him. He didn't want to do this. But he couldn't just leave them here, and setting them free would risk the lives of his friends. He reached up and took Mesha from his shoulders, then turned to hand her to Sera.

"I want you to take Mesha. Go back to G'Nor and follow me along this road. But . . . follow at a distance. I don't want you to see this."

Sera nodded, placing the shadowcat on her shoulders. She squeezed Enoch's hand and turned to go. She *paused.*

"I would walk with you, Enoch. You don't have to do this alone."

There was a low growl, and they both looked up to see that G'Nor was approaching.

Sera smiled. "He would come with us, too. He says we are a pack."

Enoch smiled grimly. He was grateful for their offer, but he didn't know how to tell them that he didn't want them to see this. He didn't have the energy to even try. This was going to be . . . hard.

He turned and looked up at the specter, wondering if there was anything to be said.

Sera read his thoughts. "Sometimes, the angels delivered eulogies at the passing of honored people. Would you like me to say something, Enoch?"

He nodded gratefully, eyes somber. Sera stepped up to the girder with the flailing, one-legged specter and raised a hand. Her voice was clear and carried in the thin desert air—and it sounded richer, more volumetric than anything Enoch had ever heard before. He realized that he was hearing the finely-tuned voice of a messenger Seraph, custom-crafted for its regal, momentous tones.

"We are here to mark the passing of this . . ." She pursed her lips in thought. "We are here to mark the passing of *these* poor souls who have been trapped in this wasted land for reasons we do not understand, and for a space of time beyond our comprehension. We are here to bring an end to their suffering."

She turned to look at Enoch, who appeared to be satisfied by her words. The specter above them had ceased his rattling movements, staring down at Sera intently. His sanity had returned, for a moment.

"You deliver a mercy many do not deserve, angel. I have railed against this iron for centuries, broken my arms and leg off into the sands below. I do not try for freedom, though. I try for death."

Enoch tried to take advantage of the dead man's clear mind for some answers.

"Why are you up there? Do the Swampmen hang all their

criminals on these iron trees?"

The specter trembled, tilting his head to the sky.

"The Swampmen, those eroded gene-whores, they only bring us to the desert. They only care to rid the earth of the post-mortems, those who rely on tiny robotics to survive rather than evolved flesh. It is a twisted continuation of an ancient argument between the two great transhuman schools. Sure, most of us whom you call specters have devolved into lunacy," and here he jerked his bony head towards the rows of girders trailing behind him, "but there are many of us here whose only crime was to try and live beyond our era."

Enoch narrowed his eyes.

"Then I won't kill you. Or any of those who are innocent here. Will you help me separate them from the rest?"

The specter's trembling grew more violent. His leg began to beat a slow march on the hot iron girder. Sanity was fading.

"Won't kill me? Won't kill me? But, but you promised mercy! You promised! There *are* no innocent here, boy. Liar boy. Nobody who has lived these long centuries is innocent!"

The specter was kicking faster now, and Enoch saw that his window for information was closing. He stepped closer to the girder.

"If the Swampmen only released you to the desert, then who put you up here? Who drove the nail through your chest? Who did this?"

"Oh, just follow the road and you'll see, liar boy. You will see how our payment is just and our jailer is fitting. Maybe maybe maybe he will have a nail saved for you? Maybe mercy maybe maybe maybemaybemaybe . . ."

Enoch stepped back and lowered his head. *I can't do this. He is twisted and crazy and sad, but he doesn't deserve to die.*

Sera's voice, now just her normal tone, came softly from behind him. "End his torture, Enoch. He has suffered too long."

"But why me? Why do *I* have to be the killer here?"

"Because you are their only hope for mercy. You are the only one who can end this."

Enoch's shoulders slumped, his head dipped even lower. There was a moment of quiet, of resignation. Then the specter gasped and went still. Enoch imagined that he heard a contented sigh as the ghoul's skull rolled back to rest, open-mouthed, against the girder.

"Let's go," said Enoch. "We have a road now and a purpose here."

Sera climbed on G'Nor's broad back, unfurling her one unbroken wing to cast a shadow over the trio. It made the heat more bearable, and travel was going to be slow. There was another specter up ahead, and he had seen what Enoch had done. Already they could hear his cries for mercy.

* * * *

The girders seemed to be part of some unfinished construction—a jagged frame thrusting up from the sand-strewn road for miles. Occasionally the sand drifted apart under the path in the ever-present breeze, and Sera could see deeper spaces under the girders—spaces filled with dark and massive machinery. This "road" was only part of some greater construction that wound throughout the heart of the desert. That was interesting but hard to focus on in the face of more dire concerns.

"If we keep going at this pace, we are going to run out of water in another few days," said Sera.

Enoch walked just ahead of her and G'Nor, at the edge of where her wing shadow could reach. Killing the mad specters for the past several hours was draining him, but he ignored her repeated requests to stop and rest. He had a look of numb determination on his face and would only *pause* in his steady trudging from girder to girder to take the occasional drink from his rapidly shrinking water skin.

G'Nor rumbled something to Sera, and she looked down to see his forepaw move through a series of signs.

"I know, my friend. He needs to stop. I am almost ready to get down and knock him over before he kills himself."

G'Nor exhaled, blowing sand from between his claws.

"No, I don't think you should knock him over. He might not get back up if you do it."

So they followed Enoch. It was long, miserable work. The girders were evenly placed about ten yards apart—just far enough to keep the specters out of conversation range, another cruel element of this torture—and some were vacant. Sera gave up trying to figure out the meaning behind it all. Some of the specters were wild, lost in their insanity and unable to make a coherent sound, just an unending babble of broken words. Some boasted of their crimes and threatened to do horrible things to Enoch once they were down. They spoke of vile deeds with some sense of nostalgic glee, as though their long lives gave them the right to bring horror, fear, and pain down on "the mortals."

Those seemed to be the easiest for Enoch, and he learned to push them dead as soon as they were in earshot. Harder were the ones who seemed genuine and decent, the ones who begged to be let down, who promised anything, everything to be set free. These ones Enoch spoke to, tried to find more answers about what had happened to them, and how they had ended up here. Again, stories differed. Some blamed the Swampmen, some blamed the devil, witches, ghosts . . . and some claimed to have nailed themselves to the girder to atone for their evil ways. No two stories were the same. There was no way to know which were liars, and so many had obviously perfected the art of doubletalk after centuries of practice.

So Enoch had no other choice but to offer them solitude or death. All of them chose death. No matter how incoherent, how insane—every specter had an animal longing to finally, at long last, die rather than hang in solitude. They left a trail of silent, windblown corpses behind them.

As night fell, and a cooling wind began to stir, Enoch staggered to a halt. Sera gasped to see dark lines running from his ears, down his neck, and staining his vest. It was blood. Dried blood.

"Water," he croaked, and Sera hurried from G'Nor's back to bring him her skin—his hung empty at his side. He lifted it to his lips and drank deeply, then held it back to her. "I think . . . I think I'll stop here."

With that, he collapsed to the ground and slept. Sera pulled him up against a silent girder and called G'Nor over to help her unpack the tent. They made camp there, among the dark, metal trees. The sand was warm enough to sleep comfortably, especially after days of soggy marsh, and neither felt safe lighting a fire. Enoch hadn't moved since they laid him between them, with G'Nor at the mouth of the tent. Even Mesha seemed to know that there was no hunting here—she curled up on Enoch's chest, her fur as gray as the sand, and scowled. Sera gave the shadowcat a piece of meat and then shared a dry meal with G'Nor as the stars came out.

"We can't hope to continue like this for much longer," she said, partly to herself and partly to the large beast breathing softly at her side. "Even if we had enough food, Enoch is killing himself."

She could see G'Nor's signed response silhouetted against the stars through the open tent flap. He told her that Enoch had found his vigil and must be allowed to see it through. Sera shook her head.

"People are not Ur'lyn. And Enoch is more than this. There is more to what he can do than killing these sad relics. And every begging, pleading specter that he kills takes something from him. I'm watching the light go out of his eyes."

G'Nor thought for a while, then exhaled with a growl. His forepaw made three simple movements.

"No," said Sera. "I don't believe he was born to kill. He has a different destiny than that."

And with that, she laid her head back against Enoch's shoulder. Mesha sniffed at her hair and then turned over, preferring to sleep away from the interloper. Soon the slow, easy sounds of slumber were all that could be heard.

CHAPTER 22

The glory of the world is in the patterns, in music and war and love.
Thus music, and war, and love combine in a pattern that glorifies all of the world.

—*Pensanden chiasmus*

Enoch awoke to Sera's gentle nudging. His head still ached from the dark, heavy work of the day before, but a night of deep sleep had helped. He sat up and rubbed at his eyes, then gratefully took the skin of water Sera offered him. The sun was already up and gently warming the eastern side of the tent.

"G'Nor left at dawn," said Sera, nodding towards the open front of the tent.

Enoch felt stupid for not having noticed the absence of the giant predator, but he decided to forgive himself a little fogginess after a day spent killing specters.

Sera's voice had a softness in it, a concern that he'd never heard before. She leaned over and brushed something off the side of his neck in a way that Enoch imagined could be considered "motherly." Enoch was comforted by the gesture, but he found himself wondering if he really wanted her to feel *that* way towards him.

"He signed that he scented water—that we need water if we are going to continue like this." Here she took a small swig from the skin, barely a mouthful, before pushing the stopper back in and swinging the bag around her back. Enoch just nodded, still feeling cloudy-headed and strangely distant.

Wake up. Focus. Another day of killing.

He rubbed his eyes again and crawled from the tent, then helped Sera fold it up into a portable size. Without G'Nor here, he would have to carry the canvas packet. It wasn't that heavy, but he knew that over time the walking and direct sunlight would make the weight oppressive. Luckily one of the straps that bound the tent could be slung over his shoulder, allowing Enoch to carry it like a satchel. He adjusted the strap so that it rested snugly against his vest and turned to face the path.

The nearest girders were empty, stretching on up the ridged dune in front of them. There was an odd randomness in the placement of the specters, sometimes heavily clumped in row after row, and sometimes spaced apart. Enoch realized that this was why he had stopped last night—his mind had been searching for a pattern in the placement of the impaled creatures and had determined—correctly—that this would be a good empty stretch. Enoch peered into his *afila nubla* and found the pattern: the bodies were placed in a representation of the mathematical constant *pi*. The impaled group counted as a number, and the empty girders represented every other number. So the first three girders had been occupied, then one left empty, then four occupied, then another empty, then five occupied—3.1415 and so on. Yesterday had ended on a long stretch of nine corpses and finished with what appeared to be a comfortable space of seven naked girders. With the even, syncopated spacing of these sand-brushed steel teeth, that meant that the night had passed beyond the shouting distance of whichever specter awaited them over the top of the dune. And, if this pattern held true, it would be a single occupied girder followed by another empty set of six.

Let's just hope that whatever circularly-obsessed madman has created this pattern is willing to stop at the 40th decimal place. I've got a few nines on the road to 50 . . .

"You're . . . smiling?"

Sera had come up beside him while he was lost in thought, and her face held an expression halfway between amused and worried.

Enoch blinked his eyes and blushed. *Was I really smiling about pi?*

Sera walked around to face Enoch, placing her hands on his shoulders. The amusement was now entirely replaced by concern.

"Enoch?"

"Oh, it's nothing, I . . . I just found this pattern in the specters and—" He looked down at his feet, unsure of how to describe this. He shrugged and ran a hand through his hair—releasing a surprising cascade of sand that seemed to be timed perfectly with an errant gust of wind. Sera took a step back, sputtering, wings spread in alarm. It was too much for Enoch—he started laughing.

Sera blinked the sand out of her eyes. Enoch tried to cover his mouth, but after a moment she joined in laughing. Enoch imagined that it was the first time that such sounds had echoed off these gray dunes in centuries.

The laughing angel brushed a tear from her eye, and Enoch had a worried thought about water conservation. This only generated further paroxysms of laughter that left him winded.

Sera finished before him and tried to pull a serious face. "Ok, ok. If we're done laughing, it might be smart to put our minds towards surviving this trek through the desert."

Enoch tried to stifle the last few giggles that bubbled up from his chest.

"I'm sorry," he gasped, the words trailing up as he fought to gain control of himself. "I . . . I just . . . it just feels so good to laugh."

She nodded.

"Of course it does. Things have been pretty grim for a while—it's nice to remember that we are still kids." She brushed some of the sand off of his vest. "I mean, it's nice to remember that *you're* still a kid."

He smiled, noticing that this conversation was the first one in a while that he'd had with Sera where he didn't feel awkward. *Maybe we are really starting to become friends now. Maybe I don't have to worry about whether or not she likes me.*

Sera, as though guessing his thoughts, smiled and shrugged,

stretching her one functional wing to its full extent. Enoch found the gesture to be incredibly charming and expressive. Not wanting to ruin the moment, he tightened his lips into a pragmatic line and turned to survey the road ahead.

"As I was saying before you started acting *childish*, there is a pattern at work here. Whoever is responsible for placing the specters here is doing so in a numbered sequence, a mathematical constant that represents the ratio of a circle's circumference to its diameter."

He looked up to see Sera rolling her eyes.

"Are you really trying to explain simple geometry to an angel? To someone who has been tailored with an innate sense of shape, distance, and perspective?"

Enoch was blushing. Luckily, Sera took pity on him.

"But no, I didn't catch the pattern."

Not sure what to think about that, he decided to plow on ahead.

"It means that whatever mind is behind this corpse path is one familiar with numbers. With patterns. It's a mind I can figure out—maybe a mind I can defeat."

"Well," said Sera, "you may have some idea of how the mind works, but you have no idea what kind of fangs, claws, and muscle lays at its command." She pointed up the road. "We should probably get moving and trust that *our* fangs, claws, and muscle get back from their hunting trip before we find out."

Enoch nodded and started taking down the tent. Mesha hissed and tumbled out of the collapsed canvas, furious to have her morning nap interrupted. Enoch just smiled and lifted her onto his shoulder, immediately regretting the decision as she shared her opinion of him with slowly retracting claws. Satisfied at his wincing and sharp intake of breath, she gave a short sigh and curled around his neck like a furry scarf.

"At least we've got our backup claws with us until then."

* * * *

The numbers proved to be true. The pattern continued in sequence, and the happy sense of discovery began to be replaced with a feeling of foreboding. It is one thing to deal with cold numbers—another thing entirely when the numbers are raving souls hung in the desert sun by some mad design. Enoch and Sera's cheer soon dwindled and evaporated with the heat. G'Nor did not return. The water disappeared quickly.

And then they found Rictus.

He was at the tail end of the line of nine completing the 50th place of the sequence. Enoch had stopped looking too closely at the specters since it made his task more difficult—especially when dealing with the quiet ones. Rictus was quiet. It wasn't Sera's hand on his shoulder that caused him to look up; it was her sharp intake of breath.

"What . . . is this one *doing*?"

Rictus had his bare face lifted to the sun, arms spread and legs hanging limp and motionless. The specter's toothy mouth was open, his back arched, and he appeared to be frozen in the final gasp of a lightning strike victim.

At first Enoch feared that he might have already pushed the specter, his mind dazed from the sun, thirst, and a morning of killing the dead. He stumbled towards the base of the pillar and banged the side of his fist against the hot metal. "Rictus, no."

Sera gasped. "Enoch? Is this . . . ?"

But then Rictus's right arm windmilled around in an arc and rested against the spike protruding from the center of his chest. Sera let out a cry of surprise.

Enoch looked up. "Rictus?"

The specter's fingers were moving now. They were sliding through an odd sequence of straight and curled gestures, rhythmically—a rhythm that his head began to nod to as well.

Enoch took a step back. Still nodding his head, Rictus opened his eyes and windmilled his arm around again.

"Ok, that was the longest air guitar solo of my life. Little help, Shepherd Boy?"

* * * *

The hole in Rictus's chest had already begun to close by the time Enoch and Sera got him to his feet, the nanites from his LifeBeat working furiously to fix the previously irreparable damage with an intensity that turned the visible metal cables running through his ribcage bright red with expended heat. Enoch tried to fill Rictus in on all that had transpired since that horrible battle under Babel, his time with the King, and the discovery of G'Nor and Sera. They wept over the loss of Cal and were silent for a long while after Enoch had finished.

Sera was silent during the reunion, kindly recognizing that the two friends needed time to unwind their grief and sudden, unexpected joy at finding each other again. Kindness aside, Enoch noticed that she kept staring at Rictus' wound, seemingly fascinated by the odd motion of rippling, steaming flesh that writhed across the specter's chest.

Rictus finally noticed the angel's focus on the puckering wound as well and pointed at Enoch with a frown.

"Your new friend here should know that it's not polite to stare at a gentleman's sucking chest wound."

Sera blushed and looked away.

Rictus chuckled and held up his hand to the angel. "Enoch will tell you that my sense of shame rotted away years ago, miss. Not too long after I lost my ears, if memory serves."

She bit her lip and shook his hand with an apologetic nod. Enoch thought it was brave of her to shake hands with one of the raving ghouls they had just spent long hours destroying.

"You've never seen nanotech biomolding at work?" said Rictus. "I assumed the angels would know about this sort of thing. Your kin should have pretty extensive records of it all—should be the few remaining folk around who couldn't be surprised by remnant tech."

Sera frowned. "Most of our archives were destroyed when Koatul cut down the Spires. We've been trying to recover what we can ever since, but . . ." She fluttered her hands in frustration. "There is not much left that has not already been destroyed or corrupted. Any recovered disks must be blessed through a dozen cleansing ceremonies, and our Windroost only has one aging librarian.

"But no, I haven't seen nanotech like this. Your kind have grown scarce since years before I was born. That's what the elders say."

Rictus looked beyond Sera, nodded towards the path of now-quiet pillars that disappeared into the distance. "I had always assumed that it was just the expired warranties, well, that and the gradual descent into suicidal madness. But when I saw what has been done here, how many of us have been hung out to dry here . . ." He turned to Enoch, teeth gritted.

Mesha tightened her grip around his neck, sensing Rictus's anger.

"I think I've found my purpose, etherwalker. I know what you have been doing along this path, and I know it was a mercy. There is no *saving* my kind. But I can return a little vengeance on those who have caused this anguish."

Enoch heard something new in his friend's voice. *Resolve?*

"Who, Rictus? Who put you up here?"

"The Swampmen?" said Sera, frowning.

Rictus chuckled. "Oh no. Those soggy zealots couldn't hold me captive for long—their poisons are less than effective against my nano." He pinched the parchment skin on his cheek.

"They ambushed me during a particularly moving ballad, which is unforgivable. It cost them four nets, seven arms, and a pair of lives before depositing me on the sand."

He *paused* to adjust his leather jacket, clucking his tongue as he emptied sand from the pockets. Enoch knew that Rictus was just drawing the tale out and rolled his eyes.

Sera raised an eyebrow. "So how did you—"

"Lose my guitar?" Rictus interrupted, frowning. "Swampmen took it. Dropped it in the damn swamp. That's when I stopped lopping off arms and started *really* hurting them. They were able to get enough lassos around me to take my sword, too."

The angel realized she was being toyed with and decided to let it slide. Enoch liked that about her.

She raised a finger, then sighed and lowered it. "So once you arrived in the desert, you noticed all your skinny friends were hanging from iron posts and decided to hop up and join them?"

Rictus smiled and gave Enoch a lidless wink, a gesture the specter had mastered which involved an interesting choreography of brow and cheek muscles.

"No ma'am. I was brought here by Váli."

It was an odd, foreign-sounding name, like something from a dead language.

Sera just smiled and nodded. Waited.

She can be patient through one of Rictus's jokes. I like that.

Rictus cleared his throat, realizing that the game was over. Which was good because Enoch had been through some of the hardest days of his life. His head hurt and he was thirsty. As happy as he was to see his friend alive—or at least mostly alive—this wasn't the best time for light talk.

"At least, the Swampmen call him Váli. They've got this thing for old Germanic names—something from before the machine times. The Germans thought their gods were messed-up whack jobs who could be selfish and lusty and violent. Not the perfect, loving gods we dreamed up afterward. The Swampmen feel like it was the all-powerful tek gods—your folks, Enoch—who ruined things. In fact, that and your friend's pretty wings may be why they decided to bring you here for sacrifice rather than just killing you outright for crossing their sacred lands. Their hatred is like a holdout from the bad, old neo-luddite days after the Schism."

Rictus tapped at the box at his chest.

"You're lucky you didn't have one of these. Anybody more . . . closely tied to tek from the fallen gods—say, someone kept alive by microscopic robots weaving organic polymers into their dying flesh—is given to Váli. He lives at the center of the desert, but he travels the Path of Agony whenever a new specter is delivered. I was his most recent 'gift.'

"Váli is a monster. That word doesn't have as much meaning as it used to, back in my day. But even in a world thick with witches and manticores, he is terrifying. Váli is . . . something that the Swampmen revere. He is the sum total of all that they hold most sacred. Biology without restraint. Strength without steel.

"And," said Rictus, "I am going to kill him."

He pointed towards Enoch's swords, ignoring the stunned look on his friend's face.

"Are you using those?"

Enoch blinked and then reached around his side to unhitch his *derech*. It was nowhere near as long as Rictus's massive blade, but it was at least a more similar weapon than the curving *iskeyar*. Rictus took the sheathed short sword—it almost looked like a dagger in his long fingers—and strapped the scabbard around his bony hips.

"Yeah, keep the bendy one," he said, grumbling. "I'm half-tempted to march back to that stinking swamp and root around for Caroline."

"Caroline?" Sera asked, now utterly lost. "Your guitar?"

"No, no, no, no. Caroline is no name for a guitar, silly. Caroline was my sword."

Rictus exhaled breathily, eyes closed.

"My guitar was named Tess. And I *am* going back to get her after I cut Váli into little pieces. The swampfolk will leave me be if I'm wearing their god's ears as a new pair of boots."

Enoch knew that Rictus couldn't be turned once he was in a mood like this one. But he knew that Sera would probably try. The angel was trying to instill some order on the situation.

"I know that you're angry, but . . . but if this monster has been able to capture hundreds of other specters—"

"One hundred and twenty-nine," interrupted Enoch. "One hundred and twenty-nine other specters."

She rolled her eyes and continued. "—if this monster has been able to capture so many other specters, what makes you think you can kill it? The Swampmen think this 'Vah-Lee' is a god for a reason, Rictus. Besides, we are out of water and Enoch's ears are bleeding from snuffing out all of . . ." Here she trailed off, apparently unsure if this would be offensive to Rictus.

The specter just waved his hand. "Don't worry about it. He

was doing them all a favor. Truth is, another few weeks up there and I would have lost it as well."

Enoch looked up at Rictus. "How many more? How many more are there?"

Rictus shrugged. "Pretty sure I was the most recent addition. You see any more behind me?"

They all turned to see. Nothing but empty girders climbing the dune behind him.

Enoch blinked his eyes. "You . . . you're right. There should be a sequence of eight following Rictus here. The pattern is . . . is ended." His mind had begun to ache just thinking of that circular sequence again. He tried to shrug it off but found his stomach rising at the thought of that endless, unrepeating pattern . . .

"Good thing, too," said Rictus, interrupting the thought. "You should see how the Path of Anguish responds to a new tenant. The girders all shake, lift into the air, and grind sideways back and forth across the path. All the specters start screaming—pretty disturbing stuff, even for the undead."

Enoch had been so relieved about his vigil coming to an end that he almost missed what Rictus said.

"They what? The girders move? I thought they were anchored below the sand."

The specter rolled his eyes. "I forget that this must all seem so meaningless to you primitives. Yes, Enoch, they move. The girders you see were once part of a complex transport system. The hooks me and my brethren decorated are just the broken ends of a glorified conveyor belt. Its original purpose was to deliver materials to the factories and silos that used to honeycomb this place."

Enoch couldn't believe what Rictus was saying. He had been using his ability to kill specters all along this path—never once had he sensed any machinery beyond their synthetically beating hearts.

Rictus grabbed the boy's hand and placed it on the warm metal girder behind them. Mesha leaped to the ground and began sniffing at the base.

"Follow the girder to its roots, kid. And then follow those

even deeper."

Enoch closed his eyes and looked. Yes, the girder was nothing more than simple metal . . . but . . . following the static lines of the steel shaft deep into the sand, Enoch saw a simple machined joint—a spring-bearing elbow. And then a piston supporting the elbow. And then a linked panel, and another, and another layered over each other like the scales on a serpent's back all the way back to the root of the following girder. The girders were like spikes along a flexible spine of metal, and yes, there was a trickle of electricity thrumming through all of it.

He should have noticed. This was something easily within his range, something that now seemed obvious to him. *Why didn't I see this?* Now that he was focused, he could see that this entire path was part of some gargantuan mechanical system. All buried beneath his feet. Enoch's mind was already sore from his grim work during the past few days, but he could sense greater systems at work even deeper in the darkness below the sand. Massive shapes, shifting silently. Tirelessly.

Enoch stumbled, falling back into Rictus's arms. Fresh blood dribbled warm from his ears. He wiped at his burning eyes, and his hand came away red.

"It's . . . it's moving down there."

Sera put her hand on his shoulder. She turned to Rictus. "What does he mean, *moving*? Where are we? What kind of desert is this?"

Mesha hissed.

"This desert is a stain that your kind left on my home," came an unnaturally loud voice from the dune above them, "when your bombs burnt this green land to glass."

They all turned at the sound. Váli had arrived.

A misshapen shadow loomed over dune behind them. Váli was three times as tall as the specter and thickly built. His shape was roughly humanoid but dense and twisted in a way which seemed oddly powerful to Enoch's blurred vision. The words *"barely contained"* came to his mind, and he wasn't sure why.

Váli's heavy form *writhed* with trembling, muscular tension.

His skin—pink, red, and webbed with pale scars—bulged and rippled as though schools of fish fought through a current beneath his flesh. His knotted limbs trembled and shook—not with any sort of palsied weakness, but with the potent energy of a spring pressed to its limit. Enoch realized, with revulsion, that Váli was unclothed: what he had assumed to be some sort of leathery tunic was actually the creature's twisted flesh flowing slowly across his giant frame. It was hard to make out any surface details on that viscous landscape, but Enoch thought he saw wetness gleaming from the crevasses between the waves of muscle. Eyes, mouths, and sinuous tongues slid in and out of folds.

Every inch of the monster moved and winked and licked and quivered. Váli spoke from several mouths, but the large, crooked grin on his face remained shut. Enoch saw bits of flesh stuck between jagged teeth and surmised that this one, largest mouth was probably reserved for eating. The two "original" eyes above this smiling maw were mismatched in both size and color, and they rolled inside their orbits in tandem with the smaller eyes scattered around Váli's body. He took another step closer, and Rictus raised his blade higher.

Mesha hissed again and backed up against Enoch's leg, nudging him to flee. Rictus unsheathed Enoch's blade and pointed it at Váli.

"Your brain has been baking in the sun for one century too many, pal. This 'green land' was honeycombed with missiles, chem-bombs, and worse—enough hardware to fry the planet to a crisp, as you may recall. All because your shortsighted ancestors wanted to beat the rest of the world to digital checkmate, no matter the cost. Nuking your warmongering patch of the Old World was the smartest thing the etherwalkers ever did."

The creature stopped and turned to regard Rictus.

"You are much more talkative than the last time I harvested you, specter. Has the *Pensanden* freed your tongue?" He spat the word "Pensanden."

"I was here when their fire sealed this place, abomination," said Váli. "I was deep beneath, but I could still feel the heat. My flesh boiled while everyone around me died. I watched them. I fed on their roasted bodies as I dug free." Váli's voice was moist and seemed to come from a dozen throats.

Rictus laughed. "It has been a while since I've faced something older than *me.* Even longer since I faced something uglier. And I'll bet it's been a while since you've come up against an armed specter who was sane enough to face you head on, Váli."

The monster stopped and seemed to consider what Rictus was saying.

The specter bowed. "I look forward to reminding you of what pain feels like. And then introducing you to death. You're due."

With his free hand, Rictus gently pushed Enoch back, gesturing for him to take Sera and go. Enoch wanted to resist, but he was in no state to fight. He fumbled for his *iskeyar*, but couldn't seem to unsheathe it while his hands were so sticky with blood. His head still ached.

Why am I so powerless? Something to do with the girders . . . the specters . . . the circular pattern . . .

Enoch gasped as another wracking pain cut through his brain. Sera gripped onto his arm tightly and started to pull him away. Mesha hopped from his shoulder and backed away, hissing at the thing at the top of the dune.

Váli opened his large, grinning mouth, and three tongues slid across his lips, across the top, the bottom, and his teeth.

"You are welcome to try, specter." Váli's voice was like the rumblings of a crowd of people—men, women, children—all speaking in cold, careful tones. All speaking hungrily. Dangerously. "The mudfolk have brought me countless offerings, as I have instructed them to since the Pensanden first burnt my homeland. You are not the first, nor shall you be the last to try and break my atoning round."

Enoch's aching head cleared for a moment, and he pulled back, resisting Sera's hands.

"Atoning round?" he called out, voice breaking. His head pounded. "You mean the circular constant that you coded into the path? Is there some other reason for the pattern?"

Rictus scowled and moved towards the monster. "Get out of here, kid. Stop asking your damn questions and go."

Váli snapped his maw shut with a clacking sound, exhaling from several mouths with a sound that could have been laughter.

"There are meanings within every ritual sacrifice, *Pensanden*." Váli turned the word into a curse, and his attention was heavy on Enoch. "Some meanings add depth and power to what is given at the altar . . ."

He took a step towards the boy. Rictus tensed.

". . . and some meanings merely to distract. To draw attention."

The hatred in Váli's voice was a physical force, ancient and chilling. Enoch imagined the long centuries of anguish, of singular, driving anger. Hatred was the black energy that roared through this monster's quivering flesh, the poisonous blood which had sustained it for days without end. And that hatred was focused with dire precision on the Pensanden boy standing in the sand before him.

To distract? Is that why I didn't notice the machinery under the—

Váli lurched towards Rictus, sweeping a heavy arm around to crush the specter into the ground. Somehow, unbelievably, Rictus was prepared for the attack, and he ducked under the arm with a smooth swing of Enoch's sword. Blood sprayed across the sand, and the monster gasped from its mouths. Apparently Rictus was right—it had been a long time since Váli's blood had been spilled.

Spinning to place himself between Váli and his friends, Rictus hissed, "Stop trying to talk with the crazy radioactive man, Enoch."

Váli whipped around with another arm—an arm that seemed to have grown yellow, bony claws. This was faster than Rictus had expected, and the specter's rolling dodge only barely avoided a blow that ripped into the sand next to him. He came to his feet and charged the monster in a daring *flèche* that surprised even Enoch with its speed.

The muscles at Váli's chest pulsed and then burst apart as a thick, muscled tentacle shot forward to wrap around Rictus's sword arm and slam him down into the sand. Rictus struggled to his feet and tilted his wrist down to slice clean through the new tentacle—he had fought Váli unarmed before, and the veteran swordsman had been planning for this. Váli grunted and took a step back. The tentacle writhed on the ground, and Rictus kicked it at its owner with a laugh.

"Got any more of those, Beautiful? I can stand here all day, cutting 'em off as fast as you squirt 'em at me—can't wrap me up so easy now, can ya?"

Váli pulled the severed limb into his largest mouth and took another step back, devouring his own flesh while another tongue licked at his bleeding stump. The monster settled back into the sand, and Enoch wondered if it had given up. A dozen smiles flashed across Váli's chest. Rictus raised his other hand and beckoned for Váli to attack.

The sand exploded at Rictus's feet, and two more tentacles wound around his legs. Váli had sent them snaking through the sand underneath the specter's feet and was now pulling him down. Rictus stabbed into the ground around him as he sank, filling the air around him with sand as he struggled in vain to cut his bonds. Again, Váli laughed the landslide laughter of a crowd.

Enoch cried out, shook free from his lethargy and drew his sword. He pushed Sera aside and ran towards his slowly sinking friend.

"Enoch!" she cried. "Stay back! We need to keep clear of his—"

Another wave of tentacles burst from the sand at Enoch's feet, wrapping around the boy. He fell to the ground, sword tumbling. Mesha pounced on the tentacles in a hissing assault of claws and teeth that blooded them but was ultimately futile. One of the tentacles snapped at her, cracking like a whip, and she tumbled across the sand and was still. Enoch cried out and reached for the shadowcat, but he was pulled through the sand towards Váli.

Sera turned to run in a panic to get clear of those tentacles. The sand was already stirring at her feet, powerful undulations almost causing her to lose her balance. She spread her broken wings with a cry of pain, flapping them once, twice. For a second, she was free of the flailing tentacles, but then her right wing collapsed and she fell into the monster's waiting embrace. Like Rictus and Enoch, she was pulled into the sand, her arms, legs, and wings pinned painfully tight inside the crushing grip of the muscular limbs.

Enoch watched Sera's failed flight with impotent horror and lifted his head to see the captor. Váli had lost any similarity to a human form. A dozen limbs sprouted from his torso, limbs which bent with a writhing, serpentine strength as they pulled a struggling Rictus, Enoch, and Sera out of the sand and towards him. The limbs were absorbed back into Váli's frame as they pulled, and Enoch could feel the flesh wrapped around his arms trembling with strange biological heat as the creature consumed itself. He could tell that the explosive transformation had cost the creature a significant amount of energy—the tentacle flesh had grown hotter still, and Váli dragged them all more slowly across the sand. Several of his mouths were panting.

"He's weaker!" Enoch shouted. "Rictus, see if you can't break free!"

Rictus turned his head to respond, but another tentacle slid around his neck and tightened like a noose. Váli smiled from his eating mouth, and a flotilla of tongues clicked at him disapprovingly.

"You think I would expend myself like this unless it guaranteed a checkmate, little Pensanden? I had this encounter calculated and won before you even drew your sword."

That was when Enoch understood. This monster, it thought like he did; it knew his mental abilities well enough to trap him and drain his flagging energies with a meaningless, infinite pattern. Váli had been trained—built? bred?—to think like a Pensanden. It was a monster, all right. *A monster like me.*

Enoch shouted, trying to find some meaning in this chaos.

"You . . . you are an etherwalker? You are what I will become?"

The smile on Váli's mouth grew wide and then literally cracked through the sides of Váli's face—around to where his ears would have been, had he been human—and transformed the creature's head into a gaping maw. New teeth pushed through the freshly bloodied gums—teeth more edged and carnivorous than those at the front. Váli meant to feed.

Rictus was closest, and the tentacles around the specter bulged and then lifted him into the air above the maw. The monster turned its eyes on Enoch.

"You think your Mesoamerican godfathers were the only ones playing with organic computers and human wetware? They were just the lucky first out of the gate, boy. The first ones to grab hold of the net and shake off those behind them."

He released the uppermost length of the tentacle holding Rictus, and the specter's sword arm was free. Rictus tried to double over and slash at the tentacles binding his legs, but Váli was too quick—with a hiss, he lunged and bit into his victim's shoulder. The specter's sword dropped to the sand as bones crunched under spade-like teeth. Rictus flailed against the monster, digging his fingers into the venous flesh of Váli's lips and pulling away bloody handfuls of flesh. It was a painful, if fruitless, gesture—the creature moaned from his mouths and then took another bite, severing Rictus's pelvis and legs from his torso. The specter now hung, spine and withered entrails dangling above the chewing maw, silently clawing at the bleeding flesh around the creature's mouth. This actually turned Váli's moan into a scream, and like that Rictus was stuffed into his mouth. Trembling tentacles moved to put oddly delicate pressure on the bleeding, wounded lips, and the rhythmic sound of crunching, snapping bones filled the dry air. Váli's voice, now smoldering with pain and rage, echoed from the unengaged mouths.

"I'll credit your specter friend—I've not been bloodied in a century. His reward will be to slowly digest in a stomach I've grown just for specters—a stomach filled with a thick bile that suspends his nanites in mucus so the acid can do its work. I've made sure to swallow his skull intact so he can witness his own dissolution."

Váli now began to pull Enoch towards him. Even though he

knew it was useless, the boy continued to struggle against the tentacles. He could hear Sera struggling as well as she was dragged beside him. He turned his head, tried to see if he couldn't help . . . *somehow.*

"Sera! I can't—"

She was staring at him, face steady, mouthing two words over and over. Enoch couldn't make sense of what she was saying. He shook his head, confused.

Sera whispered, not wanting Váli to hear. It was a barely audible hiss over the rasping of the sand.

"Suspend. Nanites."

Suspend nanites? Isn't that what Váli is doing to Rictus?

"Sera," Enoch whispered back. "What do you mean? You want me to *help*—?"

But Váli was now lifting him into the air, drawing Enoch to a mouth still spotted with Rictus's remains.

"Don't worry, I will only bite off your limbs—nothing vital. Like your specter friend, I can help you suffer for ages—nearly as long as him, in fact. I'll have to connect you to my circulatory system so that you don't bleed to death every time I peel the skin from your body."

Sera spoke from the sand underneath him now, her voice strained. "You . . . you're just a *troll.* A freak tumor of uncontrolled cancer cells. You were made to match the Pensanden. But you'll never be more than an ugly shadow. A shadow smart enough to understand what he can never be!"

Enoch knew what she was trying to do—stall Váli to give him time. Time to figure out what she had meant by *suspend nanites.* Enoch's head still ached from *pushing* the specters. He couldn't focus, couldn't . . .

And then he understood. *Suspend nanites! She wanted me to realize what those words meant when the monster said them. Váli wouldn't have to create this special bile of his, he wouldn't have to take any of these crude measures with the specters if he could do what I do. He has my ability to see and create patterns—but cannot see with the* afila nubla*! That is where he is helpless!*

Enoch knew what he had to do now. He just needed Sera to keep stalling Váli. Just a little longer . . .

Luckily, Sera had hit a nerve. Váli tightened his grip around her, and she let out a gasp. His voices were burning hotter.

"Ah, the trained bird finally speaks! Even in death, you sing the praises of your false god. You, my dear, are the saddest of this lot. An entire race of beings bred as decorative messengers in a world where communication is fast as light. A people made dependent on silly metal wings—in an age when man could fly around the world in hours aboard vessels that matched the speed of sound."

Váli focused his attention on Sera now. Enoch fought to keep his focus, pushed away his fear for Sera by holding to his *afila nubla* with ferocious determination. *This is why Master Gershom trained me*, he thought. *So that I could keep my mind in focus when it mattered most.*

Váli lifted Sera into the air and used another tentacle to pull her broken wing free, extended to its quivering limit.

Sera screamed. "Can't you *feel* the insult done to your kind just by the Pensanden? To be born a decoration. A useless, archaic decoration."

He lifted her high and opened his monstrous jaws, this time meaning to bite her in half. Váli did not care to keep the angel alive.

Enoch's will crumbled, and he screamed the last air from his lungs.

"Sera!"

There was a roar, and something large flew through the air, landing on Váli's twisted face with a heavy *thump* and knocking Sera to the ground. Gasping for breath, Enoch blinked the tears from his eyes.

G'Nor crouched on Váli's face, thick claws deep in the tentacled monster's flesh. With another roar, the beast tore into Váli with a flurry of powerful swipes that sent torn flesh and blood into the air.

Váli was screaming and roaring back, cursing in fear and rage at this unexpected intruder. The monster rolled to shake G'Nor from his face, but couldn't loose the beast's predatory grip. The tentacle around Enoch shivered loose and whipped around to beat at his attacker. With deadly feline reflexes, G'Nor twisted his head back to snap the tentacle between long dagger fangs and then shook the prize with feral violence. The bucking tentacle was torn to shreds between the beast's razor teeth, and G'Nor turned back to sink his fangs into Váli's jaw. G'Nor ripped the monster's jawbone from its mouth in a shower of blood, and Enoch couldn't help but process the contrast between the two beasts—the blunt clumsiness of twisted human creativity against millions of years of predatory evolution.

Váli was screaming now. More tentacles erupted from his torso, wrapping around G'Nor's powerful body—and being flayed to ribbons by the beast's ebony claws. But they were growing heavily tangled around G'Nor, and Enoch saw Váli's strategy: the tentacles were a distraction to the beast, much like the pattern had been to him. As the wildly flailing limbs kept G'Nor preoccupied, Váli was detaching his vital organs from the bloody mess. A slug-like portion of the creature extended from behind the bleeding torso—a featureless lozenge of pulsing flesh half the size of the original creature. It sprouted thin, finlike limbs and started to burrow into the sand beyond the reach of G'Nor.

* * * *

Sera saw and stumbled to her feet, casting around for Enoch's sword. "G'Nor! He's escaping! If he gets away, he'll heal and come back again!"

G'Nor heard her, but he was so wrapped in dying, constricting tentacles that he could not break free. Váli detached completely, slid into the blood-soaked sand and disappeared.

Sera turned to Enoch, desperate. He was standing, one hand at his temple, the other extended forward in the direction Váli had gone. Again, blood was running from his ears.

"Enoch! We've lost Váli. We need to leave here. Now. If he can heal even half as quickly as the trolls, then we . . ." Her voice drifted off.

Enoch was trembling.

"Enoch?"

G'Nor had freed himself from the tentacles and left the convulsing mess to check on Sera. He signed to her with blood-soaked paws. Sera waved him away and stumbled towards Mesha, who stirred at her touch.

"Oh . . . oh, good. She is alive. Just knocked out for a bit. But we need to go! That . . . that *thing* will be back soon. We need to grab Enoch and . . ."

G'Nor roared, and Sera spun to see the sand shifting, boiling up from the spot where Váli had disappeared only moments earlier. She took a step back, hand weary against G'Nor's wet fur.

"N-no. No. We can't fight him again, not like this."

The sand parted, and a hand reached into the air. Sera screamed.

Enoch scrambled forward and, against Sera's protests, reached down to wrap his hand around the wrist. He leaned back—and pulled a *man* from the ground in a cascade of sand. The man was tall and slender, and he was dressed in some dark material that was . . . glowing. *He* was glowing. Glowing with a strange blue light that seemed to course through his frame, trickling from his fingers, down his wrists, along his arms, streaming into his torso—and culminating in the almost piercing light emanating from his chest. The light beat in time to a low, thudding sound that vibrated across the sand like an elemental heartbeat.

Sera watched as the man steadied himself against Enoch and then stood straight. He flicked the sand from his shoulders and made a vain attempt at straightening his hair . . . and then caught sight of his hands.

Turning to Enoch, the man crumpled to his knees and began to weep. Enoch stumbled forward, blood running from his ears, and put his arm around the crying figure.

"It's ok, Rictus. It's ok."

CHAPTER 23

So we can't imitate their technopathy, fine.
We will do what clever men have always done—
build tools that will render their advantage obsolete.

—Joseph Chabran, Commander of the EurAsian Rebellion

Mosk left the dying draconfly where it lay—the creature had more than fulfilled its purpose, and its last, shuddering breaths were crumpled against the muffling immensity of the surrounding shadows. He was grateful the draconfly had lived long enough to navigate the final descent, using its antennae to weave through monolithic limbs of dead machinery in the blind drop that had ended here. But Mosk was here, that was the important thing. His destination was near, a prize that his prey would not be able to resist. This Pensanden Enoch would not be trapped by the Arkángel's plan, would not fall to Kai and her awakened sisters. He would not be heading to Tenocht without the tools created by some of his people's earliest enemies. It would be a prize too tempting for him to resist.

Somewhere above him, machinery whispered in soft and sand-brushed motion.

* * * *

There was water at Váli's den. Under the ersatz shade of five broken towers, beneath the dry webbing of dead cables and the fluttering silver leaves of metallic cloth, there was a modest lake, still and cool and surprisingly deep. Nothing grew in the wet gray sand surrounding the water, and G'Nor had signed to them that the water was safe, but "smelled of old metal." Váli had obviously spent some time shaping this ruined facility into something comfortable for his unfathomable needs—indeed, he had been the one to stretch the strange silvery tarp between the jagged antenna towers surrounding the facility to provide a simulacrum of oasis here. Enoch imagined the twisted creature sighing from its mouths as it took a leisurely swim in the cool waters, and the thought turned his stomach.

Rictus had taken some time to walk along the shore, noting the oddly circular perimeter. He returned with a theory that the floor of this lake had originally been used for listening—listening to messages from the stars. Before Váli had rerouted the facility's plumbing for his own personal bathtub, this giant dish could be angled towards any section of the sky. Enoch had been fascinated, both by the concept of communicating at such distance and by the powerful-yet-delicate machinery that would be required for such a feat.

He winced as the pain in his head flared up again. It was a sharp, driving pain that seemed to penetrate his skull just above his right eye and then lance all the way through his head. The pain had faded over the past few weeks, only surging whenever Enoch thought in numbers or patterns—something he hoped would heal in time. Apparently the loop that Váli had used to break his mind had left some shrapnel.

He felt a cool hand on his shoulder.

"Is your head bothering you again?"

It was Sera, leaning down over him with her brow furrowed in worry.

"You make a face when it bothers you—like you're angry at something."

Enoch smiled and reached out his hand to touch Sera's. The two had grown closer as they had been laid up healing. The confrontation with the monster had been traumatic, and finding this odd, synthetic oasis was an unexpected reprieve. Enoch felt guilty for bringing them here, and helpless about their current situation. Once he was fully healed, they could make another attempt to strike out north . . . but how would they get past the Swamp-men after another tiring journey through the desert? Even with G'Nor's claws, it would be a short fight.

Enoch sighed and sat up, pushing his blankets aside. Mesha, who had been napping on his legs, scowled at the interruption and sauntered off towards the lake. The shadowcat had made a full recovery since the attack but seemed more jumpy. At any loud noise or unexpected movement, she would shift to a gray that made her disappear against the sand.

Enoch smiled. He was safe, they had food and water, and his friends were here. Rictus and Sera had constructed a bower just inside the entrance to the den using the same odd, silvery cloth which Váli had stretched across the towers outside. It was tissue thin, but strong and surprisingly warm once wrapped around your body. G'Nor used the nights to patrol the area, returning each morning with meat from some swamp creature which had wandered into the desert. Unremarkable fare, but sufficient for their flagging appetites.

The thought made Enoch's stomach growl. He grinned sheep-ishly and got to his feet. The motion made his head ache, and he rubbed his brow gingerly. Sera handed him a bit of venison from G'Nor's most recent hunt.

"How are your wings feeling today?" Enoch said between bites.

She shook her head and made a strained smile.

Enoch frowned, and motioned to her bandaged wings with his scrap of meat.

"You know, I've already set up the repair protocols with the nanites in Ric's blood to help to realign your bones. Maybe we could try and have his LifeBeat generate some more for us. Even a few drops could help you feel less pain—"

Sera's face went cold, and Enoch knew immediately that he had said something wrong.

"I will be fine, thank you." She stood and brushed her hands off. "Besides, Rictus needs them all to keep him from reverting back into a ghoul. You said so earlier. I wouldn't want to take that from him to cure my own monstrosity."

She walked out of the room, ignoring Enoch's sputters: "No, I meant we could just generate *more* of them . . ."

There was a chuckle from the corner.

"I know I shouldn't expect you to be smooth with the ladies, but that was surprisingly bad, kid."

Enoch turned to see Rictus sitting against the wall behind him, half in shadow. The sunlight streaming through the doorway revealed a tall, lean man in his mid-thirties, long cobweb hair with dark roots swept back behind narrow, muscular shoulders.

"No woman wants to know that you've got plans to fix her, Enoch."

Even though Enoch knew at a microscopic level what had taken place, he was still taken back by Rictus's new look . . . *or, I suppose this is actually his* old *look.*

He had seen Rictus bitten into pieces, chewed apart, and ground under the monster's teeth. It was hard to believe that this vigorous, handsome man had recently been a dismembered specter.

"Stop staring at your handiwork, Enoch," Rictus said, eyebrow raised. "I'm not going to thank you any more than I already have."

Rictus pulled at the sleeves of his leather jacket, and a few blue lights sparkled from the folds. The lights had been dimming since he emerged from the sand.

This had been a major topic—the miracle Enoch had performed—ever since he'd regained consciousness. The worst part was that Enoch himself couldn't fully describe what he had done; much of it had happened on instinct. As far as Rictus could gather, the etherwalker had rebooted and supercharged the LifeBeat reactor, tapping into the bioelectrical energy of the host—Rictus—as normal, but also into the monster that had ingested him as well. That was a serious power boost.

Then, Rictus surmised, Enoch had cleared out what he called

"the redundant code" and "set the box to factory defaults." But that wasn't all—Enoch had modified Rictus's aging nanites to shift into high gear as well, tearing down the lining of Váli's digestive system and transplanting the regenerative cells into the specter's body. But unlike Váli's barely-controlled cellular growth, the nanites kept Rictus's new cellular activity within the confines of the original blueprint contained in his dusty old DNA strands.

Enoch scratched his head, still unclear on most of it.

"I still don't understand how you got out of its stomach, Rictus. After charging your LifeBeat, I was just hoping you'd have enough strength to survive until we found it and killed it. I didn't think that I could—"

"Don't know your own strength, kid?" said Rictus with a grin. "Whatever you set my blood bots to do didn't agree with Váli's tummy. When they revamped his stomach lining, the poor bastard's own bile ate through his unprotected guts. By then, I was whole enough to do the rest. I tore him apart from the inside out. It was the sort of vengeance he deserved.

"I'm still not sure how you got his cells to shake hands with mine. That sort of cellular manipulation should be well outside of your wheelhouse . . . at least by any description that I ever heard of the Pensanden."

Enoch leaned back, chewing thoughtfully.

"I've been thinking about that a lot, actually. It was all on instinct, like I said—" Here, Rictus raised his eyebrows and motioned for Enoch to go on. "But," said Enoch, "I never felt like I could actually *see* or *feel* that part. It felt more like the nanites knew what to do with those cells, and I just had to clear away the noise in their instructions so that they could follow them. Does that make sense?"

Rictus held out his hands—long, strong, fleshy fingers.

"It does, in a way," said the one-time specter. "It was a lovely reboot.

"The LifeBeat was top-of-the-line hardware back then," continued Rictus, "a learning micro factory that produced and refined iterative generations of nanites that would keep its owner alive—a customizable army that could handle aging cells, inefficient cells, cancerous cells. Even adapt to new diseases. But, like any complex machine, it can build up . . . sediment over time. Wasteful data, inefficient processes, fuzzy layers of binary gunk. I've been needing a good scrub for a few hundred years now."

Rictus smiled. "I'd been debating about whether to ask you about poking your head in and clearing out the cobwebs, but was worried that your inexperience with software this complex might end up breaking the only thing keeping me alive.

"Guess all you really needed was the threat of my death to kick you into high gear."

Enoch shook his head.

"It wasn't that I would have been unwilling before . . ." he said. "I think that I would have been too focused on *thinking* my way through the problem rather than feeling it. It seems like trying to reason my way through algorithms I have never been trained in is less effective than just allowing my instincts to set things in order.

"All this talk about *rebooting* and *setting protocols* for your system is beyond me. But when I looked into your LifeBeat, I could see some messy tangles in the numbers, some loops that were wasting energy. I straightened them out and then found the emergency commands that are meant to save your life. They had been buried under a lot of muck."

Rictus shrugged. "Emergency commands that I wasn't even aware of. Enoch, you resurrected some wickedly complex code that tricked my nanites into thinking that Váli's tissue was my own severed flesh. They went into full transplant mode. And then they did what good little nanites do—they reigned in the growing cells and made sure that they stayed in the right place."

Enoch shrugged. "Whether she wants to hear it or not, I think Sera should take some of your blood—if we can get your LifeBeat to generate more nanites, that is. It wasn't hard for me to give them the patterns that she needs . . ." And here Enoch looked up at Rictus, knowing this didn't sound right ". . .Or that *I* think she needs. They're supercharged right now, saturated with the bioelectrical energy from Váli and set into restorative mode on your tissue. You can't spare any, but I'm sure I could figure out how to trigger your factory confab to build some more."

"Can't spare any?" mused Rictus, standing and patting his chest. "I feel better than I have in centuries. I'm sure I could spare a few drops of *sangre*, a couple million of my bloodbots."

Enoch shook his head. "I'm sure you feel great, Ric, but that's because your blood . . ." he struggled to remember the terms he had learned in Babel, " . . . your *circulatory* and your *respiratory* systems are functioning again. But before I blacked out, I saw the nanites swarming into your gut. I think they're spending their extra energy to rebuild your digestive system. After that runs out, they'll shift back to maintenance—and I can't stop it. That's part of their cycle, one that has been long overdue. But losing any right now would leave you with a half-finished digestive system, and that . . ." Here Enoch shrugged, not really familiar with the anatomical terminology.

Rictus finished for him, patting his stomach. ". . . that would be bad. The funny thing, Enoch, is that in a few hot minutes you were able to synthesize disparate engineering and biological technologies in a way I'd never imagined. Imagine how much *more* dangerous Váli would have been with the focused nanite healing power harnessed to his explosive cell generation."

A fully-mutable, rapid healing warrior who could shape himself to look just as monstrous—or as beautiful—as he wanted to. That is *a frightening concept.*

And a powerful one.

Thoughts like this sprung into Enoch's head from time to time, and he didn't like them. The fear that he might be helpless against an ancestral destiny as a power-mad dictator weighed heavily on him sometimes.

He pushed himself to his feet and walked to the doorway that Sera had left through, gathering his *derech* and *iskeyar*.

"I'm going out to exercise," said Enoch. "I don't want to be tired out by cutting off tentacles when we meet Váli's brethren. Do you want to spar?"

Rictus stood up and brushed sand off of his leather pants.

"Sure," he said, "although I get the feeling that he was kind of a collector's item."

The morning sun made them both blink as they exited the den, although Rictus enjoyed the sensation much more than Enoch. The shade from the metal towers—*antenna clusters* is what Rictus called them—slanted away from the entrance at this hour.

The previous occupant of this artificial oasis had not been concerned with upkeep, apparently—Váli's sense of hygiene matched his physical form. There were piles of desiccated garbage, bones, and assorted refuse scattered all around the pond. Many of the mounds were more than twice as tall as Váli had been. Rictus said the place had probably been a very advanced, automated entry point to the caverns below, but now it looked very much like a monster's dwelling place, a den. So that's what they had named it.

They had made some attempt to clear the space around the entrance, and Sera had helped G'Nor construct some drying racks to preserve the meat and skins that the Ur'lyn's hunts brought them. Nobody knew how long they'd be here, but it seemed wise to plan for the worst. On a corroded metal platform just past the racks, Enoch had begun gathering bits of useful—or seemingly useful—odds and ends that they found as they cleared away the garbage. Some water containers, a small folding knife, rolls of that silvery cloth, and a tiny lantern the size of an apple which Rictus claimed could take energy from the sun and store it to generate light.

Enoch had wanted to take the lantern and explore deeper into the den, but both Rictus and Sera had overruled that—they said it was time to heal and recover. Enoch had protested, claiming that they might be able to find some way *out* of this desert. But he didn't have enough fight in him to overrule their worry.

Fine then. Let's get healed.

He walked to the edge of the lake, followed by Rictus. It was a warm morning, but the full heat of the day hadn't set in.

The Pensanden grabbed his swords by the scabbards and handed them to his friend, hilt first. "Which do you want? You prefer the straighter blades, as I recall."

Rictus reached around to his back out of habit, forgetting that his trusty sword was long gone. He closed his eyes when the memory hit and frowned.

"Naw, you're best with both of those little swords, kid. I don't want you to lose your edge just because I got declawed. Besides, Váli taught me that I'm next to useless trying to wield your toys. Let me see if I can find something more fitting to swat at you with . . ."

Rictus dug through a nearby pile, lifting a bleached human thigh bone, hefting it for weight, and then discarding it with a "tsk tsk." He dug a bit deeper and finally found something that felt better. It was a long steel bar, once part of a support structure, from what Enoch could tell. With a snap, it came loose, and Rictus staggered back a few paces. The bar was almost as long as he was tall and had a jagged point at the end where it had broken off. Rictus eyed it with a grin and then looked over his shoulder at Enoch, laughing maliciously.

Unfortunately, the bar had been supporting a critical point in the stack of refuse. There was a shifting sound and then a loud "galumph" as a wall of garbage avalanched down around Rictus's shoulders. When the dust cleared, the one-time specter was standing waist-deep in junk with a bucket on his head. But he was still holding his bar.

Enoch tried not to laugh. He really did. But the look on Rictus's face when he took the bucket from his head was just too priceless.

"That's right, enjoy yourself," Rictus said, brushing his shoulders off. "You'll be whining in a minute." He bent over to pull himself out of the mess and then *paused.* "Enoch, come check this out."

The pile of garbage had been stacked on top of—and concealing—a low building. A building with the same sturdy construction Enoch had noted in the den. It was wide, windowless, and—like everything else here—half buried in sand and garbage. It was entirely unremarkable except for the broad, slatted door that covered its face. It wasn't the type of door meant for people to move through. It was much larger.

Rictus was looking at Enoch with an eyebrow raised. "Did you know this was under here? Did you rig this to fall on your poor Uncle Rictus? I thought you couldn't use your powers without popping a lobe."

Enoch shook his head. "I thought this was all trash, I swear. Even *thinking* about looking to see what's behind that barn door is giving me a headache," he said, frustrated.

Now it was Rictus's turn to laugh. "That's right—you've never seen a garage before." He waded through the garbage and dug down through the base of the door. "Here we go—looks like this piece of junk gets to be my sword *and* crowbar today."

Enoch walked over to help Rictus dig around at the base until they uncovered a lock securing the door to some aged and crumbling cement. Then Rictus wedged his bar between the lock and leaned backwards, pulling the rod back and forth. There was a pop and the bar swung loose. It didn't take much longer, with their combined efforts, to pry the door from the base and slowly slide it up into the ceiling.

The cool air that crumbled out from the garage was stale and smelled of oil—this place had obviously been sealed away for a long, long time. In the shadows, covered in a layer of that same metallic cloth, was what Enoch could only surmise was a vehicle. It was larger than a shipping wagon and perched on four knobby wheels that splayed out from under the tarp, each plated with steel scales.

Rictus whistled, a habit he had taken to now that he had lips, and grabbed the tarp by one corner. He pulled it from the vehicle with a flourish, sending a cloud of dust into the air. Enoch coughed, blinking tears from his eyes.

The vehicle crouched low in the warm light, a powerful, almost feline shape formed of curved steel in a craft lost to this world. Enoch could not help himself, and with a painful gasp he sent his mind into the machine. It was a fascinating taste of directed power and redundancies constructed through a more communal set of thoughts than any Enoch had experienced before. It was delicious to his mind, even though it hurt. It hurt a lot.

"Enoch . . ."

Rictus was trying to get his attention, but Enoch couldn't look away from the vehicle. The four large wheels were balanced on oddly jointed rods, like spokes on a wagon that could move independent of one another. The chassis was a combination of aerodynamics and structural strength, balanced to allow the vehicle to move swiftly and nimbly without putting too much stress on any one point. There were weapons fitted to the chassis as well—weapons of focused light and ballistics.

"Enoch. Kid . . ."

It was all driven by a compact yet powerful engine nestled in the heart of the machine—a machine which had been left oiled and prepared for a long wait. It just needed a . . . needed . . .

The floor came up to meet Enoch's face, but luckily Rictus had been moving towards him and caught the boy just in time.

"Enoch! Get out of your trance, kid!" Rictus shook Enoch gently, cursing as the Pensanden shuddered.

"It just needs some power, Ric."

"And you need to snap out of it. I thought you were more cautious than that. Here, drink some water."

He took the pouch Rictus offered him, drinking deeply. The pain in his head was already waning, but Enoch had seen enough.

"We have a way out of this desert. That vehicle is ready to carry us, Rictus. It just needs a power source."

Rictus chewed on that, trying to look less concerned about Enoch's condition than he actually was. "Well, it shouldn't need much of a one—most of the cars from this era had solar cells worked into their skin, similar to that lamp you found. The battery just got them going when the sun was down—or if they'd been in the shade for millennia. I'm sure there's another one kicking around down here somewhere."

Enoch got to his feet, wiping his hands on his pants. His head felt a little foggy, but the feeling was already fading. He walked around the vehicle, waving off Rictus's muttered concern.

"I'll keep my mind out of the *car*, Ric. I just want to see what else is in here."

In the warm light that slanted through the opening, it was clear that the building was meant for vehicle storage and nothing more. There was a panel on the rear wall with a cracked glass screen, and several inert hoses and steel arms hung from the ceiling. Even without using his mechanical sight Enoch could tell that it had been used for analysis and upkeep of the vehicle. But there was no battery.

"Odd that they didn't keep a power source here," he said. "Seems like the most convenient location."

"Not really," said Rictus, who had followed him to the back. "This was a military facility. That was certainly a military vehicle. It wouldn't make sense to leave the keys to the daddy's sexy new wartank sitting on the dashboard."

Enoch rolled his eyes—Rictus might now *look* like a young man with oddly gray hair, but he still spoke like someone from a bygone age.

Sera poked her head in—she had come out to see what was going on—the noise of the falling garbage had alarmed her. When she saw the vehicle, her mouth went wide. Rictus answered her insistent questions on how they had found the thing and mentioned the missing battery.

Her earlier anger at Enoch was forgotten—this was obviously a topic that excited her. Like the rest, she had been worrying about how they were going to escape this desert. And she knew that this was the solution. Apparently Sera's mentor had shown her schematics of vehicles like this, and she eagerly bent over and used her finger to draw a schematic of the battery in the sand.

"This shouldn't be too hard to recognize. It's a cylinder about the size of your thigh," she said, "with a steel handle on one end and a thicker knot of circuitry on the other. It should be heavier than it looks and will most likely be stored somewhere cold."

Enoch nodded, engrossed with the picture. After his exploration of the vehicle's makeup, he knew exactly where the battery fit and even how it functioned . . . and that thought only made his brow ache a *tiny* bit.

Rictus pointed to the surrounding piles of refuse. There were at least a dozen other piles around the den that could be hiding similar garages. "It's possible that one of these holds a refrigerated unit storing the batteries, but my guess is that they are held deeper under the facility. Easier to keep them cool and more secure."

"Let's see what else we can uncover here," said Sera, standing up from her drawing. "Rictus, can you find me another one of those pry bars?"

The specter-made-man smiled and started digging into the refuse around where they stood. It was a dashing smile, thought Enoch, and he caught a glimpse of the "international heartthrob" status that the specter was always reminiscing about.

"I'm going to go back inside and lay down," Enoch said. "My head is still ringing."

Rictus waved as Enoch stumbled back to the den, hearing the sound of Sera scolding the specter for letting Enoch near machinery in his weakened state. Even in the scolding, Enoch could hear a new energy and hopefulness. They were going to get out of here.

And I'm going to find that battery.

For his part, Enoch hoped that his feigned weakness was convincing. He knew where he could find a battery, and he knew that Rictus and Sera were too distracted to stop him.

* * * *

The doors at the back of the den had been easy to pry open with his *derech*—the locks had corroded over time, and it appeared that Váli had not cared to reinforce them. Time had not left much of a mark on the space. Apart from some dust, the pale floor and walls seemed much like Enoch imagined they had looked centuries ago. They were paneled with a pale, lightly textured material that didn't appear to corrode. The ceiling was more utilitarian—pipes, cables, and more structural pieces naked to the eye.

The long hallway slanted down into darkness, extending beyond the reach of Enoch's lamp. The little device emitted a cold, bluish light that was surprisingly powerful. Enoch figured that he had several hours of illumination remaining. He was sure that he would be able find a battery in that time.

And the extra water, meat, and note I left back at the den were just . . . just a precaution.

Enoch smiled, finally able to admit the truth to himself—he had wanted to explore the depths of this place ever since he'd arrived. The mystery of it all! Why had Váli been so driven to keep Pensanden from discovering his den? Why the centuries of preparation and solitary vigil? And there was the memory of Master Gershom, who had suggested coming here for something. A key? The memory was too vague.

But there was something more. This place just felt *right*. It felt familiar. Enoch had somehow known that the doors at the rear of the den would lead down to . . . to something important. This wasn't his metallic vision guiding him. This was a place which had been built by brilliant minds, minds which echoed his own. They were not Pensanden, but they had been people who understood numbers and systems.

The hallway continued down, then began branching to the sides. Again and again. Yet Enoch knew which path to follow. He felt a surge of adrenaline. He felt . . . welcome.

His head felt better the deeper he went into the facility. There was something about the layout, the precision of the place that just seemed to soothe his thoughts. It was the exact opposite effect of Váli's number trap—a place engineered so soundly that it nurtured a mind bred to create order.

Enoch didn't hesitate now to send his mechanical vision along the cables in the ceiling. The pain was gone. The cables led to junctures that led to more cables that led further down into vast generators nestled deep beneath the sand. Most of them were dead and cold, but not all. A pair of these engines still flickered with atomic life, could be brought back to full power with a shift here, some new cabling there.

The structure and design of Babel had been similar to this, but now Enoch understood why it had never resonated with him like this place—generations of city-dwellers had built over and around the place, spoiling the cleanly purposed order of a rocket construction site and turning it into a chaotic city. The conflicting, incongruent layers had been jarring for his mind—still untrained at that point—and he instinctively drew away from exploring. That was why he had never really discovered the dark secret slumbering in those cold chambers.

The memory came with a pang of grief, and Enoch quickly shifted his thoughts back to the here and now. *This* place had remained untouched by the chaos. Even the horrific weapons that had transformed the land above into gray sand had been unable to penetrate the majestic order that reigned underneath. And it was suddenly obvious to Enoch that this had been the purpose of the place. It had been built by people who wished to hold something—to protect something. And to hide something from the Pensanden.

And I am getting closer.

Rooms branched off from the hallway now, and Enoch caught glimpses of incredible machinery in each of them. There was a room full of articulating arms and tools, a room that could build—or tear apart—anything one desired. There was a room with magnetized rails, which could lift, spin, and manipulate a metal object in any direction or speed. One room held hundreds of glass pistons, delicate cylinders that slid over and around each other in infinitely varied patterns. The purpose of these rooms was beyond Enoch's ken, but the power and mystery they contained stoked his curiosity. He knew that he could spend an eternity here, wandering from room to room. But he had to reach the bottom of this facility. He had to find its purpose. He had to . . .

Ok, just one room.

He chose the smaller door to his right, one that seemed almost hidden beneath layers of bolted steel. At his touch, the layers folded back and parted—it was a simple matter to unlock the codes that held them shut.

He chose the room because it was small and because it felt like something he could pop in and out of without wasting any time. Just a taste of the fascinating machinery that filled this facility. But the room turned out to be fairly . . . disappointing. Just a simple steel table surrounded by twelve tall-backed chairs—steel chairs that resembled enormous ladles, with the handles coming down from the ceiling and bending into cupped cushions. Those were odd, but not very interesting. At the end of the room was a thirteenth chair, one that looked down over the others. It was empty, however.

Hovering over the center of the table, however, was something interesting. It was an object made of light—a *hologram.* Enoch remembered the word from his time in Babel. The hologram was a sphere decorated with various symbols and colors, and other symbols spun around the sphere like flies circling a light.

Enoch supposed it held some great meaning for whoever used to sit here, but he was almost glad that he had chosen the least interesting room here—now he had to get back to the reason he had come down here. He walked around the table, thoroughly unimpressed by the simplicity of this room. Rictus and Sera and G'Nor would come looking for him soon—

And that's when he saw the body. It was sitting in the chair with its back to the door, which was why Enoch hadn't seen its occupant behind the tall back. Enoch grimaced—the body had been here for centuries and had withered into a slumped skeletal corpse, which had dried into a husk under endless years of cool, dry air whisked through the tireless ventilation system. There was no smell, no mess or rot. Just a dark, lonely little figure sitting patiently in front of the spinning hologram.

A cave full of wondrous rooms, and I choose the one with a dead guy in it.

Enoch turned to go, but something caught his eye—a glimmer on the thin wrist of the corpse. The light from the hologram had reflected on something. This was interesting—the clothing had dried and warped to become almost indistinguishable from the withered flesh of the corpse's body, but there was bright, untarnished jewelry still adorning its wrists, throat, and a single ear. Maybe Enoch could bring something back for Sera? He blushed at the thought, but it emboldened him to approach the corpse. *Just one little cadaver, right?* After all, hadn't Enoch waded through troll blood, mudman poison, and the guts of a regenerative monster?

He decided on the bracelet, a beautifully crafted tracery of silver and steel that wrapped around the thin bones of the wrist like the wings of a bird. It felt beautiful and *correct,* much like Sera. Enoch smiled. Careful not to touch the dry, leathery skin, he grasped the bracelet and slid it from the corpse's hand.

All that time traveling with Rictus—who knew it was preparing me to be an unflinching grave robber?

He lifted the bracelet up to his lamp to get a better look and gasped. The bracelet was a delicately rendered eagle, with a large ruby set as the eye.

An eagle. On the right wrist.

Enoch checked, and sure enough, there was another bracelet on the corpse's left wrist that resembled a coiling serpent. The silver scales wound towards another ruby eye.

Enoch regarded the corpse again, feeling a sort of pity. He knew that this place had been built by those wishing to oppose his kind, the Pensanden. It appeared that they could not help but imitate them as well, even wear their symbols. This person, whomever he had been, had wished to wear the Eagle and the Serpent. Had wished for what Enoch had.

He almost returned the bracelets to the corpse, an act of guilt, but instead frowned and slid them onto his own wrists. Whoever this person had been, he was an enemy to the Pensanden. When living, this person and his people had created the creature that had almost killed Enoch and his friends. Enoch would take the bracelets as a reminder of that. They fit his wrists perfectly, after all.

And maybe Sera will wear the other one.

The thought made him blush, and he liked the sensation.

As Enoch left the room, the hologram winked out. The door slid closed behind him.

Enoch wasn't sure how long he continued down that hallway with endless rooms on either side that teased at mysteries beyond mysteries. It seemed like he continued for an hour before it eventually led down to another series of stairs, and then a pair of doors that were sealed with an enormous mechanical lock. The lock was easily dealt with, as Enoch's *afila nubla* pushed the scrambled notches back into order. Pushing the actual door open was more difficult, as hinges that had been still for centuries squealed in protest.

The next turn brought him to a massive open space, a cavernous room with a ceiling so distant that his lamp could not reach its height. And there was a breeze here, an artificial wafting of air that came from some circulation system in vents far above. Enoch had been walking for hours now, and the soft wind on his skin brought his mind back to his body. His mouth was dry, and his stomach growled.

Sitting back against one of the thick girders that supported this place, Enoch drank from his pouch. He shut off his lamp to conserve energy, finally accepting the fact that he was going to be down here for a while.

Besides, it won't take me too long to route some of that stored power into the light fixtures running through here. The vent system is still working—some filters set to ensure that this cavern stays dry and clean.

Even without the lamp on, Enoch could sense the motes of energy running through this place. Could sense the slowly turning fans, the dilating vents, the weight-bearing girders all around him. A measured and silent order that held reign.

And that was when he heard the breathing.

It was ragged and dim, but it was deep. It came from something big. Something close. Enoch froze, grateful that his light was off.

That's assuming this thing can't see in the dark . . .

Images of another shapeless monstrosity like Váli rose up in his mind, and Enoch shuddered.

Constrain. Calm. Control.

The words of command came more difficult than normal—he supposed the recent nightmarish battle had left some marks in his mind.

Constrain. Calm. Control.

The breathing hadn't moved. And it seemed to be getting weaker. He recognized the nature of the sound from his days as a shepherd, taking care of animals that had been injured. The halting, wet noise of ruptured lungs.

Whatever it is . . . it is dying.

Emboldened, Enoch silently rose to his feet. He slid the lamp into his pocket and slowly drew his blades.

Just like the front room back at the farmhouse—remember the layout. Slip through it like a fish.

There had been another girder just ahead at the edge of the lamp's light. Twenty-seven steps and Enoch's toe felt the slight rise of the platform at its base. The breathing was closer. And weaker.

Ten more steps, and whatever it was stopped breathing. Not a careful attempt at being silent, but a rattling, wheezing halt.

Another ten steps.

It is dead.

Enoch counted a full minute.

Constrain. Calm. Control.

He sheathed his *derech* and pulled out the lamp. His thumb felt towards the smooth button on the side, and the light clicked on.

Enoch gasped.

It was a dead draconfly. Bulbous compound eyes, a mountain of black carapace, splayed segmented legs, and the insectile undeath of twitching antennae. One of the beasts that had brought the coldmen to his farm. The coldmen who had killed Master Gershom and cast Enoch's life into the nightmare it had become.

How did it get here? Was it from *this place? Did my ancestors leave a draconfly nest buried here under all this sand?*

As soon as Enoch thought the question, he knew the answer. This creature was definitely not from here. Something this large would have left marks passing through the narrow hallways and doors he had just been through. This thing had arrived through some other entry—

And . . . it was dead. A yellow fluid had pooled underneath

the creature, and Enoch could see several worn fractures along its thorax and wings. It had been driven hard. Someone had raced here, heedless of the cost.

"I knew you would come."

Enoch spun, dropping the lamp to draw his *derech*. The lamp bounced twice and landed at the feet of a large man only a few steps behind where Enoch stood.

A coldman.

The light angled up along his thick armored legs, as broad around as Enoch's chest. This coldman was larger than the ones he had seen back at the farm. Taller than Rictus. The plates on his shoulders curved up into horns, and Enoch had to remember that fearsome armor was not worn, it was a *part* of the coldman just as the twitching antennae were part of the dead creature behind him.

I must remember the corpse behind me. The floor slick with blood.

Enoch had drawn his blades and instinctively began mouthing the *pensa spada* as he took a step backwards. The coldman didn't move, just regarded Enoch with flat, hooded eyes that reflected the blue light from the lamp.

"It has been so long."

Its voice was dry and coarse. Enoch didn't respond.

"I could have killed you as you stood there. I could have killed you when you sat to rest. I have been following you since you first entered this chamber."

It was not bragging, merely stating a fact. Now it took a step forward. Enoch held his ground.

"I wanted you to see me before you died. To know who brought an end to your kind."

"Now you have seen me."

The coldman crushed the lamp underneath its heavy foot, and there was only blackness.

Enoch fought the panic brought by the dark, by the words of this killer. He closed his eyes, retraced the distances around him.

Hear.

The coldman was quiet, but he was large. The air would move

around it and betray any swift movements. Enoch realized that it must be standing still. It was watching him. He slid into a simple defensive position and waited.

The voice, when it came, was behind him. "You have seen me. Now hear me: I am the Mosk d'Abaddon. I am the Hiveking."

Enoch whirled, but too late. Something heavy and sharp drove into his shoulder and sent him tumbling across the floor.

"You and I both represent new paths for life – new ways for intelligence to bring order to chaos. Your path is through mechanical understanding and cooperation. Mine is through hunger and obedience."

Enoch pulled himself up on his elbows, despairing. The coldman was moving slowly, deliberately. Noiselessly. It could see in the dark. It knew his moves before he made them.

"Your path has ended."

Now the voice was closer. This *Mosk* was circling him. Enoch laid his face against the cold plastic floor. Maybe he would be able to feel the heavy footsteps. Blood ran down his shoulder, his arm, pooled on the floor around his elbows.

"I was raised on a farm. I'm not what you think I am."

The kick whistled through the air, again too fast to avoid and from an unexpected angle. It thudded into his ribs with an audible crack, and Enoch rolled across the cold floor. He was gasping.

"I know where you were raised. I know of the blademaster who raised you. I dug his body from the ground and tasted your hands in the soil of his grave."

Enoch had kept his swords in hand. Somehow. But he was dead. He could not see his enemy. He could not hear his enemy. He could not even feel his enemy's footsteps rippling in his own blood. A last act of numb defiance, Enoch refused to let this killer enjoy this torture. Refused to put up a fight. He lay back in the pooling blood and waited for the final blow.

The Hiveking did not laugh. But there was something like dark humor in its voice.

"Why else would I confront a Pensanden here, of all places? Only if I knew of the primitive way he was raised. Your blademaster hid you by severing your power, young one. In keeping you safe amongst shepherds, he hobbled you like one of your lambs. No amount of swordplay can replace what he took from you."

It was standing over him now. The dry voice drew terrifyingly close to his face. Enoch held his breath. He *paused.*

How do you defend against what you cannot see?

"So this is how the last Pensanden dies. In a mausoleum left by his first primitive foes."

You turn on the lights.

And suddenly the chamber was bathed with light. It coursed from the massive panels overhead as power roared through circuits long dead. Enoch pulled it from the generators that still held life, from the forgotten corners of this complex that still held charge. The light bore down from the ceiling high above, and it struck the coldman's lidless eyes without mercy.

He staggered back, hissing. "But you cannot know how to—"

His words were cut short as Enoch's *derech* drove into his right eye. The Hiveking hissed and struck out, knocking Enoch back to the ground. Enoch, bleeding and broken, groaned as he crawled to his feet.

The Hiveking hissed again and turned to regard Enoch with his one eye. The other was shattered and dripping pale blood that glistened in the bright light. In the full illumination, Enoch could see that Mosk was as different from a man in armor as he was from the smaller coldmen Enoch had witnessed on that fateful night.

The Hiveking did not bear a sword. He wore no armor. His weapons and defense came from the bladed shell carapace that covered his body. His shoulders and forearms bore curving spikes, like ebony spurs. His thick fingers ended in claws, and as Enoch watched, the Hiveking reached down to pull the plates over his ribcage apart . . . only it wasn't a ribcage. It was another pair of arms, folded tight under its thoracic shell. The arms were thinner and did not end in clawed fingers—each arm tapered to a curving, scythe appendage that resembled the talons of a mantis. One of them snapped forward, faster than Enoch could blink.

No human reflex is that fast. This is how he kills the Nahuati.

The Hiveking hissed again, spreading his arms out to a lethal range. His mouthparts separated, opening toothy segments as the hiss became a roar.

Losing an eye only made him angry.

Enoch crawled to his feet, swords drawn, and backed away. The Hiveking let loose with another roar, and one of the light fixtures overhead exploded in a shower of sparks. The roar was a challenge, and Mosk pointed at Enoch's wrist.

"You found the Eurym! But it cannot help you here, larva. Your enemies built this tomb well - she cannot hear you this deep!"

What? Who is She? He's gone mad . . . The light is all I can control here. I have to take him deeper.

Enoch turned and ran. Not out the way he came, but past the Hiveking and towards a series of four doors which were in a line along the wall several dozen meters to his back. There were bright lines there. There was motion. Things that Enoch could use.

The footsteps hammering behind him attested to the fact that his pursuer was no longer attempting to be quiet. Mosk was in a rage, a passion that had slept for a decade. The hunter had stepped outside of his training, outside of his patterns—and that had saved Enoch's life. Enoch wasn't sure why the creature had chosen to go against the behavior that had worked to such deadly effect for so long, why he had chosen to be melancholy and reflective and *human* at such a critical point, but Enoch had used the flaw to his advantage.

He wouldn't be able to surprise the Hiveking like that again.

Faster.

Enoch's side raged with pain, each footstep sending an agonizing blast of fire. But the footsteps were getting closer. He had to go faster.

There was a whistle, and a sharp line of pain laced across his back. Enoch saw the door ahead, triggered the mechanism that opened it. The Hiveking drew even closer, saw that Enoch was hoping to reach the opening and close it behind him.

At the last second, Enoch leapt—but not at the open door. He dove through the door *next to it*, a door that he had also unlocked but left closed until the last second. The Hiveking had too much mass to change course now, and he slid through the other door entirely with a roar. Enoch as he came to his feet, slamming both doors shut and sealing the locks.

He knew that he didn't have a lot of time. Already, the Hiveking was pounding on the door beside him. Powerful blows that shook the air. Enoch turned and ran, his mind reaching out to the architecture around him.

This room was cold, and there was a distinctive sound of dripping coming from above. But no machinery. Nothing that he could use.

Enoch found a gantry connected to a staircase that ran along some massive pipes. He began climbing the staircase, which circled around a tall shaft lifting up into the darkness above. And suddenly Enoch realized where he was.

If I can climb high enough . . . I might have a chance.

The lights in here flickered, were not as robust as those from the wide chamber he had just left. But at least he could see here. At least he could fight. He remembered that the *derech* and *iskeyar* were meant to kill coldmen. That the shifting patterns of straight and curved blades were too complex for their minds.

But he also remembered that even his Master had been overpowered. And this was the Hiveking, who had already bloodied him and broken his rib.

I just need to hold him off and stay alive long enough to get higher.

With a roar, the Hiveking smashed through the door below and charged into the pool of flickering light at the base of the stairs. He cast around for a second, raging at the limited sight his one eye offered, but spied Enoch already on the third level above. The Hiveking hissed and turned to face the boy, crouching.

He cannot possibly think to—

In one tremendous leap, the coldman bounded from the ground up to the second floor just under Enoch's feet. He grabbed onto the railing with his scythe claws and pulled himself onto the slatted floor below. Enoch could see him from between the slats under his own feet. He had less time than he thought. The Hiveking spun and leapt onto the railing next to Enoch.

I've made him angry and careless. The Hiveking has been out of practice, and I can use that against him.

Enoch chopped down with his *iskeyar*, lopping off the tip of one scythe claw that held the coldman to the railing. The Hiveking roared again and lashed out with another scythe, a flash of movement that tore across the boy's chest. Enoch stumbled back, even now horrified at the thing's inhuman speed. Hissing, the Hiveking scrambled over the railing and faced Enoch, who continued moving up the staircase with sidesteps, his swords aimed at his assailant. He began chanting the *litania eteria*. Everything came into focus.

The one scythe is neutralized. I need to be wary of the other. I have to be moving before he strikes. I have to read his movements, the step he takes before—

In a blur of movement, the Hiveking lunged at Enoch. And Enoch was already moving, dodged out of the way just in time. His clawed hand carved lines into the railing as Enoch dodged to the other side.

The other hands are just as deadly. But I can see them coming.

It lunged again, and again Enoch barely dodged the blow.

And another, but this time Enoch followed the swipe with a jab from his *derech*. It wedged into the creature's rib shell, piercing it a good two inches. The Hiveking returned the attack with a flurry of blows from his remaining scythe arm, and Enoch answered them with a blur of metal. Still, he was driven back up the next staircase.

Higher. There's nothing I can use *down here.*

The Hiveking's next attack was met with a lightning-quick series of parries and ripostes—Enoch's reflexes had returned and he was seeing the patterns of the creature's attacks. The tells he gave before a lunge, the way he leaned into a parry.

He tilts his head into a lunge—

And suddenly the patterns changed. A tell wasn't a tell, but a fake that fooled Enoch into committing himself too deeply into his lunge. The scythe lashed out across Enoch's right hand and severed his two end fingers. The *derech* spun away and clattered on the floor far below. Enoch stifled his cry, and a hoarse groan escaped his lips.

Now the Hiveking came at him hard and fast. Enoch was pushed back up the stairs again and again, his *iskeyar* flashing right and left in a desperate attempt to keep the assassin's claws from his vital organs. His movements were purely defensive now—the aggressive maneuver had cost him too much. It dawned on Enoch that this creature had been *designed* to kill him. Had killed his people for years before he had been born. Enoch's time was running out, and another of the Hiveking's attacks got through his defense.

Blood spattered the stairs, and they had reached the highest platform. Enoch stumbled back against one of the enormous pipes that bent down from high above. Above them, darkness and the dripping of water.

The Hiveking loomed over Enoch, red blood dripping from each of his claws in syncopation with the water. Enoch pulled back against the pipe, trying to tuck himself under its bulk in a primitive, animal instinct to *get away from that predator.* He was bleeding from dozens of cuts and lacerations, and his remaining blade slipped from his wet fingers. It clattered down the stairs and was lost in the darkness far below.

Enoch wrapped his arms around the pipe and shut his eyes, whispering the *litania eteria.*

* * * *

Mosk d'Abaddon, once Hiveking and Swarmlord, Him without Brother, and Master of the Hunt, had the last Pensanden trapped and defenseless at his feet. There was nowhere to run.

Mosk stepped forward, shaking drops of water from his armored skin.

"So this is how the Pensanden line is ended. With a boy cowering in the shadows.

Far above, distant hinges creaked and hidden machinery shifted. The dripping above suddenly became a stream, a torrent. Became an avalanche. A roar of water and sunlight as the floor of the lake above split apart along seams that had been bound for centuries, then tilted and emptied itself. The deluge drove down and bent the steel gantry, ripped the stairs from their moorings, and dragged the Hiveking into the darkness below. The water was a howling storm of torn metal and electricity, sizzling as broken wires fed lethal power into the flood. Mosk was torn to pieces in the darkness.

* * * *

The storm ended as quickly as it began. Warm light now filled the open space, gilded the last rivulets of water as they thinned in streams through the routed tunnel. Enoch crawled out from under the lee of the pipe he had taken refuge in, coughing. He held his hand pressed tightly against his chest, the slow stream of blood lost among a dozen others that coursed down his body.

Enoch tried to crawl out onto the remaining edges of the gantry, his arms trembling. He was so tired. His lips still whispered the mantra, voiceless, repeating; even though the machinery overhead had now spent itself and gone still, the servos of the reservoir had obeyed his command and could do no more.

"Enoch! Enoch!"

The voice echoed from high above. It was Rictus. Squinting against the brightness, Enoch looked up, tried to wave to his friend. The top was too far away, the sun . . . too bright.

"Ric . . ." His voice came out as a whisper.

I can't . . . I can't . . .

Enoch's hand slipped on the bent steel, and he slid over the edge, only stopping when his scabbard belt caught on the jagged tip. Enoch swung over the darkness. He couldn't fight any more. There was nothing he could do.

"Ric . . . help me . . . help me . . . please."

* * * *

Rictus couldn't see into the blackness, even with his new eyes.

I'd give my eyes, left arm, and functioning digestive system for one damn rope right now.

He looked over to Sera, who was leaning precariously out over the ledge. She flipped her goggles up and carefully crawled back towards him. Her face was pale.

"He's bleeding heavily. We have to get him up here. Now."

G'Nor had already circled the pit twice, and he returned again, signaling to Sera in frustration. Rictus knew what the beast was saying without Sera's translation.

No dice.

"The ledge that Enoch is on—I can barely see it from here," muttered Sera. "G'Nor says there is nothing to hold on to for a hundred feet. We can't climb down there."

G'Nor growled, lowered his haunches as if to size up the jump. Sera grabbed his shaggy neck.

"No, my friend. The landing is too narrow."

There was silence as it sank in—they were going to have to watch Enoch bleed to death. There was no way down. After all of the danger they had passed through with the boy, it was ending here.

Sera looked back at her limp wings, shaking her head. Rictus looked down at his hands. His smooth, strong hands.

Damn it.

"There is a way."

Sera looked up at the specter. She knew. They both knew.

"I . . . I'm afraid of what they would do," she said. She gathered the primary feathers in one hand, and the metal gleamed in the sunlight. Her voice was soft.

"The . . . what did he call them? The workers in your blood?"

"Saturated, overcharged nanites, Sera," said Rictus, his old heart heavy. "They are still set on transference and regeneration."

Eyes closed, Sera nodded.

"He said that they could . . . *fix* me. That they would know what to do."

Rictus tried to smile. He tried to show something, anything, besides the dread in his stomach.

She has to know that this is going to hurt.

"You don't have to do this, Sera. Maybe if we look for another way—"

"There is no other way. You know there isn't."

Rictus couldn't stop looking at his hands. In the bright sunlight, a thin sheen of sweat sparkled with grains of sand over firm, taut skin. He clenched his fingers once, twice, and released them with a sigh.

"Let's do this. Let's do this now."

G'Nor signed to Sera, who relayed to Rictus. "He wants to know if this is dangerous."

"Not for you," said Rictus, eyes down. "We don't have time to worry about that now. Enoch is dying."

He grabbed Sera by the wrist. She was staring down the pit, at the boy whose life was ebbing away in drips and gasps far below.

"We will need a knife," said Rictus, voice soft.

G'Nor had come up behind the two, and he extended the razor sharp claws on one paw, signing with the other. Sera nodded.

"G'Nor can do it quickly, and he says his saliva has an anticoagulant—it might keep your . . . your *nanites* from stitching you up before enough of them are transferred."

Rictus smiled and pulled back his sleeve. "I need to remember that our shaggy friend here probably knows more about field-surgery than any of us. Here," he said, offering his wrist, "dig in."

Taking their wrists, G'Nor looked at them both in turn.

So polite, for a purebred predator.

Rictus nodded back, and then Sera. G'Nor ran his rough tongue over their skin from palm to elbow. Then he ran a razor-sharp claw down the specter's wet wrist, parallel to the tendons to avoid unnecessary damage. Rictus grimaced as bright blood welled out, still sparkling with the supercharged nanites.

Before they could seal the wound, G'Nor deftly cut into Sera's wrist as well and then softly pushed their arms together. There was a jolt that caused both of them to catch their breath as the nanites tapped into Sera's bioelectrical field. Rictus was surprised that he could *feel* this, feel the vitality draining through his arm.

Off you go, little buddies. Do your business, but please be gentle with the lady.

G'Nor sensed the transfer as well, his sensitive nose following the chemical tang as it passed from the specter to the angel. He wrinkled his snout and exhaled sharply, shaking his head. This was not natural.

Sera began breathing hard. Her back arched, and her wings extended fully behind her—particles of light flowing from her arm, to her shoulders, to her wings.

Rictus kept his eyes down, locked to their joined wrists.

"Let it pass . . ." mumbled Rictus. "The pain is only temporary. Let it . . ."

He couldn't continue. He remembered his first resurrection. The nanites were wonderful healers, but they didn't numb the pain. The pain served up valuable analytics, the most accurate gage of nervous system functionality.

And the little buddies can't let you pass out—you have to stay awake the whole time. That's how they know everything's working.

Sera screamed. Her bones twisted inside of her, slid back into the tight spaces where irritated flesh had swollen and filled. Her own bright blood ran down her feathers, feathers that quivered as pain rifled through her wings like a hot breeze. She staggered away from Rictus and G'Nor, breaking the bond as the newly energized nanites shifted into the patterns that Enoch had set them to.

G'Nor huffed in worry, took a few tentative steps towards the trembling angel. He looked back at Rictus, who had his face in his hands.

The Alaphim convulsed and wrapped her wings around herself in one quick moment, transforming into a dome of bronze and crimson-spattered feathers. Lights flashed from within the dome, and Sera screamed again. And again.

Damn it. I remember this. The pain. I shouldn't have let her do this. What kind of monster am I?

G'Nor growled and took another step forward, but Rictus

grabbed at his mane with a thin hand.

"Stay, my friend," he said, voice weak. "She chose this and she knew what would come of it—Enoch warned her. Let her take this choice on her own."

G'Nor bowed his great head down to sniff at the specter, suddenly looking up in surprise.

Remember that? The smell of rot?

"Yeah, I made my choice as well."

Sera's screaming had stopped, and her wings had grown still. Rictus leaned on G'Nor's sturdy shoulder and pulled himself to his feet. With a sudden whoosh, Sera's wings spread wide, extended in a bright crescent over her head.

The angel stood triumphant. Even speckled in her own blood, she gleamed with a new power and vibrancy that echoed the lost glory of her people. The metal of her wings now wove into her flesh with a smooth, muscular curve that echoed the sweep of her feathers. Thin leaves of bronze swept from her shoulders, her brow, her wrists—the feathers that had once seemed so artificial in their juxtaposition with her human features now felt natural. They felt right. The lenses which had once snapped into place on crude joints were now part of a regal headdress which wove through Sera's cerulean hair like an eagle's crown.

Rictus smiled a thin smile and nudged the beast at his side.

"That's worth the ticket price, eh?"

The Alaphim raised her head, and the crown slid down over her eyes like an elaborate eyelid. Sera crouched, and with a mighty lunge she was airborne.

Rictus and G'Nor flinched as a cloud of dust and sand rolled over them. Sera rose into the air with a few powerful flaps of her gleaming wings, circled around the pair, and then dove into the pit behind them.

G'Nor helped Rictus over to the edge, but already the angel had disappeared into the darkness. A minute passed. Two. The beast signed to Rictus, who weakly shook his head.

"I don't know. She . . . she should have found him by now. She should be—"

And then the sound of beating wings, rising from the darkness. Sera rose into the sunlight, feathers flashing in the noonday sun. She carried Enoch in her arms, and the boy had never seemed so small to Rictus. He was soaked, still, and far too quiet.

Rictus and G'Nor hurried over to Sera as she landed. She gently placed Enoch on the sand, using one wing to shade the boy.

"He's still warm," she said. "Still breathing."

G'Nor sniffed Enoch, motioned urgently to his companions.

"Yes," said Rictus. "He needs to be cleaned and bandaged, and . . ." here he lifted up Enoch's mangled hand, ". . . he appears to have lost a few digits." G'Nor licked at the bleeding stumps as Rictus tore a leather strap from his own jacket and wrapped it tightly around the wound.

"That won't be enough, though."

The ailing specter pulled his sleeve back and leaned over Enoch. He sighed.

"Looks like I'm donor of the year . . ."

"No, Ric," said Enoch. "I need you alive."

Everybody gasped. Enoch opened his eyes and gave a weak smile, motioned at Sera's resplendent new wings.

"Do . . . do you like them?"

Rictus rolled his eyes, letting out an exasperated sigh.

"Half dead and half drowned, and *now* you decide to flirt?"

Sera smiled, leaned over, and pushed a strand of wet black hair back from his forehead. "They're perfect, Enoch. You fixed me."

She leaned down and kissed him on the cheek.

Enoch blinked and blushed, then closed his eyes. He coughed, shaking his head. Sera tried to quiet him, put her hand to his mouth. Enoch turned his head, amber eyes staring into hers.

"No, that's where I was wrong. I was wrong the whole time. The pattern was inside of you, Sera. Hidden in the adaptive cells on the boundary between your flesh and the metal—a place far too chaotic and *messy* for an etherwalker to see. Your people created this within themselves . . .and there is a lot more there that I barely caught a glimpse of."

Enoch coughed again, and waved away her help.

"The Alaphim were not just fancy letter carriers. I finally realized that. Sera, in a world where Koatul can break through any coded message, your people became *vital* for communication amongst those who fought the Serpent. They transformed themselves into so much more than their original design, and Koatul hunted them just as hungrily as he did the Pensanden. That's why he turned the Arkángels. He knew that you were capable of . . .of this.

"I don't know why, but the design was a part of your frame, a hidden code that only you could find. You had to open it yourself. Sacrifice yourself. That was the only way to—" and here he waved at the transformed angel with a weak hand— "to set these changes free.

"You were already perfect. Already whole."

Rictus looked at Enoch, then looked over at Sera. Finally he looked across the two of them at G'Nor.

"Can you give me a lift out of here? I'm going to be sick."

CHAPTER 24

Don't say that it's two against one,
The sky will shiver and the rivers will run,
Lucky for us, we're not alone
Lucky for me, I'm not the only one.

—Dogfish Knights, chorus for "Roam"

Sera flew again. She *flew.*

She spun and whirled through the sky, opening her mouth to taste the clouds as she splashed through their thick bellies. She couldn't remember feeling so strong before this, feeling so much in control of the wind that she caught beneath her pinions.

I can't wait to show Lamech. To show the rest of them. This *is what we can be. Not a faded decoration, not some useless reminder of past decadence. Not a twisted spider like the Arkángel. But* this. *A being meant to fly, meant to master the sky and shape it beneath crafty wings.*

She could see the caravan below, familiar sounds muffled by the soft wind blowing down from the north.

I am not something made. Not something unfinished.

The sun warmed her wings, and she *felt* it. Her feathers spread wide under the heat, gathering energy that would sustain the new guests in her blood.

Enoch had thought of everything.

"You don't *need* to keep the nanites going once they've triggered your nascent transformation," he had said. "But I figure you might want to share some of them with your family when we're done."

She wasn't quite sure what "done" meant. Enoch spoke of traveling to Tenocht and looking for more of his kind. He meant to find his home, his real home.

Oh yeah, and to destroy any of the Vestigarchy that he finds there.

Against her better judgment, Sera was beginning to like this shepherd boy.

* * * *

The vehicle crested the rise, and from the driver's seat, Enoch could see where the swamp finally rose into the dryer ground that signified the borders of Garron. Overhead, he saw the golden flash of Sera's wings as she scouted out their path. The Alaphim had spent more time in the air than on the ground since Enoch had recovered, and he had decided that the risk of detection was worth her renewed sense of freedom.

"You do realize that's the last time she will ever let you help her, right?"

Rictus was smiling from the passenger seat, his skeletal grin just as toothy and wide as when Enoch had first met him. After G'Nor had performed an emergency vivisection on the specter to get rid of a half-formed, dying digestive tract, Rictus had been able to rally his remaining nanites to recover—at least, to help him recover back to his withered specter appearance. He promised everyone that he was fine with it. Besides, after returning to the swamp, the Lodoroi had recognized his sacrifice (and Enoch's gift of death to the undying) by returning his sword. And his guitar. The specter was tuning it as they drove.

Mesha purred from Enoch's shoulder, apparently having grown fond of Rictus's music. The shadowcat had forgiven Enoch for his foray into the darkness without her and seemed to have expected this more comfortable passage north. She still snuck out at night for her gifts from the Swampmen, however.

The Lodoroi had followed them from the desert and across the swamp, astride their large reptilian steeds, their hairless swamp murs, and even on foot. Six hundred of them, armed with venomous spears, darts, and clay pots filled with a thousand poisons. Seven chieftains had come to Enoch after he drove from the desert—they came and they offered their fealty. Apparently the Vestigarchy had not left a good impression on them.

G'Nor appeared beyond the rise and signaled a clear trail ahead. He now led a scouting party of veteran Swampmen, and their ability to track and scent potential threats—combined with Sera's view from above—had lead the small army to the lands just south of Tenocht without incident.

Enoch left the vehicle idling and stepped out of his seat to stand in the crisp wind coming down from the forested hills. Tenocht was still many days journey to the north, and he imagined that an army this size wouldn't escape the Vestigarchy's notice for long.

I am ready for them.

He brought his wrists together and watched as the gems on his bracelets glowed a cool blue. The bracelets had a name: the Eurym. This name was one of the first things Enoch had learned in reading through the complex code hardwired into the bracelets—a code language developed by brilliant people outside of the Pensanden sphere. The things Enoch could do with these tools . . .

A holographic sphere formed in his cupped hands, only now Enoch had learned what the sphere was—and what it meant.

It was a map of the world, a map as seen by the satellites that still orbited the planet. Their vision was now his vision, and he could see the forces arrayed around Tenocht—as well as those resisting them from behind the walls.

Then he took the disc from his neck—the disc that Rictus had salvaged for him—and held it in his cupped hands. Light spun from the Eurym, dancing across the disk. They were reading the information left there, he knew. Using the code stored there to open a channel.

The hologram flickered, and for a moment the globe became something else. It was a face, a face made of stars. The endless eyes found his and then smiled before the image began to break apart.

"Enoch."

It was Ketzel. Enoch had found a channel to Her, to the sky goddess, but the link was not strong enough to hold for more than a few seconds. He would find a clearer connection in Tenocht, he knew. He knew it without knowing how.

And then he would seal earth and sky.

Enoch spread his hands, and the hologram disappeared. He climbed back into the vehicle and drove forward, towards Tenocht. Under the sound of the engine and the brush crunching beneath the wheels, the melody of Rictus's guitar was sharp and bright.

EPILOGUE

These, then,
were the names of they who spoke together.
It was there that they came to await the dawn.
They would look
all calm,
all silent,
all motionless,
all pulsating,
awaiting the star that precedes the face of the sun
when it is born.
"We came from there, but we were split apart," they
said among themselves.

—Popol Vuh 587:1, Maya-Quiché Genesis, New Century Revised Edition

She spun through the blackness over the broken world and ::Watched.

And now . . . now there was one who ::Answered. This one was small, yes. This one was weak. But this one brought the seeds that ::Ended.

And the seeds that >//Began.

NEVER MISS A FUTURE HOUSE RELEASE!

Sign up for the Future House Publishing email list:
www.futurehousepublishing.com/beta-readers-club

Connect with Future House Publishing

www.facebook.com/FutureHousePublishing

twitter.com/FutureHosePub

www.youtube.com/FutureHousePublishing

www.instagram.com/FutureHousePublishing

ABOUT THE AUTHOR

With over fifteen years writing for blockbuster franchises from Blizzard Entertainment, Electronic Arts, and Epic Games, Cameron has gained a reputation for bringing riveting, powerful storytelling to games. Cameron wrote the script to *Advent Rising* with best-selling novelist Orson Scott Card, and co-founded the story-centered game development studio Chair Entertainment. At Blizzard, he built narratives for some of the most popular games in the world, including *The World of Warcraft*, *StarCraft*, *Hearthstone*, *Overwatch*, and *Diablo*. He also wrote Blizzard's first web-comic, *Kerrigan: Hope and Vengeance*, which ranked #1 on Amazon. Cameron's short stories are featured in several anthologies: *Wendigo Tales*, *Paragons*, *War Stories*, and *Heroes Rise, Darkness Falls*.

Made in the USA
San Bernardino, CA
20 April 2017